Mary Balogh is a *New York Times* bestselling author. A former teacher, she grew up in Wales and now lives in Canada.

By Mary Balogh

Mistress Couplet:

No Man's Mistress
More Than a Mistress

The Secret Mistress (prequel to the Mistress Couplet)

Huxtables Series:

First Comes Marriage
Then Comes Seduction
At Last Comes Love
Seducing an Angel
A Secret Affair

Simply Quartet:

Simply Unforgettable
Simply Love
Simply Magic
Simply Perfect

Bedwyn Series:

One Night for Love
A Summer to Remember
Slightly Married
Slightly Wicked
Slightly Scandalous
Slightly Tempted
Slightly Sinful
Slightly Dangerous

Survivors' Club Series:

The Proposal
The Arrangement
The Escape
Only Enchanting

Slightly Scandalous

Mary Balogh

piatkus

PIATKUS

First published in the US in 2003 by Bantam Dell,
A division of Random House, Inc., New York, USA
First published in Great Britain in 2007
as a paperback original by Piatkus Books

9 10 8

A CIP catalogue record for this book
is available from the British Library.

ISBN 978-0-7499-3755-3

Printed and bound in Great Britain by
Clays Ltd, St Ives plc

Papers used by Piatkus are from well-managed forests
and other responsible sources.

MIX
Paper from
responsible sources
FSC
www.fsc.org   FSC® C104740

Piatkus
An imprint of
Little, Brown Book Group
Carmelite House
50 Victoria Embankment
London EC4Y 0DZ

An Hachette UK Company
www.hachette.co.uk

www.piatkus.co.uk

Slightly Scandalous

B Y THE TIME SHE WENT TO BED, LADY FREYJA Bedwyn was in about as bad a mood as it was possible to be in. She dismissed her maid though a truckle bed had been set up in her room and the girl had been preparing to sleep on it. But Alice snored, and Freyja had no wish to sleep with a pillow wrapped about her head and pressed to both ears merely so that the proprieties might be observed.

"But his grace gave specific instructions, my lady," the girl reminded her timidly.

"In whose service are you employed?" Freyja asked, her tone quelling. "The Duke of Bewcastle's or mine?"

Alice looked at her anxiously as if she suspected that it was a trick question—as well she might. Although she was Freyja's maid, it was the Duke of Bewcastle, Freyja's eldest brother, who paid her salary. And he *had* given her instructions that she was not to move from her lady's side night or day during the journey from Grandmaison Park in Leicestershire to Lady Holt-Barron's lodgings on the Circus in Bath. He did not like his sisters traveling alone.

"Yours, my lady," Alice said.

"Then leave." Freyja pointed at the door.

Alice looked at it dubiously. "There is no lock on it, my lady," she said.

"And if there are intruders during the night, *you* are going to protect *me* from harm?" Freyja asked scornfully. "It would more likely be the other way around."

Alice looked pained, but she had no choice but to leave.

And so Freyja was left in sole possession of a second-rate room in a second-rate inn with no servant in attendance—and no lock on the door. And in possession too of a thoroughly bad temper.

Bath was not a destination to inspire excited anticipation in her bosom. It was a fine spa and had once attracted the crème de la crème of English society. But no longer. It was now the genteel gathering place of the elderly and infirm and those with no better place to go—like her. She had accepted an invitation to spend a month or two with Lady Holt-Barron and her daughter Charlotte. Charlotte was a friend of Freyja's though by no means a bosom bow. Under ordinary circumstances Freyja would have politely declined the invitation.

These were not ordinary circumstances.

She had just been in Leicestershire, visiting her ailing grandmother at Grandmaison Park and attending the wedding there of her brother Rannulf to Judith Law. She was to have returned home to Lindsey Hall in Hampshire with Wulfric—the duke—and Alleyne and Morgan, her younger brother and sister. But the prospect of being there at this particular time had proved quite intolerable to her and so she had seized upon the only excuse that had presented itself *not* to return home quite yet.

It was shameful indeed to be afraid to return to one's own home. Freyja bared her teeth as she climbed into bed and blew out the candle. No, not *afraid*. She feared nothing and no one. She just disdained to be there when *it* happened, that was all.

Last year Wulfric and the Earl of Redfield, their neighbor at Alvesley Park, had arranged a match between Lady Freyja Bedwyn and Kit Butler, Viscount Ravensberg, the earl's son. The two of them had known each other all their lives and had fallen passionately in love four years ago during a summer when Kit was home on leave from his regiment in the Peninsula. But Freyja had been all but betrothed to his elder brother, Jerome, at the time and she had allowed herself to be persuaded into doing the proper and dutiful thing—she had let Wulfric announce her engagement to Jerome. Kit had returned to the Peninsula in a royal rage. Jerome had died before the nuptials could take place.

Jerome's death had made Kit the elder son and heir of the Earl of Redfield, and suddenly a marriage between him and Freyja had been both eligible and desirable. Or so everyone in both families had thought—including Freyja.

But *not*, apparently, including Kit.

It had not occurred to Freyja that he might be bound upon revenge. But he had been. When he had arrived home for what everyone expected to be their betrothal celebrations, he had brought a fiancée with him—the oh-so-proper, oh-so-lovely, oh-so-dull Lauren Edgeworth. And after Freyja had boldly called his bluff, he had married Lauren.

Now the new Lady Ravensberg was about to give birth to their first child. Like the dull, dutiful wife she was, she would undoubtedly produce a son. The earl and countess would be ecstatic. The whole neighborhood would doubtless erupt into wild jubilation.

Freyja preferred not to be anywhere near the vicinity of Alvesley when it happened—and Lindsey Hall was near.

Hence this journey to Bath and the prospect of having to amuse herself there for a month or more.

She had not drawn the curtains across the window. What with the moon and stars above and the light of numerous lanterns from the inn yard below, her room might as well have been flooded by daylight. But Freyja did not get up to pull the curtains. She pulled the covers over her head instead.

Wulfric had hired a private carriage for her and a whole cavalcade of hefty outriders, all with strict instructions to guard her from harm and other assorted inconveniences. They had been told where to stop for the night— at a superior establishment suitable for a duke's daughter, even one traveling alone. Unfortunately, an autumn fair in that town had drawn people for miles around and there was not a room to be had at that particular inn or any other in the vicinity. They had been forced to journey on and then stop *here*.

The outriders had wanted to take shifts sitting on guard outside her room, especially on learning that there were no locks on any of the doors. Freyja had disabused them of that notion with a firmness that had brooked no argument. She was no one's prisoner and would not be made to feel like one. And now Alice was gone too.

Freyja sighed and settled for sleep. The bed was somewhat lumpy. The pillow was worse. There was a constant noise from the yard below and the inn about her. The blankets did not block out all the light. And there was Bath to look forward to tomorrow. All because going home had become a near impossibility to her. Could life get any bleaker?

Sometime soon, she thought just before she drifted off to sleep, she really was going to have to start looking seriously at all the gentlemen—and there were many of them despite the fact that she was now five and twenty and always had been ugly—who would jump through hoops if she were merely to hint that marriage to her might be the prize. Being single at such an advanced age really was no fun for a lady. The trouble was that she was not wholly convinced that being married would be any better. And it would be too late to discover that it really was not after she had married. Marriage was a life sentence, her brothers were fond of saying—though two of the four had taken on that very sentence within the past few months.

Freyja awoke with a start some indeterminate time later when the door of her room opened suddenly and then shut again with an audible click. She was not even sure she had not dreamed it until she looked and saw a man standing just inside the door, clad in a white, open-necked shirt and dark pantaloons and stockings, a coat over one arm, a pair of boots in the other hand.

Freyja shot out of bed as if ejected from a fired cannon and pointed imperiously at the door.

"Out!" she said.

The man flashed her a grin, which was all too visible in the near-light room.

"I cannot, sweetheart," he said. "That way lies certain doom. I must go out the window or hide somewhere in here."

"*Out!*" She did not lower her arm—or her chin. "I do not harbor felons. Or any other type of male creature. Get out!"

Somewhere beyond the room were the sounds of a small

commotion in the form of excited voices all speaking at once and footsteps—all of them approaching nearer.

"No felon, sweetheart," the man said. "Merely an innocent mortal in deep trouble if he does not disappear fast. Is the wardrobe empty?"

Freyja's nostrils flared.

"Out!" she commanded once more.

But the man had dashed across the room to the wardrobe, yanked the door open, found it empty, and climbed inside.

"Cover for me, sweetheart," he said, just before shutting the door from the inside, "and save me from a fate worse than death."

Almost simultaneously there was a loud rapping on the door. Freyja did not know whether to stalk toward it or the wardrobe first. But the decision was taken from her when the door burst open again to reveal the innkeeper holding a candle aloft, a short, stout, gray-haired gentleman, and a bald, burly individual who was badly in need of a shave.

"Out!" she demanded, totally incensed. She would deal with the man in the wardrobe after this newest outrage had been dealt with. *No one* walked uninvited into Lady Freyja Bedwyn's room, whether that room was at Lindsey Hall or Bedwyn House or a shabby-genteel inn with no locks on the doors.

"Begging your pardon, ma'am, for disturbing you," the gray-haired gentleman said, puffing out his chest and surveying the room by the light of the candle rather than focusing on Freyja, "but I believe a gentleman just ran in here."

Had he awaited an answer to his knock and then addressed her with the proper deference, Freyja might have betrayed the fugitive in the wardrobe without a qualm. But he had made the mistake of bursting in upon her and then treating her as if she did not exist except to offer him information—and his quarry. The unshaven individual, on the other hand, had done nothing *but* look at her—with a doltish leer on his face. And the innkeeper was displaying a lamentable lack of concern for the privacy of his guests.

"Do you indeed believe so?" Freyja asked haughtily. "Do you *see* this gentleman? If not, I suggest you close the door quietly as you leave and allow me and the other guests in this establishment to resume our slumbers."

"If it is all the same to you, ma'am," the gentleman said, eyeing first the closed window and then the bed and then the wardrobe, "I would like to search the room. For your own protection, ma'am. He is a desperate rogue and not at all safe with ladies."

"*Search my room?*" Freyja inhaled slowly and regarded him along the length of her prominent, slightly hooked Bedwyn nose with such chilly hauteur that he finally looked at her—and saw her for the first time, she believed. "Search my *room?*" She turned her eyes on the silent innkeeper, who shrank behind the screen of his candle. "Is *this* the hospitality of the house of which you boasted with such bombastic eloquence upon my arrival here, my man? My brother, the Duke of Bewcastle, will hear about this. He will be interested indeed to learn that you have allowed another guest—if this gentleman *is* a guest—to bang on the door of his sister's room in the middle of the night and burst in upon her without waiting for a reply merely because he *believes* that another gentleman dashed in here. And that you have stood by without a word of protest while he makes the impudent, preposterous suggestion that he be allowed to search the room."

"You were obviously mistaken, sir," the landlord said, half hiding beyond the door frame though his candle was still held out far enough to shine into the room. "He must have escaped another way or hidden somewhere else. I beg your pardon, ma'am—my lady, that is. I allowed it because I was afraid for your safety, my lady, and thought the duke would want me to protect you at all costs from desperate rogues."

"Out!" Freyja said once more, her arm outstretched imperiously toward the doorway and three men standing there. "Get out!"

The gray-haired gentleman cast one last wistful look about the room, the unshaven lout leered one last time, and then the innkeeper leaned across them both and pulled the door shut.

Freyja stared at it, her nostrils flared, her arm still outstretched, her finger still pointing. How *dared* they? She had never been so insulted in her life. If the gray-haired gentleman had uttered one more word or the unshaven yokel had leered one more leer, she would have stridden over there and banged their heads together hard enough to have them seeing wheeling stars for the next week.

She was certainly not going to recommend *this* inn to any of her acquaintances.

She had almost forgotten about the man in the wardrobe until the door squeaked open and he unfolded himself from within it. He was a tall, long-limbed young man, she saw in the ample light from the window. And very blond. He was probably blue-eyed too, though there was not quite enough light to enable her to verify that theory. She could see quite enough of him, though, to guess that he was by far too handsome for his own good. He was also looking quite inappropriately merry.

"That was a magnificent performance," he said, setting down his Hessian boots and tossing his coat across the truckle bed. "Are you *really* a sister of the Duke of Bewcastle?"

At the risk of appearing tediously repetitious, Freyja pointed at the door again.

"Out!" she commanded.

But he merely grinned at her and stepped closer.

"But I think not," he said. "Why would a duke's sister be staying at this less-than-grand establishment? And without a maid or chaperone to guard her? It was a wonderful performance, nevertheless."

"I can live without your approval," she said coldly. "I do not know what you have done that is so heinous. I do not *want* to know. I want you out of this room, and I want you out *now*. Find somewhere else to cower in fright."

"Fright?" He laughed and set a hand over his heart. "You wound me, my charmer."

He was standing very close, quite close enough for Freyja to realize that the top of her head reached barely to his chin. But she always had been short. She was accustomed to ruling her world from below the level of much of the action.

"I am neither your sweetheart nor your charmer," she told him. "I shall count to three. *One*."

"For what purpose?" He set his hands on either side of her waist.

"*Two*."

He lowered his head and kissed her. Right on the lips, his own parted slightly so that there was a shocking sensation of warm, moist intimacy.

Freyja inhaled sharply, drew back one arm, and punched him hard in the nose.

"Ouch!" he said, fingering his nose gingerly and flexing his mouth. He drew his hand away and Freyja had the satisfaction of seeing that she had drawn blood. "Did no one ever teach you that any ordinary lady would slap a man's cheek under such scandalous circumstances, not punch him in the nose?"

"I am no ordinary lady," she told him sternly.

He grinned again and dabbed at his nose with the back of one hand. "You are adorable when you are angry," he said.

"Get out."

"But I cannot do that, you see," he said. "That grandfatherly soul and his pugilistic henchman will be lying in wait for me, and I will be doomed to a leg shackle as surely as I am standing here."

"I do not want to hear any of the sordid details," she said, the significance of his dishabille suddenly borne in upon her. "And why should I care if they *are* lying in wait?"

"Because, sweetheart," he said, "they would see me coming from your room and draw their own slightly scandalous conclusions, and your reputation would be in tatters."

"It will doubtless survive the shock," she said.

"Have pity on me, O fair one," he said, grinning again—did he take nothing seriously, this man? "I fell for an old trick. There were the elderly gentleman and his granddaughter—a damsel lovely beyond words—in the parlor downstairs with nothing to do to while away the evening hours, and there was I, similarly employed—or unemployed. It was the most natural thing in the world for the grandfather and me to play a few hands of cards while the said damsel watched quietly and sweetly, always in my line of vision. After I had retired for the night and she came to my room to offer further entertainment—I daresay you have noticed that there are no locks on the doors?—was I to point virtuously at the door and order her to be gone? I *am* made of flesh and blood. As it turned out, it was just fortunate for me that I was still up and still half dressed and that the grandfather did not wait quite long enough before bursting in, all righteous wrath, with the innkeeper and his ferocious-looking thug in tow as witnesses. It was fortunate for me too that they came rushing into the room in a great zealous body, leaving the door unguarded. I made use of the exit thus provided me, dashed along the corridor as far as I could go, and . . . took the only door available to me. This one." He indicated the door of her room with a sweeping gesture of his arm.

"You were going to debauch an innocent girl?" Freyja's bosom swelled.

"Innocent?" He chuckled. "*She* came to *me*, sweetheart. Not that I was in any way reluctant, I feel compelled to admit. It is a way some men have of marrying their daughters or granddaughters to advantage, you know—or at least of extorting a hefty sum by way of compensation for lost virtue. They lie in wait in places like this until a poor fool like me happens along, and then they go into action."

"It would serve you right," she said severely, "if you *had* been caught. I have not the least bit of sympathy for you."

And yet, she thought, it was just the sort of scrape that Alleyne might get into, or Rannulf before his recent marriage to Judith.

"I am going to have to stay here for the rest of the night, I am afraid," the stranger said, looking around. "I don't suppose you would fancy sharing your bed with me?"

Freyja favored him with her coldest, haughtiest look, the one that froze most normal mortals in their tracks.

"No?" He grinned yet again. "It will have to be the truckle bed, then. I'll try not to snore. I hope you do not."

"You will leave this room," she told him, "before I count to three, or I shall scream. Very loudly. *One.*"

"You would not do that, sweetheart," he said. "You would expose yourself as a liar to your erstwhile visitors."

"*Two.*"

"Unless," he said with a chuckle, "you were to explain that I must have tiptoed in and hidden myself in the wardrobe while you still slept and then jumped out on you as soon as I surmised the coast to be clear."

"*Three.*"

He looked at her, raised his eyebrows, waggled them, and turned with studied nonchalance toward the truckle bed.

Freyja screamed.

"Jesu, woman," he said, one hand coming up as if to be clapped over her mouth.

But it must have been clear to him that that would have been akin to shutting the stable door after the proverbial horse had bolted. Freyja had considerable lung capacity. She screamed long and loud without once having to stop to draw breath.

The stranger grabbed up his coat and boots, dashed to the window, threw up the sash, poked his head out, tossed down his garments, and then disappeared.

The drop to the ground must be at least thirty feet, Freyja estimated, feeling a moment's remorse. His mashed remains were probably splashed over the cobbled yard below by now.

The door burst open to reveal a veritable mob of persons in various states of dress and undress, the innkeeper bringing up the rear, the gray-haired gentleman and the unshaven, leering thug with him.

"He burst in upon you after all, did he, my lady?" the gray-haired man asked above a hubbub of voices demanding to know what was the matter and who had been murdered in his bed.

But she despised the man—both on her own account and on that of the stranger whom he had tried to trap by using a woman—*if* the story was to be believed, that was. It was altogether likely that the stranger had made off with all the man's valuables.

"A mouse!" Freyja cried, gasping and clasping her throat. "A mouse ran across my bed."

There was a great to-do as a few ladies screamed and looked about them for chairs to stand on and a few men dashed into the room and went on a spirited mouse-hunt, under the bed, behind the washstand, behind the wardrobe, under the truckle bed, among Freyja's bags.

Freyja meanwhile was forced into maintaining a part quite unfamiliar to her. She shuddered and looked helpless.

"I daresay you dreamed it, ma'am—my lady, I mean," the innkeeper said at last. "We don't often have no mice in the house. The cats keep 'em out. If there *was* one, he's gone now, right enough."

Alice had arrived in the midst of the commotion, all wild-eyed terror, probably imagining what she would say to the Duke of Bewcastle—or, more to the point, what *he* would say to *her*—if her mistress's throat had been slashed from ear to ear while she was sleeping elsewhere than the room where she was supposed to be.

"Your maid will stay with you, my lady," the landlord said as the other guests drifted away, some indignant at having been so rudely awakened, others clearly disappointed at not having witnessed a mouse caught and executed for its transgression in having run across a bed with a human in it.

"Yes. Thank you." Freyja thought she sounded suitably pathetic.

"I'll sleep on the truckle bed, my lady," Alice announced bravely after everyone else had left and the door was closed. "I am not *very* afraid of mice, not as long as they stay on the floor. You wake me if it bothers you again and I'll chase it away." She was obviously terrified.

"You will go back to your bed, wherever it was," Freyja told her. "I would like to *sleep* for what remains of the night."

"But, my lady—" Alice began.

"Do you think I am afraid of a *mouse?*" Freyja demanded scornfully.

Her maid looked understandably mystified.

"Well, I didn't *think* you were," she said.

"Go." Freyja pointed to the door. "And may this be the last interruption any of us suffers for the rest of this night."

As soon as she was alone, she hurried to the window, put her head out, and peered downward, fearful of what she would see. He was a rogue and a villain and deserved whatever was coming to him. But surely not death. No, she would feel sorry, even a little guilty, if that had been his fate.

There was no sign of either the stranger or his boots or his coat.

It was then that she noticed the ivy growing thick on the walls.

Well, that was a relief anyway, she thought, closing the window and turning back into the room. Perhaps now she could expect a few hours of peaceful sleep.

But she stopped suddenly before she reached the bed and looked down at herself.

That whole scene—or series of scenes—had been enacted while she was clad in nothing but her nightgown, her feet bare and her hair loose and in a voluminous bush of tangled waves down her back.

Gracious heavens!

And then she smiled.

And then chuckled.

And then sat on the edge of the bed and laughed aloud.

The utter absurdity of it all!

She could not remember when she had enjoyed herself more.

CHAPTER II

Joshua Moore, Marquess of Hallmere, was on his way from Yorkshire, where he had been staying with a friend, to spend a week with his grandmother, the Dowager Lady Potford, in Bath. He could name a dozen other places he would rather be without even stretching his mental faculties, but he was fond of his grandmother and he had not seen her for five years.

He left his horse at a livery stable, found the correct house on Great Pulteney Street, rapped the door knocker against the door, and noted with amusement how the ex-pression on the face of the manservant who opened it changed from one of practiced deference to a look of haughty disdain.

"Sir?" he said, half closing the door and blocking the gap between it and the door frame with his black-clad per-son. "What might be your business?"

Joshua grinned cheerfully at him. "See if Lady Potford is at home and ask her if she will receive me, will you?" he asked.

The servant looked as if he were about to inform him without even bothering to check that his mistress was from home.

"Tell her that it is Hallmere," Joshua added.

The name obviously meant something. The man's expression underwent another change, becoming a blank, polite mask as he opened the door wide, stood to one side, and bowed.

"If you would wait here, my lord," he murmured.

Joshua stepped onto the black-and-white marble checkered floor of the hall and watched the servant—no doubt the butler—ascend the stairs, his ramrod-straight back bristling with polite disapproval, and disappear from sight. No more than two minutes later he reappeared.

"If you will follow me, my lord," he said from halfway down the stairs. "Her ladyship will receive you."

Lady Potford was in a square, pleasingly appointed sitting room overlooking the wide, classical elegance of Great Pulteney Street. She was still slim and straight-backed and fashionably clad and coiffed, Joshua saw as he strode into the room, though her hair was grayer than he remembered. It was, in fact, quite white at the temples.

"Grandmama!" He would have strided all the way toward her and caught her in his arms if she had not lifted a lorgnette from a fine gold chain about her neck and raised it to her eyes, looking pained as she did so.

"My dear Joshua," she said, "how foolish of me to have imagined that acquiring the title must surely have made you respectable. It is no wonder Gibbs was wearing his most woodenly incommunicative expression when he came to announce your arrival."

Joshua cast a rueful glance down at himself. Although his coat and pantaloons were decent enough, his Hessian boots lacked all shine and still bore traces of mud from last night. So did his coat actually. His shirt was yesterday's and wrinkled. Much of it was hidden beneath his coat, of course, but there was the lamentable absence of a neckcloth to make it look marginally respectable or a waistcoat to hide more of it. He was also without a hat or gloves. He had not shaved since last evening—or combed his hair for that matter. In plain terms, he must look quite remarkably disreputable. He must look like someone who had just staggered away from an all-night orgy.

Of course, he *had* kissed two different women last night, but on neither occasion was he given the time or chance to indulge in anything resembling an orgy—more was the pity.

"I ran into a spot of bother at an inn last night," he explained, "and escaped literally as you see me. I did manage to rescue my horse from the inn stable, but, alas, I was forced to abandon all my possessions. My valet will doubtless rescue them and bring them on here later. It is not the first time he will have awoken to find me already flown."

"As I can well believe," Lady Potford said tartly, dropping her lorgnette on its chain. "Well, am I to be given a kiss?"

He grinned, took the remaining three strides toward her, caught her up in his arms, swung her once about, and kissed her heartily on the cheek as he set her back on her feet. She shook her head, half in exasperation, half in acknowledgment that she might have expected as much of him.

"Saucy boy," she murmured.

"It is good to see you, Grandmama," he said. "It has been a long time."

"And whose fault is that?" she asked severely. "You have been gallivanting all over the Continent for years, if gossip and your infrequent letters have reported matters correctly, though how you could have done so while the wars were still being fought I shudder to imagine. It is a pity that it took the death of your uncle to bring you home to England."

The death of his uncle had brought Joshua his title and property and fortune—and all the burdens that came with them.

"It was not quite that, Grandmama," he said. "It was the end of the wars that brought me back to England. With Napoléon Bonaparte imprisoned on Elba and Englishmen free to roam about Europe at will again, there was no more fun to be had from dodging danger."

"Well, no matter," she said, shaking her head again. "You are home now, whatever the reason—or almost home, at least. It is as it ought to be."

"I have no intention of going to Penhallow if that is what you have in mind," he told her. "There are too many other places to go and other experiences to be lived."

"Oh, do sit down, Joshua. You are too tall to look up at." She seated herself. "You are the Marquess of Hallmere now. You belong at Penhallow—it is yours. You have duties and responsibilities there. It really is time you went back there."

"Grandmama." He grinned at her as he took the chair she had indicated and ran one hand ruefully down the stubble of one cheek. "If you intend to preach duty at me for the next week, I shall have to ride off into the sunset in search of another scrape to get into."

"You doubtless would not have to look far," she said. "Scrapes seem to come riding in search of *you*, Joshua. Your eyes are bloodshot. I suppose you did not sleep last night. I will not ask what else you *did* do last night apart from riding toward Bath in such a shockingly disheveled state."

He yawned until his jaws cracked—a most unmannerly thing to do in a lady's presence—and at the same moment his stomach rumbled quite audibly.

"You look an absolute *mess*, Joshua," his grandmother observed bluntly. "When did you last eat?"

"Sometime last evening," he admitted rather sheepishly. "I was forced to abandon my purse too, you see." He had been forced to make a few intricate and time-consuming detours about tollgates on his way.

"It must have been a large spot of bother indeed," she said, getting to her feet and pulling on the bell rope beside the hearth. "I am *almost* tempted to ask if she was at least pretty, but it would be quite beneath my dignity to do so. I shall leave you to the ministrations of Gibbs. He will feed you and shave you and then you may wish to sleep. There will be little else for you to do until your valet arrives with a change of clothes. I have several calls to make."

"Food and a shave and a sleep, in that order, sound quite like heaven to me," he said agreeably.

LADY HOLT-BARRON REVELED HAPPILY IN THE COUP OF having enticed Lady Freyja Bedwyn, sister of the Duke of Bewcastle, to Bath as her houseguest. Charlotte was more pleased just to have a friend of her own age there.

"Mama *would* insist upon coming to Bath again, Freyja," she explained as the two of them strolled in the Pump Room early on the morning following Freyja's arrival while Lady Holt-Barron, ensconced at the water table with a glass of the famous waters in her hand, beamed with pride as she conversed with a group of acquaintants similarly occupied. "She believes that a month of the waters puts her in good health for all the rest of the year. I suppose she may be right, but Papa and Frederick and the boys have gone shooting, as they always do at this time of the year, and I would far prefer to be with them. I am *so* thankful you agreed to come."

There was not much opportunity for such private exchanges. The Pump Room was the fashionable place to gather each morning for exercise and gossip—and for the drinking of the waters for those so inclined—but really, Freyja discovered, the amount of exercise one gained from walking about the high-ceilinged, elegantly appointed Georgian room was minimal. In fact, one took a few steps and then stopped to greet acquaintances and converse with them for a few minutes before taking a few more steps and stopping again. And because she was a new arrival, and a titled one at that, she found that everyone wished to speak with her, to greet her, and to quiz her for news from beyond the confines of Bath.

The day proceeded in no more energetic a fashion. They went shopping on Milsom Street after breakfast. Freyja had never delighted in that almost-universal feminine obsession. She shuffled from dress shops to milliners' shops to jewelers' shops in Lady Holt-Barron's wake, an enthusiastic Charlotte at her side, and wondered what the reaction of all around her would be if she were to stop in the middle of the pavement and open her mouth and scream—as lustily as she had done two nights ago. She found herself smiling at the memory. She had never been a screamer, but there had been an enormous exhilaration in letting loose with that one and seeing the grinning, overconfident stranger dive out the window.

God's gift to womanhood put to rout.

"Oh, you *do* like it, Freyja," Charlotte said, noticing the smile. She was sporting a dashing hat with a startlingly bright scarlet plume in place of her own more modest bonnet. "I do too, and I do not believe I can resist buying it even though I already have more hats than I will ever need. Shall I, Mama?"

"If Lady Freyja likes it," Lady Holt-Barron said, "then it must be all the crack, Charlotte. And indeed it looks very handsome indeed."

During the afternoon they paid a few social calls and then took tea at the Upper Assembly Rooms, where there were more people to converse with. The Earl of Willett was there—he was staying in Bath with his uncle, from whom it was rumored he was like to inherit a hefty fortune. He had paid pointed attention to Freyja ever since Jerome's death, but she had never encouraged him. He was short and sandy-haired and sandy-eyebrowed and blond-eyelashed—though it was not his undistinguished looks that made him unattractive to her as much as his humorless, always rigidly proper demeanor. After all, she was no beauty herself. But she was never rigidly proper.

In the setting of Bath, though, where most of the inhabitants were elderly, she had to admit that the earl's youth was an attraction in itself. She greeted him more warmly that she would have done if they had met in London, and he seated himself at Lady Holt-Barron's table and made himself agreeable to all three ladies for well over half an hour.

"My dear Lady Freyja," Lady Holt-Barron said after he had taken his leave of them, her eyebrows raised significantly, "I do believe you have made a conquest."

"Ah, but, ma'am," Freyja said haughtily, "*he* has *not*."

Charlotte laughed. "I believe it would be a waste of your time, Mama," she said, "to try playing matchmaker for Freyja."

In the evening they returned to the Upper Rooms for a concert. Freyja was not averse to music. Indeed, there was much that had the power to enthrall her. Operatic sopranos did not. But, as luck would have it, the guest of honor was a soprano with an Italian name and a large bosom and a large voice, which she displayed at full volume throughout her recital. Perhaps she believed, Freyja thought, her eardrums contracting against the piercing high notes, that superior volume was to be equated with superior quality.

The Earl of Willett somehow contrived to sit beside her during the second half after conversing with her during the interval.

"One's hearing could be permanently affected by a performance such as this," she commented.

Alleyne or Rannulf would have answered her in kind and they would have found themselves after a few such exchanges fighting to contain the laughter attempting to bellow forth.

"Yes, indeed," the earl agreed solemnly. "It is divine, is it not?"

And *this* was only the first day.

The second began the same way, the only difference being that yesterday morning the buzz of excitement had been over Freyja's arrival in Bath, whereas today it was over that of the Marquess of Hallmere. Everyone waited with eager anticipation for his appearance in the Pump Room with the Dowager Lady Potford, his maternal grandmother. Freyja knew Lady Potford but had no acquaintance with the marquess. When the lady arrived, though, she came alone. The air of disappointment in the room was really quite palpable.

"He is a young man," Lady Holt-Barron explained, "and is said to be very personable. He is, of course, one of the most eligible bachelors in England." She looked archly at Freyja.

And so he would be deemed personable even if he looked like a gargoyle, Freyja supposed.

It took the arrival of someone new—preferably someone titled—to titillate the spirits of these people, Freyja thought with a great inward sigh as they left the Pump Room to return home for breakfast. She had surely made a dreadful mistake in coming to Bath. She would be insane within a fortnight—within a *week*! But she remembered the alternative—being at Lindsey Hall, awaiting the imminent announcement from Alvesley—and decided that she must somehow bear her exile for at least a month. Besides, it would be unmannerly to leave the Holt-Barrons so soon.

She could not, however, endure another morning of shopping. She made the excuse of some unwritten letters not to accompany Charlotte and her mother and did indeed, as a salve to her conscience, sit down at the escritoire in her room and write to Morgan, her younger sister. She found herself describing what had happened at the inn where she had spent a night on the way to Bath, embellishing the story considerably, though indeed the bare facts were sensational enough in themselves. Morgan would appreciate the humor of it all and could be trusted not to show the letter to Wulfric.

Wulf would certainly not be amused.

It was a lovely day for early September, if a little breezy. Freyja thought wistfully of a ride—the hills beyond Bath were made to be galloped among. But if she sent a servant to hire a horse and waited to have it brought around, Charlotte and her mother might already have returned from their shopping trip before it came and there would be a great deal of fuss over sending a groom with her for protection. She had never been able to endure having servants trailing along behind her while she rode. She decided to walk instead, and set out alone as soon as she had changed, her dark green walking dress swishing about her legs as she strode down the steep hill from the house on the Circus. Her bushy fair hair was confined in a coiffure that was almost tame beneath her feathered hat, which sat jauntily to one side of her head.

She strode through the center of Bath, nodding at a few acquaintances and hoping that by some ill fortune she would not encounter her hostesses and be forced to spend the rest of the morning in the shops with them, took a shortcut through the Abbey churchyard past the Pump Room and the Abbey itself, turned to walk along the river, and then noticed up ahead the very grand Pulteney Bridge, which she had forgotten, since she had not been in Bath for many years. On the other side of the bridge, she remembered now, was the splendidly wide and elegant Great Pulteney Street. And were not Sydney Gardens at the end of *that*?

She had not intended to walk quite so far, but she felt as if she were drawing air deep into her lungs for the first time in days, and she had no desire to return to the house just yet. She turned to walk across the bridge, looking briefly in the little shop windows as she passed, and then discovered that memory had not deceived her. A short distance ahead of her stretched one of the most magnificent sights of an admittedly magnificent city.

At the end of Great Pulteney Street she turned onto Sydney Place, intending to cross over to the Gardens. But then she noticed the sign indicating that Sutton Street was to her left and frowned and stopped abruptly. It did not take more than a few seconds to realize why that name sounded familiar. It was on Sutton Street that Miss Martin had her school for girls. Freyja hesitated, grimaced, hesitated again, and then struck off firmly along Sutton Street. She even knew the number of the house.

Five minutes later she was standing in a shabby genteel parlor, awaiting the arrival of Miss Martin herself. This was definitely *not* a good idea, Freyja decided. She had never come here in person before or written—or even allowed her solicitor to use her name.

Miss Martin did not keep her waiting long. She was as pale and tight-lipped and straight-backed as Freyja remembered her. Her dark gray eyes looked as steadily into Freyja's as they had ever looked, but now she dared to look with hostility only barely masked behind civility.

"Lady Freyja." She inclined her head but did not curtsy. She did not offer a chair or refreshments or express surprise or gratification. She did not point at the door and order her visitor to leave. She merely looked, an expression of polite inquiry in her face.

Well, Freyja thought, she liked the woman the better for it.

"I heard that you had a school here," Freyja said, masking her own embarrassment with more than usual haughtiness. "I was passing by and decided to call on you."

Asinine words!

Miss Martin did not dignify them with a reply. She merely inclined her head.

"To see how you did," Freyja added. "To see if there was anything your school was in need of. Anything I could provide."

It was amazement that was in Miss Martin's eyes now—and far more open hostility.

"I am doing very well, I thank you," she said. "I have both paying pupils and charity pupils and several good teachers. I also have a benefactor who has been both kind and generous to me and to my girls. I have no need of your charity, Lady Freyja."

"Well." Freyja had taken note of the barely concealed shabbiness of the place and decided that the benefactor was not nearly generous enough. Or that the person acting for the benefactor had different notions than his employer of what adequate funding was. "I thought it worth making the offer."

"Thank you." Miss Martin's voice quivered with an emotion her person did not show. "I can only hope that you have changed in nine years, Lady Freyja, and that you have come here out of a genuine goodness of heart rather than out of a malicious hope of finding me desperate and destitute. I am neither. Even without my benefactor's generosity my school is beginning to pay its way. I certainly do not need your assistance—or any further visit from you. Good day. My pupils are missing their history lesson."

A short while later Freyja was walking in Sydney Gardens, her heart still beating erratically, her ears still ringing from the rebuke and the obvious dislike with which it had been delivered.

It must not be a fashionable time to be here, she concluded with some relief. She passed very few other people as she walked the meandering paths, and no one at all that she knew. This was not, she supposed, the place to be walking without a maid trailing decently along behind. But she had never cared about the proprieties and at this particular moment she was very glad indeed to be quite alone. She sat on a rustic bench for a while, close to an ancient oak, feeling the sunshine on her face and the merest suggestion of autumn in the air, and watching a pair of squirrels foraging around for anything visitors to the park might have left behind by way of food. They were remarkably tame. But she sat very still anyway. She did not want to frighten them away.

She had frightened away a whole string of governesses when she was a girl. She had never taken kindly to being confined, to having to do as she was told, to giving her mind to lessons she found excruciatingly boring, to accepting the authority of insipid gentlewomen. She had been a horror, in fact.

Wulf had always found her governesses other employment after dismissing them or accepting their resignation, and Freyja had never given them another thought. Until, that was, Miss Martin had shown unexpected spirit by walking away from Lindsey Hall—literally *walking*—her head high, having refused any assistance whatsoever from Wulf.

For once in her life Freyja had been genuinely upset by a governess—an ex-governess, in this particular case. She had tolerated the next one, even though she was the most insipid of all, for the rest of her time in the schoolroom.

It was only by accident that she had heard of Miss Martin again. She had opened a school in Bath, but she was struggling dreadfully and must soon close it down. The story had been told maliciously to Freyja by an acquaintance who had expected her to be delighted. She had not been. She had sought out a solicitor, disabused him of the idea that she needed a man to accompany and do business for her, and paid him very well indeed to find Miss Martin, determine the needs of her school, and announce to her that an anonymous benefactor was prepared to answer those needs, provided she could prove to an inspector each year that the education she provided her pupils was up to an acceptable standard.

Since then Freyja had warmed to her unaccustomed role as a carer of deserving humanity and had sent Miss

Martin several charity pupils and even one needy teacher, providing all the necessary funding for their keep.

Poor Miss Martin would have an apoplexy if she knew the identity of her benefactor.

And she herself would be mortified indeed, Freyja thought as she absently watched the squirrels, if anyone were to discover her secret softness. For softness it was. Any governess who could not control her charges deserved to be dismissed. And any dismissed governess who was too proud to accept her employer's assistance deserved to starve.

She chuckled softly. How she had liked Miss Martin this morning. How she would have despised her if she had fawned all over her former tormentor.

And then a scream jerked her back to reality—a feminine scream, coming from somewhere down the hill and around a bend in the winding path. Trees hid the screamer from Freyja's view, but there were the distinct sounds of a scuffle, a deep male voice, another less frantic scream, and a high-pitched female voice. The squirrels scampered to the nearest tree and shot up its bark to disappear among branches and foliage.

Freyja surged to her feet. She was female herself. She was small. She had no one with her, not even a maid. She was in a park that seemed almost deserted and was made even more secluded by the hills and trees of which it was composed. It was certainly not the occasion for heroics. Any normal woman in this particular situation would have turned right and hurried away in the opposite direction as fast as her legs would carry her.

Freyja was not any normal woman.

She turned left and strode down the path, almost breaking into a run as she did so. She did not have far to go. As she rounded the bend, a stretch of lawn came into view just ahead. On it stood a great tall beast of a man—a *gentleman*, no less—clutching a small slip of a serving girl. Her arms were imprisoned against his chest and he was lowering his head with the lascivious intent of claiming his prize—though to complete the process he would doubtless be dragging her off into the bushes within the next few moments.

"*Take* your hands off her!" Freyja commanded, lengthening her stride. "You uncouth villain. Let her go."

They sprang apart and turned identically startled faces her way. And then the girl—wise wench—screamed again and made off down the hill as fast as her feet would carry her and did not look back.

Freyja did not slow her pace. She strode onward until she was almost toe-to-toe with the villain, drew back her arm, and punched that assaulter of female innocence in the nose.

"Ouch!" he said, his hand jerking up to cover the offended organ. And then his watering eyes focused on her. "Well, now, I *thought* I recognized that gentle feminine touch. It is you, is it?"

He was fashionably dressed in a blue riding coat with buff breeches and shining top boots, a tall hat on his head. But with a shock of recognition Freyja noticed the long limbs and perfectly proportioned body, the very blond hair beneath the hat, and the very blue eyes of the man she had last seen diving from her inn window three nights ago. Adonis and devil all rolled into one. She drew an audible breath.

"Yes, it is I," she said. "And I am sorry in my heart now that I did not reveal your hiding place in the wardrobe to that gray-haired gentleman and abandon you to your fate."

"No, you are not, are you, sweetheart?" he asked, having

the gall to grin at her, watering eyes and reddening nose notwithstanding. "How unsporting of you."

"You dastardly, cowardly villain," she said. "You wretched debaucher of innocence. You are beneath contempt. I shall report you and have you run out of Bath and away from the company of respectable people."

"*Will* you?" He leaned a little toward her, his eyes dancing with watery merriment. "And *whom* will you report, my charmer?"

She swelled with indignation. "I shall discover your identity," she said. "You will not be able to show your face outdoors in Bath again without my seeing you and finding out who you are."

"Well," he said, "we both know that *you* are not a duke's daughter, do we not? Where is your retinue of guardians and hangers-on?"

"You will *not* divert my attention," she said severely. "Do you think that any serving girl is yours to take merely because she *is* a serving girl? And merely because you are too handsome for your own good?"

"*Am* I?" He grinned again. "I suppose you are in no mood to allow me to explain, are you, sweetheart?"

"I am *not* your sweetheart," she said. "And I need no explanation beyond the evidence of my own ears and my own eyes. I *heard* the girl scream and I *saw* you with her clutched in your arms, about to have your wicked way with her. I am not *stupid*."

He crossed his arms over his chest and regarded her with dancing eyes and pursed lips. She was very tempted to punch him again.

"No," he said, "perhaps not. But are you not afraid that with my wicked will freshly thwarted and my raging appetites left unappeased I may choose to pounce upon you instead?"

"I invite you to try," she said coldly. "You would, I promise you, return home with more bruises than you would find comfortable."

"A tempting invitation." He laughed. "But, of course, you can scream far more loudly than that wench who just escaped my clutches. I think I would be wise not to risk it. Good day to you, ma'am."

He touched his hand to the brim of his hat, made her a mocking half-bow, and strode at a leisurely, long-legged pace down over the lawn to the path at the bottom.

Freyja was left victor of the field.

JOSHUA CHUCKLED SOFTLY TO HIMSELF AS HE STRODE along. Who the devil *was* she?

He had thought of her a few times in the last couple of days, every time with amusement. She had looked quite enticingly shapely in her nightgown. Her fair hair, all wild, unconfined waves about her shoulders and down her back, had done nothing to lessen her appeal. Her anger, her boldness, her total lack of self-consciousness or fear, had aroused his interest. Her unexpected refusal to let him call her bluff had won his admiration, even though he would probably have broken his neck going through that window if he had not noticed the ivy just in time.

His first impression this morning had been that she was ugly. Not from the neck down. She was small, but in her well-cut walking dress she had looked quite as shapely as she had the other night. Even her hair, confined decently today beneath her fetching little hat but still managing to look wavy and rather wild, was not unattractive. But her eyebrows were quite incongruously dark in contrast to the almost blond color of her hair, and her nose was prominent,

with a bend in it. She had fierce green eyes and an unfash-
ionably dark complexion.

There was nothing delicately feminine about her facial
features. She was not beautiful, or even pretty. But she was
not ugly either. There was too much character behind
those looks for that. If he were to be charitable, he might
call her handsome. If he were to be honest, he would call
her attractive.

Whoever had taught her to punch had certainly done
his job well. If many more of those landed on his nose,
Joshua thought ruefully, he might well acquire a bend in it
to match her own.

A week in Bath was going to seem endless indeed, he
had thought just an hour ago, pleased as he was to see his
grandmother again after so long. Yesterday, although he
had taken a stroll up to the Pulteney Bridge and back and
had gone for a ride, as he had done this morning, and then
taken a shortcut from the livery stables back through Sydney Gardens to Great Pulteney Street as he was doing
again now, he had spent altogether too long indoors, being
sociable to his grandmother's visitors during the afternoon
and accompanying her to Mrs. Carbret's private card party
in the evening rather than to the concert at the Upper
Rooms.

It still felt strange to be presented to people as the Marquess of Hallmere even though he had been in possession
of the title for longer than six months, and to see the added
deference in people's manner once his title had been mentioned.

He had never wanted the title or any of the trappings
that had come along with it—least of all Penhallow, the
marquess's seat in Cornwall. He had lived there from the
age of six to the age of eighteen, and had hated almost
every moment of it. The orphaned son of the marquess's

brother, he had not been made to feel welcome at his uncle's home. There had been a few visits to his grandmother and to his maternal uncle, Lord Potford, her son, over the years, but he had never complained to them or asked to stay indefinitely—he had been too proud and perhaps too stubborn for that. He had left Penhallow as soon as he was able, though. At the age of eighteen he had begged a local carpenter to take him on as an apprentice, since he had always loved working with wood, and he had moved into the village of Lydmere across the river from Penhallow. He had been happy there for five years, until circumstances had forced him to leave.

The title, Penhallow, and all the emotional burdens he had left behind him in Cornwall felt like a particularly heavy millstone about his neck. He had dismissed his uncle's steward six months ago and installed his own. He read the monthly reports and wrote back with specific instructions when his personal input was needed. Apart from that, he ignored the place. He never wanted to see it again.

He would stay here in Bath for the full week, he decided as he neared his grandmother's house, but not a day longer. He had friends all over the country and now he had ample funds with which to travel—the one aspect of his changed circumstances that he admittedly liked. He would spend the winter moving about the country, staying a week here, two there. He would think about a more permanent occupation when next spring came.

He grinned to himself as he took the stairs inside the house two at a time. That little Amazon from the park the daughter of a duke, indeed! But she must be staying somewhere in Bath. She probably showed herself at some of the fashionable places even if she was not in the forefront of society—the Pump Room, the Assembly Rooms, the Royal Crescent, for example. He was almost bound to meet her again—and discover who she really was.

Perhaps he would flirt with her. That should be endlessly amusing, given her opinion of him and her bristling temper. He must be watching for that fist next time, though. He had already been taken unawares twice too many times by it.

As he let himself into his room and tossed his hat and whip onto the bed, he remembered her threat to find *him* and to report him to... Well, to someone in authority, he supposed. It might not be wise to try calling her bluff this time. He must be prepared for a few interesting moments when they did come face-to-face in public. Of course, he could beat her at her own game....

Joshua sat down on the side of the bed and hauled off his riding boots without bothering to summon his valet. He hoped she did not plan to leave Bath within the next day or two. She might be his one hope of avoiding death via boredom.

Devil take it, he thought, touching his nose gingerly—it was *still* sore.

Chapter III

"No, indeed I do not drink the waters," Lady Potford told her grandson the following morning as the carriage they rode in passed the Abbey and approached the Pump Room. "Do you think I wish to kill myself?"

"But are they not healing waters?" he asked with a twinkle in his eye. "Are they not the reason so many people flock here?"

"Most people, once they have tasted the waters," she said, "are wise enough to decide that they prefer the infirmities with which they are comfortably familiar. Actually bathing in the waters, of course, is somewhat out of fashion. No, Joshua, one comes to the Pump Room each morning, not for one's health, but in order to see and be seen. It is the thing to do when one is in Bath."

"Like promenading in Hyde Park when one is in London," he said, vaulting out of the carriage as soon as the door was open and setting down the steps himself before handing his grandmother down. "Except that that is done at teatime, a far more civilized hour than the crack of dawn."

"Ah, that hint of early autumn," she said, pausing on the step and inhaling the air. "My favorite season—and my favorite time of day."

She was dressed with consummate elegance—as was he. When in Bath one must do what the Bathians did, he had concluded yesterday. And that meant participating in all the tedious public displays that were so much a part of the daily routine here, starting with the early morning stroll in the Pump Room.

He wondered if the dark-browed little virago would be here. If so, he would discover who she was—as she would discover his identity. That might lead to interesting developments. At least his morning would not be dull if she was here—even if she chose to give him the cut direct.

She was not there. But a whole host of other people were, and large numbers of them had not yet been introduced to him. He felt like someone masquerading as a grand hero as people converged on his grandmother to congratulate her on having her grandson to stay with her, and remained to be presented to him. He resigned himself to smiling and conversing and exercising his charm.

He grimaced inwardly when he saw Mrs. Lumbard bearing down upon him. She was one of his uncle's neighbors in Cornwall, and one of his aunt's bosom bows. She had never had the time of day for him while he was growing up at Penhallow, especially after, at the age of ten or so, he had taught her daughter a swearword he had learned in the stables and she had used it in her governess's hearing. He had been even farther beneath her notice as a carpenter. Now she was approaching him, all heaving bosom and ample hips and nodding bonnet plumes, like a ship in full sail, that same daughter in tow, and sank into a gracious curtsy.

"Lady Potford," she said, addressing his grandmother though she was looking at him, "how very gratified you must be to have Hallmere with you at last. *Such* a handsome, distinguished gentleman he has grown into. Has he not, Petunia, my love? And I remember the time when he was such a dear mischief." She simpered at her own joke. "My dearest Corinne used to weep tears of despair over him. My dear Hallmere, I suppose it is too much to hope that you remember me?"

"I remember you well, ma'am," he said, bowing. "And Miss Lumbard too. How do you do?"

"We are both tolerably well," Mrs. Lumbard replied, "if I ignore a few twinges of the rheumatics, which are always at their worst this time of year. But I never complain. How very kind of you to ask. My dearest Corinne will be beside herself with delight when she knows I have seen you. Every day she expects you to come home. She is quite pining for a sight of you."

Joshua thought it altogether more likely that his aunt was holding her breath in the hope that he would never come, even though she had written more than once recently to invite him home. It had struck him as faintly amusing that the letters had been phrased just that way— as gracious *invitations* to his own home. She need not fear. She was welcome to live out her life there undisturbed by him.

He inclined his head stiffly to Mrs. Lumbard.

"Ah," she said, suddenly distracted, "there are Lady Holt-Barron and her daughter and Lady Freyja Bedwyn. I simply must go and pay my respects to them. Come along, Petunia."

Joshua offered his grandmother his arm again and prepared to stroll onward. But he glanced in the direction of the new arrivals and stopped abruptly, his lips pursed.

Well! Here was something to enliven what had promised to be an intolerably dull morning. Here she was.

She was dressed today in a russet walking dress and bonnet and looked tamer than she had yesterday. She also had a look of bored hauteur on her face as if, like him, she would far prefer to be somewhere else altogether more lively.

"Who is the lady—" he began to ask his grandmother.

But the lady in question caught sight of him even as he spoke. She held his gaze, her eyes growing noticeably more steely despite the distance between them.

And then he heard the echo of what Mrs. Lumbard had just said—*and Lady Freyja Bedwyn.*

That prominent nose went up in the air and with it the aggressively set chin. The green eyes grew arctic.

Joshua was already enjoying himself.

"—in russet with the two other ladies Mrs. Lumbard is approaching?" he asked, completing his question.

"Lady Freyja Bedwyn?" his grandmother asked, following the line of his gaze. "Lady Holt-Barron has been displaying her all over Bath since she arrived a few days ago, like some sort of trophy. Which is, of course, what I will be accused of doing with you."

"*Lady* Freyja Bedwyn?" he asked.

The woman was tapping an impatient tattoo on the floor with one foot. She was taking no notice at all of Mrs. Lumbard, who was fawning all over her, but was still gazing narrow-eyed at Joshua.

"The Duke of Bewcastle's sister," his grandmother explained.

Uh-oh. Joshua grinned slowly and deliberately.

Lady Freyja Bedwyn was leaving her group without a word or a backward glance and was moving purposefully across the room with long, manly strides. The inappropriateness of her movements in such confined, genteel surroundings drew attention even before she came to a halt less than a foot in front of Joshua, glaring at him with what he could now correctly interpret as aristocratic disdain.

"Lady Potford," she said without taking her eyes off him, "would you be so good as to inform me of the identity of the gentleman who is with you?"

There was a brief silence, the only indication his grandmother gave of the surprise she must be feeling at this quite unmannerly demand.

"Hello, sweetheart," Joshua murmured, and thought that if Lady Freyja Bedwyn only had a chimney in the top of her head she might not look quite as if she were about to explode.

"Lady Freyja," his grandmother said with admirable poise, "may I have the honor of presenting my grandson, Joshua Moore, Marquess of Hallmere? Lady Freyja Bedwyn, Joshua."

She glared at him with flared nostrils, apparently quite uncowed by what she had just learned. He returned her look with amused admiration. By God, she did not mind making a spectacle of herself before a large audience of Bath society. And the buzz of conversation had indeed hushed considerably as heads turned to see what it was that was threatening to disturb the genteel routine of the morning stroll.

"I believe," Lady Freyja said in strident tones that must be carrying clearly to every farthest corner of the room, "he would be more appropriately named the Marquess of *Hell*mere." She pointed one kid-gloved finger directly at his chest. "*This man* does not even deserve the name of gentleman."

There was an audible gasp from all around them, followed by shushing sounds. No one wanted to miss a word of this delicious scandal that was developing before their very eyes.

"My dear Lady Freyja—" his grandmother began, sounding quite dismayed.

"*This man*," Lady Freyja continued, "likes to amuse himself by preying upon innocent, helpless women."

There was a swell of shocked sound followed again by more frantic shushing sounds.

"I do beg you, Lady Freyja—" His grandmother tried again.

Lady Freyja poked her finger, like a blunt dagger, into Joshua's chest.

"I warned him that I would discover his identity and expose him to Bath society for the villain he is. I vowed I would have him ejected from the society of decent people." She poked him with her finger again. "If you thought I was bluffing, my man, you were sorely mistaken."

"Again," he said, smiling sheepishly and calculating that the expression would further enrage her. "I really ought to know better by now, ought I not?"

There was no further pretense of anyone's strolling. Even the water tables had been deserted. Joshua realized that he and his grandmother and Lady Freyja Bedwyn had become isolated in the middle of a rough circle that had formed about them. Their audience seemed about equally divided between those who were acutely embarrassed that a lady should behave with such lack of decorum and those who gazed with hostile eyes at the man who preyed upon innocent, helpless women.

But someone was coming to their rescue—or to join

the fray—a man with self-important air come to deal with the sudden crisis. Joshua recognized him as James King, the master of ceremonies at the Upper Assembly Rooms, who had called upon him two afternoons ago at Great Pulteney Street. It was the man's job to maintain Bath's gentility and see to it that every visitor was welcomed and properly entertained—and that every visitor kept the strict rules of decorum.

Even marquesses and the daughters of dukes.

"My lady," he said, addressing Lady Freyja, "surely you are mistaken. This gentleman is the Marquess of Hallmere and grandson of Lady Potford, a longtime resident of our city. Perhaps this slight misunderstanding can be cleared up quietly outside?"

His voice was courteous, but it held a thread of steel. He took Lady Freyja by the elbow, but she shrugged him off and looked at him along the length of her nose as if he were a worm.

"This *slight misunderstanding?*" she said with haughty emphasis. "A peer of the realm assaulted a poor serving girl on a lonely stretch of lawn in Sydney Gardens yesterday despite her piteous screams for help and was about to drag her off into the bushes to complete his wicked designs on her while I witnessed all, and it is a *slight misunderstanding?* It is something to be hushed up discreetly beyond the confines of this room? I do not believe so. This matter will be cleared up here and now and before the respectable citizens of Bath. Have the courage to perform the duty for which you are employed and expel *this man* from Bath without further ado."

There was a smattering of applause from the gathered spectators.

Joshua grinned at Lady Freyja, who was looking magnificent enough to be a queen of the Amazons. He even made a slight kissing gesture with his lips.

Mr. King sighed and turned his attention to Joshua.

"Do you have anything to say on this matter, my lord?" he asked.

"Yes, indeed," Joshua said. "The lady has a vivid and lurid imagination."

She looked at him with haughty contempt. "I might have predicted," she said, "that you would deny it all."

"*Did* you see Lady Freyja in Sydney Gardens yesterday, my lord?" the master of ceremonies asked.

"Most certainly I did," Joshua said. "She was alone and wearing a dark green walking dress with a feathered hat. And she punched me in the nose."

There was another gasp from the spectators, followed by a buzzing, followed by the inevitable shushing noises.

Mr. King looked pained.

"For nothing at all, my lord?" he asked. "You expect us all to believe that she struck you, a stranger to her, for no reason whatsoever?"

"She came rushing upon me when I was holding a serving girl in my arms," Joshua explained. "Probably she had heard the girl scream a few moments before. She appeared to have concluded that I was about to—ahem!—have my wicked way with the wench."

"But you were not, my lord?" the master of ceremonies asked.

In the short pause Joshua allowed to fall before he replied, he could see the suddenly arrested look in Lady Freyja's eyes, the dawning realization that perhaps she had made a ghastly mistake. That she had just made a prize ass of herself, in fact.

"A squirrel had stepped into the girl's path as she crossed a lawn in the park," Joshua explained. "It startled her and she stopped abruptly. But instead of bounding away as any sensible squirrel would have done under the circumstances, it attempted to take refuge under her skirts and she screamed. By the time I hurried to the rescue, having witnessed the whole catastrophe, the poor girl was hysterical, though the squirrel had long ago recovered its wits and made off for the nearest tree. I, ah, gathered her into my arms to steady her."

He had, of course, been about to kiss her too, with her full and enthusiastic compliance, but there was no need to add those incriminating details.

"It was at that moment," Joshua added, "that Lady Freyja Bedwyn rushed onto the scene, frightened the poor serving girl into screaming again and taking flight, and punched me in the nose."

Mr. King transferred his gaze from Joshua to Lady Freyja. So, Joshua estimated, did everyone else in the Pump Room.

"*Could* this be the explanation of what you witnessed, my lady?" he asked.

To do her credit, she did not crumble or look as if she were searching the Pump Room floor for a deep hole to crawl into. Neither did she bluster or make a further idiot of herself by trying to insist upon the truth of her story. Her eyes narrowed and she continued to stare haughtily at Joshua.

"Why did you not explain all this to me yesterday?" she asked imperiously.

"Now let me see." He lifted one hand and stroked his chin with his thumb and forefinger. "I asked if I might be permitted to explain, and you replied to the effect that you knew perfectly well what you had seen and what you had heard. You added, I believe, that you were not *stupid*. It would have been quite ungallant of me to contradict you."

There was a titter from some members of their audience.

Her eyes grew steely again. "This was deliberate," she said. "You led me into this quite deliberately."

"I beg your pardon for contradicting a lady." He made her an elegant half-bow. "But I believe it was *you* who approached *me* this morning."

"It would appear," the master of ceremonies said, raising his voice slightly, looking about him with genial affability, and speaking with firm finality, "that this altercation has been over a slight misunderstanding. We must have you shake hands, my lord, my lady, so that all will see that there is no remaining rancor between the two of you."

Joshua, with a deliberately courtly gesture extended his right hand, palm up. He smiled. He was enjoying himself enormously. He was very glad she had not collapsed into an ignominious heap of feminine mortification—that would have lessened his pleasure in besting her. Her nostrils flared again, her chin came up and with it that splendid aristocratic nose, and like a queen conferring a favor on some poor inferior mortal, she set her hand on his.

He closed his own about it and raised it to his lips.

Again there was a smattering of applause, and then everyone got back to the serious business of strolling and gossiping or—for the intrepid few—drinking the waters.

"I will get you for this," she murmured.

"The pleasure will be all mine, I do assure you, my lady," he murmured in return—and smiled at her with the full force of his considerable charm.

Lady Holt-Barron was so severely discomposed by the scene in the Pump Room that she was quite unable to go shopping after breakfast. Indeed, even her breakfast had to be reduced to dry toast and weak tea, the only items she thought herself capable of digesting. She retired to her room afterward to lie quietly upon her bed.

"Oh, dear," Freyja said to Charlotte when they were alone in the morning room, "I forget that there are ladies with such inconveniences as delicate constitutions. Ought I to apologize to your mama, do you suppose?"

But Charlotte had turned purple in the face and was attempting to stuff her linen handkerchief into her mouth. Nothing, though, would stifle the laughter that came bubbling out of her.

"Oh," she wailed, "if Mama hears me she will have a major fit of the vapors and we will end up having to send for the physician."

She stifled further whoops as best she could.

"It might all have seemed like the farce at the end of the drama to you," Freyja complained. "I could cheerfully have died."

"If you could just have *seen* yourself," Charlotte said. "Stalking across the Pump Room like an avenging angel while all the dowagers gaped after you. And then speaking to the marquess *just* as the headmistress at my school used to talk to us when we were in major trouble. And jabbing at his chest with your finger."

But the memories were too much for her composure. She spread her handkerchief over her face and rocked with merriment.

"He *knew* that I would do it," Freyja said, thinking with indignation of the grinning marquess, whose immaculate good looks had only fueled her wrath. "That was why he did not insist upon telling me the truth in the park."

"And if you could have *seen* Mama trying to make herself invisible," Charlotte continued, "and that horrid Mrs. Lumbard swelling to twice her size and Miss Lumbard's eyes fit to fall out of her head and—oh, *everyone*." She went off into whoops again.

"At least," Freyja said, "I have given everyone enough to talk about and write home about for a month or more. The letters will all be book-length, I daresay."

"Oh, don't!" Charlotte rocked back in her chair.

"The Pump Room is going to seem deadly dull forever after," Freyja said, "even to those who have never realized that it always is. They will all be looking to me for an encore. I will be *famous*."

Charlotte giggled.

"Actually," Freyja admitted, "I would have loved nothing better, Charlotte, than to have punched the Marquess of Hallmere in the nose again for leading me into that trap. But I really thought I had better not. Perhaps he will offer me some provocation to do it tomorrow."

She looked at her friend with a frown for a few moments before her lips twitched at the corners and she first chuckled and then laughed aloud.

He was a worthy foe. She must admit that much about him.

LADY HOLT-BARRON LEFT HER ROOM SOMETIME AFTER noon, looking pale and martyred, though she smiled cheerfully and assured her daughter and Freyja that she was quite rested and had only the smallest of headaches remaining. She did not believe she would go out calling on anyone during the afternoon, though, and she did not advise the younger ladies to go out walking. She rather fancied it was going to rain, and they would both catch chills if they were caught out in it.

She looked sharply at Freyja for a moment.

"My dear Lady Freyja," she asked, "what on earth were

you doing alone in Sydney Gardens yesterday? Why did you not wait for Charlotte to accompany you? Or why did you not at least take your maid with you?"

"I felt like air and exercise, ma'am," Freyja told her. "And I am far too old for chaperones."

Lady Holt-Barron looked somewhat shocked, but she did not pursue the matter. Freyja rather suspected that her hostess was a little afraid of her.

"Perhaps," Freyja continued, "you would be happier if I left Bath, ma'am. I can see that I embarrassed you this morning." And that was doubtless a massive understatement, she thought. She had embarrassed even herself, and she did not embarrass easily.

"Oh, *no*, Freyja," Charlotte cried.

"It is a generous offer," her hostess replied. "But I will not accept it, Lady Freyja. Within a few days the unfortunate incident will have been forgotten, I daresay. Tomorrow morning we will put a brave face on it and make our usual appearance in the Pump Room. Perhaps the Marquess of Hallmere will be tactful enough to remain at home."

"I am certainly not afraid to face him," Freyja said. "And of one thing I am quite convinced. He was about to steal a kiss from that serving girl. I would like to hear him deny *that*."

"Oh, my dear Lady Freyja," Lady Holt-Barron said, her voice faint with anxiety again, "I beg you not to confront him with any such accusation."

She jumped with alarm at the sound of the door knocker coming up from below, and she stood up to do a hasty hand-check of her dress and hair.

"I do hope this is not a caller," she said. "I really do not feel up to entertaining today. I expected all our acquaintance to leave us in peace until tomorrow."

As if her behavior this morning had plunged them all into quarantine, Freyja thought.

But a caller it must be. The housekeeper scratched on the door and handed her mistress a calling card.

"Gracious me!" Lady Holt-Barron exclaimed after reading the name on it. "The Marquess of Hallmere! And he is waiting below, Mrs. Tucker?"

"Waiting to see if you are at home, ma'am," the housekeeper explained.

Now what was he up to? Freyja wondered, her eyes narrowing.

Lady Holt-Barron glanced nervously at her. "*Are* we at home?"

"Oh, absolutely." Freyja raised her eyebrows. She was not going to hide from anyone, least of all him.

"Show his lordship up, Mrs. Tucker," Lady Holt-Barron said.

It was plain to see as soon as he set foot in the room that the Marquess of Hallmere patronized the famous Weston as a tailor. So did Wulfric and Freyja's other brothers. The marquess showed to distinct advantage in a green superfine coat that was so close-fitting that it looked as if he must have been poured into it and in gray pantaloons that clung to every impressive curve and muscle of his long legs. His linen was snowy white, his Hessian boots so shiny that he might have used them as twin mirrors if he looked down. His hat, gloves, and cane must have been left below.

Clearly the man had come here intending to impress them. And he did look impressive, Freyja was forced to admit. Even his teeth were perfect, just crooked enough to be interesting, but very white.

Lady Holt-Barron was obviously impressed too. She fluttered, a tendency she had when in the presence of someone of superior rank. She was also simpering, an unfortunate reaction to the sight of a handsome man. Charlotte was also impressed. She blushed.

Freyja crossed one leg over the other in a posture that a string of governesses during her growing years had told her was inelegant and unladylike, swung her free foot, raised her chin, and stared haughtily.

"I thank you, ma'am, for admitting me when I was not expected," he said, addressing himself to Lady Holt-Barron.

She fluttered and simpered more than ever and assured him that he was most welcome. She offered him a chair and he seated himself.

Just don't apologize for me, Freyja urged her hostess silently. And if he expected any apology from *her* he might wait until hell froze over.

"I will not take much of your time, ma'am," he said, still addressing Lady Holt-Barron. "I have come with an invitation from my grandmother for you and Miss Holt-Barron and Lady Freyja Bedwyn to join a small party for dinner tomorrow evening. We both consider it desirable to dispel any lingering fear anyone may be harboring that there is lasting animosity between Lady Freyja and myself over our, ah, slight misunderstanding this morning."

Freyja bared her teeth.

"I am sure there can be no such thought in anyone's mind, my lord," Lady Holt-Barron assured him. She was even batting her eyelids, though it was probably a nervous reaction rather than a flirtatious one, Freyja conceded.

"I feel no animosity," he said, finally turning his head and looking with wide, guileless eyes at Freyja. "I trust *you* do not, Lady Freyja?"

"No, why should I?" she said with studied nonchalance. "You gave a satisfactory explanation for what I observed in the park—for *most* of what I observed."

For a moment she saw laughter in the depths of his eyes and knew that he understood her meaning perfectly well. He had certainly been about to kiss that girl. But this afternoon he was playing the part of impeccably courteous gentleman and did not see fit either to grin at her or address her as sweetheart.

"I trust you will all come to Great Pulteney Street tomorrow evening, then?" he asked.

Lady Holt-Barron almost tripped all over herself in her eagerness to accept. The marquess took his leave five minutes later after they had all—with the exception of Freyja—engaged in a lively discussion of the weather.

"Lady Freyja!" Lady Holt-Barron said, clasping her hands to her bosom, her headache apparently dissipated. "I do believe all will be well after all and no shadow of scandal will be allowed to hang over your head. I even sense that the marquess is smitten by you."

Freyja snorted.

"He is *gorgeously* handsome," Charlotte said with a sigh.

"My love," her mother said reproachfully. "Remember Frederick."

The absent Frederick Wheatcroft, Charlotte's betrothed, was off shooting with her father and brothers.

Gorgeously handsome, indeed! *Too* handsome by half. And doubtless he thought now that he could charm her out of her indignation over his trickery—he had oozed charm from every pore of his body. They would see about *that*.

She should have let him be caught in that wardrobe like a mouse in a trap.

She should have been sure to take an inn room with all the ivy shaved off its outer walls.

She should have punched him in the nose again this morning while she had had the chance.

She should have . . .

She was so desperately *glad* that there was at least something of interest to look forward to tomorrow. The Marquess of Hallmere might be—and undoubtedly *was*—all sorts of nasty, unsavory things, but at least he was not *bland*.

CHAPTER IV

THE PLANNED DINNER AT LADY POTFORD'S WAS turning into a grand affair as she kept adding names to the guest list.

"You have been the Marquess of Hallmere for longer than six months, Joshua," she explained when he asked if she had one more leaf to add to the dining room table— and perhaps one more wing to add to the dining room itself. "It is high time you took your rightful place in society instead of chasing all over the country in search of amusement with low companions."

"But amusement is so . . . amusing, Grandmama," he said with an exaggerated sigh. He did not add that some of his "low" companions were aristocrats and the sons of aristocrats.

"It is time too that you returned to Penhallow," she said, not for the first time. "It is yours, not just as a possession, but as a responsibility too."

"My aunt lives there," he reminded her, "and my cousins. It would only upset them—and me—if I went to live there too. My aunt always had the running of the place, you know, even when my uncle still lived. He did not mind. I would."

"Well, and so you ought," his grandmother said, rather exasperated as she folded the last invitation and rang the bell to have a servant take it and deliver it. "You must go and exert yourself and make other arrangements for the marchioness and her daughters, Joshua. There is a dower house at Penhallow, is there not? Goodness! When your grandpapa died and Gregory became Potford, I would no more have dreamed of remaining at Grimley House than I would of flying to the moon. Gladys would not have liked it, and I would have liked it less."

Joshua stretched his legs out in front of him along the sitting room carpet and crossed them at the ankles. "*Exert* myself?" He grinned at her. "That sounds remarkably painful, Grandmama."

"Joshua." She turned in her chair at the escritoire and regarded him with some severity, "I have always chosen to believe that you were in France and other countries of Europe during the past five years risking the dangers of capture in an enemy nation merely for the amusement of indulging in such a prank. But I have always realized deep down that there was a far more alarming explanation for your presence there. Do not think now to convince me that you are a lazy care-for-naught intent upon nothing but your own amusement."

He raised his eyebrows and pursed his lips. He had, of course, been spying for the British government on the military forces and maneuvers of Napoléon Bonaparte, but not in any official capacity. He had no military rank or diplomatic status.

"Ah, but it *was* amusing, Grandmama," he told her.

She sighed and got to her feet. "What you *should* do," she said, "is choose a suitable bride, take her to Penhallow, and begin the new life that is yours whether you ever wished for it or not."

"I did not," he said decisively. "Albert was the heir and I never envied him his future prospects."

"But your cousin died five years ago," she reminded him—as if he *needed* reminding. "It is not as if your new status was sprung unexpectedly upon you when your uncle died."

"Except that he was a robust man when I went away," he said, "and died far sooner than I expected."

"Despite that ghastly scene in the Pump Room," she said, taking a seat close to his, "I cannot but admire the forthright manner in which Lady Freyja Bedwyn confronted what she had perceived as an unpardonable offense. Most ladies would have turned a blind eye or gossiped privately and blackened your name before you had a chance to defend yourself."

Joshua chuckled. "Most ladies would not have been walking alone in the park or would have turned tail and fled at the first sound of some other poor female screaming."

"She is Bewcastle's sister," his grandmother continued. "There is no higher stickler than the duke, or one of greater consequence unless one ascends into the realm of the princes themselves."

He looked more closely at her, suddenly alerted.

"You are not, by any chance," he asked her, "suggesting *Lady Freyja Bedwyn* as a bride?"

"Joshua." She leaned forward slightly in her chair. "You are now the *Marquess of Hallmere*. It would be a very eligible match for her as well as for you."

"And that is what *this* is all about?" he asked her. "This grand dinner?"

"Not at all," she said. "This dinner is to restore the proprieties in the eyes of all doubters. It really was a ghastly scene though I must admit to having enjoyed a private chuckle or two since over the memory of it."

"She throws a mean punch," he said, "as I have twice learned to my cost. Yet you think she would be a suitable *bride?*"

"Twice?" She looked sharply at him.

"We need not make mention of the other occasion," he said sheepishly. "I am sorry to disappoint you, Grandmama, but I have too great a regard for my health to launch into a courtship of Lady Freyja Bedwyn. Or of any other lady, for that matter. I am not ready for marriage."

"I wonder why it is," she said, getting to her feet again, "that every man when he says those words appears to believe them quite fervently. And why does every man appear to believe that he is the first to speak them? I must go down to the kitchen and see that all is proceeding well for tonight's dinner."

And why was it, Joshua thought somewhat ruefully, that all women believed that once a man had succeeded to a title and fortune he must also have acquired a burning desire to share them with a mate?

Lady Freyja Bedwyn!

He chuckled aloud and remembered her as she had looked yesterday afternoon in Lady Holt-Barron's sitting room—on her haughtiest dignity and bristling with barely suppressed resentment and hostility. And unable to resist at least one barbed gibe by implying that she knew very well he had been about to kiss that serving girl.

He wondered if she would appreciate the joke of his grandmother's preposterous suggestion. He really must share it with her, he thought, chuckling again—and keep a wary eye on her fists as he did so.

T HERE WAS NO ONE AT LADY POTFORD'S DINNER THAT Freyja did not know. She felt perfectly at ease in the company. It took her a while, though, to realize that most of the other guests were far from at ease in *hers*. They must be wondering, she thought, whether she was about to make another spectacularly embarrassing spectacle of herself tonight.

How foolish people were. Did they not understand that gentility had been bred into her very bones? She conversed with her neighbors at the dining table with practiced ease and studiously ignored the Marquess of Hallmere, who was seated at the foot of the table looking handsome enough in his dove-gray-and-white evening clothes to seriously annoy a Greek god or two. He ignored her too if one discounted the single occasion when their eyes met along the table. She was sure it was not a trick of the flickering candlelight that made it appear as if he blinked slowly—with one eye.

Well, every day brought something new, she thought, renewing her efforts to be sociable to the very deaf Sir Rowland Withers to her right. She had never been *winked* at before, unless it was by one of her brothers.

But she and the marquess ignoring each other was not, of course, the purpose of the evening. As soon as the gentlemen had joined the ladies in the drawing room after dinner, entertainment was called for and Miss Fairfax obligingly seated herself at the pianoforte and played a couple of Bach fugues with admirable flair and dexterity.

"Lady Freyja?" Lady Potford asked when she had finished. "Will you favor us with a piece or a song?"

Oh, dear—her close acquaintances had learned long ago that Lady Freyja Bedwyn was not like other young ladies, willing and able to trot out their accomplishments at every social gathering. She decided upon candor, as she usually did—it was easier than simpering.

"After I had had a few lessons at the pianoforte as a young girl," she explained to the gathered assembly, "my music teacher asked me to raise my hands and declared himself amazed that I was not in possession of ten thumbs. Fortunately for me, two of my brothers were within earshot and reported the remark with great glee to our father—intending the joke, of course, to be at my expense. The music teacher was dismissed and never replaced."

There was general laughter, though Lady Holt-Barron looked distinctly uncomfortable.

"A song, then?" Lady Potford asked.

"Not alone, ma'am," Freyja said firmly. "I have the sort of voice that needs to be buried in the middle of a very large choir—if it is to be aired at all."

"I sing a little, Lady Freyja," the marquess said. "Perhaps we can join our voices in a duet. There is a pile of music on top of the pianoforte. Shall we see what we can find while someone else entertains the guests?"

"Oh, splendid," Lady Potford said, and there were a few other murmurings of polite interest.

She should, Freyja realized belatedly, have made mention of rusty saws in connection with her singing voice, but she never liked to be quite untruthful. Hallmere was, as she expected, looking at her with polite interest—and a gleam of amusement in his eyes. And everyone else was observing with keen interest this first exchange between yesterday's antagonists.

She got to her feet and approached the pianoforte, near which he was standing.

"Miss Holt-Barron?" Lady Potford was asking politely, and Charlotte without a murmur of protest approached the instrument and began a flawless performance of some Mozart sonata.

The marquess picked up the whole pile of music and carried it to a wide, velvet-padded window seat. He sat on one side of it and Freyja on the other.

"Might I be permitted to observe, Lady Freyja," he said, "that you look particularly fetching in that shade of sea green? It matches your eyes. And might I apologize for not believing your claim to be the sister of a duke? No duke's sister of my acquaintance, you see, sleeps in unlocked inn rooms without any accompanying maid, or walks in a public park without a chaperone. Or punches men in the nose when they displease her."

"You would deny, I suppose," she said, picking up a sheet of music that announced itself as a song for two voices. But she saw at the very first glance that the singer of the top part had to soar to a high G and slipped the music to the bottom of the pile. "You would deny, I suppose, that you were about to steal a kiss from that poor girl?"

"Oh, absolutely," he agreed.

"Then you lie!" she retorted, snatching another sheet for a song in more than one part off the pile and glaring at him. "I am not *quite* stupid, despite your insinuation yesterday morning to the contrary."

"No!" he said, his eyes laughing at her—he was making no attempt to look through the music himself. "Did I do that? But why would I do something so ungentlemanly when the ghastly truth must have presented itself to the intelligence of everyone gathered around? It *was* rather a large gathering, was it not?"

Freyja was given the distinct impression that she might have met her match—something that rarely happened outside the members of her own family. She gave her attention to the music in her hands. It was all about cuckoos, and the songwriter appeared to have devised his whole piece so that the two voices—no, four—might deceive the audience into believing they were a flock of demented birds in a dither and unable to utter any sound but their own names. It was the sort of song most gatherings would exclaim over in delight and admiration. Freyja set it at the bottom of the pile.

"I feel compelled to defend my honor yet again," the marquess continued. "I was not about to *steal* a kiss, Lady Freyja. I was about to *convey* one and have one conveyed willingly in return. I cannot tell you how ill-timed your interruption was. She had lips like cherries and I was within moments of tasting their sweet nectar. *Does* one suck nectar from a cherry? But I daresay my meaning is clear enough anyway."

If his eyes danced any more merrily, they would be in danger of dancing right out of his head. And he was wearing some *perfume*. Freyja despised men who wore perfume, but this was subtle and musky and wrapped enticingly about her senses. Her eyes dipped to his lips, which had come so close to kissing the maid in the park, found them as perfect as the rest of him, and dipped lower to the pile of music. She had just remembered that those lips had actually kissed *her*.

"You are supposed to be helping me select a duet to sing," she said.

"I thought I would leave it to you," he said. "If you did not like my choice you would doubtless quarrel with it and with me and find some reason for punching me in the nose, and it is altogether possible that other people in the room might notice. And even if they did not, I derive no great pleasure from having my nose punched. Now why are you frowning so ferociously?"

"Nymphs and shepherds and Phyllises and Amaryllises," she said, frowning down in disgust at the music in her hands. "The last one was all about cuckoos." She set the piece with the other discarded ones beneath the pile and found another duet.

"Are you *always* so cross?" he asked her.

"In disagreeable company, yes," she said, looking coldly at him.

He grinned at her. "Do you ever smile?"

"I have been *smiling* all evening," she told him. "Until, that is, I was forced into this tête-à-tête."

"Almost, Lady Freyja," he said softly, "I am led to believe that you are trying to deliver me a resounding setdown."

"Almost, Lord Hallmere," she retorted, "I am led to believe that you must have *some* intelligence."

He chuckled softly, a sound that was drowned beneath the polite applause that succeeded Charlotte's playing. No one else took the instrument. Card tables were being set up and the guests were taking their places. No one attempted to include either of the two sitting on the window seat.

"Tonight," the marquess said, "you have been smiling what I suspect is your public Lady Freyja Bedwyn smile, the gracious expression that informs the world that you are someone of consequence and equal to any social situation. I have a mind to see your private Freyja smile, if there is such a thing."

There were not many men who would dare to flirt with her. And this was definitely flirtation—he had deliberately lowered his voice. *Mock* flirtation, of course. His eyes were still laughing at her.

"I have what my brothers describe as my feline grin,"

she told him, regarding him coldly. "Shall I oblige you with a display of that?"

He chuckled again and reached across the pile between them to take the music from her hands.

"Hmm," he said after examining it for a moment or two. "'Near to the silver Trent Sirena dwelleth.' I like the sound of her already. It gets better. 'She to whom nature lent all that excelleth.' The mind boggles, does it not?"

"*Your* mind obviously does," she said.

He did something then that had her itching to curl her fingers into fists. He let his eyes roam slowly down her body, starting with the rather wide expanse of bosom showing above the fashionably low neckline of her gown and moving on downward, giving the impression that he saw every curve beneath the barrier of her high-waisted gown and its loose, flowing skirts. He pursed his lips.

"'She to whom nature lent all that excelleth,'" he murmured again. And then he smiled—it was definitely not his grin this time but an expression of great charm clearly designed to make women turn weak at the knees. "Shall we move to the pianoforte bench, Lady Freyja, and try this one?"

She was weak at the knees with suppressed wrath, Freyja decided when she got to her feet. And then his hand came to rest against the hollow of her back. She looked haughtily over her shoulder at him.

"I am quite capable of crossing the distance between the window and the pianoforte without your guidance, I thank you, Lord Hallmere," she said.

"But I felt compelled to test a theory," he told her. "'She to whom nature lent...' Never mind."

"I suppose," she said, "you realize that I am quite immune to your flatteries and attempts at flirtation. But of course you do. *That* is why you are doing it. I suppose you hope to provoke me into some public display of temper."

"Better flirtation than courtship, I would think," he said. "My grandmother has suggested to me that I court you. She believes our marriage would be a dazzling match for both of us."

She stared at him, speechless.

He grinned at her. "We agree on one thing at least, sweetheart," he murmured, and indicated the pianoforte.

A few moments later they were seated side by side on a pianoforte bench that had not been designed to seat two. He made no attempt to perch on the very edge of his end of it, as any decent gentleman would do, but crowded her at the hip and all along her bare arm. They had apparently been forgotten by the rest of the company, who were concentrating upon their card games to the accompaniment of the low hum of conversation.

"Let us try," the marquess said, spreading the music on the stand and resting his hands on the keys—they were long-fingered, well-manicured hands, Freyja saw. Was there anything *not* perfect about him physically? Yes, there were his crooked teeth, though actually they were only very slightly crooked, and they looked more attractive this way than if they had been lined up all in a neat row. "Do you read music?"

"Of course I read music," she said. "I just cannot *play* it."

He had a pleasant tenor voice, which turned out to be rather similar to her contralto voice. Surprisingly, they made a pleasing blend of sound. The song moved slowly and melodiously so that it was fairly easy to sing it passably well even if not to master it.

"Oh, well done, indeed," Lady Potford said when, after a few false starts, they sang the song all the way through without stopping or making any major blunders.

It seemed she had not been the only one listening quietly as they had sung. There was polite applause from every table. Lady Holt-Barron was beaming her approval.

"I believe," the marquess murmured, "a crisis has been successfully weathered, Lady Freyja. I have been seen openly to have forgiven you, and you have been seen graciously to have accepted the error of your assumptions."

She leapt to her feet and glared down at him while he looked back in innocent astonishment.

"*You* have forgiven *me?*" she said with all the hauteur she could muster. "*The error of my assumptions?* When it was all your doing? I would have you know—"

But Lady Potford had got hastily to her feet too, mere moments after Freyja.

"It is time we had the tea tray brought in," she said. "Joshua, my dear, would you be so good as to pull the bell rope?"

Freyja busied herself with folding the music and bringing the rest of the pile back from the window seat. *That* had been a near escape. She was beginning to feel like a puppet dancing on the Marquess of Hallmere's string. He had done that deliberately—again. She had always been known for her outspokenness and hot temper, but she had always known where and when to use each—and, more to the point, where and when *not* to.

She went to stand at Charlotte's table, and looked at the cards over her friend's shoulder.

J OSHUA WAS FEELING READY TO MOVE ON AGAIN, though he would stay out the week in Bath since his grandmother expected it. Lady Freyja Bedwyn was avoiding him even though he went everywhere the fashionable were expected to go and so did she. It was amusing to watch her greet society with gracious, if rather bored, hauteur. He sensed that it was not entirely an act to cover the embarrassment of that scene she had trapped herself into in the Pump Room. She was the daughter and sister of a duke—arrogance came naturally to her. He ought to have believed her from the start.

He saw her two mornings in a row in the Pump Room. The first time, she was leaving with Lady Holt-Barron and the lady's daughter just as he was arriving with his grandmother, and they all exchanged the merest civilities. The second time she was strolling with the Earl of Willett, whose head was bent attentively to hers as she talked. She favored Joshua with the merest nod of acknowledgment when she saw him.

He saw her on Milsom Street that same afternoon. She was standing on the pavement talking with Willett. Lady Holt-Barron and her daughter were coming out of a milliner's shop as Joshua walked by. There was a flurry of greetings all around, and he continued on his way.

He saw her at the theater one evening. She was sitting between Miss Holt-Barron and Willett and fanning her face languidly. She raised her eyebrows when Joshua caught her eye, nodded graciously, and then turned her attention back to the conversation.

There was not much, then, by way of flirtation to keep Joshua in Bath beyond the week—not even when he accompanied his grandmother on an afternoon visit to Lady Holt-Barron's on the Circus, that splendid circle of tall Georgian terraced houses with a circular green at its center and several magnificent ancient trees. It was true that they arrived just as Lady Freyja and Miss Holt-Barron were setting out to walk on the Royal Crescent close by and that Miss Holt-Barron invited him to join them. But they already had another escort. Willett took his place firmly at Lady Freyja's side, though she did not take his arm.

She walked, Joshua noticed as he strolled along Brock Street behind them with Miss Holt-Barron, with a firm, manly stride despite her small stature. Willett's cane tapped elegantly along the cobbles. Joshua clasped his hands behind him and set about making himself agreeable to his companion.

The Royal Crescent was a magnificent semicircle of terraced houses, a deliberate complement to the Circus. Several other people were strolling along the cobbled street before the houses, enjoying the view over the park in front and down the hill to the town below. And inevitably, of course, these people exchanged greetings as they passed one another and sometimes stopped to exchange any news or gossip that had accumulated since the morning gathering in the Pump Room.

"Bath is divine," Miss Fanny Darwin declared when her group came up with Joshua's and they had all stopped, "and there are *so* many exciting things to do all the time. Would you not agree, Lord Willett?"

"Certainly, Miss Darwin," the earl said. "Bath offers a pleasing combination of outdoor exercise and indoor entertainment. All to be enjoyed in the congenial company of one's peers."

"We took the carriage to Sydney Gardens yesterday afternoon and strolled there for all of an hour," Miss Hester Darwin said. "It was wonderful exercise in delightfully picturesque surroundings. Have you seen the park, Lady Freyja?"

Her brother cleared his throat, her cousin, Sir Leonard Eston, picked an invisible speck of lint from one of his sleeves, her sister flushed scarlet, and Miss Hester Darwin clapped a hand to her mouth too late as everyone remembered what had resulted from Lady Freyja's solitary foray into Sydney Gardens.

Joshua grinned. "I do believe Lady Freyja has, Miss Darwin," he said. "So have I."

"Exercise!" Lady Freyja exclaimed. "People come to Bath for their health, and for the sake of their health they stroll in the Pump Room and they stroll on the Crescent and they stroll in the park. It is a word that should be struck from the English language—*strolling*. If I do not *walk* somewhere soon, or—better yet—*ride* somewhere where there is space to move, I may well end up in a Bath chair, being wheeled from place to place and sipping on Bath water."

Her audience chose to react to her words as if she had uttered something enormously witty. The gentlemen laughed; the ladies tittered.

"You must certainly be rescued from the Bath water," Joshua said. "Come riding with me tomorrow, Lady Freyja. We will seek out the hills and the open spaces beyond the confines of the city."

"It sounds like heaven," she said, looking at him with approval for perhaps the first time. "I will gladly come."

"But not alone, Lady Freyja," Willett said hastily. "It would be somewhat scandalous, I fear. Perhaps we can make up a riding party. *I* would certainly join it. Would you, Miss Holt-Barron?"

"Oh, I would too," Miss Fanny Darwin cried. "I enjoy nothing better than a ride, provided the pace is not too fast or the distance too far. Gerald, you must come too, and you, Leonard, and then Mama can have no objection to allowing Hester and me to join the party."

Joshua's glance locked with Lady Freyja's. He could sense the grimace she kept from her face. He grinned at her and winked.

He was pleased to see her nostrils flare with indignation.

Perhaps, he thought hopefully, tomorrow would be more amusing than the past few days had been.

CHAPTER V

NEITHER FREYJA NOR CHARLOTTE HAD HER OWN horse with her in Bath, but they were able to hire some for the day. Freyja sent back the first horse that was brought around to the house with the message that she had been riding since she was in leading strings and had never felt any inclination to bounce along on a tired old hack that looked to be lame in all four legs. The second mount met with her approval even though Lady Holt-Barron thought it high-spirited enough to need a man's firm hand on the reins and begged Freyja to ride very carefully.

"Whatever would I say to the duke, Lady Freyja," she asked rhetorically, "if you were carried home with a broken neck?"

Freyja and Charlotte rode side by side down steep Gay Street in the direction of the Abbey, outside which they had agreed to meet the other six members of the riding party. It was a glorious day, warm enough for summer but with more freshness in the air.

"If we have to amble along once we have left Bath behind at the horse equivalent of a stroll, Charlotte," Freyja said, "I shall have a tantrum. Will the Misses Darwin be so mean-spirited?"

"I fear they will," Charlotte said with a chuckle. "We are not all neck-or-nothing riders like you, Freyja. Will the Earl of Willett find some time alone with you today, do you suppose? He has been very determined during the past few days. He must be very close to making a declaration."

"Oh, dear," Freyja said. She had encouraged him rather, simply because she had wanted to *discourage* the Marquess of Hallmere, who had been deliberately amusing himself at her expense and who seemed to know exactly how to make her forget herself in public. Doubtless it was all *very* amusing to a man who had probably never entertained a serious thought in his life. Unfortunately, the Earl of Willett did not need much encouraging. "I do hope he can be saved from that embarrassment."

"You would not accept him, then?" Charlotte asked.

She *should*, Freyja thought. He was an earl with a grand estate in Norfolkshire and a fortune rumored to be very large indeed—not to mention his prospects of doubling it after the demise of his uncle. He was amiable if a little starchy in manner. He would meet with Wulfric's approval. She should marry him and be done with it. But the memory of the sort of passion she had known with Kit Butler for one brief summer four years ago came to mind unbidden. And then her eyes alighted upon the gorgeously handsome figure of the Marquess of Hallmere as they approached the appointed meeting place. And she knew that she wanted more out of life than merely making do with a marriage that promised respectability and good fortune.

He was riding a splendidly powerful and sleek black mount—the marquess, that was. Freyja was instantly envious. His long legs, encased in buff riding breeches and black top boots, showed to best advantage when he was on horseback. So did the rest of him. He might be a frivolous, licentious man, and she seemed to do nothing but bristle with hostility whenever she was near him, but at least he was alive and made her feel alive. And she was enormously grateful to him for suggesting this ride, though she hoped it was to be more than a mere sedate crawl over the countryside.

"I think not," she said in answer to Charlotte's question. "I shall try diligently to avoid riding at his side. It would quite ruin my day—and his too, I daresay—if he were to blurt out the question today."

But the Earl of Willett was not to be so easily deterred. Once encouraged—and she *had* encouraged him—he had become bold in his pursuit of her. While the marquess rode with the Misses Darwin on either side of him, their trilling laughter grating on Freyja's ears, and Charlotte rode between Mr. Darwin and Sir Leonard Eston, the earl led off the party with Freyja. They moved sedately through the streets of Bath and up the hill beyond it, taking the London road.

"We will not put our horses through their paces on this steep gradient," the earl informed Freyja, "or indeed when we reach level land. I am ever mindful of the fact that there are four ladies in the party and that you ride sidesaddle. I admire you immensely for your grace and skill in doing so, but I will be diligent in my efforts not to put you in any unnecessary danger."

Freyja leveled an appalled glance at him but said nothing. They *were*, after all, on a rather steep hill at the moment.

They all stopped when they reached the top to admire the view back down to the elegant, gleaming white buildings of Bath.

"This is what I most look forward to every time we come here," Miss Fanny Darwin said with a contented sigh. "This first sight of the city. All the white buildings are quite dazzling on the eye when the sun shines, as it does today. Are we to ride much farther, Lord Willett?"

Freyja looked sharply at her.

"There is a village not far off along the road," the earl said. "I would suggest that we ride there at a leisurely pace, drink some tea or lemonade at the inn, and ride back again. I will not suggest that we leave the road. There are always rabbit holes and uneven ground in the fields as a trap to the unwary."

It was still morning, Freyja thought. Was he intending, then, to be back in Bath for the regular activities of the afternoon? And since when had this become *his* outing?

"At a leisurely pace?" she said. "Along the road? For the mere pleasure of drinking tea? I came out for a *ride*." She pointed to her right with her whip. "I intend to ride that way, across the hills. Indeed, I intend to *gallop* across them."

"Lady Freyja—" The earl sounded genuinely alarmed.

"Oh, I say!" Mr. Darwin's voice was bright with interest.

"Gerald," Miss Hester Darwin said, "Mama made you promise not to let us ride fast and not to go galloping on ahead of us."

"I will see you all back in Bath, then," Freyja said, turning her horse off the roadway and edging it through a gap in the hedgerow into the field beyond.

Already she felt more exhilarated. She nudged her horse into a canter and did not look back to see if anyone had the courage to follow her. But if no one else did, she guessed, the Earl of Willett probably would. He would feel duty-bound to escort her. Perhaps after all she had trapped herself into a tête-à-tête with him. She urged her mount to a faster pace. Ah, she could feel the air in her face at last.

She could hear hooves thudding behind her. She hoped that if he *had* come, he was not alone. She turned her head to look and felt instant relief. Of course! She might have known that the Marquess of Hallmere would be the one to take up the challenge. It was he, after all, who had suggested this ride—for just the two of them. And it was he who had winked at her—again!—when Miss Darwin had expressed her hope that the party would not ride too far or too fast.

He was grinning. That, of course, was no surprise.

"Do you see that white rock?" he asked, coming up alongside her as she slowed somewhat and pointing ahead with his whip.

There was a white speck in the distance. At least three fields lay between it and their present position. But from the rock, jutting out over the land below, there must be a splendid panorama that included the city of Bath.

"That is to be the finishing point of our race?" she asked, anticipating what he was about to say. "Very well. I will wait for you there." She spurred her horse and bent low over its neck.

It was not her own horse, of course, but it was no slug. It responded to her commands with a surge of power. She knew only a moment's apprehension as they approached the first hedge. But it would be ignominious indeed to turn aside to find a gate. The horse soared over with surely a foot to spare, and Freyja laughed. With her peripheral vision she could see the marquess not quite one length back from her. If he was holding back out of a gallant intention to allow a lady to win, she thought, he would learn his mistake. But he was not, of course, a man from whom she need fear undue gallantry. He got past her long before the next hedge loomed near and cleared it a full length and more ahead of her. He had a splendid seat, she noticed admiringly.

The race became everything after that. She had always been intensely competitive, perhaps the more so because she had always been small and the only girl among numerous boisterous boys—her brothers Aidan, Rannulf, and Alleyne, and the neighboring Butlers, Jerome, Kit, and Sydnam. She had never felt like a girl with a sister. Morgan was seven years younger than she. She had competed with the boys and made herself their equal.

She competed now, urging her mount on ever faster and faster, hearing the thunder of its hooves beneath her, feeling the wind whip at her hat and her hair and riding habit, watching the gap between her and the horse ahead getting narrower and narrower until by the time they jumped the final hedge, they were almost neck and neck.

The marquess made the mistake after they had landed of looking across at her, perhaps in some surprise to see that she had caught up since he was certainly *not* making allowances either for the fact that she was a woman or for the fact that she rode sidesaddle. As they converged on the huge white rock, she was in front of him by a whole head. She whooped in triumph and turned to laugh at him.

"I have not had so much fun in ages," she cried.

"I am glad I allowed you to win, then," he said.

He was incautiously close. She reached out with her whip and dug him in the ribs with it.

"Ouch!" he said. "Where did you learn to ride like that? I expected to be fully rested and fast asleep here by the time you came trotting up." He swung down from his horse's back and tethered it to a tree, and then he strode over to her and reached up his arms. "Allow me."

She set her hands on his shoulders and would have jumped down, but he lifted her with strong hands at her waist, slid her all-too-slowly down his front, and then, as soon as her feet were on firm ground, dipped his head and kissed her on the lips—as he had done on another memorable occasion.

His hands circled her wrists as he lifted his head. "I graciously concede defeat with a kiss," he said, grinning. "And at the same time I protect my nose from having a fist collide with it."

He was an enormously attractive man, she thought. That was no new discovery, of course. But what surprised her was that at this particular moment it was not just an intellectual realization. She could feel her body reacting to his attractiveness with a heightened awareness and slight shortness of breath. She had not reacted physically to any man since Kit.

But the Marquess of Hallmere was certainly not the man with whom to conceive any sort of passion. Would he not be delighted if he could bring her to such discomfiture? She smiled her feline grin at him, released her wrists, and turned away to climb up onto the white rock. The wind whipped at the heavy skirts of her riding habit and at her feathered hat. She pulled the latter off impatiently, pocketing the pins that had held it to her hair, and then she could not resist pulling out her hairpins too. It was sheer bliss to raise her head and feel the wind blowing through her hair. She drew a deep breath of air and expelled it slowly.

"A Viking maiden standing in the prow of a Viking ship," he said from down below. "You would have inspired a boatload of warriors into hacking their way ashore and conquering a new land for you."

He had one booted foot up on the rock, one arm draped across his leg. In his other hand he held his hat. His hair blew about, gleaming very blond in the sunlight.

"I have often suspected," she said, "that I was born in the wrong era."

"Lady Freyja Bedwyn," he said, "I do not believe I insult you by observing that you must be well past the age of twenty, do I? Why are you still unmarried?"

"Why are *you?*" she countered.

"I asked first."

She looked out at the view and drew in another deep breath of air.

"From birth," she said, "I was intended for Jerome Butler, Viscount Ravensberg, eldest son of the Earl of Redfield, my father's neighbor. We were betrothed when I was twenty-one. He died before I was twenty-two and before we married."

"I am sorry," he said.

"You need not be," she told him. "We grew up together and were fond of each other. I mourned his death. But we felt no grand passion for each other."

"How long ago did he die?" he asked.

"Longer than three years," she said.

"And there has been no one else in all the time since then?" he asked.

"It is your turn," she told him. "Why are *you* not married? You too are well past the age of twenty."

"I grew up as a poor relation in the home of my uncle, the late marquess," he said. "He had a son, my cousin Albert. I would not have been considered a good catch until his accidental death five years ago suddenly made me the heir. My uncle had three daughters but no more sons. I suppose I became instantly eligible as soon as I became the heir, but from the time of Albert's death until the present I have scarcely been in one place long enough to form any lasting attachment."

"Am I to commiserate with you?" she asked, gazing down at him. "Or has the life suited you very well? Love them and leave them, is it?"

He chuckled. "My grandmother still wants me to court you," he said, "even after you began to rip up at me again during her party. She thinks you are merely high-spirited. She believes you need a firm hand on the rein. Mine, in fact."

"Setting aside the fact that you mentioned the last point—perhaps even invented it—entirely to arouse my ire," she said, "your grandmother is going to be disappointed, is she not? You have no wish to court me and I have no wish to be courted. At least we are in agreement over that."

He got up onto the rock then and came to stand beside her. She was reminded of how very tall he was, how well formed.

"You are quite right," he said. "I do not have marriage in mind, and, fortunately, neither do you. I need not fear, then, that you will get the wrong idea if I tell you that I feel an almost overpowering urge to kiss you properly. Will I acquire two black eyes and a broken nose if I give in to that urge?" He turned his head to smile dazzlingly at her. His eyes, as she fully expected, were dancing with merriment.

She drew breath to deliver the withering set-down that such pretension deserved. But it *was* tempting. She was twenty-five years old and had not been kissed in four years. Jerome, strangely enough, had never kissed more than the back of her hand. Sometimes the emptiness and the alone-ness of having loved and lost Kit were almost too much to bear.

And here was a man—a handsome, devastatingly attractive man—who expected nothing from her beyond a kiss and who knew that she would demand nothing in return.

"The lady hesitates," he said. "Interesting."

"You would *not* suffer any mutilation to your face," she said firmly. "Not unless you were to fall from the rock on your way down."

She felt horribly embarrassed then and horribly—and foolishly—aware of her ugliness. It was years and years since she had given up lamenting what could not be changed. Nature had given her a wild bush for hair and eyebrows that were a different color from it, and her father had handed on to her the Bedwyn nose, as he had to all his offspring except Morgan, who, like their mother, was perfection itself.

Freyja turned determinedly as he set down his hat in a sheltered hollow and then took hers from her hand and set it there too. She lifted her chin.

He flicked it lazily with the knuckle of his forefinger. His eyelids had become rather heavy, she noticed, and they had the strange effect of causing her insides to perform a flip-flop. This definitely had not been a good idea, but it was too late now to say no. He would be able to accuse her of cowardice, and with some reason.

He was certainly taking his time. She had expected him to dip his head and claim her lips without further ado. At least then she could have closed her eyes and hidden her embarrassment. Both his hands were up and touching her face, though he did that only with his fingertips. He ran his thumbs over her eyebrows, one forefinger lightly down her nose.

"Interesting," he said. "You have an interesting face. Unforgettable."

At least, she thought, he had not called her beautiful. Out of sheer principle she could not have continued if he had.

His hands cupped her face.

"You may touch me too, you know," he said, "if you wish."

"I do not wish. Yet," she added, and watched laughter flicker behind his eyes.

He rubbed his nose lightly across hers and then angled his head and touched his lips softly to hers for a moment. Her hands came to rest on either side of his waist. She had to concentrate upon not snatching herself free and breaking into a run. How mortifying that would be!

Skittish, aging maiden—unchaperoned—flees clutches of practiced rake.

His tongue was licking softly, enticingly against her lips. She gripped his waist a little harder, leaned a little closer, and parted her lips. His tongue came through and curled up behind to stroke the soft, moist flesh within. Raw sensation burst to life in every part of her, from her lips to her knees—no, to her toes. She slid her arms about his waist, stepped closer until her bosom was pressed to his chest and her abdomen to his, and opened her mouth.

He kissed her then with all the skill and expertise of what she later guessed to be a man of vast experience, who must have practiced his art on half the female population of Europe—at least half. She could only cling and press closer and use her tongue to fence with his and give as much as she could of her own meager skills out of sheer self-defense.

It suddenly felt like midsummer during a heat wave.

She had no idea how long it lasted. She *did* know that

when she started to come to herself—it was when she sensed that he was about to lift his mouth from hers at last—she could feel one of his hands spread across her bottom, holding her firmly against him. And she was not such an innocent that she did not understand perfectly well exactly *what* she was being held firmly against.

"Well," she said, her voice only slightly breathless when he lifted his head and looked down at her, his eyelids considerably more heavy than they had been before he started, "that was very pleasant."

The smile began in his eyes and spread to his lips and then had him throwing back his head and shouting with laughter as he released her.

"That was my very finest turn-the-lady's-knees-to-jelly kiss," he said. "And it was *very pleasant*? And so it was too. I had better get you back up on your horse, Lady Freyja, and myself back on mine before my self-image has been quite deflated. I do believe there is a village over the next rise or the one beyond it. Shall we ride that way and see if we can find an inn or a pastry cook to feed us? Kissing is hungry work."

He grinned as he offered her her hat and put his own on with a flourish, pulling it low over his brow to prevent its being blown away in the wind.

Her knees, she realized after testing them surreptitiously before she took a step forward, were going to bear her up. That was certainly one of the more foolish things she had done recently. She had expected little more than a peck of the nature of the other two kisses he had dealt her—one in the inn room at their first encounter and the other after he had lifted her off her horse this morning. She might have guessed when he had talked of kissing her *properly* that he had a great deal more in mind.

She felt considerably discomposed and was not enjoying

the feeling one bit. It helped that he was so careless about the whole thing that he did not seem to realize that she was not quite herself. He would surely have taken advantage of the situation if he had suspected. He would have slain her with his grinning wit.

She set her booted foot on his clasped hands, and he tossed her up into the saddle before mounting himself.

"Of course," she said in her haughtiest voice, "that was not an open invitation to maul me whenever the urge is upon you. It was a pleasant embrace, but it is not to be repeated. *That* would be a bore."

"There," he said, turning a laughing face to hers before leading the way across the hill in the direction of the village he thought was close by, "a set-down was not to be avoided after all. I am crushed, deflated, robbed of all my confidence with the fair sex for all time. Perhaps it will be the epitaph on my tombstone—*his life was very pleasant, but any repetition would be a bore*. I need some strong liquor. A tumbler of brandy at the very least."

Freyja rode after him, smiling at his back.

NOW THAT HAD BEEN A FOOLISH ERROR OF JUDGMENT, Joshua thought while they sat in a small inn parlor, eating meat pasties and drinking tea and ale, and all the way back to Bath.

She had looked really rather magnificent standing up on that rock, her hair free and wild as it had been the first time he saw her, but with the sunlight on it and wind in it this time. He had wanted to kiss her—but in the same sort of light, flirtatious way he had treated her all through their encounters so far.

He had not—he had *certainly* not—intended kissing her that way. And he had not anticipated her own wild outpouring of passion. Which was foolish of him really. Despite all her haughtiness, he had had ample evidence that she was a woman of forceful character and uncertain temper and impulsive nature.

She would, he suspected now, be all wild, unleashed passion in bed.

It was something he would have been altogether more comfortable not suspecting at all since the only way he could verify such an enticing idea was through marriage, and marriage was just not in his immediate or medium-term plans.

It was fortunate indeed that it was not in hers either.

He escorted her all the way to Lady Holt-Barron's door in Bath and took her horse back to the livery stable from which it had been hired. Then he stabled his own horse and arrived back at his grandmother's in the middle of the afternoon, feeling windblown and full of energy and determined that he must leave Bath within the next few days before he was tempted to step into some further indiscretion with Lady Freyja Bedwyn that perhaps he would not be able to step out of so easily.

His grandmother was entertaining in the drawing room, Gibbs informed him. She had asked that Lord Hallmere call on her there immediately after he returned from his ride.

Joshua followed the butler up the stairs, checking to see that his riding clothes were at least marginally respectable for a brief appearance in the drawing room. But his grandmother had said immediately. He had better not take the time to go to his room to change.

There were two ladies with his grandmother. Joshua had seen neither of them in five years, but there was no mistaking his aunt, the Marchioness of Hallmere. She was of medium height and slight build and looked sweet and frail and even sickly. She had always looked the same way. But the outer appearance, as he had discovered to his cost during his years at Penhallow, hid a steely, domineering will, and a mean, humorless disposition. The younger woman with her, less plump, less plain than he remembered her, was Constance, her eldest daughter.

His aunt never left Penhallow. It was her domain and she ruled it like a private fiefdom. Even the desirability of taking her daughters to London when they reached a suitable age for presentation to the queen and an introduction to the beau monde had not coaxed her away. It must be something of immense importance that had brought her to Bath.

Himself, no doubt.

He had ignored her invitations to come home to Penhallow. So she had taken the extraordinary step of coming to him—informed of his presence here, no doubt, by her friend Mrs. Lumbard. His heart landed somewhere in the soles of his boots.

"Aunt?" he said. "Constance?" He bowed to them both before greeting his grandmother with a stiff smile.

"Joshua," his aunt said, getting to her feet and coming toward him, both slender hands outstretched. Her voice shook with emotion. There were tears in her eyes. "My dearest boy. We have been living in anxiety for too long, my poor girls and I. Hallmere—the *late* Hallmere—is gone, and Albert is gone. We are entirely at your mercy. You were raised at Penhallow just like one of our own, of course, but the young often forget the debts they owe to those who loved them and sacrificed for them during their growing years."

Good Lord! Could she look him in the eye and utter such nonsensical drivel? But of course she could. Joshua

took her offered hands in his—they were limp and cold—
and squeezed them before releasing them.

"I am not about to toss you out on the street with my
cousins, Aunt," he said briskly. Besides, even if he did just
that, she had her more than adequate widow's settlement
from the estate.

"But you are certain to marry soon," she said, "and we
will be in the way of your marchioness, much as I would
welcome her to Penhallow with open arms. No, I have
come to Bath to arrange matters with you to the satisfaction of all of us. I have brought Constance with me."

Of course she had brought Constance with her. And
one glance at his cousin's pale, set face assured him that
she knew the reason as well as he did—and liked it as little.

*Why had she not spoken up, then? Why had she not refused
to come with her mother? Refused to comply with the scheme his
aunt was obviously concocting?*

But to be fair to Constance, he knew how near impossible it was to thwart the Marchioness of Hallmere when her
mind was once set upon a particular course.

She had obviously decided that her best chance of
keeping her home and her dominion over it was to marry
her eldest daughter to her nephew.

Lord help him!

CHAPTER VI

I T WAS RAINING HEAVILY THE NEXT MORNING, AND
Lady Holt-Barron decided against going to the Pump
Room. Freyja spent the morning writing letters to Eve
and Judith, her sisters-in-law, and to Morgan. She described yesterday's ride, including the Misses Darwins' fear
of riding at anything faster than a cautious crawl and the
Earl of Willett's fussy insistence upon treating ladies as if
they were delicate hothouse plants. She described her own
escape with the Marquess of Hallmere and their race across
country, jumping hedgerows as they went.

She did not describe what had happened after their race
was over, of course, but she did sit and think about it for
long minutes, brushing the feather of her quill pen absently back and forth across her chin.

It had been a scandalously lascivious kiss, and she feared
that perhaps she was the one who had made it so. He had
had her face cupped in his hands when he started and then

he had kissed her lips. No other part of his body had been touching any other part of hers. The whole thing would probably have ended sweetly and chastely if she had not clutched his waist for balance and then leaned right against him and then wrapped her arms about him. And then . . .

Well.

And then.

She frowned fiercely.

But she must not assume all the blame. It was he who had started licking at her lips and putting his tongue into her mouth and doing things there that he must have known very well would drive her to distraction. She felt no doubt that he was well experienced with such tactics of dalliance—and doubtless far more too. He had instigated all that had followed.

But there was no particular comfort in the thought. As usual, she had danced on his string like a brainless puppet. He had probably laughed at her all the way home and all through the evening. He was probably still laughing this morning and dreaming up ways of provoking her into making an idiot of herself again today.

Lady Freyja Bedwyn did not take kindly to being made to look a fool.

But, oh dear—she sighed aloud as she dipped her pen in the ink and prepared to resume her letter to Morgan—that one kiss had awakened hungers she had thought only Kit capable of arousing. Perhaps it was not so much Kit she had been in love with all these years as the exuberant passion of her own nature that had burst into glorious life when she had been with him four summers ago.

Now *there* was a thought.

Being a twenty-five-year-old virgin was really a rather dreary thing to be, she decided, and she debated with herself for a minute or two longer whether to add the advice to her letter that Morgan look seriously about her for a husband when she made her come-out next spring. But Bedwyns were notorious for never taking advice, even—or especially—from one another. And Morgan would think Freyja was sickening for some deadly disease if she did anything as uncharacteristic as advising her sister to participate willingly in the marriage mart. Besides, there was something mildly lowering about the thought of Morgan marrying before she did.

Her mind touched again upon the Earl of Willett as a prospective husband but she dismissed the thought without further consideration. She really would not be able to bear it. He would insist upon treating her like a *lady* every minute of every day—and of every night too, most like. She would expire of boredom and frustration and ire within a month.

She bent over her letter again.

T HE RAIN HAD EASED TO A LIGHT DRIZZLE BY THE afternoon. Lady Holt-Barron still did not like the idea of their getting their shoes and hems wet or of having to carry an umbrella rather than a parasol, but the Upper Rooms were little more than a stone's throw away, and staying at home was an unattractive alternative to the prospect of tea and conversation with their peers. They walked to the Rooms.

The tearoom was fuller than usual, probably because the weather discouraged outdoor exercise, but they found an empty table and nodded politely to various acquaintances while the tea was set before them. Within five minutes the Earl of Willett was seated with them. He had come, he explained, to assure himself that Lady Freyja had taken no harm from her dash across country yesterday.

"Hallmere really ought not to have encouraged you," he said. "He ought to have remembered that you are a lady and are therefore compelled to ride sidesaddle."

Freyja regarded him with haughty disdain—and noticed that the subject of his complaint was just then entering the tearoom, looking handsome and distinguished in brown and fawn. She was thoroughly alarmed by the mode of heightened awareness into which her body immediately launched.

Hallmere really ought not to have encouraged you.

No, he ought not. But she had not needed much encouragement, had she?

She set about pointedly ignoring him. He was escorting three ladies—Lady Potford and two strangers, the elder of whom was wearing mourning and smiling sweetly about the room while she leaned heavily on his arm. But although Lady Potford soon sat down at a table with a few of her acquaintances, the marquess and the other two ladies remained on their feet and circulated slowly about the room. He was apparently presenting them to Bath society.

The earl stood and bowed when the group approached their table. Freyja looked up and met the marquess's eyes, her own cool and—she hoped—very slightly disdainful. His smile was looking somewhat more strained than usual, she noticed.

"Lady Holt-Barron, Miss Holt-Barron, Lady Freyja Bedwyn, the Earl of Willett," he said with great formality, "may I have the honor of presenting my aunt, the Marchioness of Hallmere, and my cousin, Lady Constance Moore?"

The aunt was the one on his arm.

"How do you do?" she said. "It is a wonderful pleasure to be in Bath and to meet all of dear Joshua's friends."

She clung to his arm as if she were too frail to stand alone. She smiled sweetly and spoke in the sort of high-pitched whine affected by ladies who fancied themselves permanently indisposed. In Freyja's experience they almost invariably outlived all their more robust relatives—and drove them near to insanity while they still lived.

Lady Constance, a neatly clad and coiffed, sensible-looking girl, curtsied and murmured a how-do-you-do.

"How do you do, ma'am, Lady Constance?" Lady Holt-Barron said graciously. "You have come up from Penhallow to take the waters, have you?"

"Perhaps they would improve my health," the marchioness said. "My spirits have been low since the passing of my dear Hallmere. But I came with the purpose of seeing my dearest nephew, ma'am, and of enabling him to become reacquainted with his cousin. Constance was little more than a girl when Joshua left home to seek adventure five years ago. Five weary years," she added with a sigh that sounded weary indeed.

Ah. The woman had come with the intention of marrying off her daughter to her nephew and so securing her home and her place in it, then, had she? Freyja looked more closely at Lady Constance Moore. And then she transferred her gaze to the marquess. He was looking steadily back at her, his lips pursed, a suggestion of laughter in his eyes. It was an expression that acknowledged his awareness of her understanding of the situation.

"We are staying at the White Hart Inn," the marchioness was saying in answer to a question Lady Holt-Barron must have asked. "I was told it is the best."

"Hallmere," the earl said, "I must commend you for escorting Lady Freyja home safely from your ride yesterday. I must confess that I was filled with trepidation on her behalf when you took her away from the party we had formed and went galloping across the hills with her. But you returned her safely to Lady Holt-Barron's and so no great harm was done."

Freyja was caught between amusement and exasperation.

The marquess raised his eyebrows. "Actually, Willett," he said, "to my everlasting shame I must confess that it was Lady Freyja who won our race by a full head, and so it might be said that it was *she* who brought *me* safely back from our ride. I am much obliged to her for that."

"I am only thankful," Lady Holt-Barron said, fanning herself with her linen napkin, "that I knew nothing of this race until after it was well over. I do not know what I would have said to the Duke of Bewcastle, Lady Freyja's brother, if she had fallen off her horse and broken every bone in her body."

"Oh, never say it, ma'am," the marchioness said, sounding on the verge of a fit of the vapors. "Horse racing is extremely dangerous, especially for a lady. I hope you never persuade Constance to go galloping across country with you, Joshua, dear."

Her voice was faint, but her eyes were fixed sharply upon Freyja and bored into her like twin needle points. Freyja raised her eyebrows with quelling hauteur.

Gracious heavens, she thought, *I am being warned off. How very diverting!*

The Marchioness of Hallmere, she decided, was a lady who liked to have her own way and would get it by any means at her disposal. It would not be a comfortable thing to have such a person as a mother—or as an aunt. It would be interesting to see how successfully she was able to maneuver the marquess.

The group moved on to the next table.

"The marchioness is a very genteel sort of person," Lady Holt-Barron said approvingly.

"It is highly commendable in her to have come all the way from Cornwall to pay her respects to the nephew who has succeeded to the title of her late husband," the earl said. "It would be very proper for him to offer for his cousin."

Freyja met Charlotte's glance across the table, and her friend half smiled. Charlotte had wanted to know yesterday after the ride what had happened. And of all the things she might have spoken of—and had written of this morning at great length to her relatives—Freyja had blurted just three words.

"He kissed me."

Charlotte had clasped her hands to her bosom, her eyes dancing with merriment.

"I knew it," she had said. "From the very first moment—that hilariously awful scene in the Pump Room—I recognized the attraction you feel for each other. And now he has kissed you. I might feel mortally jealous if it were not for Frederick, even if he *is* very ordinary-looking and quite unromantic, the poor love."

"And *I* kissed *him*," honesty had forced Freyja to add. "But it meant absolutely nothing, Charlotte. We were both agreed on that when we spoke of it afterward."

Charlotte had merely chuckled and whisked herself off to change her dress.

DESPITE THE HEAVY RAIN THAT HAD KEPT HIS GRAND-mother at home during the morning, Joshua had walked to the White Hart and escorted his aunt and cousin to the Pump Room, where he had introduced them to the few people who had braved the elements and where Mrs. Lumbard and her daughter had greeted them with obsequious enthusiasm. Afterward, he had escorted them back to their hotel and had breakfast with them. He had taken them shopping on Milsom Street and returned them to the hotel after two hours, empty-handed. The prices in the shops were outrageously high, his aunt had complained. He had taken luncheon with them before returning to his grandmother's.

But he had promised to take them up again later to convey them to the Upper Rooms for tea. Afterward, although it would have been more convenient to drop them off at the White Hart and return to Great Pulteney Street in the carriage with his grandmother, his aunt invited him in, explaining that there was some business she really must discuss with him. And so his grandmother returned home alone.

It had been a wearying day for Joshua. His aunt had always been a tyrant and had ruled even her own family with an iron will, but she had reserved all her worst venom for the nephew who had arrived at Penhallow at the age of six, a bewildered, unhappy orphan, who had just lost both his mother and his father to a fever within three days of each other—though he had not even known it at the time. As he grew older, he had understood that her hatred for him was due in large part to the fact that out of four children she had been able to produce only one son. Albert was the heir, but he, Joshua, was the spare, so to speak.

There had been no love lost between him and Albert either. Albert had been smaller, weaker, and a year younger than Joshua. He had liked trying to flaunt the one great advantage he had over his cousin—and had been infuriated to discover that Joshua really had no interest in inheriting the title.

It had been a severe trial to Joshua to be forced into spending a full day in his aunt's company, shepherding her and Constance about Bath, introducing them to everyone of any social significance, his aunt's endearments and complaints in his ear every step of the way. But he could hardly abandon them to finding their own way about. They had come with the sole purpose of seeing him. Besides, he would not deliberately shun Constance even if he could. He had always been rather fond of his girl cousins.

He wondered how long they intended to stay, how long courtesy would oblige him to dance attendance upon them. There were, after all, the Lumbards with whom they could consort after today.

His aunt sank into a chair as soon as they had arrived in her private sitting room at the White Hart and her maid had borne off her bonnet and gloves and other outdoor garments.

"I am weary beyond words," she said, making Joshua wonder why she had been so insistent that he come inside, then. "And so are you, Constance, my love. Go and lie down on your bed for an hour. Joshua will excuse you."

"But, Mama—" Constance began.

"You are tired," her mother informed her. "Go and lie down."

Constance went obediently after Joshua had smiled sympathetically at her.

"I should leave you to rest too, Aunt," he said hopefully, but she waved him to a seat.

"Stay," she said. "Much time had passed since we last saw you, and you are Hallmere now. You must be very happy about that. I daresay it is what you always wanted."

He did not contradict her. What was the point? He sat down and crossed one leg over the other.

"You have grown into a fine figure of a man, Joshua," she

said, frowning disapprovingly at him. "And your title and fortune make you doubly eligible. You are well received in Bath, I see. I am glad of it." She sounded anything but.

"*Everyone* is well received in Bath, Aunt," he said with a smile. "It is not as fashionable a resort as it used to be, especially among the young. Everyone is welcomed with open arms."

"There are at least some other young people here," she said. "The Misses Darwin are fine girls."

"They are," he agreed. "But I have difficulty telling them apart even though they are not twins."

"Miss Holt-Barron is very pretty," she said.

"And amiable too," he said. "I understand she is betrothed to Mr. Frederick Wheatcroft, son of Viscount Mitchell."

"Ah, yes," his aunt said. "The prettiest girls always go the fastest. Prettiness is certainly not a malady from which Lady Freyja Bedwyn suffers." Her tone had sharpened almost imperceptibly.

Joshua pursed his lips.

"She may be the sister of a duke," his aunt continued, "the Duke of Bewcastle, I believe? But her rank has apparently not made her attractive enough as a marriage prospect. She must be all of five or six and twenty and is quite sadly ugly. There is not a great deal she can do to disguise that nose, is there?"

Joshua thought Lady Freyja's nose was perhaps her most attractive feature, although her hair, especially when loose down her back and blowing out in a wild tangle in the wind, must come a close second.

"I have heard her described as handsome," he said.

"That is what people always say about girls when they are too kind to call them ugly," she said. "You went riding alone with her yesterday, Joshua? Was that not somewhat indiscreet?"

"We went *riding* with a party of eight," he explained, feeling amused. His aunt's unerring nose had led her to the right quarry, at least. "We went *galloping* alone together since the pace was not to our liking. Lady Freyja Bedwyn is a neck-or-nothing rider."

"As your aunt who knows more of life than you, Joshua," she said kindly, "I feel constrained to warn you of the wiles that aging and unattractive spinsters will employ when more genteel methods have failed to net them an eligible husband. If you are not very careful, Lady Freyja Bedwyn will trap you into compromising her virtue and you will find yourself forced to offer for her."

His lips twitched as he thought of the inn room in which he had first encountered Lady Freyja and of yesterday's hot embrace on the white rock up in the hills. He wondered if she would appreciate the joke if he were to tell her what his aunt had just said—or would her wrath know no bounds?

"Oh, you may smile, Joshua," his aunt said, looking frail and weary. "But do not say you have not been warned."

"I will not, Aunt," he promised.

"I can scarcely believe," she said, "that Constance is already three and twenty. How times does fly. She should have been married long ago. I should have grandchildren to comfort my old age. But tragedy has kept the poor girl unwed this long. Albert died just when she ought to have been making her come-out, and since then my health has been too fragile to enable me to endure a Season in London. Then, just when I thought that perhaps I was recovering enough strength to do what was right for both Constance *and* Chastity, Hallmere suffered his heart seizure and died. Now I do not know when my dear girls

can be expected to settle in life. And as for Prudence..."
She sighed piteously.

There was a rather lengthy pause during which Joshua
knew exactly what was coming, though he was powerless
to prevent it.

"It is time *you* considered marriage, Joshua," she said.
"You are eight and twenty, and you are Hallmere now. It is
your duty to produce a male heir for Penhallow. And it is
your duty to provide for your cousins since you are their legal guardian—except for Constance, of course, who is of
age and has come into her portion. It is time you put behind you these years when you have been sowing your wild
oats, as the vulgar phrase would have it. I do not begrudge
you that time or that wildness, Joshua, though Albert
never showed any inclination to desert his home or his father or his sisters—or his mother. But I beg you now to remember your duty. And I beg you too not to resent this
gentle reminder from the aunt who has loved you and nurtured you all your life."

"Except for the first six years, Aunt," he said quietly but
firmly, "when my mother and father were still alive."

"May God rest their souls," she said. "Do you have a
possible bride in mind?"

"I do not," he said. "But I will inform you as soon as I am
betrothed, Aunt. It will be some considerable time in the
future. And I have exercised my guardianship over
Chastity and Prue—I have left them undisturbed at Penhallow with you. Constance too."

"I know you love them, dear Joshua." She regarded him
with sad, fond eyes—until they lit up, apparently with a
sudden idea. "How absolutely delightful it would be if you
were to conceive a *tendre* for Constance. It would not be at
all surprising. She is a sensible, dutiful girl, and she is in
good looks, is she not? She has always been fond of you—

and you of her, I remember. How perfectly … *right* it would be for you to marry the sister of your wards. I cannot *imagine* why I have not thought of this before now."

"Constance is my first cousin, Aunt," he pointed out.

"Cousins marry all the time," she said. "It is a sensible thing to do, Joshua. It keeps titles and lands and fortunes in one family, as well as duties and responsibilities."

"I am not about to turn either you or Constance or my other cousins off penniless, Aunt," Joshua said, "even if I had the power to do so. There is really no need for you to foist one of your daughters on me."

"Foist." She spoke faintly and wilted back into her chair. She produced a black-bordered handkerchief from somewhere and raised it to her lips. "I offer you my dearest Constance and you accuse me of *foisting* her on you? But you were ever ungrateful, Joshua. You were a difficult boy to raise, and then you shamed your uncle by spurning his generous hospitality and going to live in the village to work as a *carpenter*. And *then* you came back and forth to the house, supposedly to visit Prudence, and … Well, I try not even to think of the shameful vulgarity of your behavior. And when Albert went to confront and reprimand you … But I have made every effort to put the painful memories behind me and to forgive you. It is the Christian thing to do and has ever been my way. I have been prepared to believe that five years must have matured you, made you a better person. I have trusted you sufficiently to offer you my own daughter. Yet you speak of *foisting?*"

She had shriveled into what seemed like half of her usual self—a trick she had always had of drawing pity and remorse and ultimate acquiescence from anyone who had been foolish enough to try thwarting her will. She dabbed at her eyes with her handkerchief.

"I daresay," he said, "Constance has no desire to be foisted upon me either, Aunt."

"Constance has always been a dutiful girl," she said. "She will do as I advise. She knows that I always have her own good at heart. And how could any girl *not* wish to be the Marchioness of Hallmere? I shall relinquish the title to her without any reluctance at all. I shall delight in the title of dowager."

Joshua got to his feet. "I would not talk of this as if it were a foregone conclusion if I were you, Aunt," he said firmly. "You would doubtless be doomed to disappointment. Constance ought to have been allowed to stay for this discussion. I am convinced she would disabuse you once and for all of the notion that we will marry. You must not upset yourself, though. I have informed you before that I have no intention of returning to Penhallow to live. It is your home. You may live there in peace for the rest of your life. My cousins may live there for the rest of theirs if they do not marry."

If by some strange chance he ever *did* marry Constance and take up his residence at Penhallow, he thought, his aunt would have to go. She doubtless did not have the imagination to realize that.

She gazed pitifully up at him, her eyes brimming with tears.

"You were always a hard, unfeeling boy, Joshua," she said. "But I will not take offense. And I will not despair. I *will* consult Constance, and she will agree with me that a marriage between the two of you is the only decent way in which you can atone for your past actions."

There, Joshua thought, he had allowed her after all to get under his skin like a sharp and jabbing needle. He was angry when he ought to have kept his feelings aloof, even amused. She was going to try to wear down Constance's defenses, if she had not already done so, and then use his fondness for his cousin to make him feel guilty for resisting her suggestion—her utterly preposterous suggestion.

The trouble was he was stupidly afraid. The woman was the very fiend for getting her own way.

"There is a concert at the Upper Rooms this evening," he said. "Will you wish to go?"

"No." She sighed. "Marjorie Lumbard has invited us to a card party at her lodgings this evening. We will go to the Pump Room again in the morning, though. You may call for us here on your way. And there is to be a ball at the Upper Rooms tomorrow evening, I believe?"

"There is," he said.

"We will attend it," she said. "You may lead Constance into the opening set of dances. It would appear very strange if you did not."

She looked wan and dejected. Any man who did not know her methods of enforcing compliance with her wishes might have felt compelled to assure her that he would at least consider what she had proposed.

She needed no such assurance.

"It will be my pleasure, Aunt," Joshua said. "I will take my leave now so that you may rest before your card party."

She waved her handkerchief in a pathetic gesture of helplessness, too choked up with emotion, it seemed, even to bid him farewell.

She was, of course, absolutely determined to have him, Joshua thought grimly as he left the White Hart and strode off in the direction of the Pulteney Bridge. The drizzle had increased slightly in intensity, and he was soon damp and uncomfortable. He had realized that as soon as he set eyes upon her in his grandmother's drawing room the afternoon before. Good Lord, she had even taken the unprecedented step of leaving Penhallow.

The obvious course for him now, he supposed, was the one of least resistance. He should simply leave Bath. It was what he would do too, he decided, cheering up considerably. It was so easy to fall into old patterns of thought when under his aunt's aura of influence. For years he had had no choice but to obey or suffer the consequences. But he was free of her now. He owed her nothing except the basic courtesy of a gentleman and a relative.

He would do it the day after tomorrow. Not tomorrow, though he was very tempted to flee while the proverbial coast was clear. He had agreed to escort his aunt and Constance to the Pump Room in the morning and to the ball at the Assembly Rooms in the evening. He would fulfill those obligations, and then he would make himself scarce.

He would dance with Lady Freyja Bedwyn at the ball too. He would flirt with her one last time, perhaps find some way to provoke her into losing that very volatile temper of hers one last time. What fun if he could do it in public, in full view of all the attendees at the ball. And what a wicked thought! He chuckled softly to himself.

He was going to miss her. She was surely the most interesting lady of his acquaintance.

One of the most sexually appealing too.

A dangerous admission. Yes, for more than one reason it was time to leave Bath.

CHAPTER VII

THE PREDICTABLE ROUTINE OF LIFE IN BATH WAS wearing on Freyja's spirits. The rain had stopped, though the sky was still heavy with gray clouds, and after one day's absence they returned to the Pump Room for the usual morning promenade. The same people as usual were in attendance. There were no new faces at all, in fact, unless one counted the Marchioness of Hallmere and her daughter. The marquess and Lady Potford were with them.

Freyja strolled with Charlotte and stopped to talk with Mr. Eston and one of the Misses Darwin—she was not sure which—and then with Mrs. Carbret and her sister. The Earl of Willett joined them and walked between them until they came face-to-face with the marquess's party close to the alcove at one end of the room. Freyja thought almost with nostalgia of that morning when she had stormed up to the marquess and demanded that he be expelled from the Pump Room and from Bath itself. There had been some excitement about life in those days—it seemed eons ago.

"I do admire the cut of your dress, Lady Freyja," the marchioness said after greetings and pleasantries had been exchanged and the marquess, looking sober and respectable this morning, had half depressed one eyelid while looking at Freyja and made her bristle with indignation. "You must tell me who your modiste is and whom I should patronize in Bath. Do come and stroll with me."

She took Freyja's arm, leaning rather heavily on it as if she were an invalid just risen from her sickbed, and led her off away from the others.

"I am the very last person to consult about fashion, ma'am," Freyja said. "And I patronize absolutely no one in Bath. Shopping is surely the most tedious pastime ever invented for women. I abhor it and avoid it whenever I am able. You would be better advised to talk with Lady Holt-Barron or even with her daughter."

"Ah, but it is you with whom I wish to speak," the marchioness said.

This was interesting, Freyja thought, nodding genially to a couple of elderly acquaintances. And she would wager she knew what was coming, though she guessed that it might take her companion some time to get to the point. How very diverting! She must listen attentively so that she could report the conversation verbatim to Morgan when she wrote to her later.

"I am flattered, ma'am," she said.

"I am very grateful that you are staying in Bath for a while, Lady Freyja," the marchioness said. "There are not, I have observed, many young people here of a rank sufficiently elevated to offer companionship to Hallmere."

"Your gratitude is misplaced," Freyja told her. "I did not

come to Bath in order to offer companionship to the Marquess of Hallmere. I came to visit my friend Miss Holt-Barron."

The lady tittered. "Hallmere is reveling in the company of my dear Constance," she said. "He grew up at Penhallow with his cousins after the tragic death of his parents when he was very young. He doted on them and they on him. Indeed, very often his uncle and I forgot entirely that they were not all brothers and sisters."

The little-girl whine was annoying Freyja. She wished the woman would simply talk and show her claws.

"But now you are happy," Freyja said, "to remember that in fact he and Lady Constance are merely cousins."

"It is a match the late Hallmere and I expected almost all their lives," Lady Hallmere said with a soulful sigh. "It might have appeared an ineligible connection while my son still lived, since dear Joshua did not possess any fortune of his own. But our fondness for him was such and their attachment to each other was such that we would not have had the heart to refuse our consent to the match. Now, of course, there are no such barriers to be overcome. They can look forward to a happy ending to their long attachment."

"Happily-ever-after endings are the best possible endings," Freyja said, "especially when there has been an unnecessary separation of years and then a sudden, unexpected reunion." She nodded at a few more acquaintances.

"Ah, the separation," the marchioness said. "It *was* necessary. Constance was barely eighteen years old, far too young for matrimony, according to her papa, who had his own ideas on such matters. Yet dear Joshua's ardor was such that being so near to her every day was an unbearable torment to him. And so he went off to seek his fortune and broke all our hearts."

"How collectively painful, ma'am," Freyja murmured.

"Devastatingly so." The lady darted her a suspicious glance. "But not Constance's heart—she knew he would remain true. She knew he would not stay away forever. And now her patience and Joshua's sense of honor are to be rewarded, Lady Freyja. He will marry my daughter and Penhallow will remain my home and the home of my other daughters for as long as they remain unwed."

"I am honored indeed," Freyja said, "that you would confide such an intimate secret to me."

"I have done it," the marchioness said with a look of sad candor, "because I was given the distinct impression yesterday, Lady Freyja, that perhaps you were in danger of losing your heart to Hallmere. And the boy *does* have a naughty tendency to flirt with the ladies. He is so very handsome, you see, and cannot help but notice the admiring glances he attracts wherever he goes. But his heart is true, and it was given long ago."

Freyja discovered that she was enjoying herself immensely.

"*Now* I understand why you drew me apart with that clever ruse about the fashionable cut of my dress," she said. "I am eternally grateful to you, ma'am. If I am ever inclined to experience a weakness of the knees at the sight of the Marquess of Hallmere's handsome person or to suffer heart palpitations at one of his charming smiles bestowed upon me, I shall remember that his heart is given elsewhere and has been for five long years while his beloved has been growing up—from the tender age of eighteen to the altogether more eligible age of three and twenty. I shall remember that you brought her here to him when he was surely pining with the anxious fear that perhaps she was *still* too young to be snatched from her mother's bosom. It is a marvelously romantic story, in which your own part has been one of selfless maternal devotion. How could I ever even think about intruding upon such an affecting romance by conceiving a *tendre* for the gentleman myself?"

The marchioness's arm had stiffened beneath Freyja's. Her voice was a little more steely when she spoke again.

"I perceive that you mock me, Lady Freyja," she said.

"*Do* you?" Freyja asked. "How very peculiar!"

"I merely felt it my duty to offer you a friendly warning," the marchioness said. "I would not wish to see your heart broken."

"Your kindness is overwhelming," Freyja said.

"I daresay that by a certain age," Lady Hallmere said, "one's heart becomes even more vulnerable to disappointment. Let us say five and twenty? Or six and twenty? But I would advise you not to despair, Lady Freyja. I am confident that the Earl of Willett is quite prepared to have you."

Freyja was torn between outrage and unholy amusement. The latter won. One could hardly feel true outrage against such an unworthy foe.

"Oh, do you believe so, ma'am?" she asked. "What a balm to my worst anxieties *that* would be. At my age I must be immensely grateful to *anyone*—even the chimney sweep—who is still willing to relieve me of my single state. Now, ma'am, I believe we have exhausted the purpose of this conversation." She smiled at Lady Potford and Lady Holt-Barron, who were standing together at the water table. "I believe we understand each other perfectly well."

"I do not believe you understand me at all, Lady Freyja," the marchioness said sharply. "I will not have you come between Hallmere and his intended bride. I am wondering what the Duke of Bewcastle would think of his sister's leaving the propriety of a riding party of eight ladies and gentlemen in order to gallop off alone with one gentlemen in scandalously improper fashion."

Ah, this was better. The lady's claws were being bared at last.

"I imagine, ma'am," Freyja said, "that he would *say* nothing. He would undoubtedly, though, make deadly use of his quizzing glass, though whether upon me or upon the divulger of such foolish information I leave you to imagine. You may address any letter to his grace to Lindsey Hall in Hampshire."

"I wonder if Hallmere has thought to mention to you," the marchioness said, her sweet whine restored as she leaned more heavily on Freyja's arm again, "that he has the most adorable little bastard son living with his mother in the village close to Penhallow. She was the girls' governess until the unfortunate incident forced my husband to dismiss her. They appear not to be suffering. I understand that Hallmere still supports them."

This was somewhat surprising and displeasing, Freyja had to admit privately to herself—*if* it was true. She knew very well that her brothers were all lusty men—even Wulfric, who had kept the same mistress in London for years. But she knew too, though no one had ever come right out and said so in her hearing, that one of the cardinal rules by which they had grown up was that they were to make no amorous advances to anyone employed in any of the ducal homes or on their estates or in the villages attached to them. And not to any woman who was unwilling, either. There was a strong tradition too among the Bedwyns that once they married they remained true to their spouses for the rest of their lives.

"Well, that has sealed the matter," Freyja said briskly. "I renounce all claim on the marquess, ma'am, broken heart notwithstanding. I simply could not countenance any part of his fortune being frittered away on keeping a bastard and his mother from starvation. Lady Constance must be a saint if she is prepared to overlook such a useless expenditure."

"I do not consider your tone of levity ladylike, Lady Freyja," the marchioness complained. "I would have expected a lady of your years and unfortunate looks to be especially careful to cultivate a gentle demeanor."

The claws had raked a bloody path down her person, Freyja noted with interest, and left her for dead. Gone, for the moment, was all pretense of delicate health and sweet disposition.

"I am humbled," Freyja said, "and now understand why at the age of five and twenty I am still unwed. I daresay it is my nose. My mother really ought to have thought twice before bearing my father a daughter. The nose looks distinguished enough on my brothers. On me it is grotesque and has blighted all my matrimonial hopes. I shall not weep here, ma'am—you must not fear that I will draw attention to you. I shall wait until I am in my own room at Lady Holt-Barron's. I brought six handkerchiefs with me to Bath. That should be a sufficient number."

They had come up to the Marquess of Hallmere and Lady Constance Moore by the time she finished speaking. The marchioness smiled sweetly, Freyja bared her teeth in her feline grin, Lady Constance wore no detectable expression at all, and the marquess raised his eyebrows.

"Lady Freyja Bedwyn and I have been enjoying a delightfully comfortable coze together," the marchioness said. "We have been agreeing that you two cousins look delightful together. I trust you have been enjoying your stroll?"

"We have, Aunt," the marquess assured her.

"And now," she said, "you may escort us back to our hotel for breakfast, Joshua. Are you to attend the ball at the

Upper Assembly Rooms this evening, Lady Freyja? Joshua has insisted upon dancing the first set with Constance."

"While I," Freyja said with a sigh, "am still anxiously hoping to avoid being a wallflower."

There was a gleam of laughter in the marquess's eyes.

"I shall fetch my grandmother, Aunt," he said. "She is over by the water table with Lady Holt-Barron. May I escort you there, Lady Freyja?"

He offered his arm and she took it.

"Well, sweetheart," he said as they moved beyond earshot of his aunt. "Let me guess. She was warning you off her territory."

"Whether I felt inclined to play there or not," Freyja said. "And I am not your sweetheart."

"You displayed a great deal of admirable forbearance," he said. "I expected every moment to see you haul back your arm and plant her a facer."

"I have never yet struck a lady," she said. "It would be unsporting. My tongue is a far better weapon with them."

He threw back his head and laughed—and drew considerable attention their way from people who doubtless hoped for some renewal of the altercation between them that had so enlivened the morning scene here a few days ago.

"My guess," he said, "is that you routed the enemy quite resoundingly and sent it slinking off the battlefield in mortified disarray. That is a considerable accomplishment where my aunt in concerned. Will you dance with me this evening? May I reserve the second set with you?"

"How dreadfully lowering!" she said haughtily. "Only the *second* set?"

"Remember," he said, "that I *insisted* upon the first set with my cousin. Actually I begged and groveled, but my pride does not like to admit that too readily."

"And will you also beg and grovel for the second set?" she asked him.

"I'll go down on bended knee right here and now if you wish," he said with a grin.

"You tempt me," she said. "But these people might put the wrong interpretation on the gesture and your aunt might suffer an apoplexy. I will dance the second set with you. At least it will relieve me of the humiliation of being a wallflower if no one offers to lead me into the first set. I have just been informed that a lady of my years and looks must be careful to cultivate at least a sweet demeanor."

"No!" He grinned at her. "I would pay a sizable sum to have heard your answer."

They had come up to his grandmother and Lady Holt-Barron by that time, and the marquess bowed and took his leave, his grandmother on his arm.

"How very obliging of the Marchioness of Hallmere to stroll with you, Lady Freyja," Lady Holt-Barron said. "She is a sweet-natured lady, is she not? How sad that her health appears not to be robust. I daresay she deeply mourns her husband, poor lady."

T HOUGH SHE HAD BEEN REMINDED OF HER ADVANCED age and less than gorgeous looks, Freyja was inclined to be far more cheerful on their return to the house on the Circus than she had been when they had set out for the Pump Room earlier.

The mood did not last. There was a letter from Morgan propped against her coffee cup in the breakfast room, and since Lady Holt-Barron had several letters too and Charlotte had one fat one from her betrothed, Freyja slit the seal and read it at the table.

There was a long, witty description of a village assembly

that Morgan had been allowed to attend with Alleyne, since she was now eighteen and was to make her official come-out next spring. And there was a lengthy discussion of a book of poetry by Mr. Wordsworth and Mr. Coleridge that she had been reading. Sandwiched between the two was a brief, terse paragraph.

"A messenger rode over from Alvesley yesterday afternoon with a note from Kit," Morgan had written. "Wulf read it to us at teatime. Viscountess Ravensberg was delivered of a boy yesterday morning. Both are doing well."

Nothing else. No details. No description of the raptures Kit must have expressed in the note. No comment on what Wulfric or Alleyne had said about the news. No description of how Morgan felt—she had always hero-worshipped Kit, who had been kind to her when she was a child with the double disadvantage of being far younger than all the rest of their playmates and of being the only girl apart from Freyja.

"Bad news, Freyja?" Charlotte asked suddenly, all concern.

"What?" Freyja looked up blankly at her. "Oh, no, no. Absolutely not. Everyone is perfectly well at home. How is your Frederick?"

A son.

Kit had a son. With the oh-so-perfect, oh-so-perfectly-dull Lauren Edgeworth he had married. The viscountess was perfect to the last detail, it seemed. She had produced a son within one year of her marriage. And so Alvesley and the earldom of Redfield had its heirs for the next two generations.

Freyja pasted a smile on her face and tried to pay attention to the contents of Charlotte's letter, which she was reading aloud.

Thank heaven, Freyja thought—oh, *thank heaven* she

was not at Lindsey Hall now. Alleyne and Morgan would be studiously avoiding the topic in her hearing and the neighborhood would be buzzing with the glad tidings. She would feel honor-bound to pay a duty call at Alvesley with her family, and both families would be horribly uncomfortable. The fact that *she* had almost been Viscountess Ravensberg, first as Jerome's bride and then as Kit's, would have fairly shouted itself into every small silence that fell in the conversation. Consequently, they would all have chattered brightly without ceasing on any inane topic that came to mind.

She would have to *smile* graciously at the viscountess. She would have to *congratulate* Kit. She would have to gaze admiringly at the baby.

Thank heaven she was in Bath.

She made an excuse not to accompany the other two ladies shopping. She must write some letters, she explained. But instead she did what she very rarely did. She flung herself facedown across her bed and brooded.

She hated what had happened—and what had *not* happened—to her life. Who would have dreamed all through her growing years that she would end up like this? Unmarried, unattached, unheartwhole.

She ground her teeth and pressed her fists into the mattress.

If the Earl of Willett were to turn up on Lady Holt-Barron's doorstep at this precise moment to propose marriage to her, she thought, she would probably fly into his arms and drown him in tears of gratitude.

And what a ghastly image *that* brought to mind.

Please God, let him not do anything so stupid.

It would be far better to go to the assembly tonight and flirt outrageously with the Marquess of Hallmere. He was a far more worthy opponent, and the encounter was far less likely to bear any dire and lasting consequences. It would be worth doing if only to see the marchioness his aunt with smoke billowing out of her ears and nostrils.

Freyja rolled over onto her back and stared at the pleated silk canopy of the bed and remembered the scene in the park, when she had punched him in the nose and ripped up at him, and the scene in the Pump Room the next morning, when he had wreaked his devilish revenge. She thought of his grandmother's dinner party and their verbal sparring there. She thought of the horse race in which she had beaten him fair and square and of the embrace that had followed. And then she remembered their first encounter in her inn room on the way to Bath and first chuckled and then laughed out loud.

How ignominious it was that she had pined for Kit Butler for three long years after their brief summer of passion and had not been able to shake off her attachment to him in the year since he had spurned her and married Lauren Edgeworth instead. And how ghastly that her family was so well aware of her feelings that Morgan had felt obliged to break the news to her in such a brief paragraph that if she had blinked she might have missed it.

She would get up right now, she decided, and go out for a long, brisk walk. And tonight she would dance her feet off.

Brooding was not in any way a satisfactory activity.

JOSHUA HAD ENJOYED HIS FEW MINUTES ALONE WITH Constance in the Pump Room. She had never been a particularly vivacious or pretty girl. It had never occurred to him to find her attractive. But she had always been sensible and good-hearted. He had been fond of her, and even now he felt the pull of their relationship. They were cousins. Their fathers had been brothers.

She had answered all his questions about her sisters. Chastity, always prettier and livelier than she, was now twenty, but she had no romantic attachment. Prudence—Prue—was eighteen. She was doing well, Constance reported—remarkably well. She had blossomed with Miss Palmer as her governess, and she had made some dear friends in the village. She was happy. But when had Prue *not* been happy? No one could possess a sunnier nature.

Constance had been reluctant to talk about herself until he had decided to be frank with her and introduce the topic of her mother's hopes and plans. She had admitted to him then that she had a beau—a quite ineligible connection—whom her mother would dismiss if it were in her power to do so.

"Dismiss?" Joshua had asked. "One of the *servants*, Constance?"

"Mr. Saunders." She had blushed.

Jim Saunders was the steward he had interviewed in London and hired and sent to Penhallow—the one servant who was indeed beyond his aunt's power to dismiss.

"He *is* a gentleman," Joshua had commented.

"And I am a marquess's daughter," she had said bitterly. "But I love him dearly. I will not marry you, Joshua, even though I may never marry him. You must not fear that I will join with Mama in trying to persuade you. And even if she were to induce you to make me an offer, I would say no."

"I will not," he had said. "You are my cousin and therefore dear to me. But you are not the bride I would choose."

"Thank you," she had said, and they had looked at each other and laughed. She had looked really rather pretty as she did so.

But she spoke a somewhat different story when he led her out onto the dance floor at the Upper Assembly Rooms that evening for the opening set of country dances. She was clearly agitated, though she did not speak until they were well out of earshot of her mother.

There was not a vast crowd in attendance, and many of those who were there were elderly. Nevertheless, James King, the master of ceremonies, had done his job admirably well and had coaxed almost everyone onto the floor who was not confined to a Bath chair. Joshua's aunt was not dancing, of course—she was still wearing her black mourning clothes. But Lady Freyja Bedwyn was. She was looking magnificent indeed in an ivory gown with a gold netted tunic, her hair swept up into an elaborate coiffure and tamed with gold and jeweled combs.

But there was no mistaking the fact that something had happened to shake Constance out of her usual placid demeanor.

"Joshua," she said with considerable urgency in the few private moments before the orchestra began playing, "you must be warned."

"What is it?" he asked, bending his head closer to hers.

"Mama is determined," she said.

He grinned at her. "We will thwart her," he told her. "Never fear. I will be leaving Bath tomorrow morning."

The orchestra, sitting apart on a dais, began playing before they could say more, and for a few moments the vigorous, intricate figures of the dance, which had them twirling about with the couple next to them, precluded further conversation.

"Tomorrow may be too *late*," she gasped out when next she could.

"Smile," he told her, smiling himself. "Your mama is watching us."

Constance smiled. They clapped with everyone else as the couple at the end of the lines twirled down between them, too far apart to converse privately. Then the figures began again.

"She is going to see to it that we dance almost every set together," Constance said when they came together for a moment again, her voice breathless from her exertions. "And she is going to mention our attachment to everyone within earshot. She is even hoping to have our betrothal announced tonight."

"Preposterous!" Joshua said. "Even your mama cannot force us into a betrothal, Constance."

She twirled away on the arm of the gentleman next to Joshua.

Joshua smiled his most charming smile at the man's partner and twirled her firmly about. It seemed forever before there was a small pocket of privacy in which to exchange a few more words with Constance.

"Oh, yes, she can," she said bitterly as if there had been no interruption. "She is *Mama*, Joshua. She has spoken of my duty to her and to Chastity—and most of all to Prue. And she told me that you said you would marry me if I were to consent. *Did* you say that?"

"Dash it, Constance," he said. "Of course not."

They took up their places in their respective lines and clapped again as another couple—Willett and Lady Freyja—went twirling down the set.

His aunt had twisted his words at the White Hart, of course. She had convinced herself that he would bow to her will if only Constance would. And poor Constance was her daughter and had to live with her every day of her life. How could the poor girl resist his aunt when he could scarcely do so himself?

He would wring her neck for her. That would settle the matter once and for all.

Hoping to have his betrothal announced tonight, for God's sake!

"Joshua," Constance said the next time they were close to each other. "*Do* something. Be firm. I am dreadfully afraid I will not be able to. And if she should succeed in getting us to dance together all night or induce me to admit in public that I am fond of you or some such thing, you will feel honor-bound... Oh, I will simply die."

He grimaced.

"I'll think of something," he said. "In the meantime I have at least promised the next set to someone else."

"Thank heaven!" she said fervently.

He should run while he still had a chance, Joshua thought. His aunt could hardly maneuver him into a betrothal with Constance if he was not even here. But, dash it all, was he going to run from a mean, manipulative little slip of a thing?

It was very tempting, he had to admit. But first he must dance with Lady Freyja Bedwyn.

"The next set is to be a waltz," his aunt said after he had led Constance back to her side. She beamed at the two of them and spoke rather loudly, somehow including a whole crowd of people standing within her orbit in the conversation. "Constance knows the steps, Joshua, and I am sure you must. Do dance it together as everyone can see you both wish to do. You make such a very striking couple, and under the happy circumstances of your recent reunion no one will object to your dancing two sets in a row together."

Good Lord, Joshua thought. His cousin had not exaggerated.

"I beg your pardon, Constance, Aunt," he said with a

bow, "but I have already solicited the hand of Lady Freyja Bedwyn for the next dance."

A waltz. That was interesting. He looked across the ballroom at Lady Freyja. She really did look very fetching indeed tonight. She looked quite regal, in fact, or at least every inch a duke's daughter. She was standing with Miss Holt-Barron, her chin lifted, her fan slowly cooling her face.

"That was kind of you, Joshua," his aunt said, a sharp edge to her voice. She reduced the volume to a theatrical whisper. "She really is remarkably ugly."

He bowed to Lady Freyja a few moments later and led her onto the floor, where other couples too were gathering.

"I was delighted to see," he said, "that you were not a wallflower for the first set."

"So was I," she said. "Doubtless I would have gone home and put a bullet in my brain."

He laughed and set his hand behind her waist as she set hers on his shoulder. He took her other hand in his. Except when he was with her, he always tended to forget how small she was. She was also very shapely.

"How clever of me, sweetheart," he said, "to have chosen a waltz."

"I just hope you can dance it well," she said. "You can have no idea of the peril ladies put themselves in during this particular dance, when their slippers are in such close proximity to their partner's dancing shoes. And I am not your sweetheart."

The orchestra began playing, and for a while he forgot everything but the sheer pleasure of moving with her through the lilting steps of the waltz. He was going to regret not seeing her again after tonight, not matching wits with her. Not kissing her.

She looked up at him and arched her eyebrows.

"No squashed toes yet," she said.

"If I do anything so clumsy and unmannerly," he said, "I will allow you to use your fist on my face without even trying to defend myself."

She laughed.

"How is your courtship proceeding?" she asked him. "Your aunt looks very pleased with herself this evening."

He grimaced. "Parson's mousetrap hovers," he said. "According to Constance, who is about as eager for the match as I am, she is determined to throw us together tonight with such frequency that for very decency's sake we will be obliged to announce our engagement. It might be of interest to add that the woman's will has almost never been thwarted."

"Nonsense!" she said. "I found her quite an unworthy foe when I spoke with her this morning."

"Perhaps Connie and I should let you loose on her then, sweetheart," he said. "I don't suppose you feel like entering into a fake betrothal with me for a day or two, do you?"

He grinned at her.

She stared at him, an arrested look on her face. Her eyebrows rose haughtily. He waited for the lash of her tongue.

"Actually," she said, "it would be rather fun, would it not?"

They were still waltzing, he discovered with some surprise.

CHAPTER VIII

HE WAS MAD.
She was mad.
They grinned at each other like a pair of prize idiots.

It was a wild, mad suggestion. Surely he had not been serious. But the chance of getting even for this morning's insults in the Pump Room was irresistible to Freyja. Besides, she had been in the mopes all day because of that infernal letter—or rather, because of that one brief infernal paragraph in the letter. And this really did sound like fun.

A mock betrothal! Just what she had suspected Kit of last year, some part of her mind told her. She pushed the thought firmly aside. She was sick to death of Kit Butler, Viscount Ravensberg.

She had always been a madcap. Those many governesses she had plagued had been forever trying to explain to her that if she only learned to think before she acted instead of dashing impulsively onward with every scheme that presented itself to her vivid imagination, she would land herself in trouble far less often.

Freyja had always rather enjoyed trouble.

She found herself suddenly, irrationally, and quite inappropriately happy.

"By all means," she said to the marquess. "Let us do it. Tonight. Now. We can break it off tomorrow. It is doubtless what people will expect of us anyway."

She had always loved performing the energetic, slightly scandalous waltz. She had been particularly enjoying this one. But she was quite happy to abandon it before it ended. The marquess waited until they were close to the doorway leading to the tearoom, then waltzed her through it before releasing his hold on her, taking her by the elbow, and going in search of the master of ceremonies, who was absent from the ballroom.

Mr. King was in the tearoom, circulating among the tables there, conversing with their occupants. He beamed genially at them, rubbing his hands together as he did so.

"My lord," he said. "I am delighted to have such illustrious guests at the assembly as you and Lady Freyja Bedwyn—and the marchioness, your aunt, and her daughter, of course. A table for two, my lord?"

"No, thank you," the marquess said, smiling amiably. "Perhaps you would be willing to make a public announcement at the end of the waltz, King. I wish all my friends and acquaintances in Bath to share my joy. Lady Freyja Bedwyn has just made me the happiest of men by accepting my marriage proposal."

Mr. King looked almost speechless with wonder for a few moments. But it did not take him long to recover himself and puff out his chest with importance. He beamed with delight.

"It will give me the greatest pleasure, my lord," he declared, taking one of the marquess's hands between both his own and pumping it up and down. He made Freyja a deferential bow. "My lady. I cannot tell you how gratified and honored I am."

They left him as he called for the attention of everyone in the tearoom and informed them that if they proceeded to the ballroom when the music ended, they would hear a happy announcement indeed.

"You have just saved me from a situation akin to walking on eggs, sweetheart," the marquess murmured as he led Freyja back to the ballroom. "Perhaps I can repay you in some way one day."

"You may depend upon it," she said. "Though I do believe that just the look on your aunt's face is going to be reward enough for now. Indeed, I would not miss it for worlds."

The waltz was ending. The marquess offered Freyja his arm and led her to where Lady Holt-Barron was sitting. Very properly he bowed before returning to his own party, but his eyes were dancing with merriment, Freyja noticed, unfurling her fan and cooling her hot face with it.

She schooled her features to their customary hauteur. What on earth had she done now? Wulf would freeze her solid with a glance if he ever heard about it. How *soon* tomorrow could they end the joke?

But she could not deny that her heart was dancing with merriment. This was *just* what she needed to pick herself out of the mopes.

People were coming into the ballroom from the tearoom and the card room. They were buzzing with heightened interest, and soon their mood conveyed itself to the ballroom crowd too. Bath society thrived upon news and gossip—as did society everywhere. But rarely was there something really new to titillate their spirits and enliven their conversation. Mr. King did not need to clap his hands for attention when he mounted the orchestra dais, though he did so anyway.

The Marchioness of Hallmere, Freyja saw, looking frail and sickly in black, was nevertheless smiling graciously as she rested one arm upon the marquess's sleeve and had the other tucked through Lady Constance's arm. She clearly thought she had the evening well in hand.

Lady Constance was looking tense and unhappy. The marquess was looking nonchalant. But he caught Freyja's eye across the room and depressed one eyelid in that slow wink of his.

"I have been honored with the privilege of making an important and happy announcement," Mr. King told his avidly attentive audience. "It is a betrothal between two of the most illustrious members, not only of Bath society, but of the whole of English polite society. It is a dazzling match by any standards."

Freyja plied her fan a little faster. The marchioness turned her gracious attention to her daughter, clearly having decided that the announcement had nothing of interest to offer her.

"The Marquess of Hallmere has asked me," Mr. King said, beaming about him with pride and pleasure, "to announce his betrothal to Lady Freyja Bedwyn, who, as you all know, is the sister of the Duke of Bewcastle."

The marchioness jerked about to look up at her nephew, saucer-eyed. Lady Constance looked at him too, her eyes shining with happiness.

And then Freyja became aware of the swell of sound around her and the exclamations of surprise and delight coming from both Lady Holt-Barron and Charlotte. She became aware that the Marquess of Hallmere was striding across the ballroom toward her, his charming smile firmly in place, one arm outstretched. Freyja took a few steps forward and met him on a stretch of empty dance floor. He took her hand in his, bowed over it with courtly elegance, and raised it to his lips.

The crowd sighed with pleasure and then applauded enthusiastically.

It was all very horribly theatrical.

And very alarmingly real.

Freyja quelled a horrifying urge to relieve her feelings by throwing back her head and bellowing with laughter, and smiled instead.

The marquess raised his head, still holding her hand, and smiled into her eyes. Behind the charming, radiant smile, far back inside his eyes, he laughed.

"Now we have got ourselves into a famous scrape, sweetheart," he murmured.

It was the last private word they were to have for some time to come. Numerous people—almost everyone in attendance, in fact—wished to shake them by the hand or bow and curtsy to them and wish them well. A few even claimed to have predicted such an outcome immediately after the fracas in the Pump Room. Lady Holt-Barron was weeping delicately into her handkerchief and smiling at the same time. Charlotte hugged Freyja tightly and whispered that she had never been happier in her life—except when her own betrothal had been announced. The Earl of Willett looked sadly stricken. Lady Potford kissed Freyja on the cheek, turned to her grandson, and tapped him sharply on the sleeve with her fan before accusing him of being a rogue for keeping such a delightful secret from her. Mrs. Lumbard fawned all over them, reminding them and everyone else within earshot that they would be neighbors when the marquess and his new marchioness came home to Penhallow to live.

Mr. King clapped his hands for silence again after a good ten minutes of noise and congratulations, and announced that the program for the evening would be modified slightly in order to include another short waltz, to be danced by the newly betrothed couple. Everyone stayed to watch before the cardplayers drifted back to their room and the tea drinkers to theirs.

It was all remarkably ridiculous—and shamefully exhilarating.

"There is going to be an even greater stir tomorrow," Freyja remarked as their own private waltz was drawing to an end, "when we break off the engagement."

"Ah, not tomorrow, sweetheart," he said. "If it is all the same to you, we will remain betrothed until my aunt has returned home. I daresay she will not remain above a day or two now that her will has been thwarted. She will return home in high dudgeon."

"The moment she leaves, then," Freyja said, "we will have the announcement made." Actually, she did not mind prolonging this amusing farce for a day or two.

"There is no *we* in it," the marquess said. "*You* will break the betrothal. It is something a gentleman never does."

"Wonderful!" she said tartly. "It would serve you right if I neglected to do so and you were forced to marry me."

"Better you than Constance, my charmer," he said.

"I shall lull myself to sleep tonight with the memory of those ardent words of devotion from my betrothed," she said.

He grinned and then acknowledged the smattering of applause from the spectators with a more appropriate smile.

"Shall we go and discover what my aunt has to say?" he suggested.

"Absolutely," she told him, setting her hand along the sleeve of his offered arm. It had not escaped her notice that the marchioness was one of the few guests who had not come to congratulate them before their waltz.

The lady had recovered from what must have been a very nasty shock indeed. She was looking frail and sweet and about half her usual size—it was an impressive performance. She extended both hands to Freyja as they approached, clasped them unnecessarily tightly—Freyja countered by clasping hers more tightly still—kissed the air first at Freyja's left cheek and then at her right, and smiled warmly and graciously.

"What a delightful surprise, Lady Freyja," she said rather loudly, for the benefit of those around them. "I can think of no one I would more gladly welcome into the bosom of my family. I have always thought of dear Joshua as a son, you know." Her eyes were doing that needlepoint glare into Freyja's again.

"Thank you, ma'am," Freyja said. "I knew you would be happy for us."

"And my dear Joshua." The marchioness transferred her attention and her hands to her nephew. "What a naughty surprise, indeed. You would not confide in either your grandmother or your aunt?"

"I plucked up the courage to make Lady Freyja an offer during the waltz, Aunt," he said, "and she said yes. We were both so bubbling over with joy that we wanted everyone to share our happiness without any further delay. I thought you and Grandmama would appreciate the happy surprise."

The marchioness's smile did not falter. "Of course, dear," she said.

Mr. Darwin was bowing to Freyja then and requesting the next set of country dances with her. They were, after all, she realized, only two sets into the ball. There was much of the evening remaining. She smiled as she set her hand on his sleeve, remembering her resolve to cheer herself up by flirting with the Marquess of Hallmere tonight.

Well, she had done a great deal better than flirting. She had entered into a mock betrothal with him. Just for the sheer fun of it.

She was, she discovered, looking forward to the next few days with more exhilaration than she had looked forward to any day since she did not know when. At least they would take her mind off Alvesley and Kit's new son and the dreary state of her own life.

JOSHUA WALKED UP TO LADY HOLT-BARRON'S HOUSE on the Circus late the following morning. He had avoided the Pump Room, especially as his grandmother had expressed her intention of remaining at home after the late night. But he had not succeeded in avoiding the issue that had kept him awake much of the night, alternately chuckling and breaking into a cold sweat.

His aunt had invited herself and Constance to breakfast, and she had joined enthusiastically in his grandmother's plan to host a large betrothal party at Great Pulteney Street one week hence.

"I cannot tell you how delighted I am, Joshua," his aunt had said, "that you have decided to settle down at last. Though I daresay you will wish to take your bride traveling on the Continent for a year or two after the nuptials, now that the wars are over."

"I sensed Lady Freyja was the right woman for you from the first moment," his grandmother had agreed before laughing. "Well, from *almost* the first moment. You will never find life dull with her, Joshua."

Constance had found a moment to have a private word with him.

"Thank you, Joshua," she had said. "How quickly you thought and acted! But I do hope you did not offer for Lady Freyja Bedwyn only to thwart Mama. It would be unfair, would it not? I do not think she is ugly. I think she is distinguished and handsome. But, even so, she must have feelings to be hurt."

"Lady Freyja and I understand each other perfectly well," he had assured her. "We share the same enjoyment of a good lark."

"Ah," she had said. "It is not a real betrothal, then. I suspected as much. But I am rather sorry. I cannot help thinking, as your grandmother does, that she is perfect for you."

His aunt was planning to stay for at least another week, then, he thought ruefully as he strode up the steep incline of Gay Street. He had not expected her to stay so long. Neither had he expected his grandmother to insist upon a grand party. This betrothal business might yet prove a deuced embarrassment—and perhaps fun too, he admitted. That *was* the word she had used, was it not?

He knocked on the door of the house on the Circus, was admitted by a smirking housekeeper who had clearly heard the news—had anyone in Bath *not*?—and was taken up immediately to a sitting room where the ladies were gathered, mother and daughter looking as if they had just recently returned from an outing.

Lady Holt-Barron beamed at him and her daughter smiled. Lady Freyja looked wary.

"I have come to invite Lady Freyja to walk with me," he said after the first pleasantries had been exchanged.

She got to her feet after folding a letter she must have been writing at the escritoire.

"I need some fresh air," she said.

"And today, Lady Freyja," her hostess said with a broad smile, "you do not need any chaperone while walking with your betrothed."

A few minutes later they were striding back down Gay Street, not touching—she had refused to take his arm.

"You were writing to your family?" he asked her. "Breaking the glad tidings?"

"Doing no such thing," she said. "I was writing to my sister, as I do most days. I was describing the assembly to her—part of the assembly, at least."

"But you were omitting the insignificant detail of your betrothal being announced during it, no doubt," he said, grinning. She was looking out of sorts this morning.

"Exactly," she said. "They need not know. In a day or two's time we will be free to put an end to this foolishness. Your aunt will leave Bath, severely disgruntled, I sincerely hope, and then I can either have an announcement made or else you can leave too and I can go home soon after and no more need ever be said on the matter."

"Do you really believe it is going to be as simple as that, sweetheart?" he asked, chuckling.

They had reached the bottom of the hill and were winding their way toward the Abbey and the river beyond it. The sun was shining, though the breeze was fresh.

"Of course it will," she said with brisk confidence.

"My grandmother is even now planning a grand betrothal party for next week," he said.

She grimaced. "Then we must both leave Bath before then," she said.

"It would be unsporting," he told her, touching the brim

of his hat in acknowledgment of a couple they were passing. "All the invitations are being sent out today."

"Dammit," she said.

He laughed out loud. He had never before heard a lady utter such a word. He wondered if she had other such gems in her vocabulary and guessed she probably did.

"And my aunt has decided to stay for the party," he told her.

She stopped walking and looked at him severely as if he were to blame—as to a certain extent, of course, he was.

"Double dammit," she said. "*You* appear to be enjoying yourself enormously."

"I cannot help remembering," he said as they resumed their walk, "that things were looking grim last evening and that my aunt might just as easily have trapped me into announcing my engagement to Constance. I would far prefer to have you."

"I am overwhelmed," she said haughtily.

"Because you can be shed after a week or so," he said.

"Like a worn coat," she retorted.

"Unless you choose to hold me to the promise, of course," he said, "and make me marry you."

"Heaven forbid," she said.

"Will feigning a betrothal to me and a romantic fondness for me for a whole week be quite anathema to you?" he asked. "Culminating in a grand party and then freedom and sanity again? Last evening you thought it might all be fun."

"Last evening I did not *think* at all," she said. She looked at him assessingly as they reached the river and turned by unspoken consent in the direction of the Pulteney Bridge. "However, life in Bath *is* excruciatingly dull under normal circumstances."

"It is," he agreed. "Shall we agree, then, to enjoy the

less-than-normal—or *more*-than-normal—circumstances that the next week promises?"

She smiled slowly at him, the same slightly reckless light in her eyes that had appeared there last evening when he had asked her as a kind of joke if she would care to enter into a fake betrothal with him.

"Since it would appear that the week must be endured anyway," she said, "we might as well enjoy it, I suppose. Where are we going?"

"Sydney Gardens?" he suggested. "It is rather far away, but not *too* far a walk for you, I seem to remember. I may even be able to find another serving girl there being accosted by a squirrel and impress my betrothed by rescuing her."

"No, not the Gardens," she said. "Beechen Cliff. I have heard that it is a steep climb but that the view from the top is quite spectacular. I wish to go there."

"Good," he said.

At least dancing attendance upon Lady Freyja Bedwyn for the next week was not going to be boring. He had intended being on his way from Bath this morning. He was not on the whole sorry for the excuse to spend more time in her company. He found her amusing—and increasingly attractive.

FREYJA DID NOT PLAY FAIR. SHE HAD DONE THE MARquess of Hallmere an enormous favor, and she exacted payment in any way she could devise over the week following their betrothal announcement.

It was true that the Pump Room still had to be endured most mornings and the occasional concert or play or card party during the evenings. But she really did not mind those activities very much. At least the obligatory stroll in the Pump Room got everyone up and moving at a decent hour of the morning, and she enjoyed good music and lively acting and even the occasional game of cards. It was the rest of each day that had always been unbearably tedious.

Now the tedium was gone.

Each day she dragged the marquess off walking or riding. They clamored up Beechen Cliff that first day and up Beacon Hill and across the fields to the village of Charlcombe another day. They walked to the village of Weston one afternoon. They rode up Lansdown Hill and to Claverton Down. Even on the day it rained steadily from morning until evening she insisted upon riding as far as the village of Keynsham halfway to Bristol. Having a betrothed, she quickly discovered, was quite as good as having one of her brothers resident in Bath, since Lady Holt-Barron put up no protest about the propriety of their going off alone together so often.

But if truth were known, she enjoyed the marquess's company better than that of any of her brothers—and he enjoyed himself as much as she, she was sure. She enjoyed looking at him—he was undeniably one of the most handsome men of her acquaintance. And he was witty company. Verbally she could never get the better of him—or he of her. He never suggested to her that as a lady perhaps this walk or that ride might be too much for her. When she demanded the ride in the rain, he did not even so much as look surprised, though Lady Holt-Barron warned of all the dire consequences to their health of not simply taking tea in the Upper Rooms instead.

Freyja was not looking forward to the party at Lady Potford's, which was to be a grand squeeze of an affair since almost everyone with any pretension to gentility in Bath had been invited. She liked Lady Potford and did not relish the thought of such deception as the party would involve. But the more she saw of the Marchioness of Hallmere and Lady Constance Moore during the week, the more she realized that it would have been cruel indeed to have abandoned the marquess to what might well have been his fate—marriage with his cousin, who did not want him any more than he wanted her.

No, for this one week she was betrothed—again!—and she would act her part until the end and then retreat into her normal self and her normal life again when the party was over and the marchioness had left for Cornwall.

Life next week was going to seem very dull, she thought as she arrived back at Lady Holt-Barron's after the ride to Claverton Down. But she would think of that next week. Perhaps she would simply return home to Lindsey Hall. It should be safe to do so by then.

The marquess came into the house with her, since Lady Holt-Barron had invited him for tea. They were somewhat windblown and flushed from the outdoors, but Freyja did not go up to her room to change first. She preceded the marquess into the drawing room.

And stopped so abruptly that he almost collided with her from behind.

Lady Holt-Barron and Charlotte were both in the room. So was Wulfric.

He was just rising to his feet, looking his usual elegant, immaculate, faintly cold, silver-eyed self. His long fingers were curling about the handle of his quizzing glass and raising it halfway to his eye.

"Ah, Freyja," he said, his voice haughty and distant.

"Wulf!" she exclaimed.

"And . . . ?" His glass went the rest of the way to his eye, magnifying it horribly.

"May I present the Marquess of Hallmere?" she said,

standing to one side. "My brother Wulfric, my lord. The Duke of Bewcastle."

What in heaven's name had brought Wulf to Bath at this of all times? But she knew the answer without having to pummel her brain any further. Of course! Wulf, she sometimes thought, shared the quality of omniscience with God. It was *this of all times* that had brought him.

Someone had told him.

He knew!

His next words dispelled any shadow of doubt she may have felt.

"Ah, yes," he said softly, lowering his glass but still looking at the marquess with cold eyes. "Freyja's betrothed, I believe?"

CHAPTER IX

BEWCASTLE HAD A DISTINCT ADVANTAGE OVER him, Joshua thought an hour later as the two of them walked down Gay Street, Lady Holt-Barron's housekeeper having made arrangements for the horses to be returned to their stables. There was the advantage of rank, of course—Bewcastle was a duke while he was a marquess. But the difference between them was far vaster than that. Bewcastle had been born to his present role. He was an aristocrat to the marrow of his bones, while Joshua, even after being heir to his title for five years and holder of the title for seven months, still felt like a usurper.

They had conversed on a variety of topics over tea, the five of them, and consequently nothing of any significance had been said. Now Bewcastle spoke of the attractive appearance of Bath and Joshua agreed with his every word, trying not to feel like a whipped boy—or, rather, like one who was about to be whipped. But this really was a devilish coil. It had been too much to hope, he supposed, that word of the betrothal would not somehow come to the ears of Lady Freyja's brother, but who could have predicted that he would come in person like this instead of merely writing to his sister for more information?

"You will step into the Royal York with me?" Bewcastle asked as they reached level ground. It was phrased as a question, but Joshua recognized a command when he heard one.

"It would be my pleasure," he said.

The duke had a private suite of rooms at the hotel. His valet took their hats and gloves and brought a tray of drinks into the sitting room. Bewcastle indicated one empty chair and took another himself. The valet poured two glasses, handed one to each of them, and then left them alone, closing the door silently behind him.

Bewcastle regarded his visitor with pale, keen eyes that had Joshua thinking of wolves—the man was named appropriately, it seemed.

"You will doubtless explain to me," Bewcastle said in a pleasant enough voice, though his eyes were as cold as ice, "why your betrothal has been publicly announced to Bath society and not announced at all to Lady Freyja Bedwyn's family."

Joshua crossed one leg over the other. "It was an impetuous decision," he said. "I proposed marriage to Lady Freyja during a waltz at the Upper Rooms, she said yes, and we decided to invite our fellow guests to share our joy." His explanation sounded remarkably silly even to his own ears.

"Ah, impetuosity," Bewcastle said. "But you did not wish to invite her family also to share your joy, perhaps the next day or the day after—or the day after that?"

There was an unfortunate pause while Joshua tossed about in his mind a few possible answers. There *was* no convincing answer, of course. This was all devilishly embarrassing.

"Perhaps," the duke suggested, "you intended to wait upon me at Lindsey Hall after the first euphoria of your engagement had passed?"

"Lady Freyja is of age," Joshua said. "Strictly speaking, we do not need your consent. We would have sought your blessing in time, yes. During this past week, as you have suggested, we have been enjoying each other's company rather too much to consider what ought to be done."

"You have, then," the duke said softly, "conceived a passion for each other?"

Oh, Lord. He was wading in deep waters, Joshua realized.

"One might say so," he said.

"One might," Bewcastle agreed. "But do *you* say so, Hallmere?"

"I rather believe," Joshua said carefully, "that my feelings for Lady Freyja and hers for me are our private concern."

"Quite so." Bewcastle set down his half-empty glass, leaned back in his chair, set his elbows on the arms, and steepled his fingers. Silences, it seemed, did not embarrass him. It was a while before he continued. "It would seem, Hallmere, that you have always been an ambitious man."

Joshua raised his eyebrows.

"It would be strange if you were not," Bewcastle said. "All during your growing years you were one life removed from the heirdom to a marquess's title and property and fortune—a frustration, no doubt, to a penniless boy. And then that one life was extinguished under somewhat mysterious circumstances."

Good God! Joshua turned cold inside. At least it was

now clear who had informed Bewcastle of the betrothal and why he had lost no time in coming to Bath.

"Under *tragic* circumstances," Joshua said. "Are you insinuating that you believe I had a hand in my cousin's death?"

"I insinuate nothing," his grace said, raising haughty eyebrows. "Very probably they were merely *fortunate* circumstances for you. You celebrated your new expectations by traveling extensively and, ah, sowing some wild oats, I believe?"

"I spent five years in France," Joshua said somewhat testily, "doing undercover spy work for the British government. I resent this interrogation, Bewcastle."

"Do you?" The duke still spoke softly. He was not to be drawn into any angry exchange, it seemed. "But you wish to marry my sister, Hallmere. I will interrogate any man who aspires to her hand, even if he has forced *my* hand by announcing his betrothal before speaking with me. You refused to marry the lowly gentlewoman you impregnated at Penhallow before you left there?"

Joshua pursed his lips. It would be interesting to read the letter his aunt had written the Duke of Bewcastle. But he would not allow her malice to put him on the defensive before a stranger.

"She never even asked me to marry her," he said, grinning. "But I have supported her and the child for longer than five years."

Bewcastle showed no sign of sharing his amusement. He picked up his glass again and sipped from it. "Lady Freyja Bedwyn is the daughter of a duke," he said. "She is also an extremely wealthy woman, as I daresay you know."

"I suppose I would have guessed it," Joshua said, "if I had given the matter any thought."

"She is, in fact," the duke said, "a quite brilliant match for you."

"And since we are speaking of rank and fortune," Joshua said, grinning again, "I am something of a brilliant match for her too. It is what Bath society has been saying since the announcement was made, anyway."

The duke regarded him with cold hauteur. Too late, it struck Joshua that perhaps he should simply have told Bewcastle the truth. This mock betrothal was going to be over within the next week, after all. Why leave it to Lady Freyja to have to explain to her family?

"You are not at all sure you approve of me," he said. "I can hardly blame you. I proposed marriage to your sister without first consulting you as head of her family, and then I compounded that error by having the betrothal publicly announced during an assembly and by neglecting either to write to you or to call upon you immediately after. My aunt, I perceive, has performed that task for me. I can only say now that I have the deepest regard for your sister and will accept her decision if she should see fit to break off our engagement after listening to your advice."

There—perhaps that would give them a decent way out of their predicament when the time came. This awkward visit of her brother to Bath might turn out for the best after all.

The ducal eyebrows had risen.

"Extraordinary!" Bewcastle said softly. "You would not fight for the woman you love, Hallmere?"

"I certainly would not force any woman into a marriage against her will," Joshua said.

The duke set his empty glass down on the table beside him and Joshua took the gesture as a sign that the interview was at an end. He got to his feet.

"I will be escorting Lady Freyja to a concert at the Upper Rooms tonight," he said. "I will see you there?"

The duke inclined his head.

"I will bid you a good afternoon, then," Joshua said, and left the room.

He blew out air from his puffed cheeks as he stepped out of the Royal York Hotel. The Duke of Bewcastle was not going to grow any fonder of him when he disappeared from Lady Freyja's life in a few days' time. That would not matter one iota to *him*, of course, but it might matter a great deal to her, whether she then divulged the full truth or not.

Devil take it! Life was getting just too complicated for comfort.

But he grinned suddenly. It would be interesting indeed to be an invisible witness to the interview between Bewcastle and Lady Freyja that must be pending.

I T WAS ONE THING, FREYJA THOUGHT, TO HAVE BECOME involved in a betrothal in the eyes of Bath society; it was quite another suddenly to have one pair of those eyes belonging to Wulfric. Such inscrutable eyes too. They always had been. They had always been his single greatest asset when dealing with underlings, including his brothers and sisters.

His other great asset was his patience—if that was the right word. Wulfric was never in a rush. He could bide his time forever while his quarry fidgeted and dithered and waited for him to pounce.

All through tea at Lady Holt-Barron's he had made no further mention of the betrothal but had conversed politely about his journey and the state of the roads and about Bath and the weather and a dozen other topics. Then he had gone off walking back down into the city with the marquess, elegant and urbane, his eyes like two chips off a glacier.

He sat beside Freyja during the orchestral concert in the Upper Rooms that evening, Lady Holt-Barron on his other side, the marquess on Freyja's other side. They did nothing but listen to the music and talk about the music, though Wulfric was mobbed during the interval by people eager to make their curtsy or their bow to the Duke of Bewcastle. There was hardly a moment during which to snatch a private word with the marquess.

"What did he *say*?" she asked during one of those moments. "Did you tell him the truth?"

"Good Lord, no," he said, confining his answer to the second question. "Ought I to have done? I thought you might have been in more trouble over the masquerade than over a broken engagement next week."

"Wulf is not my keeper," she said haughtily. "There is no question of there being *trouble* either way."

"Then why are you so very out of sorts, sweetheart?" he asked, grinning at her.

Someone was in the process of informing Wulf that he must be gratified indeed at the betrothal of his sister to the Marquess of Hallmere, and Freyja caught the marquess's eye and chuckled mournfully.

There was going to be a *pile* of trouble.

Wulfric went back to his hotel after the concert. He appeared in the Pump Room the next morning, immaculately dressed in black and gray with white linen. He acknowledged Freyja and Charlotte and Lady Holt-Barron and proceeded to speak with other people, most notably Lady Potford, with whom he strolled twice all about the room.

Freyja walked arm in arm with Charlotte, who confessed herself mortally terrified of his grace, though she giggled at her own foolishness.

"Does he *ever* smile, Freyja?" she asked.

"Never," Freyja said. "It is beneath the ducal dignity."

They laughed together and she felt horribly disloyal. She adored all her siblings, Wulf included.

The crowds were beginning to disperse for breakfast when Wulfric sought her out and informed her that she would be taking the meal at the Royal York Hotel with him.

Should she confess the full truth to him and be done with it? she wondered a few minutes later as she took his arm and they set off at a brisk walking pace. But, oh, dear, he already knew—Lady Holt-Barron had told him, enraptured by the romance of it all—that for the past week she and the marquess had been going off walking and riding together, not a maid or chaperone in sight. How would that appear if it were suddenly revealed that they were not really betrothed after all?

And since when, she asked herself, had she been afraid to tell the truth or admit to a little indiscretion? She had never pretended to live by the code that hemmed other ladies in from all quarters until they had less freedom than servants or pets.

She drew breath to tell Wulfric exactly what had happened.

"Lady Potford has gone to great pains to arrange this large betrothal party for you tonight," he said.

Ah, yes, the party. Tonight. Well, this deception must continue until tomorrow, she thought. Surely tomorrow or the next day the marchioness would return home. She must be weary of smiling sweetly at Freyja whenever their paths crossed—at least two or three times each day—while darting private venom at her with her eyes. She had been looking rather pleased with herself this morning, but perhaps that was because she anticipated trouble for her nephew and Freyja with Wulfric's unexpected arrival in Bath.

In fact, Freyja thought with a sudden rush of insight, it was probably Lady Potford who had informed Wulf.

"She has been most kind," Freyja replied, winning for herself a rather sharp glance from her brother, who must have wondered at the docility of her answer.

They did not talk any more as they walked.

If the marchioness left tomorrow, Freyja thought, then the marquess would probably leave the day after. She would then confess all to Wulfric and go back to Lindsey Hall with him. It would all be very easy. No one here need know. No announcement of the ended betrothal need ever be made. After a while people would forget and stop wondering when the wedding was to be. She had never much cared what gossip was circulating about her anyway.

They ate breakfast in Wulfric's private suite of rooms. His valet was dismissed as soon as he had carried in the food and poured their coffee.

"We have seen two of our brothers married in the past few months," Wulfric said conversationally as Freyja buttered a slice of toast. "Both quite suddenly and ineligibly."

She would have agreed with him on both counts when she first met each of her sisters-in-law.

"Eve's father might have been a coal miner," she said, "but she was brought up as a lady, and she has spirit and a tender heart. Besides which, Aidan dotes on her. Judith is a gentlewoman even if her father *is* just an obscure country parson. Grandmama adores her and so, of course, does Rannulf. Eligibility is not everything, Wulf."

"Quite so," he said, taking his time about chewing a mouthful of sausage. "You, on the other hand, have made a perfectly eligible choice, Freyja."

She had been quite prepared to argue and fight. She had

nothing to say to these words of approval. She looked at him suspiciously.

"Though an equally sudden one," he added.

"It was an impetuous thing," she said. "He proposed marriage to me during a waltz at the Upper Rooms, I said yes, and we wished to invite our fellow guests to share our joy."

"Ah," he said softly in that way Wulf had of making one's flesh crawl with apprehension, "almost word for word the explanation I had from Hallmere himself."

"Because that is the way it was," she said. "Look here, Wulf, if you have come to Bath to play elder brother and head of the family and scold me for betrothing myself to the marquess without first weeping all over you and begging you to give your consent, you may jolly well go home again. I have been of age these past four years. I would think you would be delighted to see me marry eligibly."

"I would rather a marquess than a footman, certainly," he said. "But I do feel constrained to ask if Aidan's marriage and Rannulf's provoked you into this, Freyja."

"Eh?" she asked inelegantly, a forkful of egg halfway to her mouth.

"You are, as you have just observed," he said, "four years past your majority. Five and twenty is an uncomfortable age for a single lady. Have you been made suddenly aware of that this year?"

"No!" she exclaimed hotly. Though there might be a grain of truth in what he had said, she supposed. She had not attended Aidan's wedding—no one in the family had even known about it until weeks after the event. But she had been at Rannulf and Judith's just before coming to Bath, and she had felt some envy. She had even considered putting an end to her single state by grabbing some eligible gentleman in Bath—the Earl of Willett, for example.

Wulfric appeared to hesitate before speaking again. He stopped to take a drink from his coffee cup.

"It did not escape my notice," he said, "that the announcement of your betrothal was made two days after Viscountess Ravensberg was delivered of her son. One day, I believe, after Morgan wrote and informed you of the event. Probably the very day you received her letter."

"If you have a point to make, Wulf," she said when he paused, "there is no need to take all day about it. You think that because Kit has a child I am prostrate with grief and self-pity? You think I hurled myself into the arms of the first available man after I heard the news? You think it was I who proposed marriage to the *marquess* during that waltz and begged him to have our betrothal announced? All to cover for a broken heart? I do not care *that* much for Kit Butler." She snapped her finger and thumb over the table between them with a satisfying click. "Or for his viscountess. Or for their son." She tore off a piece of toast and popped it vengefully into her mouth.

"This is, then," Wulfric asked after a brief silence, "a love match, Freyja?"

How could she deny it now after that impassioned outburst, from which she was still breathless?

"I *adore* him," she said. "And he adores me."

"Ah," he said, gazing at her with his inscrutable eyes. "Quite so."

The tension was almost too much to bear. What a bouncer she had just told. And if he believed it, she was going to look that much more pathetic in a few days' time after she had been abandoned. She leaned across the table, her eyes sparkling with merriment.

"Have you heard about our first encounter in Bath?" she asked him. "Or rather about our first *two* encounters. They are inextricably linked. If you have not heard yet, someone is bound to bring up the matter this evening. I had best tell you myself now."

He looked slightly pained. "I have a feeling," he said, "that it might be something I would rather not know about."

She laughed and told him about the misunderstanding in Sydney Gardens, about her punching the Marquess of Hallmere in the nose and his neglecting to insist upon telling her what had really happened.

"Of course," she added, "I did not know his identity at that time or he mine. He refused to believe that I was a duke's sister because I had no chaperone with me."

"It is very clear," Wulfric observed dryly, "that you were behaving perfectly normally."

She proceeded to describe the scene in the Pump Room the following morning, complete with all the gruesome details.

"You are to be commended," Wulfric said when she had finished. He sounded rather weary. "You must have provided Bath society with enough conversation to last a week, Freyja. And then, just when it was dying down, you refreshed it with that unexpected announcement at the assembly. Now that you have described the commencement of your acquaintance with Hallmere, of course, it makes perfect sense to me that the two of you would have fallen head over ears for each other and you would have decided upon a life's commitment to each other in the course of a single waltz." He sighed and set down his knife and fork.

Freyja wondered what he would have to say if she were to describe her first encounter with the marquess *outside* of Bath.

"Are you going to be happy in this marriage, then?" he asked.

Sometimes—just occasionally—one had a sudden glimpse

into the humanity of Wulfric. Not often. If he had feelings, he almost never displayed them. If he had dreams or secrets or personal concerns, he never shared them. She often wondered about his relationship with his mistress—if it was strictly business, serving only the obvious function. But sometimes, for the merest moment, there came the shocking realization that perhaps he cared for them all, not just as brothers and sisters who were his responsibility, but as persons whom he might love.

She had one of those stabbing glimpses when he asked his question. And she did something horribly ignominious. Her eyes filled with tears.

"Yes, I am," she said fervently, leaning a little toward him across the table. "Yes, we are."

And then she swallowed and heard a nasty gurgling sound in her throat as she remembered that what she had just said with such uncharacteristic emotion was all a lie.

She almost wished that she really *were* betrothed to the Marquess of Hallmere and that she really *were* in love with him and looking forward to a lifetime of happiness with him. She wanted to be able to give her happiness as a gift to Wulf, who, she suddenly thought, was quite probably a lonely man.

"I suppose, then," Wulfric said, setting his napkin on the table and leaning back in his chair, "I had better give my blessing to this match, Freyja, for what my blessing is worth. It *is* rather akin, I daresay, to shutting the stable door after the horse has bolted."

There was still food left on Freyja's plate, but she had lost interest in it. She pushed the plate away. She felt wretched. She was impulsive and headstrong and frequently indiscreet, but she was unaccustomed to lying to Wulf or anyone else in her family. She was so far into this deception business, however, that there was nothing else to do now but go forward with it until it ended. Fortunately that would be soon.

"Hallmere had better come back to Lindsey Hall with us unless he has some pressing obligation elsewhere," Wulfric said. "We will need to present him in the neighborhood and celebrate your betrothal properly. And we will need to make plans for your wedding."

Freyja suddenly wished she had not eaten at all.

CHAPTER X

LADY POTFORD'S HOME ON GREAT PULTENEY Street was filled with guests on the evening of the betrothal party. She had opened the drawing room, her private sitting room, a salon, and the dining room in order to accommodate all her guests. Each room blazed with the lights of many candles. The long table in the dining room with its crisp white linen cloth was covered with dishes laden with a wide variety of appetizing foods. Two footmen hovered to help guests make their selection and fill their plates. Others carried large trays of filled glasses from room to room.

Lady Potford was, as she had told Joshua and Freyja numerous times and the Duke of Bewcastle once during her morning stroll with him in the Pump Room, more than delighted by the happy turn of events.

"I was dreadfully afraid," she had told Joshua, "that you would drift on as you have drifted for the past several years, tasting the ephemeral pleasures of life without realizing that there is an even greater pleasure to be had from fulfilling one's appointed role in life and from forming one's own family. You will go back to Penhallow after marrying Lady Freyja and set up your nursery there and see to the administration of your estate and the well-being of your people. She is *just* the bride for you, Joshua. I am very happy."

"I have an able steward, Grandmama," he had pointed out to her, "and I keep in constant communication with him." Jim Saunders was, in fact, the one person who always knew where he was. "Lady Freyja may prefer to live in London—or she may not," he conceded.

All the guests appeared happy too. It was not often that there was an event of such a dazzling nature to celebrate in Bath—and involving two such illustrious persons as a marquess and a duke's daughter. There was a great deal of merry conversation and laughter in every room.

The Marchioness of Hallmere, clad regally in a black satin gown with tall black hair plumes, appeared as happy as anyone. She smiled with sentimental joy at anyone who greeted her and occasionally dabbed at a happy tear with her black-bordered handkerchief. She kissed the air close to Freyja's cheek and took Joshua's face between her two hands before kissing him tenderly and assuring him and everyone else within earshot that his dear departed uncle would be proud of him tonight.

And then she sought out the Duke of Bewcastle in the drawing room.

"I am gratified and relieved that you saw fit to come to Bath at such short notice, your grace," she said, presenting him with her hand.

He took it and bowed over it, though he did not carry it to his lips.

"Ma'am," he said.

"Lady Freyja has taken Bath society by storm," she said. "She is *such* a sweet young lady."

His grace inclined his head in acknowledgment of the strange compliment, his silver eyes flat and quite unreadable.

"One can only hope," she said, "that she will be as happy as she deserves to be."

"Indeed, ma'am," he agreed with chilling hauteur.

"And one can only hope," she said, dabbing delicately at one eye with her handkerchief, "that Joshua did not rush into this betrothal simply for a lark."

The ducal eyebrows arched slightly, but he did not ask the question she clearly expected him to ask in the pause that succeeded her words.

"He is the dearest boy," she said with a deep sigh. "It was always impossible not to love him despite all his mischief. He was devoted to his cousins, especially Constance, my eldest girl, to whom you were presented in the Pump Room this morning."

The duke inclined his head again.

"But he acquired what the late Hallmere referred to as cold feet when he was on the verge of offering for her five years ago," she said, "and ran away to amuse himself on the Continent, though why he would go *there* when there was a war on I cannot imagine. It became clear to me after my dear husband's passing that he was still too embarrassed and ashamed to come home, and so I came here. It was soon obvious that the attachment between Joshua and Constance was still very much alive, but foolishly—parents can be *very* foolish, your grace, when they wish for nothing more than the happiness of their children—foolishly I pressed the match on them instead of allowing the courtship to take its natural course. It was my dearest wish that their betrothal be announced during last week's ball in the Upper Rooms, and I was under the distinct impression that it was Joshua's dearest wish too. But then he dashed off to waltz with Lady Freyja, that mischievous, reckless look in his eye that I recognize so well, and at the end of the set he had Mr. King announce his betrothal to *her*."

The Duke of Bewcastle had grasped the handle of his quizzing glass and raised it halfway to his eye.

The marchioness tittered and then let the happy expression fade. She looked fragile and wan.

"I fear," she said, "that my nephew has taken advantage of a fine lady who has perhaps reached the age at which— I am sure you will pardon me for such plain speaking, your grace—she is so eager for a marriage proposal that she is unable to distinguish between a serious offer and one that was made merely for his own convenience until he can disappear on one of his wild escapades again."

For a moment the marchioness found herself undergoing the disconcerting experience of being regarded through the lens of the duke's quizzing glass. But he soon let the glass fall on its ribbon.

"I must congratulate you, ma'am," he said coldly, "on your narrow escape."

"My . . . ?" Clearly she did not know what he was talking about. She took refuge behind her handkerchief and then smiled bravely and sweetly at a guest who greeted her as he passed.

"It would have been painful to you, ma'am," he said, "to see Hallmere married to your daughter when you suspect that he was somehow responsible for your son's death."

She stared at him. "Oh, I do beg your pardon," she said, her eyes widening in shock. "Is that the impression I gave in the letter I felt bound to write you, your grace? It was an accident. Joshua was with Albert before it happened. He was the last person to see him alive. There was never any question, though, that he *caused* the accident or even witnessed it."

"Ah," his grace said. "But there would still be the painful knowledge that the man who married your daughter had also fathered a child on her governess."

"Oh, not *Constance's* governess," she said. "Constance was already out of the schoolroom. Miss Jewell was governess to my other daughters, your grace. It was an unfortunate incident." She simpered and looked archly at him. "But young men will be young men, as I am sure I need not tell *you*, your grace. You have several younger brothers, I believe?"

The cold silver eyes regarded her in silence.

"Well." She dabbed at her eyes once more. "I considered it my duty to warn you, your grace, that your sister may be in danger of having her heart broken. Joshua is such a handsome boy and such a heartless rogue. I do not know why I love him, but I do. Lady Freyja is such a sweet lady. I would hate to see her hurt."

His grace was fingering the handle of his quizzing glass again and regarding her with haughtily raised eyebrows and arctic eyes.

"Oh." She smiled brightly and waved to someone across the room. "If you will excuse me, your grace. I see that I am wanted."

The duke bowed slightly to her, and she hurried away.

W HAT IS IT, SWEETHEART?" JOSHUA ASKED. "CAN'T keep your hands off me, can you?"

He was lighting a single branch of candles on the mantelpiece in the small downstairs room his grandmother used as her office and writing room. There were a desk and chair in there, as well as a few bookcases and two matching armchairs with gilded arms and legs.

"Ha!" she said with haughty disdain.

He turned his head to grin at her. She had told him that she needed to have a private word with him, and he had brought her in here. She was wearing a transparent silver tunic over a low-cut pale blue gown with a great deal of silver thread and embroidery and was looking quite dazzlingly handsome. Her hair was threaded with silver too.

"I may well not be able to keep my hands off *you*," he told her, perching on the edge of the desk with one foot braced on the floor and the other leg swinging free. "I believe your modiste must have run short of fabric when she reached your bodice. With magnificent results, I might add."

"Such lascivious talk does you no credit," she said severely. "I would wager you would not dare talk thus to any other lady."

"Good Lord, no," he agreed. "I never enjoy having my face slapped. You will note that I set half a room between us before talking thus to *you*. I like my nose the shape it is."

"We have got ourselves into a dreadful coil," she said.

"We have," he agreed. "Somehow I suppose I imagined that Mr. King would announce our betrothal, everyone would smile and nod and assure us and one another that that was very pleasant news, and then we would all go about our business more or less as usual until you and I could decently go our separate ways again. I did not envisage this party—or the extravagance of my grandmother's delight."

"And I did not foresee Wulf's coming to Bath," she said, frowning. "It has made the whole thing horribly and embarrassingly complicated."

"Has he tried to persuade you to end the betrothal?" he

asked. "I have been under the distinct impression that he is less than delighted with me." He wondered if her brother had shown her his aunt's letter or told her any of the damning things she appeared to have included in that letter.

She shook her head. "Wulf would not do that," she said. "He does not give orders. Not to his brothers and sisters anyway. Though I have often thought that he is quite expert at maneuvering us into doing what he wants us to do, apparently of our own free will."

"Perhaps, then," he said, smiling at her, "you can allow him to maneuver you into giving me my marching orders. It would be the perfect answer to our dilemma, would it not? Just give me enough warning, though, if it happens before my aunt leaves Bath so that I can flee before I find myself betrothed to someone else instead."

"I assured him," she said, "that I adore you and that you adore me. I have promised him that we will be happy."

Despite himself he threw back his head and laughed.

"You might try frowning less ferociously," he said. "I might almost believe that you do not mean a word of it."

"Is everything a joke to you?" she asked, coming closer to him. "I have never lied to Wulf before. I have always scorned lies."

He reached out and took one of her hands in his and shifted his weight so that he was sitting fully on the desk.

"At the moment," he said, "I am feeling something akin to adoration."

"He expects you to accompany us back to Lindsey Hall within the next few days," she said, "so that you can be presented to the rest of my family and our neighbors. So that our betrothal can be celebrated there. So that our wedding can be planned."

"Ah," he said, possessing himself of her other hand too. "We find ourselves in a coil indeed."

"You are *not* to agree to it," she said, glaring at him haughtily along the length of her nose. "You are *not* to come. You are to make some excuse about another commitment, and then after you have gone I will break the truth to Wulf."

"Ah, sweetheart," he said, "I *have* made life difficult for you."

"You have indeed," she said. "But I agreed to your mad scheme and on the whole I am not sorry. This past week has been far less tedious than it would have been if we had not been betrothed. Indeed, it has been downright enjoyable."

"For me too." He grinned at her.

She opened her mouth and drew breath to say something else, did not say it, but locked glances with him instead. It was an awkward, unexpectedly silent moment in which it seemed they both simultaneously realized that they were alone together in a small, private room lit only by the flickering light of three candles.

He was very aware of the enticingly bare expanse of her bosom, of the cleavage between her generously rounded breasts, of her gracefully arched neck, of her bold, strangely attractive face, of the shining mass of her fair hair. He felt his temperature rise a notch, his breath quicken, his groin tighten.

He drew her forward until she stood between his spread legs, and drew her arms about his waist until she locked them behind him. He cupped her face with his hands, smoothed his thumbs over her dark eyebrows and then down her cheeks to rub over her lips.

He ran his tongue over his own lips as he lowered his head and then over hers—they were soft and warm and unresisting. He drew down her bottom lip with his thumb, ran his tongue back and forth over the soft flesh inside, and then, when she opened her mouth with a low sound of acquiescence, he kissed her fully, sliding his tongue deep inside.

Desire exploded in him with furnace heat. He wrapped one arm about her shoulders and the other about her waist to draw her closer, and lost himself in sheer carnal lust.

"What are we doing?" she asked suddenly a short while later, jerking back her head and glaring at him with bright eyes and flushed cheeks.

"Kissing?" he suggested, rubbing his nose across hers and grinning at her. "We *did* both just agree, did we not, that it has been an enjoyable week? Why not make it more so?"

"Perhaps," she said, her hands on his shoulders as if to push away from him, "you need to be reminded that we are not really betrothed."

"Yet this is our betrothal party," he said, "and you have assured your brother that we adore each other and are going to live happily ever after together. You never lie to your brother."

He had better be careful, he thought, or he was going to talk himself into something he could not talk himself out of.

"I do not kiss every handsome stranger I encounter," she retorted.

"Only the ones you temporarily betroth yourself to?" He grinned and wrapped both arms about her waist. It was very small, a delicious contrast to her bosom and hips.

She stared at him. "Promise me you will not be persuaded to come to Lindsey Hall," she said. "This needs to be ended now—as soon as possible after tonight."

"You are afraid," he asked softly, rubbing his nose over

hers again and teasing her lips with his own, "that you will not be able to resist my body much longer?"

She tutted. "I have never in my life met such a conceited man," she said.

"I am mortally afraid," he said, "that I will not be able to resist yours."

He meant it too. Having Lady Freyja Bedwyn in bed, he suspected, would be the sensual experience of a lifetime. Unfortunately, he would never know for sure. She was a lady—an aristocrat. She was out of bounds. But a betrothal, he was finding, even a fake one, was setting severe temptation in his way. In hers too, it appeared—despite her words she was making no concerted effort to get away from him.

"I could begin the feast here," he said, nibbling at her lips with his teeth, "and work my way down to your toes. Toes are a marvelously erotic part of the anatomy. Did you know that?"

"I did not," she said firmly, drawing her head back a few inches to glare at him. "And this is quite improper talk. You are laughing at me. Your eyes give you away every time."

"Do they, sweetheart?" He dipped his head to nuzzle her neck where it joined her shoulder. She hunched the shoulder and tipped back her head. Her fingers twined in his hair and clutched it. "And do they also tell you that I might never reach your toes? I might be distracted by something altogether more erotic halfway down."

He heard breath hiss into her. This might be the moment to protect his nose from acquiring a bend of its own, he thought, but when he lifted his head he could see that her lips were parted and her eyes heavy-lidded. She did not have fisticuffs on her mind, then.

"We ought not to be here," she said. "We ought to be

with your grandmother's guests. They will wonder where we are."

"They will think that we are stealing a few moments for ourselves," he told her. "They will be charmed."

She moved her head forward then, closing her eyes as she came, and kissed him fiercely on the lips, opening her mouth, opening his, and invading him with her tongue.

She had both arms coiled about his neck and he had both hands splayed over her buttocks when the door opened.

"Ah," the cold, rather languid voice of the Duke of Bewcastle said as Joshua opened his eyes, lifted his head, and slid his hands up to a more decorous position on either side of her waist, "here you both are."

He stepped into the room and closed the door quietly behind him as Lady Freyja spun around, flushed and slightly disheveled.

"Do you ever think of knocking, Wulf?" she demanded haughtily.

He raised his eyebrows and looked faintly surprised. "No," he said after pausing to give her question some consideration. "A servant directed me here."

FREYJA WAS HORRIBLY EMBARRASSED — PARTLY BECAUSE she had launched herself with such lascivious intent at the marquess, partly because Wulf had walked in and caught her at it. It was only after the marquess had moved his hands that she had realized where they had been. And of course they would have been in full view to Wulf—she had had her back to the door.

She glanced down hastily but was reassured to find that the low bodice of her gown still covered everything it had been designed to cover. Now, she thought crossly, she was going to look doubly pathetic in a few days' time when this farce was all over.

Wulfric had not come to drag her back to the party by the hair, it seemed. He settled into one of the gilded chairs, rested his elbows on the arms, and steepled his fingers—a characteristic pose when he had something of some import to say.

"Sit down, Freyja," he said, indicating the other chair before joining his fingertips again. "I understand that there was a great deal more at play during the infamous ball at the Upper Rooms one week ago than presented itself to general observation."

Freyja, seating herself and feeling the marquess come to stand behind and slightly to one side of her chair and set a hand on the back of it, suddenly felt no doubt at all that Wulfric knew everything.

"It would appear," he continued, "that quite unknown to most of the guests present, there was an unseemly rush to win the race over which of two betrothals, both involving the same gentleman, was to be announced first. Am I correct in this assumption, Hallmere?"

There was a predictable thread of laughter in the marquess's voice when he answered.

"Not exactly," he said, "though according to my cousin Constance, the marchioness was hoping to advance our apparent courtship to such a degree that an announcement would have seemed superfluous. I preferred to defend myself with offense."

Wulfric leveled upon him the sort of keen, icy look that had most ordinary mortals withering up in the vain hope of disappearing altogether. Freyja did not look to see if the marquess was one of them. She should, she supposed, be feeling enormous relief. The worst part of ending the masquerade—telling Wulf—was to be avoided. She might have guessed that he would discover the truth for himself.

"This betrothal is to end as soon as the Marchioness of Hallmere and her daughter have left for home, I assume?" Wulfric asked.

"With heartfelt thanks to Lady Freyja for saving me from a life sentence and apologies for any inconvenience to her, yes," the marquess agreed.

"It has not been inconvenient, Wulf," Freyja added firmly. "Indeed I agreed gladly to the scheme. And the tedium of life in Bath has been considerably alleviated during the past week."

"During which time you have been enjoying excursions into the hills and surrounding countryside at all hours of the day, alone with a gentleman who is not your betrothed," Wulfric said. "And embracing him."

"That was just tonight," she said. "And on one other occasion," she added for honesty's sake now that the lies had been dispensed with. "You are not going to be gothic about this whole thing, are you, Wulf? I am five and twenty years old. I do not need to be hedged about with chaperones and guardians as poor Morgan does."

He transferred his inscrutable gaze to the marquess.

"Your aunt's prediction, made to me not one hour ago, will prove perfectly correct when you abandon my sister within the coming week," he said. "She will be delighted. Lady Freyja Bedwyn will be humiliated."

"Nonsense, Wulf," she said crossly.

But he did not even deign to look at her. His silver gaze was fixed on the marquess, who chuckled softly.

"Neither of which outcomes is to my liking," he said. "What are you suggesting, Bewcastle? That I marry Lady Freyja after all? I doubt she will have me."

"That—publicly, at least—should be her decision," Wulfric said. "Would you not agree?"

Freyja shot to her feet. "Nonsense," she said again. "I agreed to this scheme because it amused me to do so. I did *not* do it in order to trap the Marquess of Hallmere into marrying me. I do not want him—or any other husband for that matter."

His eyes were laughing, she saw when she strode past him on the way to the desk. She sat down on the chair behind it, as far from the two men as she could get. How very stupid all this was.

"Perhaps," the marquess said, "we can stage another scene in the Pump Room in a few days' time. Have you heard of the first one, Bewcastle? I am afraid Lady Freyja showed to less than advantage on that occasion. On the next, I can assure you, everyone's sympathy will be with her as she punches me in the nose and invites me to go to hell. Everyone will congratulate her for so publicly freeing herself from her betrothal to a rogue."

Wulfric, Freyja could see as she stared broodingly at him, was not amused.

"The day after tomorrow, Hallmere," he said, "you will accompany Lady Freyja and me to Lindsey Hall, where you will formally make the acquaintance of our family and neighbors. We will have your betrothal properly announced and celebrated. If by Christmas or the spring she has decided that after all she does not wish to join herself in matrimony to you, then the necessary announcement will be made—by me. She will be frowned upon, of course—*that* cannot be avoided now—but she will not be pitied."

"I believe," the marquess said, turning to glance at her, "Lady Freyja does not wish me to come to Lindsey Hall."

She compressed her lips. How many minutes had passed

since she had assured the marquess that Wulf never gave orders to his brothers and sisters? This all sounded very like a firm ducal command to her.

"Lady Freyja will be glad of an escort for the next week or two," Wulfric said. "Her brothers and their wives will be coming to Lindsey Hall, having been invited to attend the christening celebrations for the new grandson of our neighbor, the Duke of Redfield."

Freyja sat bolt upright in her chair. Celebrations for the christening of Kit's son? And she was now trapped into going home, with or without the Marquess of Hallmere? She was going to have to attend? To smile and grin at everyone and pretend to be happy for Kit and the viscountess and the earl and countess?

The marquess had turned to face her fully, his hands clasped behind his back. He was looking far more serious than usual—almost grim, in fact.

"If it is Lady Freyja who is to decide if and when our betrothal is to end," he said, "then it is she who must decide whether I come to Lindsey Hall or not."

She should set him free here and now. Indeed, she should march out into the party right at this moment and make a public announcement of the end of their betrothal. It had been a ridiculous farce from the start. At the same time the marquess could make a public announcement that he was¯ *not* going to marry his cousin Constance. There would be an end of the whole stupid mess.

With the pathetic humiliation of a broken engagement behind her—news of it was bound to drift homeward sooner or later, probably sooner—she was going to have to attend the christening party for Kit's baby and smile and smile until her face felt permanently stretched.

"You had. better come for a week or two, then," she said

ungraciously. "We will contrive to quarrel at the end of it—it should not be difficult."

Wulfric got to his feet. "I believe," he said with distant hauteur, "you have neglected Lady Potford's guests for long enough."

He strolled to the door and let himself out without a backward glance.

The marquess looked at Freyja.

"Good Lord," he said.

"Triple damnation," she said.

He grinned and then—quite predictably—laughed.

"So we live to kiss again," he said, waggling his eyebrows and offering her his arm.

"Over my dead body," she assured him, lofting her nose into the air and passing him on her way to the door.

"A cliché unworthy of you, sweetheart," he said. "But I sincerely hope you do not mean it. I would be incapable of enjoying such a kiss—as would you too, of course—and I would hate that for both of us."

CHAPTER XI

TWO DAYS LATER JOSHUA FOUND HIMSELF RIDING along the king's highway in the midst of the impressively large entourage of liveried coachmen, footmen, and outriders escorting his grace's crested traveling carriage and baggage coach to Lindsey Hall in Hampshire. Who could have predicted the bizarre sequence of events that had brought him to this moment? He could not decide whether he should be quaking with terror or doubled over with helpless laughter.

But he was not a man much given to terror. And watching people in every village through which they passed gawking in awe and bobbing curtsies or pulling at forelocks and the drivers of every vehicle they passed respectfully pulling over to one side of the road until the procession had gone by was endlessly amusing. *He* could probably behave this way if he wished, he supposed—he was the Marquess of Hallmere, after all. The thought tickled his fancy.

He wished he could share the joke with Lady Freyja. But she, much against the grain, he suspected, was riding inside the leading carriage with the duke. Besides, it was possible that she was so accustomed to this form of travel that she would not see anything humorous about it. He wondered what they were talking about. Probably nothing at all, or else the weather or the passing scenery. Bewcastle had made no further mention of the betrothal since the evening before last.

Joshua was feeling perfectly cheerful as he looked forward to arriving at Lindsey Hall. It was true that he was fairly caught in parson's mousetrap until Lady Freyja in due course decided to set him free. He was entirely at her mercy. But she was a woman who would always play fair even if she also played rough, he believed. Besides, she had no more wish to marry him than he had to marry her. In the meantime he liked her. He had not yet tired of her company. Quite the contrary—he found her conversation and wit and spirit quite as stimulating as those of any of his male friends. And he found her dashed attractive. Maybe too attractive—he was going to have to tread carefully in the coming days or weeks or however long he was expected to stay in Hampshire.

They reached Lindsey Hall during the middle of the afternoon. Joshua followed the carriage through the gates and along a straight, wide avenue lined with elm trees. The house soon came into view at the end of it. It was neither medieval nor Jacobean nor Georgian nor any other single architectural style. It was a mix of many styles and clearly a mansion that had been in the family for generations and "improved" upon and added to many times. The result was surprisingly imposing and pleasing.

The wide avenue divided into two not far from the house in order to skirt about a large circular garden with a marble fountain at its center. There were not as many flowers blooming at this time of the year as there probably were in July, but the water had not yet been turned off for the winter. It spouted at least thirty feet into the air before spilling over into the wide basin like the sparkling spokes of an umbrella.

There was a young boy standing precariously on the edge of the basin, probably getting wet. A tall, solid-looking man with dark, forbidding countenance and large, hooked nose—the Bedwyn nose?—stood on the grassy verge of the avenue not far from the boy, a young girl perched on one of his shoulders and clinging to his hair. A slender, pretty, brown-haired young lady and a voluptuously endowed redhead were with them. All had turned to watch the approach of the carriage. The ladies smiled as it passed. The little girl waved. They all looked curiously at Joshua.

Three other people dressed for riding were walking out of the stable yard as the carriage made its final turn onto the cobbled terrace before the great double doors of the house. One was a slender, willowy, dark-haired young beauty. The other two were men, one tall, broad, fair, and dark-browed, the other dark, slim, and good-looking. Both had the family nose.

He was about to meet the Bedwyns, Joshua realized. He wondered how he would be introduced. He had not discussed with Bewcastle whether or not the family was to be party to the farce that must be acted out for decency's sake until the betrothal could be properly ended—if there *was* a proper way to end a betrothal.

There was a great deal of noise as everyone converged upon the terrace while the carriage door was opened wide and the steps set down. The big, fair-haired brother reached inside and swung Lady Freyja out without benefit of the steps. She proceeded to hug the ladies and the little girl. She shook hands like a man with the boy and her brothers. The duke meanwhile descended, nodded to them all, and looked faintly taken aback when the brown-haired lady hugged him.

Joshua dismounted and turned his horse over to the care of a groom who had come running from the stables.

Freyja came striding over to him when she had completed her flurry of greetings. Her chin was lifted proudly. There was a martial gleam in her eyes. It was not, perhaps, a moment she had anticipated with any great joy. She took him firmly by one hand.

"I want you all to meet the Marquess of Hallmere—Joshua," she said, her voice raised haughtily. "My betrothed. There is no marriage date set. I daresay it will be next year sometime. Perhaps next summer."

There was a chorus of sound, but she held up one hand and it subsided.

"Let me complete the introductions first," she said and proceeded to name all the strangers about him. Lady Morgan Bedwyn, the dark young beauty, curtsied to him and looked him over with frank, dark eyes. Lord Alleyne, the dark-haired young man, looked amused. The fair-haired giant was Lord Rannulf, the gorgeous redhead, his wife, Judith. The pretty, brown-haired lady was Eve, Lady Aidan Bedwyn. Her husband was the dark, dour man, who looked as if he might have spent a year or ten in the military. The children, Davy and Becky, belonged to the latter couple.

"So *that* is why you dashed away to Bath without a word to anyone just when we were expecting Aidan and Eve and Ralf and Judith to arrive," Lady Morgan said to her eldest brother. "You heard about the betrothal and went to see for yourself. Why is it that Wulf hears all the interesting stories and we do not?"

Lord Rannulf was shaking Joshua's hand with a warm, firm grip.

"This is sudden," he said, grinning. "But we Bedwyns have a recent history of sudden betrothals and marriages. Why would Free be different?"

"Hallmere?" The dark, granite-faced Lord Aidan Bedwyn shook his hand with a nod but no smile.

His wife was hugging Lady Freyja again, tears in her eyes.

"I am so happy for you, Freyja," she said. "I knew it must happen soon."

The little boy had wormed his way between Joshua and Freyja and was pulling on the skirt of her carriage dress.

"Aunt Freyja," he said, and tugged again. "Aunt Freyja, I brought my cricket set with me."

"Hey, rascal." Lord Aidan suddenly looked almost human as he reached down to scoop the child up and deposit him astride his shoulders. "Let your aunt get her foot inside the house before pestering her to play with you. Besides, this is not the season for cricket. We will find something else energetic to do tomorrow."

"But cricket it will be first, in season or out," Lady Freyja said, smiling up at the boy and even winking at him. "I want you on my team, Davy. I'll hit a six in my very first over at bat."

Joshua looked at her with some interest. She played cricket? He might have known it.

"May I play too?" he asked. "I am a famous bowler and have been known to prevent a single six being hit for a whole inning—or even a four."

"Ha!" she said.

The boy was laughing with delight and Lord Aidan made himself look entirely human by smiling.

"I suppose," he said, "any season is good for cricket if the Bedwyns say it is."

"Perhaps," the Duke of Bewcastle said without at all raising his voice, though all of the boisterous Bedwyns fell silent to listen, "we should step into the house and gather for tea in the drawing room in half an hour's time?"

"The master has spoken," Lord Alleyne said with a low chuckle after Bewcastle had preceded them all into the house. He set one arm about Lady Freyja's shoulders and hugged her to his side. "I am happy for you, Free, if *you* are happy. And you, Hallmere. We had better file inside like docile lambs." He strode off ahead of them.

"Whew!" Joshua said, grinning down at Lady Freyja and offering her his arm.

"I have decided," she said, looking at him haughtily as she took it, "that I will call you Josh. I refuse to 'my lord' you, I do not wish to call you Hallmere, and Joshua is too biblical. You may call me Freyja."

"Or Free, as your brothers do?" he suggested.

"Or Free," she agreed. "But only as long as we are betrothed. Until Christmas at the latest."

"I will make free with Free until then," he said.

She cast him a sidelong look, which assured him that she had not missed either the pun or the double entendre.

They ascended the steps and entered the house. Joshua found himself in an impressive medieval great hall complete with an oak-beamed ceiling, a gigantic fireplace large enough to roast an ox in, whitewashed walls bedecked with coats of arms, banners, and weapons, a minstrel gallery above an intricately carved wooden screen, and a massive oak table filling up much of the floor space.

It looked like the perfect setting for a feast and an orgy.

THE CHRISTENING WAS TO TAKE PLACE TWO DAYS after her return home, Freyja discovered, and it was to be a grand affair indeed. After the church service late in the morning, all the guests were to proceed to Alvesley

Park, home of the Earl of Redfield—and of Kit, Viscount Ravensberg, too—for dinner and a party that would probably last into the evening.

Rannulf and Judith had come all the way from Grandmaison in Leicestershire, where they lived with the Bedwyns' ailing maternal grandmother, whose heir Ralf was—he and Kit had always been best friends. And Aidan and Eve and the children had come because they were not far away in Oxfordshire and because, according to Aidan, he had been away at the wars for so many years that he had missed a decade and more of family and neighborhood events.

It was all going to be a severe trial, Freyja decided. She dreaded the day even with the added security of a betrothed to take along with her. It was stupid to have allowed herself to be so discomposed by an ancient passion—it was four years since she had fallen desperately in love with Kit Butler, and it had lasted for precisely one month. But, of course, there had been the added bother of last year and all its hideous embarrassment. She had behaved badly. She had made an idiot of herself. She had ended up practically begging Kit to give up Lauren in order to marry *her* and then slamming her fist into poor Ralf's jaw, perhaps because Kit's had not been available at that precise moment.

She would think of tomorrow when tomorrow came, she decided the morning after she arrived home. And she would think of the problem of Josh after tomorrow was over. He was in her debt, she had decided, despite all the walks and rides in Bath. After all, he had enjoyed those walks and rides too. So he owed her his escort for tomorrow. After that she would find some way of drawing him into a ghastly, very public brawl, and she would break off the engagement. She had no intention of waiting until

Christmas or later, as Wulfric had suggested. It would be unfair. And she might find it harder to do if she allowed more time to elapse. He was quite alarmingly attractive. That was in addition to his good looks, of course, which had not escaped notice among her family.

"You have been in Bath for a couple of weeks, Freyja," Morgan had said the night before when all the women had gathered briefly in Freyja's bedchamber, "and you have come home with a Greek god. All *I* will discover when I go to town in the spring for my come-out and exposure to the marriage mart is a whole gaggle of awkward-mannered, pimply youths. It is most provoking."

Both Judith and Eve had laughed.

"But you will wait for your prince to arrive, Morgan," Eve had said. "And he *will*, you know, just as Freyja's has."

"Freyja's prince just happens to be absolutely *gorgeous*," Judith had added, her right hand placed theatrically over her heart, her eyelids batting. "All that shining blond hair. Arghhh!"

"And those laughing blue eyes," Morgan had added mournfully. "How will I ever find any man to match him for myself?"

"But one's own particular prince always appears more splendid than any ordinary mortal, Morgan—or even any other extraordinary one," Eve had said kindly. "Aidan does to me, and I am certain Rannulf does to Judith."

Freyja had looked at them both, slightly envious.

She would feel no negative emotion today, though, she decided after getting out of bed early and looking out the window to note that the clouds were high and might even move off by midmorning to offer a sunny day. The air coming through her open window was cool but not cold. It was a fine morning for cricket. It was a fine day for all sorts of strenuous outdoor activities.

How *wonderful* it was to be away from the confining atmosphere of Bath.

They all joined in the game of cricket after breakfast—all except Wulfric, of course, who disappeared into his study. Even Eve and Judith decided to play, though Rannulf tried to talk Judith out of it, directing all sorts of significant glances across the table at her, all of which she ignored.

Gracious heavens! Freyja thought. Was Judith with child? How very interesting *that* would be if it were true. She and Ralf had been married no longer than a month. Was it possible... But that was absolutely none of her business.

Freyja and Joshua were on different teams—deliberately so. He was determined to bowl her out; she was equally determined to hit a six off him. She had Eve, Morgan, Rannulf, and Davy on her team. Joshua had Judith, Aidan, Alleyne, and Becky on his.

Fortunately, Rannulf was a decent bowler. Although he went easy on Judith and very easy indeed on Becky, making sure that she hit a number of balls and scored a total of eight runs while all the fielders became remarkably clumsy and simply could not throw her out, Aidan hit one six and a couple of fours off him before Freyja caught him out close to the boundary, and Joshua hung in for a total of twenty runs. Alleyne went out ignominiously to the very first ball bowled at him—it shattered the wickets behind him while Davy went wild with glee.

Freyja's team needed fifty-two runs to win when they came up to bat. Rannulf scored fifteen before being caught out. Eve scored sixteen and Morgan eleven, both with very lenient bowling from Josh, who looked distractingly virile and handsome without his coat or waistcoat and with his shirtsleeves rolled halfway to his elbows. Davy, also the recipient of friendly bowling, was at nine runs when Morgan finally went out and Freyja came in.

Joshua's first ball came hurtling down between the wickets, a wicked spin making its course almost impossible to judge. Freyja could do nothing better with it than fiercely protect her wickets and then glare at a grinning bowler.

"Can't you do any better than that?" she yelled, and flexed her wrists and made a few showy air shots with the bat.

He could.

The next ball hopped awkwardly just in front of her, sending up a shower of grass and dust and almost taking her front teeth out as it whizzed past her face.

"Can't you do any better than that?" he yelled, while his team catcalled and Freyja's clapped their hands and called out encouraging words to her.

She watched the next ball every inch of the way, saw it as if it were coming at half speed, judged the spin with clear, unhurried mind, adjusted the bat, gripped it tightly, and hit the ball with a satisfying crack. She watched it as it soared over the lawn in a beautiful arc and cleared Aidan's head at the boundary by a good three feet. Then she ran between the wickets, her bat in one hand, her skirts caught up in the other, laughing as she went, passing a wildly whooping Davy halfway down.

The game had been won by Freyja's team.

"I believe," she said, when she had finished running, stopping not far from Joshua, panting, her hands on her hips, her hair in wild disarray about her shoulders—she had pulled out the last of the pins long ago, "I have proved a point."

"You have," he said, with a look of abject dejection belied by his laughing eyes. "You have won our wager, Free. I had better pay the penalty."

And there, before her brothers and sister and sisters-in-law and the two children, he took two long strides forward, tangled his hand in her hair so that he was cupping the back of her head, tipped back her head, and kissed her with lingering thoroughness on the lips.

She was glad she had been running, she thought, when he finally lifted his head and she found herself the interested object of her relatives' grinning attention. It would account for her hot cheeks. It would be just too lowering to be seen to blush.

"I must be suffering from memory loss," she said. "I do not recall any wager."

"I will never again be able to hold up my head among my cricket-playing peers," Joshua said. "I must confess that game was quite fairly won. I had no intention of allowing you to get a hit off me."

"I know." She smiled dazzlingly at him.

"What are we going to do next?" Davy was jumping up and down in his excitement and addressing them all in a piping yell. "You said we would find something else strenuous to do, Uncle Aidan. Can we go riding or play hide-and-seek or climb trees or—"

Aidan caught him up and suspended him by his ankles.

"What we will do next," he said, while Davy squealed and giggled and demanded to be put down, "is have luncheon. And then we will see." He set the boy gently down on the grass and tickled him with the toe of his boot.

"*Uncle Aidan?*" Joshua asked, as they walked back to the house, taking Freyja's hand in his and lacing his fingers with hers.

"Becky and Davy were Eve's foster children when Aidan met her earlier this year," she explained. "Their parents were dead and none of their relatives were willing to take them in. More recently Eve and Aidan have been given legal custody of them. Becky calls them *Mama* and *Papa*. Davy calls them *Uncle* and *Aunt*. Eve has told me that they are careful not to try to take their parents' place or to encourage the children to forget their parents. I could never have imagined Aidan with children. But, as you can see, he is as fond of those two as any father."

"He has been a military man?" Joshua asked.

"For twelve years," she said. "From the age of eighteen to a few months ago, after he married Eve." She glanced down at their hands. "Did I give you permission to hold my hand, Josh—and in quite so intimate a manner?"

He looked down too and then up into her face before laughing at her.

"No," he said. "But we have a masquerade to maintain. Apparently you and Bewcastle agreed between you that our betrothal is to appear real to your family. I am merely doing my part."

"If you imagine," she said severely, "that I am going to stand idly by while you maul me about in the name of realism, I am here to tell you that you are mistaken."

"Stand idly by?" He laughed again. "Oh, I hope not. It is no fun mauling about a marble statue or a limp fish. I suppose you were quite a hoyden when you were growing up?"

"Of course," she said.

"Good." He lowered his head closer to hers, and for one moment she thought he was going to kiss her again. "I have a definite weakness for hoydens."

This masquerade, she realized, had given him all the license in the world to flirt outrageously with her—and even to slip beyond flirtation at times.

Why was it such an exhilarating thought?

THE BEDWYNS WERE A BOISTEROUS, FUN-LOVING family, Joshua had decided before the day was out. The children were not hidden away in the nursery while the adults found something decorously dull with which to occupy themselves. After luncheon they all decided to walk down to the lake, which was hidden from sight among the trees to the east of the house. There were plenty of hiding places there, Rannulf said—all of them had invited Joshua to an informal use of their names—for a game of hide-and-seek. He would take the swing with him, Alleyne added, and set it up in one of the trees. The trees were there to be climbed too, Freyja said.

"And there is always the water," Aidan said.

"In September?" his wife asked.

"A *warm* September," Aidan said, looking toward the window.

The sun indeed was shining.

"If anyone is going swimming," she said firmly, "I shall sit on the bank watching and attempt to look as decorative as I possibly can."

"Me too, Eve," Judith said. "We can take turns on the swing for exercise."

It was as active and strenuous an afternoon as it had promised to be. The children, Joshua suspected, were merely an excuse for the adults to kick up their heels and have a rollicking good time.

Alleyne and Joshua both climbed a tall, stout tree not far from the picturesque, man-made lake and secured the ropes of the swing to a high branch. The children swung there for a while, but inevitably a game of hide-and-seek began and continued for an hour or more until it was Joshua's turn to hunt and he had unearthed everyone but Freyja. He found her eventually perched high in an old oak tree, her back against the trunk, her feet drawn up against her, her arms clasped around her knees. He had already searched around and past that tree half a dozen times.

"Hey!" he called. "That is cheating. One rule was that we must keep in contact with the ground."

"The tree trunk is in contact with the ground," she said, looking down without giving any sign that she might be afraid of heights. "And my back is in contact with the tree trunk."

"Hmm," he said. "There is a flaw in that logic somewhere. But you are fairly caught now."

"You have to touch me first," she said.

"Are you going to make me come up there?" he asked, narrowing his eyes on her.

"Yes." She tipped back her head to admire the sky.

They admired it together after he had climbed up and touched her arm to make her officially out. A few little puffs of white were rolling slowly in a wide expanse of blue.

"Summer is almost over," she said. "Well, it *is* over, but it is lingering on into autumn. I wish winter were not ahead."

"But there are invigorating walks and rides to take in winter," he said. "And if it snows, there are sled rides and snowball fights and skating and snowmen to build."

"It never snows," she said with a sigh.

He stood on the branch slightly below the level of hers and looked at her. She had left her hair down since the morning. She looked like a wild fairy creature of the woods—but in a pensive mood.

"We will have to stay betrothed, sweetheart," he said. "And I will show you so many interesting ways of using winter that you will want summer never to come."

She turned her head and half smiled at him.

"Don't worry," she said. "I will have decided long before winter arrives in earnest that you have repaid the debt you owe me. Tomorrow will be tedious."

"Tomorrow?" he said, and then remembered that they

were to go to a christening party for the neighbor's new baby. "Redfield and his family are a dull lot?"

"I was engaged to the eldest son once," she said. "I was supposed to be the Viscountess Ravensberg. The first son—the first heir of the next generation—was to have been mine. But Jerome died."

"Ah, yes," he said. "Pardon me, I knew that. You loved him?" She had said not when she had told him about the betrothal at the white rock above Bath.

She looked slightly disdainful. "We grew up to expect the marriage," she said. "We did not dislike each other. We were even fond of each other. But *love* is not a requisite for such matches."

Nevertheless, today she was feeling understandably low-spirited about the whole thing. Tomorrow might be somewhat difficult for her, he supposed. She would see another woman in the place that should have been hers with a child that should also have been hers—though with a different father.

"Do you swim, Josh?" she asked.

"Of course I swim," he said. "You are not about to propose a race, are you, Free? If so, I give you fair warning—I grew up by the ocean. I would race to win. You have severely dented my self-esteem, first by winning our horse race in Bath, and then by hitting one of my best balls this morning during your first over—for a six, no less."

"To the far bank and back," she said.

He turned his head to look down and could see that the men and children were already in the water. Now that he was paying attention, he could hear their shouts and the children's laughter. Eve and Judith were sitting decorously on the bank. Morgan was on the swing, propelling herself almost dangerously high and looking very pretty indeed. That young lady, he thought, was going to be mobbed by prospective suitors when she made her come-out next spring, regardless of the fact that she was a duke's daughter.

"What do you intend to wear?" he asked.

"My shift," she said. "If you believe you will be just too embarrassed, you may make your way back to the house and find a good book."

"Embarrassed?" He started down the tree without offering her a hand—that might be provocation enough for one of her famous punches in the nose. "I can hardly wait. I'll give you a head start for our race, shall I? I'll count slowly to ten before coming after you."

He chuckled as she sputtered and fumed and came down after him.

CHAPTER XII

THE CHRISTENING OF THE HONORABLE ANDREW Jerome Christopher Butler was indeed a grand occasion, as Freyja realized as soon as the Bedwyns arrived at the church and were shown to their pews. The church was filled with neighbors and with both Kit's relatives and the viscountess's. Her cousin, the young Viscount Whitleaf, was there and her grandfather, Baron Galton. Then there were all her illustrious relatives by her mother's second marriage—the Duke and Duchess of Portfrey, the Duke and Duchess of Anbury, the Marquess of Attingsborough, the Earl and Countess of Kilbourne, the dowager countess, and her widowed daughter, Lady Muir.

Such a fuss, Freyja thought, for a baby who was supremely indifferent to all that was going on around him in his honor. He was dressed gorgeously in a long lace christening robe, a family heirloom, but he slept through the whole service, waking only once to squawk with indignation when the baptismal water was poured over his head. He soon fell asleep again, rocked in Kit's arms.

Freyja tried not to pay too much attention to the central group, but how could she avoid seeing Kit, fairly bursting with pride and happiness, and his viscountess—Freyja had never been able to think of her as Lauren—glowing with her new motherhood.

The viscountess had a certain beauty, Freyja conceded. She had dark, lustrous hair and a flawless complexion and eyes that were startlingly violet. But she was always dignified, always the proper lady, with never a word or a hair out of place. It seemed to Freyja that she lacked all spirit and charisma. She hated the woman—if only because everyone else admired and loved her.

Freyja was looking at her gloved hands in her lap when Joshua took one of them, squeezed it tightly, and drew it through his arm. She looked up at him with her is-this-not-a-dead-bore look. He smiled at her, his eyes softer, less merry, less mocking than usual, and covered her hand with his free one.

She could cheerfully have gone at him with both fists then. She knew very well what this was all about. He *pitied* her. Just before he had handed her into one of the carriages this morning, when she had been feeling out of sorts and irritated with everyone, he had bent his head to hers and spoken for her ears only.

"Courage," he had said. "Your Jerome is gone. But there will be someone else for you one day." He had grinned then. "And in the meanwhile, maybe I can be of some service, sweetheart."

He thought she was depressed because of *Jerome*. And so she was—or so she ought to be. He had died so young and so foolishly—of a fever contracted when he rescued several of his neighbors' laboring families from a flood. And she *had* been fond of him. He had been one of her playmates all through her growing years. But she had dragged her heels about marrying him, and he had not seemed over-eager for the event either. Whenever she had made some excuse not to make the betrothal formal just yet or—after their betrothal—not to set a wedding date just yet, he had offered no objection.

The interminable service was over at last, and Kit and the viscountess left in the first carriage, it being close to the time when the baby would need to be fed. It would appear that the viscountess was nursing her child herself. She certainly was not perfect in that, Freyja thought with a moment's satisfaction. Many ladies of good *ton* would frown and even call her vulgar for not hiring a wet nurse.

It was an enormous blessing having Joshua with her after they arrived at Alvesley. Introducing him to everyone as her betrothed occupied both her time and her attention and deflected any embarrassment or pity any of those people who knew about last year might have been feeling. And there was an appallingly large number who did know that last summer's celebrations for the birthday of Kit's grandmother—she had died suddenly earlier this year—were to have included the announcement of his betrothal to Lady Freyja Bedwyn.

Just before dinner Kit and his viscountess came down from the nursery, and there was the painful moment of coming face-to-face with them. Kit was wearing the somewhat wary smile he always wore in Freyja's presence. The viscountess was wearing her corresponding bright, warm smile. Freyja smiled dazzlingly. What varying thoughts and emotions must be turning over behind those three smiles, she thought.

"I must congratulate you both on the birth of your son," she said.

"Thank you, Freyja," Kit said. "And thank you for coming."

"We are so very delighted that you came home from Bath in time to join us today," the viscountess said—surely lying through her teeth.

"May I present the Marquess of Hallmere, my betrothed?" Freyja said. "Viscount and Viscountess Ravensberg, Josh."

"Lady Freyja's *betrothed.*" The viscountess smiled with warm pleasure at Joshua. "How pleased I am to make your acquaintance, Lord Hallmere. And how *happy* I am for you, Lady Freyja."

She took one step forward and for a horrified moment Freyja thought she was about to be hugged. She raised her eyebrows and lifted her chin, and the viscountess hesitated and contented herself with another warm smile.

"Hallmere?" Kit shook hands with him. "You are a fortunate man. I hope you realize that you have won a treasure."

Freyja's knuckles itched as she curled her fingers into her palms.

"And Freyja." Kit set both hands on her shoulders. "I knew you would find happiness one day soon. My sincerest best wishes." He did not hesitate as his wife had done. He kissed her warmly on the cheek.

Fortunately dinner was announced at that moment and so there was no need to make further conversation. Freyja took Joshua's arm and smiled dazzlingly at him.

"What *fun* we are having," she murmured.

J OSHUA DID NOT STAY AT FREYJA'S SIDE ALL THROUGH the afternoon. It would have been bad form, and it seemed to him that once dinner was over the terrible tension he had sensed in her body earlier despite her smiles and seemingly perfect composure had dissipated. She was circulating among the guests, bright-eyed, poised, and sociable and looking remarkably fetching in a muslin dress with loose, floating skirts in varying shades of turquoise and sea green.

He was not at all sure she had not loved Jerome Butler very much indeed. Certainly today seemed very hard for her.

He mingled with the guests too for most of the afternoon. But eventually he sat down on the window seat in the drawing room beside the Earl of Redfield's youngest son, Sydnam Butler, who had been sitting there for a while. The man's right arm and eye were missing, and the right side of his face and neck were disfigured with the purple marks of old burns.

"War wounds?" Joshua asked.

"Right," Sydnam Butler said. "I was captured by a French scouting party when I was on a reconnaissance mission in Portugal. I was out of uniform."

Joshua grimaced. "It was my greatest fear for five years," he said. "I was in France doing some spying for the government, but in an entirely unofficial capacity. No commission, no uniform, no rescue had I been caught. You were not given the honorable treatment your uniform would have ensured, then?"

"No," Butler said.

They chatted for a while about the wars and about Wales, where the man was now living on one of Bewcastle's estates in the capacity of steward. Then Butler nodded in Freyja's direction—she was in a group with Rannulf and Judith, Lady Muir, and a Butler cousin whose name had escaped Joshua's memory.

"I am very glad indeed to see Freyja happy again," he said. "You are obviously good for her."

"Thank you," Joshua said. "Today has been something of a strain for her, though. I believe she must have been deeply attached to your brother when she was betrothed to him."

"Oh, they were never actually betrothed," Butler said. "When Kit came home last summer he brought Lauren with him as his fiancée, and there was an end of the match Bewcastle and my father had arranged." He paused briefly and Joshua was aware that he grimaced slightly. "I do beg your pardon. You were speaking of *Jerome*. Yes, of course. They were always fond of each other. But I would not worry if I were you. That was a long time ago, and she looks happy today. *Very* happy."

Ravensberg and his wife, who had been absent from the room for a while, came back into it at that moment. The viscountess was carrying the baby, no longer in his christening robe but wrapped cozily in a white blanket. Two little hands were waving above its folds. They proceeded to move from group to group, showing off their treasure while the ladies cooed and smiled over him and several of the gentlemen looked faintly sheepish.

They were a remarkably good-looking couple. And they were still in the throes of a deep romantic attachment to each other, if Joshua was not mistaken.

He also had not mistaken what Sydnam Butler had just said before he had realized his mistake. A marriage had been arranged for Freyja and the present Ravensberg. It made sense. If the two families had planned the alliance with the eldest son from the children's infancy, would it not be natural a suitable time after his demise to revive the plan with the second son as the projected husband? But the second son had brought home a bride of his own choosing and so had spoiled the plan.

Had it been deliberate? Had he known of the marriage his father and Freyja's brother were arranging for him? Had he—rather like Joshua himself in Bath—rushed into a betrothal with someone else in order to avoid a marriage he did not want? Or had he not known?

Either way Freyja would have felt spurned.

She would not have liked that!

What part of her being had been most hurt by the rejection? he wondered. Her pride? Or her heart?

Watching from his position on the window seat— Sydnam Butler had been drawn away by his father and a cousin—Joshua could see Freyja's smile become brighter as the couple and the baby approached her group. He could see her fingers flexing at her sides and one foot tapping a rapid tattoo on the carpet. The smile looked somewhat feline to him. She darted a look at the viscountess, who was not far from her now and who had just laughed with warm delight as she gazed down into the face of her baby. Freyja's look, brief as it was and quickly veiled as it was, was pure venom.

In a few moments more, the couple and their baby were going to be moving on to Freyja's group, and she was going to be called upon to admire the child. Judith was already beaming in happy anticipation of the moment and glancing a tender look at Rannulf.

Joshua got to his feet.

"Freyja." He touched her elbow, and she jumped as if he were holding a branding iron. "I see that a few brave souls are strolling out on the terrace. Would you care for a breath of fresh air?"

"I would *love* it," she said rather loudly. "I am going mad from inaction."

The weather had changed overnight. Yesterday had been almost like summer. Today was cold and gray and blustery, more like November than September. They wore their cloaks outside. Joshua pulled his hat down over his brow so that it would not blow away.

"I hope," Freyja said, "you are not expecting me to stroll with mincing steps along the terrace, Josh. I need to draw air into my lungs. Are not such gatherings unbearably insipid?"

She turned right to walk in the direction of the stables, and as soon as they were past the formal gardens before and below the house, she struck off across the lawn to walk parallel to the driveway. She moved along with her usual manly stride. Joshua fell into step beside her.

"Ah." She tilted back her face. "This is better."

He did not attempt to make any conversation, and she was clearly not in the mood. They walked until they reached the stone bridge that crossed a river and formed the boundary between the inner cultivated part of the park and the woods beyond. It must be later than he had realized, Joshua thought. Already early dusk was falling.

"What now?" he asked. "Back to the house?"

"Not yet," she said. "That party will go on for hours yet. No one knows when to end events like this."

"Where next, then?" he asked.

She looked about her. "There is the lake," she said, pointing to it over to their right. "But I do not fancy a swim today." She shivered as a cold blast of wind buffeted them.

"What?" he asked, waggling his eyebrows. "I do not get to see you in your shift again today?" More accurately, he had seen her in her *wet* shift yesterday, and it had been very akin to no shift at all. His temperature threatened to rise a notch at the mere memory.

"Let's go to the gamekeeper's hut," she said. "It is through there." She pointed into the woods to the left of the driveway. "It was actually more like a family retreat, since I can never remember any gamekeeper living there. But it was always kept in good repair. Perhaps we can light a fire there and be cozy for a while before going back."

It sounded good to him, Joshua thought, leading the way across the bridge.

They wandered about in the darkening woods for a while since it seemed she did not remember quite where the hut was. But she cheered up considerably even while she was searching for it.

"I spent several hours of a hot afternoon there once," she told him. "I was locked in and Jerome and Kit stood guard outside. They had kidnapped me. But the adventure got dismal for them when Aidan and Ralf refused to ransom me. When Kit finally went up to the house to try to steal some food from the kitchen, I yelled and swore so foully that Jerome let me out for fear that I would attract the attention of some wandering gardener. I dealt him a bloody nose, and then I went home and left a few bruises on Ralf and Aidan too."

"And you were never kidnapped again?" Joshua said, grinning at her. "Sweetheart, kidnapped maidens are supposed to weep and wilt and make their captors fall in love with them."

"Ha!" she said. "Oh, *there* it is. I knew it must be just here."

It was locked, but he felt above the lintel and she lifted a few mossy stones beside the door until she found the key. It opened the door so easily that he knew even before stepping inside that the hut must still be used. The interior was dark, but he could see in the faint light from the doorway that there was a small table against the far wall, and on it were a lamp and a tinder box. He fumbled around for a few moments until he had the lamp lit.

There was a fireplace with a fresh fire laid in the hearth and a box of logs standing beside it. There was an old wooden rocking chair with a faded blanket thrown over the back and seat. There was a narrow bed against one wall, neatly made up with blankets and a pillow. Everything was clean, including the dirt floor.

This, Joshua thought, was definitely someone's retreat.

Freyja stepped inside and closed the door. She stood with her back against it while Joshua knelt and lit the fire.

"Yes, this is it," she said. "My prison house."

"But a prison no longer, sweetheart," he said, straightening up and brushing off his hands before turning and stepping against her. He dipped his head and touched his lips to hers. "A haven instead. Soon to be a *warm* haven, I hope."

It was also a very private, secluded haven. A dangerous haven for a man and a woman who were trying to avoid having their betrothal extended into the life sentence of a marriage. He stepped back and indicated the rocking chair.

She unfastened her cloak, tossed it over the back of the chair, and sat down. He set his hat and cloak on the table and took a seat on the edge of the bed.

"The big ordeal is almost over," he said.

She laughed softly, her eyes on the fire. "It would serve you right if I refused to release you after all," she said. "Am I really such a big ordeal? How lowering. *You* are, of course, but am *I*?"

"I was not referring to us," he said. "Tell me about Ravensberg."

"Jerome?" she said.

"Kit."

She turned her head to look at him. "What do you want to know about Kit?"

"Were you in love with him?" he asked.

"With *Kit*?" She frowned ferociously at him.

"Jerome was not the only brother you were betrothed to," he said, "or *almost* betrothed to. You were fond of Jerome. Were you fonder of Kit?"

She continued to glare at him. "It is none of your business," she said.

"I *am* your betrothed," he reminded her.

"You are *not*," she said scornfully. "And you are *not* going to play the part of jealous lover now, Josh. The very idea! It is none of your business whom I have loved or whom I do love, if anyone. *Kit* is none of your business."

"Did he know," he asked, "that you loved him?"

"Of course he *knew*," she said, turning her head back toward the fire again and then setting it back against the chair and closing her eyes. "He desperately wanted me to marry him. He wanted me to give up everything—all the expectations of his family and mine—and go follow the drum with him. I was everything in the world to him and he to me. But Wulf would not give his consent. I was one and twenty and did not *need* his consent. It was not that he forbade me exactly—Wulf rarely does that, and of course he knew that I would have fought to the death against any such attempt at tyranny. But there was a speech on family duty and I allowed myself to be talked into announcing my engagement to Jerome. Kit fought Ralf bloody when he came storming over to Lindsey Hall and was refused admittance. Then he went off back to his regiment in the Peninsula. Last year, with Jerome dead before our nuptials had been solemnized and Kit on his way home, his father and Wulf arranged for *our* marriage at last. But Kit had not forgiven me. He had his revenge on me by bringing home that perfect, insipid woman, Lauren Edgeworth."

Joshua wondered if she had yet realized that even if it had started out as revenge—or simply escape—the marriage was now a love match. And he wondered how much real love Freyja still felt for Ravensberg, mingled with the very real hatred and bitterness.

"Poor Freyja," he said softly.

She surged to her feet then and closed the gap between them in three strides. He clamped one hand about her right wrist when her fist was two inches from his nose, and about her left wrist as her fist brushed the underside of his chin. He came to his feet and bent her arms behind her back. He held them there by the wrists—her hands were still fisted.

Her eyes flashed at him. Her teeth were bared.

"Don't you *dare* pity me," she told him in her coldest, haughtiest voice. "My story and my feelings are *my* concern and no one else's. Certainly not yours. We are not even really betrothed. We are nothing but strangers who happen to have been thrown together by circumstances. We are nothing to each other. You are nothing to me. Do you understand me? *Nothing.*"

He lowered his head and kissed her. He was taking a mortal risk, he knew—she might well take a chunk out of his lip with her teeth. But she needed comforting. Not that his motive was entirely selfless. Freyja Bedwyn in a raging temper was an infinitely exciting woman.

"Nothing at all, sweetheart?" he murmured. "You wound me."

"What I *will* do is knock your head off your shoulders if you will just stop playing the coward and release my wrists," she said, her eyes still flashing fury. "Are you afraid of facing the anger of a woman unless you have pinioned her arms?"

He grinned and released her. And chuckled aloud as he parried blows without grabbing hold of her again.

"Ouch!" he said as one of her fists connected with his ear.

But she was not finished with him and would not be, he suspected, until she had milled him to the ground and stamped him into the dirt with her heel. It was a good thing for him that she was not wearing her riding boots. To give her her due, though, he noticed that she did not attempt to use either her fingernails or her teeth. She fought fair.

There was only one course of defense open to him short of planting his own fist in her face. He caught her up in his arms, one about her waist, the other about her shoulders, hauled her tightly against him so that her fists flailed helplessly out to the sides, and kissed her again—openmouthed.

"I dislike you intensely," she said coldly when he lifted his head a good while later. The rage had gone from her eyes and the fury from her voice. "And you are absolutely nothing to me. Less than nothing."

"I know, sweetheart," he said, and kissed her again.

Her anger might have subsided, he realized during the next few moments, but her passion certainly had not. She opened her mouth beneath his, somehow got her arms about him, and pressed as close to him as their clothes and their anatomy would allow.

"Don't stop," she told him fiercely when he lifted his head, desperately trying to hold on to his sanity. "Don't stop!"

"Freyja—"

"*Don't stop!*"

Who tumbled whom to the bed he did not know, but there they were moments later, wrestling and panting together in the narrow space, their hands all over each other in a desperate effort to find bare flesh. She pulled off his coat and waistcoat with a little cooperation from him, and she was tugging his shirt outside his pantaloons and sliding her hands underneath to press against his naked back while with his thumbs he hooked the low neckline of her muslin dress beneath her breasts and took them in his hands, rolling her nipples between his thumbs and forefingers. With his mouth he found the racing pulse at the base of her throat.

Somewhere sanity was trying to attract his attention. And another thought occurred to him too.

"Sweetheart." He lifted his head and looked down into her face. "Are you a virgin?"

Perhaps she was not if there had been that passionate interlude with Kit Butler. If she was not...

"Lift your arms."

He lifted them, and his shirt was off over his head and sailing over the edge of the bed to land in a heap with his coat and waistcoat.

"Are you a virgin?"

"Don't you dare stop." With one hand she pulled his face back down to hers. With the other she fumbled at the flap of his pantaloons.

He took it that the answer was yes. If it had been no, she would have said so and dispensed with his scruples. His bare chest came down onto her bosom and he pressed his tongue into her mouth. She sucked it deep.

"Let me do this," he whispered a few moments later, moving off her and undoing his buttons himself.

But she helped him remove the pantaloons after he had pulled off his Hessian boots and stockings. He drew her dress down her body, taking undergarments with it. Sanity, he half realized after he had pulled off her silk stockings too, had been stripped away with their clothes.

They came together again with fierce passion. If she *was* a virgin—and he would wager she was—there was no shrinking self-consciousness in her for either her own nakedness or his. But then he had known that being in bed with Freyja would be akin to lying with a pile of explosives with the fuses lit.

When he touched her between her legs, she opened to him, feverish and urgent. She was hot and wet and ready. He was hard and throbbing with need. He rolled fully on top of her, pushed her legs wide with his own, slid his hands beneath her to lift and tilt her, and mounted her.

She was a virgin. She was small and tight, and there was a barrier to impede his progress. She was also hot and wet, and her inner muscles were contracting about him and her hands were pressing down on his buttocks while her feet pushed her up from the bed. He pressed inward, heard her involuntary cry as he broke through, and embedded himself fully in her.

He might have taken her slowly and carefully after that, but she would have none of it. She was hot and fierce with passion, and he, God help him, felt an answering hunger that needed no further encouragement.

What followed was more like a wrestling match than lovemaking. He had no idea how long it lasted. He only knew that somehow he held on to some measure of control until she cried out and shuddered into a powerful release. Then he plunged toward his own pleasure and allowed his seed to spill into her.

They were both slick with perspiration, he discovered moments or minutes later—he had become strangely unaware of time—though the fire in the hearth had died down. They were also panting as if they had run ten miles apiece into a stiff wind. He lifted his head and looked down at her in the dim lamplight.

Her hair was in wild, wavy disarray about her head and shoulders. She was flushed. Her lips were parted, her eyes heavy-lidded.

"Well, sweetheart," he said, "if we were not in a scrape before, we certainly are now."

CHAPTER XIII

FREYJA'S LEGS WERE TREMBLING AS SHE DRESSED. So were her hands as she fumbled with her hairpins, dragging them all out and trying to tame and re-arrange her hair without benefit of either a mirror or a comb. She was very thankful that Joshua had dressed faster than she and was at the moment kneeling at the hearth, cleaning out the remains of their fire and building a new one.

Glancing at him, she had a stomach-churning feeling of *knowledge*.

Gracious heavens, that splendid male body had just been naked and...

Well, never mind.

"This," she said in a firmly practical voice, "was all my fault."

He came to his feet and turned toward her, his eyes laughing, though there was a certain grimness about his mouth.

"Will you put a further dent in my self-esteem, then?" he asked her. "Have I just been *seduced*, Free?"

"You would not have done it," she said, "if I had not insisted. I will never blame you. It was all my fault."

Don't stop. Don't you dare stop.

How excruciatingly humiliating.

"If that were a bird's nest," he said, nodding toward her hair, which she was holding on top of her head while she jabbed in hairpins to keep it in place, "it would be impressive indeed. But I would guess it is meant to be an elegant coiffure?"

He came closer, batted her hands away, and then, when the hair came cascading down about her shoulders again, he sat her down on the end of the bed and played lady's maid with surprisingly deft fingers.

"It was a mutual outpouring of lust, Freyja," he said. "It was mutually satisfying too, though I cannot see that I did not hurt you rather badly. I daresay you would rather be stretched on the rack than admit to that, though, and so I will not ask. You do agree, I suppose, that we are now in a very serious scrape indeed."

"If you mean," she said, holding still as he anchored her hair in place with the pins, "that we are now obliged to marry, then of course you are speaking nonsense. Don't you dare propose marriage to me. I am five and twenty years old, and I imagine you are older. Why should we not go to bed with each other if we wish? I thought it was remarkably pleasant."

"Pleasant." He chuckled softly and stood back to admire his handiwork. "Remarkably chic, even if I do say so myself. *Pleasant*, sweetheart? You certainly know how to wound a man where it hurts. But I can answer your question in one word. Why should we not bed each other if we wish? Babies! They have an annoying and sometimes embarrassing habit of resulting from such activity as we just indulged in."

How utterly foolish of her not to have thought of that—especially on the day of a christening.

"It will not happen," she said briskly, getting to her feet and setting the bed to rights again.

"If it *has* happened," he told her, "we have both of us acquired a leg shackle, sweetheart. For now we had better get back to the house and hope that no one has noticed quite how long we have been absent."

They bundled up in their cloaks, and she waited outside, getting her bearings in the dark woods, while he extinguished the lamp, locked the door, and put the key back where they had found it. They walked back to the driveway and across the bridge without talking.

It was strange that she should feel so strongly opposed to marrying Joshua, she thought. It was not that she did not want to marry at all. She did. And she was five and twenty already. Joshua was handsome, charming, witty, and attractive, and he liked the same sort of vigorous outdoor activities as she. They had been to bed together and it had been a glorious experience.

Why did she not wish to marry him, then?

Because *he* did not wish to marry *her*? Because she might be in danger of falling in love with him? Why would that be undesirable?

Because she would feel disloyal to Kit? Or because she would destroy her foolishly romantic dream of love by proving that it was possible to love two different men in the course of a lifetime?

Because she was afraid that her heart might be broken—again?

But Lady Freyja Bedwyn did not fear anything or anyone. *Ever.*

"If I were an enemy army watching you march into battle against me," Joshua said, "I would not wait and stand my ground but turn and flee in panic and terror."

"What nonsense you speak," she said.

"Why the grim look and the long, purposeful stride, my charmer?" he asked her.

"It is cold, if you had not noticed," she said. "I am eager to get back to the house."

"Our outing has served its purpose, then, has it?" he asked.

She turned her head and looked at him in the darkness.

"You must understand," she said, "that everyone in my family and Kit's, everyone in the whole neighborhood, I daresay, knew that he was coming home to marry me. And then he came with Lauren Edgeworth and presented her as his betrothed. I have never been accustomed to humiliation. I thought it a ploy to anger me, to punish me. I thought it a fake betrothal because they seemed so very unsuited to each other. In fact, the circumstances seemed very similar to yours and mine now. Except that I thought he really meant to have me in the end. But he married her instead. I am not abject, Josh. I am not an object of pity. I am just . . . angry."

"It is a love match," he said. "Take it from someone who has met them for the first time today. It is very much a love match, Free."

She laughed softly as they approached the house across the lawn. "Are those meant to be words of comfort?" she asked.

"I would not so insult you," he said. "You like straight talk, sweetheart. You like the truth more than falsehood and directness more than evasion. Your Kit is very deeply in love with his wife."

"My Kit." She laughed again. "He was raw with pain

that summer four years ago. He had just brought Sydnam back from the Peninsula, broken and maimed and closer to death than life. He blamed himself. He was Sydnam's only companion on that reconnaissance mission and his superior officer. When they were trapped by a French scouting party and one of them had to court capture so that the other could go free to complete the mission, Kit was the one who went free. He was mad with guilt that summer— and he turned to me. My Kit—he was never mine."

She had never faced up to the truth of all this before now. While he had been as desperately in love with her as she with him that summer, for him it had been a transitory thing, a way of coping with his guilt and anxiety. She wondered if Wulfric had realized that and so had taken the unusual step of interfering in her life, of actually lecturing her about duty. She wondered if the Earl of Redfield had realized it. And Jerome.

Everyone but her.

There was no one strolling on the terrace now. Everyone was indoors.

"This is the moment," Joshua said, "at which we must hope that our absence has not been too particularly remarked upon and that every pin in your hair does not decide to clatter to the carpet as soon as we step into the drawing room."

Their long absence had not, of course, escaped the notice of Freyja's family. Aidan raised his eyebrows when they entered the drawing room, Alleyne waggled his, Morgan smiled knowingly as she caught Freyja's eye, and Wulfric fingered the handle of his quizzing glass. Only Rannulf did not react—he was deep in conversation with Kit and the viscountess and Judith.

Kit was sitting next to the viscountess, his arm draped along the back of her chair, his fingertips just touching her shoulder on the far side. It was an almost shockingly informal pose, but it was late in the day and everyone seemed more relaxed than they had been earlier. They were both engrossed in listening to something Judith was saying.

Yes, it was true, Freyja thought. She had known it for a long time, of course—perhaps even from the beginning. It was a love match. And perhaps they were even suited, the two of them. Certainly they were a handsome couple.

She did not wait to consider whether or not the admission brought pain with it. She glanced at Joshua, who was looking down at her quizzically, linked her arm through his, and strode across the room with him.

"I hope," he murmured, "I am not about to be embroiled in a *scene*, sweetheart. I do find scenes embarrassing."

Freyja smiled, first at Kit, who looked suddenly wary, and then at the viscountess, whose gracious smile hid any sign of trepidation she might have been feeling.

"I do apologize," Freyja said, "for missing seeing the baby when you brought him down a while ago. Josh suggested a walk, and I was longing for some fresh air and dashed off without a thought. I should, of course, have waited a few minutes."

Although she was eating a great deal of humble pie—or perhaps because of it—she was also speaking in what she recognized as the haughty voice she always used when on the defensive. Nevertheless, all four of them looked at her in some astonishment. Joshua, she noticed, was hugging her arm tightly to his side.

"Oh, but he is still awake," the viscountess said, her smile bright and warm as she got to her feet. "It just did not seem kind to leave him down here when he is used to the peace and quiet of his nursery. Will you come up and see him now?"

Freyja grimaced inwardly but maintained her smile.

"If you are not afraid I will disturb him," she said.

"Oh, no." The viscountess looked at Joshua and a certain merriment danced in her violet eyes. "But we will not drag you up there, Lord Hallmere. Do take my chair."

For a moment Freyja thought that the viscountess was going to link an arm through hers, but if she had had such an intention she thought better of it and led the way out of the room and up the stairs to the nursery floor.

"I am afraid," she said, turning her head to smile at Freyja as they approached the nursery, "new parents can be very tedious, Lady Freyja. We dote upon our children and make the assumption that everyone else must be as charmed as we are."

"Perhaps it is time," Freyja said, "that you dropped the 'Lady' every time you address me."

The viscountess looked quickly at her. "And you must start calling me Lauren," she said. "Will you?"

The baby was lying on a blanket in the middle of the nursery floor, his arms punching the air and his legs kicking while his nurse sat in a chair close to him, knitting. But it was not exactly a place of peace and quiet. There were several other children present, some of them babies, a few older, including Becky and Davy, who waved cheerfully at Freyja before returning their attention to their paints. There were three other nurses in attendance.

Freyja would have been quite contented to stand looking down at the baby and to make a few appropriately admiring comments. But Lauren bent down, scooped him up into her arms, and deposited him in Freyja's before leading the way into an inner room, which was obviously the baby's bedchamber, and closing the door.

Freyja held him gingerly, terrified of dropping him. He had Kit's brown hair, lighter than Lauren's. But he was going to have her eyes. He was soft and warm and weighed almost nothing at all. He smelled sweet and powdery. He made little gurgling noises and gazed at her with eyes that were not yet quite fully focused. She was alarmed by the rush of tender emotion she felt.

For Kit's baby—and Lauren's.

"He is beautiful," she said—lame words indeed. She handed him back to his mother.

"Freyja," Lauren said, "I cannot tell you how happy I am that you have met Lord Hallmere and are betrothed to him. I will not pretend to know him on such short acquaintance, of course, but in addition to his extraordinary good looks he has smiling eyes. I always trust eyes like his. He looks happy, and *you* look happy. How becomingly flushed your cheeks are! I knew this must happen for you one day, but until it did I have been anxious for you. I know how you felt, you see—I was abandoned at the altar by the man I had loved all my life. I thought my life had ended. I certainly never expected that I would love again. But I did—and the second love has been many times more powerful and satisfying than the first. I believe you must be discovering that too. It will only get better as time goes on. Believe me."

She really was extremely lovely, Freyja admitted grudgingly to herself. And she glowed with her new motherhood—and perhaps with more than just that.

That man—the one Lauren had grown up with and almost married—was the Earl of Kilbourne. He was downstairs with his wife. Their daughter was one of the babies in the nursery. It was clear that Lauren felt not one twinge of lingering bitterness regarding him and what might have been.

"I never really loved Jerome," Freyja said. "I was fond of him. I mourned him far more deeply than I could ever have predicted. But I did not love him."

Lauren smiled her acknowledgment of Freyja's deliberate misunderstanding and looked down at the baby, who was being lulled to sleep in her arms.

"I wish I had known Jerome," she said. "Kit adored him."

Yes. But their last encounter had been a bitter, violent one. Kit had broken Jerome's nose before riding over to Lindsey Hall and fighting Ralf and then returning to the Peninsula.

"I should tell you," Freyja said, "about the time the two of them kidnapped me and locked me in that gamekeeper's hut in the woods."

Lauren looked up and laughed. "Kit has told me," he said. "How delighted I was to hear that you came out the victor. Did you really swear the air blue? And did you really punch Jerome in the face? Childhood memories *are* wonderful, are they not? We use that hut quite often, you know, Kit and I. It is our own quiet, cozy retreat."

Freyja was suddenly reminded of what had happened there just an hour or so ago—she had been trying not to think about it. Perhaps even now she was with child herself. Perhaps even now she was fated to marry Josh—against both their wishes. But if it were not so, then she was fated to end their betrothal soon and never see him again.

It was a strangely dreary thought.

The baby was sleeping. Lauren kissed him softly on the forehead and set him down gently in his crib before covering him with his blankets. Then she turned back to Freyja, and this time she did link arms with her before they went back downstairs.

"I am so glad we can be friends at last," she said. "I have always liked and admired you. Sometimes I wish I had your bold spirit. But I must confess that I have also been a little afraid of you."

Freyja let out a short bark of laughter. "One would never have known it," she said. "Do you remember that first time you came to Lindsey Hall with Kit?"

"And you all tried to make me as uncomfortable as you possibly could?" Lauren said, laughing too. "How could I possibly forget? I could cheerfully have curled up and died."

"But instead you dealt me a magnificent, oh-so-ladylike set-down," Freyja said. "My brothers were crowing with delight after you left."

The party was breaking up, Freyja saw when they entered the drawing room. Some of the neighbors had already left. Wulfric was on his feet. So were the other members of her family. The carriages must have been sent for.

"Gracious, Free," Alleyne said, appearing at her side as Lauren made her way toward Wulf, "has there been a grand reconciliation between you and Lauren? Life is threatening to grow very dull indeed."

"It is time you got a life for yourself," she said severely.

He winced. "A hit, Free!" he said. "A palpable hit, to quote some authority I cannot quite identify at the moment. I shall have to go out into the world to seek my own happy ending. Aidan, Ralf, you . . . Happy endings are becoming an epidemic among us."

Joshua was standing talking with Lady Kilbourne and the Duchess of Portfrey. He was using all his considerable charm on them and looking devastatingly handsome in the process. The light from the chandelier overhead made his hair gleam very blond. Again Freyja felt that rush of knee-weakening knowledge. Just an hour or so ago . . .

He had tried to stop it from happening.

She had dared him to stop.

How complicated life had become.

And how undeniably exhilarating!

He turned his head and smiled at her, and she raised her eyebrows. And then he slowly depressed one eyelid and she bristled with indignation.

JOSHUA WAS NORMALLY AN EARLY RISER. HE WAS NOT late up the following morning, but he was later than usual. He had scarcely slept all night, only to fall into a deep sleep when it was already light. All the Bedwyns except Freyja and Judith were at breakfast.

"She is feeling indisposed this morning," Rannulf said, looking rather sheepish, when Joshua asked about Judith, "just as she was yesterday morning until it was almost time to leave for church. I have just been admitting to the family that she is in a delicate way. We were going to keep it to ourselves for a while, but morning sickness is a great spoiler of secrets."

"Poor Judith," Eve said. "I'll go up and keep her company for a while after breakfast—unless I discover that she would rather be alone."

"And Freyja?" Joshua asked. Surely she was not still in bed, unless she had had as sleepless a night as he. It was altogether possible.

"Did you two quarrel yesterday?" Alleyne asked, grinning. "She would not come back inside after riding with us before breakfast. She said she needed more air and went striding off on foot."

"Quarrel?" Joshua said. "With your sister? How could one ever provoke a quarrel with a sweet-natured lady like Freyja?"

Everyone at the table laughed. Even Bewcastle looked faintly amused.

"I winked at her across the drawing room just before we

left Alvesley last evening," Joshua said, "and sent her into a towering rage. People, she told me when we had a moment alone together before getting into the carriage with Morgan and Alleyne, might have *noticed* and thought us remarkably vulgar. Where might she have gone?"

"You might be wise," Aidan said, "to wait for her to walk off any lingering indignation and return to the house in her own good time."

"Ah," Joshua said, "but no one has ever been able to accuse me of excessive wisdom."

"There is a wilderness walk out behind the house," Morgan said. "She usually goes there when she wishes to be alone. And if *I* had quarreled with my betrothed, Aidan, I would want him to come after me even if I had told everyone that I wished to be left alone and even if I had warned him not to follow me."

"Eve is still in the process of teaching me how to understand women," Aidan said. "I spent too many years in the military, it seems."

It was not that they had quarreled exactly, of course, Joshua thought as he strode off beyond the stables half an hour later to where the wilderness walk began. And she had not been in a towering rage over the wink—only hotly indignant. He had made a kissing gesture with his lips and called her sweetheart when she had scolded him, and had watched her nostrils flare, and then they had been in the carriage with her brother and sister and he had deliberately drawn her hand through his arm.

No, they had not quarreled. But last evening they had had conjugal relations and everything had changed between them. What had begun as a light flirtation to alleviate the boredom of being stuck in Bath for a week had escalated into an impulsive and very temporary betrothal to stave off his aunt's dastardly entrapment scheme and then into something rather more lengthy with his grandmother's decision to give them a betrothal party. And then Bewcastle had arrived in Bath and quickly discerned the truth, and *that* had led to *this* prolonging of the connection. He had *known* the danger. He had prepared himself for it, steeled himself against it, for both her sake and his own. But now look what had happened. They were in dire peril of having their temporary lark transformed into a lifelong commitment. If it so happened that she was with child, they would have no choice at all. And even if she was not . . .

Good Lord, she was *Lady Freyja Bedwyn*.

Last night she had seemed not to realize the seriousness of what had happened. Or perhaps she had, but had simply refused to admit it. This morning, if his guess was correct, she had faced reality and found it disturbing indeed.

The wilderness walk began with a series of wide, earthen steps with wooden borders leading up between rhododendron bushes to larger trees farther up the hill. Then a well-worn, shaded path turned sharply to the right to weave among the trees and give the walker an impression of total seclusion, of being miles from any habitation. It was fragrant with vegetation even though the height of summer was past, and loud with birdsong.

So had he—faced reality this morning, that was—or last night, to be more accurate. He was Hallmere now, whether he wanted to be or not. The wars were over with Napoléon Bonaparte imprisoned on the island of Elba. His job was done. He was twenty-eight years old. It was true that he had no intention of returning to Penhallow—ever. But he was a peer of the realm. He was going to have to take his seat in the House of Lords one of these days. He was going to have to acquire a permanent home somewhere—

probably in London. He was going to have to *settle down*—those dreaded words.

Though why he should think them with dread he did not know. He had settled down once before, years ago, when he had learned and practiced the trade of carpenter. He had expected to live his life out there in the village of Lydmere. He had even been starting to look about him at some of the village girls.

Perhaps it was time he married. And if he *must* marry, why not Freyja? Socially he could not do better. He would never be bored with her. He found her attractive. He had discovered last evening that she was quite as explosively passionate in bed as he had expected. He would certainly enjoy the opportunity of bedding her under less frantic circumstances in order to discover if her nature was as sensual as it was passionate—he would wager it was.

Why *not* Freyja?

Perhaps because he had never set out to woo her. Perhaps because she had never shown any inclination to be wooed. Perhaps because his nature was still too restless or because her feelings were still too tied up with a thwarted passion for Ravensberg.

But perhaps now they had no more choice in the matter, he thought, striding along the path and peering into the occasional grove or folly set aside for rests along the way. There was no sign of Freyja. It was possible, of course, that she had not come this way at all. Or, if she had, she might have returned to the house another way by now.

The path had been climbing steadily upward from the beginning, though not with any steep gradient. He was about to move over the crest of the hill, Joshua realized, and begin the gradual, curving descent to the end of the walk. A stone tower, artfully built to look romantically ruined, had been built on the crest. If there was a winding stairway inside the narrow doorway with its Gothic arch—and he rather believed there must be—the energetic walker could get up to the crenellated battlements and have a magnificent view out over the treetops to the surrounding countryside.

He looked up—and grinned.

Her hands were resting on the battlements. Her face was raised to the sun and more than half turned from the path on which he stood. If she had been wearing a hat for her ride earlier, there was no sign of it now. Or of any hairpins. Her hair was billowing out loose behind her in the breeze.

Once more he was reminded of Viking maidens or Saxon warrior women. Or perhaps this morning she looked more like the medieval lady of the castle, holding it against all assailants while her lord was away in battle.

She had told him once that she sometimes felt she had been born in the wrong era.

"If I come closer," he called, cupping his hands on either side of his mouth, "will I be greeted with boiling oil and poisoned arrows raining down on my head?"

She turned and looked down at him, raising her hands to hold her hair back from her face.

"No," she called back. "I thought I would give myself the more personal pleasure of pitching you over the battlements. Come on up."

She favored him with one of her feline smiles.

CHAPTER XIV

"Look," SHE SAID AFTER HE HAD COME UP THE spiral stairs inside the tower and joined her at the top. She gestured about her with a wide sweep of her arm. "Is there a view more lovely anywhere, do you suppose?"

There was a view for miles in all directions. The house was back behind her, but she preferred to look into the wind the other way, over the trees, over the back part of the park, and on out over farmland and farm buildings and hedgerows and winding lanes. The tower was one of her favorite places in the world—wild and secluded, dwarfing her little problems and heartaches, blowing them away in the wind.

She did not like sharing it with anyone, but it would have been petty to send Josh away. She wished she could have done so, though. Hearing his voice calling unexpectedly from below and then looking down and seeing him had turned her knees to jelly and sent her stomach somersaulting and taken her breath away for an unguarded moment. She was terribly aware of him physically, more so now that he had come up beside her, tall and virile in his riding clothes—and hatless.

She did not like the feeling one little bit. Passion had been all very well four years ago when she had also fancied herself in love and headed toward a happily-ever-after—how *young* she had been in those days. But now it suggested only a loss of control, a fear that she could somehow lose her hard-won sense of strong independence. She was not in love with Josh, but she was certainly and ignominiously in lust with him. She did not like it. She did not *choose* to be either in love or in lust—especially not with a man who found everything in life amusing and rarely seemed to entertain a serious thought.

Joshua Moore, Marquess of Hallmere, was not worthy of her love, even if she was prepared to offer it. She was not.

"Not that I have seen in any of my travels," he said in answer to her question, looking about appreciatively at the view. "The fields have all been harvested and some of the trees are beginning to turn color. In another few weeks they are going to look more glorious yet. Ah, pardon me." He turned his head to look down at her. "You do not like autumn, do you?"

"Only because winter comes so close behind it," she said. "Winter always reminds me of—" She shivered.

"Your mortality?" he suggested. "Have you read *Gulliver's Travels*?"

"Of course I have," she said.

"Do you remember those characters who were doomed to live forever?" he asked her. "I cannot remember which part of the book they were in, but they were born with a mark on their foreheads that meant they could never ever die. Instead of being envied, they were the most pitied members of their race. It was a terrible fate to be born with such a mark. Jonathan Swift was wiser than most of us, it seems, and understood how undesirable it would be to live forever. And if we live always in constant dread, Free, how can we enjoy the time that *is* allotted to us?"

"I do not live in constant dread," she told him.

"Only in winter?" he said, smiling at her. "And in autumn because winter comes next? Half of every year?"

She shook her head. "This is foolish talk," she said. "Who told you that you would find me here?"

"Were you hiding from me?" he asked her.

"I *never* hide from anyone," she said crossly—she had, of course, been doing just that, or at least postponing seeing him as long as she could this morning. "I think it is time we quarreled, Josh. It is time I set you free and sent you on your way. It is time to end this farce."

"It cannot be done, sweetheart," he said, leaning one elbow on the battlements and turning to look fully at her. "Not yet. Not until we know if you are with child or not."

She had lain awake most of the night worrying about just that. About having to marry Josh. About his having to marry her. About being forever trapped in a marriage that neither of them had freely chosen and both of them would forever resent. About having a soft, warm, living baby of her own.

"I am *not*," she said firmly. "And there is always something or another. When we started this, we were going to end it the next day. Every day since then we seem to have dug ourselves a deeper hole."

"Am I to understand, my charmer," he asked her, "that you do not *want* to marry me?"

"You know I do not," she said irritably, "any more than you want to marry me. Do be serious for once in your life,

Josh. I begin to think that your laughter and your carefree manner are masks that you wear. What I have not yet decided is whether they mask nothing at all or whether there is a person behind them that I would not recognize if I were to meet him without the disguise."

He gazed at her with squinted eyes, the smile still playing about his lips. "It would be nothing at all, sweetheart," he said. "Are you sorry last night happened?"

"Of course I am sorry it happened," she said. "And it was all my fault. I ought not to have suggested the gamekeeper's hut in the first place. With a little imagination I might have guessed the danger I was leading us both into. But I did not. I had not armed myself for resisting what proved irresistible. *You* had. You would have stopped me. But I would not be stopped. It is all quite, quite lowering."

"You did not enjoy it, then?" he asked her.

"*Of course*—" She turned her head and glared at him. "Of course I enjoyed it. I am a woman and you are a man— a handsome, attractive man."

"No!" He grinned at her. "Am I?"

"Of course I enjoyed it," she said again. "But that has nothing to do with anything. Do you not see that? I wish it had not happened. Not only are we not betrothed, but we are not even thinking of becoming betrothed. We have never cultivated any deeper relationship than a light flirtation, and we engaged in *that* only because we were both stuck in Bath and were horridly bored. We have never taken our feigned betrothal seriously, though we have both enjoyed it, I believe, as a sort of lark that will soon be over and will leave us quite unscarred. Last night spoiled all that. Of course I wish it had not happened. If we are forced to marry, that one mistake on my part will have ruined both our lives."

"We had better hope that we are not forced to marry,

then," he said, the laughter gone from his eyes. "But did last evening have at least one positive result? Have you now abandoned your hatred of Viscountess Ravensberg?"

"It was high time," she said with a sigh, turning away to look back toward the house, which, with its long mullioned windows looked very Elizabethan from this angle. "My feelings had become an embarrassment to me—and to her and Kit. She is a perfect lady and kind and warm-hearted too—all qualities I have hated in her because I do not possess them myself. But, yes, we came to an understanding last evening. Perhaps we will even become friends. Who knows? Stranger things have happened."

"And Ravensberg?" he asked her. "Have you forgiven him?"

She sighed again and held her hair back from her face with one arm. "I could not help thinking all last night," she said, "that if he had come home last summer without Lauren, he would perhaps not have been able to resist the pressure of expectation from his family and mine. He might have married me simply because he could find no way *not* to marry me. And I would have known, if not immediately, then long before now. I would have been trapped in a living hell. There is nothing to forgive. He would have married me four years ago, but I would not marry him. He owed me nothing last year. And perhaps I have been clinging to something that never really existed. I was in love—desperately so, but I am not sure being in love is any closer to real loving than being in lust is."

"Are you in lust with me?" he asked.

She turned to look at him again and laughed when she saw the laughter back in his eyes.

"Oh, now *that*," she said, "I will not deny. You must know it anyway as I know it of you. It certainly would not be enough to carry us into any future, though. And so it is dangerous and must be resisted at all costs."

She was standing too close to him. His hands reached out to catch her on either side of her waist and draw her against him. He lowered his head and kissed her softly, almost lazily, with slightly parted lips. She rested her hands on his shoulders and realized with a terrible sinking of the heart that there was going to be a yawning emptiness in her life where he had been after this farce had finally come to its end.

"Though why you lust after me," she said when he lifted his head, "I will never know. I am so ugly."

"What?" His eyes were alight with merriment. "In any other woman that would be a far from subtle fishing expedition for a compliment. But you mean it. Let me see. Let me have a good look at you."

His eyes proceeded to roam her face while she wondered what on earth could have possessed her to utter such stupid words aloud. She had long ago given up lamenting her looks and envying Morgan hers. She was as she was. Anyone who did not like looking at her might simply look elsewhere.

"You are not pretty, Free, or beautiful," he said—at least he was not going to resort to lying flattery. "You are something else, though, over and above both. You, my sweetheart, are plain gorgeous. I think I may forever afterward find all the pretty girls somewhat insipid."

"How foolish!" She laughed. "Any more of such blatant flattery and I may toss you over the battlements in dead earnest."

"I am in fear and trembling," he said, and bent down to scoop her up into his arms.

"Put me down," she demanded indignantly.

But he stepped against the battlements with her and

lifted her higher. She shrieked, wrapped her arms tightly about his neck, and then found herself laughing helplessly.

"Don't struggle," he said, laughing too, "or I may d-d-drop you, Free. Oops!"

She shrieked again as he pretended to do just that.

He set her down at last and she stood close to him, her face against his cravat, recovering from leftover laughter.

"You wretch," she said. "I will get my revenge. See if I don't."

"Free," he said softly, his chin against the top of her head, "this needs to be said. If we *have* made a child, I was as much a part of the making as you. We will marry, and we will make the best of the marriage both for the child's sake and for our own. We will not waste energy resenting each other and blaming ourselves and making ourselves unhappy by imagining that the other must be unhappy. We will do our best to rub along together. Agreed?"

She was considerably shaken. She felt warm and safe standing against him, and uncharacteristically she welcomed the solid safety of his body. His words had changed nothing—and everything.

. . . if we have made a child . . .

"Agreed," she said.

They stood against each other, neither seeming to know how to proceed.

"We had better go back to the house," she said briskly, stepping back. I am hungry."

"I'll go down those stairs ahead of you," he said. "They are remarkably steep. You may take my hand if you wish."

Freyja lifted her chin to a sharp angle and glared at him along the length of her nose.

"Uh-oh!" he said, raising his hands theatrically as if to defend himself from attack. "*Now* what the devil have I said?"

"Don't you *dare* try to protect me!" she told him, her voice cold and haughty. "I came *up* the stairs without the helping hand of any insufferably hovering male. I will go *down* the stairs the same way."

"Deuce take it," he said, shaking his head and returning his arms to his sides, "one cannot even be a gentleman with you, Free, without arousing your ire. Go ahead. Break your neck on the way down and I'll stand behind you, thankful you are not taking me down with you. Better yet, you can break *my* fall when I trip all over my boots."

Freyja smiled to herself as she started down the steep spiral stairs.

Joshua liked the Bedwyns and regretted the deception that was being perpetrated against them—though of course it might not prove to be a deception if he and Freyja were forced to marry after all.

Rannulf and Judith were to return to Leicestershire the next day. They lived at Grandmaison Park with Lady Beamish, the Bedwyns' maternal grandmother, but she was in poor health and they did not want to be absent any longer.

"We will see you again soon, Joshua," Judith said when she was taking her leave of everyone, "so this is not good-bye. I just hope you do not set your wedding date for a time when I am unable to travel. But that is extremely selfish of me. I will be very happy for you and Freyja wherever I am on that day."

"You must be made of stern stuff to have taken on Free," Rannulf said, winking at him as they shook hands. "It will doubtless not be a tranquil marriage. She is not easily controlled. But my guess is that she has met her match. It is sure to be an *interesting* marriage."

"I do not believe," Joshua said, "she can be controlled, easily or otherwise. It is perhaps a blessing that I like her as she is."

Rannulf laughed appreciatively and punched him in the shoulder.

Aidan seemed dour and humorless until one got to know him. He was certainly reticent and slow to laugh, or even to smile, but it was soon evident that he adored Eve and was devoted to their children. He spent much of the day before the christening and the days after with the children—playing with them, taking them walking and riding, demanding courtesy and obedience of them, but otherwise keeping them on a very loose rein.

"They experienced all the terrors of rejection and insecurity after their parents died," he explained after Joshua had supervised the boy on his pony while Aidan gave the little girl a riding lesson one morning. "Even when they had been with Eve for a while and after I married her, someone tried to snatch them away as revenge against Eve for marrying me. It took a court case and the ruling of a magistrate to establish the fact that we are their legal guardians. If I have to spend the next twenty years of my life helping them believe that they belong somewhere, that they are loved unconditionally, that their world is a predominantly benign place, that they can dare to be happy, productive adults when they grow up, then I will consider those years well spent."

"They are fortunate children," Joshua said, remembering the bleakness of his own childhood.

"They have every right to be," Aidan told him. "Of course, we face the possibility of their insecurities surfacing again when Eve bears a child of our own, but that time is not yet, and we will deal with it when it does happen."

Alleyne reminded Joshua of himself. Cheerful and always active, he nevertheless exuded a certain air of restlessness and aimlessness.

"I envy you," he said when the two of them were alone together at breakfast after seeing Rannulf and Judith on their way. "You have your home and your estate to go to now that you have the title and your services in France are no longer required. And a marriage with someone you love to help you send down roots. I think you must love Free." He grinned. "I cannot imagine any other reason a man would want to marry her unless it was her fortune, and you obviously don't need her money."

"I do not," Joshua agreed. "You probably are not lacking in funds yourself, though, or any of the other attributes necessary to attract a prospective bride, if that is what you want."

"The trouble is," Alleyne said, "that I do not know what I want. If I were poor, I would have no choice but to take employment, would I? I suppose I would have found my niche long ago and been reasonably happy in it. And if I were poor, there would not be so many females setting their caps at me. Perhaps I would have pursued and won someone who loved me for myself, someone for whom I would happily give up my freedom. Rank and fortune are not without their problems."

"Once upon a time," Joshua said, "I had neither, and on the whole I would have to admit you have a point."

"Having said which," Alleyne said ruefully, rising from his place to help himself to more food from the sideboard, "I am not sure I would give up either even if I could. I have been thinking—with a little prodding from Wulf—of running for a seat in Parliament or taking some government appointment. As for marriage, I am in no hurry. Bedwyns are expected to be monogamous once they do marry. More than that, they are expected to love their spouses. I am not sure I am ready for that sort of commitment yet, if I ever will be. I hope you are. Freyja will demand it of you—with her fists if necessary."

"Now that is a threat to put the fear of God into me," Joshua said. "I have been at the receiving end of one of those fists—at least my nose has—on two separate occasions."

Alleyne threw back his head and laughed.

"Good old Free," he said.

Morgan was young and beautiful and on the verge of making her come-out in society. She would be presented to the queen next spring and remain in London to participate in all the frenzied social activities of the Season. With all her advantages of birth and fortune and looks, she could not fail to take the *ton* by storm and to be courted by every gentleman in search of a wife and a good number who would think of matrimony only after setting eyes on her.

But she was not living for that day. She was not a giddy young girl with nothing in her head but beaux and parties.

"It is all remarkably foolish," she said at dinner one evening, "all this faradiddle of a come-out and a Season. And the whole idea of a marriage mart is distasteful and re-markably lowering."

"You are not afraid no one will bid for you, are you, Morg?" Alleyne asked.

"I am afraid of no such thing," she said disdainfully, "so you may wipe that grin off your face, Alleyne. I am afraid of just the opposite. I expect to be mobbed by silly fops and ancient roués and earnest, dull men of all ages. All because of who I am. Not a one of them will *know* me or even wish to know me. All they will want is marriage with the wealthy younger sister of the Duke of Bewcastle."

"Fortunately, Morgan," Aidan said, "you have the power to say no to any or all of them. Wulf is no tyrant and could not force you into a marriage against your will even if he were."

"You will meet someone next spring," Eve said, "or the year after or the year after that, and there will be something about him that is different, Morgan. Something that stirs you *here*." She touched her heart. "And before you know it, even if you never intended to love or even to like him, you will know that there is no one else in the world for you but him."

"Eve met Aidan," Freyja said, sounding exasperated, though there was a certain fond gleam in her eye as she looked at her sister-in-law, "and has become a hopeless romantic."

"Yes, I have," Eve agreed, and laughed and blushed.

"Well, I certainly do not expect to meet my future husband at the London marriage mart," Morgan said with a contemptuous toss of her head. "I will wait until I am five and twenty if I must, just like Freyja. *She* waited until she met just the right man." She looked at Joshua, approval in her eyes.

"Even if there were a few hiccups along the way," Alleyne added.

Joshua found that he did not dislike even Bewcastle. The man was cold, austere, distant. He took his meals with his family and joined them in the drawing room during the evenings. But apart from that he kept very much to himself. He did invite Joshua into his library after luncheon the day Rannulf and Judith left. Joshua guessed that such invitations were rare. He sank into the leather chair Bewcastle indicated before taking the one at the other side of the hearth himself.

"You have been presented to most of the members of our family," he said, setting his elbows on the arms of the chair and steepling his fingers, "and to almost all our neighbors while we were at Alvesley for the christening. It was my intention when I came home from Bath to host an evening party or even a ball here in honor of your betrothal. But you may consider such an event undesirable. The betrothal is still of a temporary nature, I assume?"

Joshua hesitated and found himself staring into the pale, inscrutable eyes of the duke. It seemed for a moment that he could almost read in those eyes a knowledge of what had happened during the evening at Alvesley.

"As you pointed out in Bath," Joshua said, "and as I explained to Freyja before that, my betrothal is very real to me. Only she can end it. She has not yet spoken the final word on that."

He had noticed before that Bewcastle did not seem disconcerted by lengthy silences. There was one now.

"If you wish her to speak that final word," Bewcastle said at last, "then I trust you will make it desirable to her to do so. Freyja may be the last woman one would expect to be susceptible to a broken heart, but that fate is not unknown to her."

"I know," Joshua said.

"Ah." The ducal eyebrows went up.

"I will see what Freyja thinks about a party or ball," Joshua said, feeling that he had had a brief glimpse into a side of Bewcastle that he kept very carefully hidden even from his own family. He cared about Freyja—not just about her good name and therefore the good name of the Bedwyns, but about *her*. He was afraid she was going to be hurt again.

The library door clicked open behind him at that moment, and the ducal eyebrows arched even higher while his fingers curled about the handle of his quizzing glass. Joshua looked over his shoulder and saw that the intruder was young Becky, who peered around the door for a moment before stepping inside and shutting it carefully behind her.

"I just woke up from my nap," she said very precisely in her piping little voice, "and Davy was gone and Nanny Johnson said I could come down. But Mama and Papa and everyone else have gone outside and I do not want to go to join them there because it is cold today."

Bewcastle half raised his glass to his eye. "It would seem, then," he said, "that the only alternative is to remain indoors."

"Yes," she agreed. But she did not respond to the implied suggestion that she was free to make herself at home in any part of the indoors except the library.

"Hello, Uncle Joshua," she said as she passed him on her way to examine the object that had taken her attention— Bewcastle's quizzing glass. She took it from his surprised fingers, examined it closely, turned it over in her hands, and raised it to her eye. She looked up at him. "You look funny, Uncle Wulf."

"I daresay I do," he said. "So does your eye."

She went off into peals of giggles before turning and wriggling her way up onto his lap, leaning against his chest, and resuming her game with his glass.

The thing was, Joshua thought as Bewcastle began a determined conversation about Penhallow, he looked both slightly uncomfortable and slightly pleased. He also sat very still as if he feared frightening the child away. It was Joshua's guess that nothing like this had ever happened to him before.

Freyja was adamantly opposed to any public celebration of their betrothal at Lindsey Hall, as Joshua had expected.

"Gracious heavens," she said when he asked her about it as they played a game of billiards later in the afternoon, "whatever next? A mock wedding? Enough is enough. I am going to quarrel with you very soon, Josh, and very publicly, whether you like it or not. This whole business is becoming tedious and ridiculous."

"Just wait a little while," he said.

"Oh, wait, wait, wait," she said impatiently. "Will you still be saying that on my eightieth birthday? Everything has become so *stupid*. No, there is to be no soiree, no ball, no tea, no *anything*. I wish we had never started this. I wish you had not come dashing into my inn room that night. I wish I had not been walking in Sydney Gardens that morning. I wish I had ignored those silly screams. I wish I had not danced with you at the assembly. I wish—"

"If you hit that ball," he warned, "it is going to go sailing over the end of the table and smash right through that window."

She slammed down the billiard cue.

"Josh," she said, "everyone is so *happy* for me. For us. I cannot stand it any longer."

"There are two courses open to us, then," he said. "You can quarrel with me and break off the engagement and send me away, or I can discover important business that necessitates my immediate return to Penhallow and leave here. I would suggest the second course since it need not involve an immediate ending of our betrothal and will leave you open to recall me if it becomes necessary to do so."

Devil take it, he thought, surprised, he did not *want* to leave just yet. But he had to admit that the situation had become intolerable and surely unnecessary. In retrospect he was not convinced that Bewcastle had been right to insist upon his coming here and keeping the betrothal alive this long.

"Do that, then," she said, frowning. "But how? What reason will you give?"

"My steward writes to me frequently," he told her. "He knows I am here. There is almost bound to be a letter from him within the next few days."

"It cannot come too soon for me," she said.

"Such warm, romantic words, sweetheart," he said, lifting one hand and flicking his forefinger across her chin.

She picked up the billiard cue, frowning, and bent over the table again.

CHAPTER XV

T HE LETTER CAME THE NEXT MORNING. IT WAS WAIT-
ing on the silver tray on the great hall table where
the family's letters were always displayed, except for
Bewcastle's, which were delivered separately to the library.
They had all just returned from a ride, slightly damp, since a
drizzling rain had started falling. Even the duke had come
with them this morning. The children were already running
upstairs to the nursery to change.

"Oh, Aidan, here is a letter from Thelma!" Eve exclaimed, sounding delighted. "And there is one for you underneath it, Joshua." She handed it to him with a smile.

His eyes met Freyja's—she had just picked up a letter of
her own. It was a bleak moment. Here it was, then, his excuse to leave. He had already thought out what he would
say after "reading" the letter, and indeed there would even
be some truth in it—that with the harvest in and winter
not far off there was an urgent need to begin some repairs

and some rebuilding for his farm laborers, and that dreary as such business was, he really ought to be there to oversee the work, at least for a few weeks. During those weeks, of course, Freyja would learn the truth of her condition and either bring him back to arrange a hasty marriage or put an end to their betrothal. It would be up to her to think of a plausible reason for *that*.

He would leave tomorrow, he thought as he broke the seal of the letter. He would be a free man again—at least he would once he had heard from Freyja. He would be able to do whatever he wanted with the rest of his life. He could get back to enjoying himself in any way that presented itself.

Jim Saunders's letter was shorter than usual. Joshua read it quickly, and then read it again more slowly. Well, hell and damnation, he thought. He had crossed the woman's will, and now she would not be satisfied until she had destroyed him. She was prepared, it seemed, to go to extraordinary lengths to do just that.

"Is something wrong, Josh?" Freyja asked, her voice deliberately loud and concerned, and of course everyone looked at him, as she had intended they would.

"Actually there is," he said. "I am going to have to go to Penhallow without delay I'm afraid."

"Oh, what has happened?" Eve asked, all concern. "Nothing too dreadful, I hope?"

"Actually," he said, "I am about to be charged with murder."

"*Murder?*" Aidan spoke for all of them in a voice that must once upon a time have had a whole regiment of men jumping to instant attention. "Murder of whom?"

"My cousin," Joshua said, folding his letter into its original folds. "Five years ago. A witness has recently presented himself to my aunt, the Marchioness of

Hallmere. He is prepared to swear that he saw me kill Albert."

"And *did* you?" Aidan asked, his face like granite, every inch the formidable colonel he had been.

"Actually, no," Joshua said, grinning. This was not funny, he knew—not by any means—but it was playing out like a typical melodrama, with all of them standing about the great hall like well-placed actors. "Though I was, apparently, the last to see him alive."

"Might I suggest," Bewcastle said, sounding perfectly cool, even bored, "that we remove this discussion to the breakfast parlor?"

For a few moments no one moved except Bewcastle himself. But then Freyja came hurrying forward to link her arm through Joshua's.

"*I* am hungry if no one else is," she said.

She marched him off with long strides, leaving everyone else behind.

"I might have known," she said, her voice low and furious, "that you would invent a perfectly ridiculous story like this. Do you seriously expect anyone to *believe* it?"

"I'll do my best to be convincing, sweetheart," he said, slipping Saunders's letter into the pocket of his riding coat. "At least you will have a reasonable excuse to end our betrothal in a few weeks' time if it turns out that I am a vicious felon, locked up in some damp, gloomy cell awaiting a hanging."

"*Everything* is a joke to you," she retorted.

There was no chance for further private conversation. Everyone came crowding after them, avid for more information. But Bewcastle talked languidly and determinedly about the weather until they had all filled their plates at the sideboard and the butler had poured their coffee and been dismissed.

"Now, perhaps, Hallmere," his grace said when the family was alone together, "you would care to enlighten us further on the nature of these accusations against you. Or perhaps not. Freyja has some right to know, I believe. The rest of us do not."

"Albert drowned," Joshua explained. "He and I were out in a boat together during a night that became more and more stormy. He jumped overboard to swim back to shore. He was not a strong swimmer, but he refused to get back into the boat. I rowed beside him until he was close enough to the beach to set his feet down on the sand—which he did—and then I took the boat out again for an hour or so longer. It was reckless of me under the circumstances, of course, but I had things on my mind. Besides, in those days I still considered myself invincible. The next morning I heard that he was missing. Later in the day his body was washed ashore with the incoming tide."

Eve had both hands over her mouth.

"He went swimming again after you had disappeared?" Alleyne said. "That was a dashed stupid thing to do on a stormy night, especially if he did not swim well. Or did he think himself invincible too?"

"The two of you had quarreled, I assume," Aidan said.

"Yes," Joshua admitted, "though I can no longer remember over what. We were always quarreling. We grew up together at Penhallow, but there was never any love lost between us."

"And yet," Bewcastle said, sipping his coffee and regarding Joshua with steady silver eyes, "you went out rowing with him at night."

"Yes."

"And now a witness has come forward," Morgan said scornfully. "Someone who was also rowing or swimming around in those stormy seas, I suppose. Yet you did not see him, Joshua? I daresay he is someone hoping to make his fortune with a little blackmail. Is your aunt likely to pay him? You must indeed return home and see to it that she does not."

"My aunt, you must understand," Joshua explained, "lost her only son that night. He was the heir to the title and all that went with it—including the house she still calls home. I was the one who benefited from his death—it made *me* the heir. Just recently I made it very clear that I would not marry my cousin, her eldest daughter. I was already...attached to Freyja."

"So she is willing to believe this witness?" Eve said, her eyes wide with distress. "Oh, poor Joshua. How are you to prove your innocence?"

"I really do not expect it to be difficult," he said. "However, I must go down there to sort the matter out. It would appear that another cousin, my heir presumptive, has been summoned, and there is bound to be a bit of a bother. For, of course, if the accusation could be made to stick, I would not have the protection of my rank. The death occurred long before I was Hallmere."

"Oh, poor Joshua," Eve said again. "What can *we* do to help?"

"I rather fancy the idea of interviewing this witness," Alleyne said. "It sounds a havey-cavey business to me."

Freyja had been sitting silently across the table all this while, watching Joshua with cold, hostile eyes. Suddenly she got to her feet, scraping back her chair with her knees as she did so, and came stalking around the table toward him. She reached into his pocket without a by-your-leave, pulled out Saunders's letter, unfolded it, and stood there reading it. Her lips were compressed into a hard line by the time she had finished. She folded the letter and set it down beside his plate.

"That woman is behind this," she said. "She needs to be taught a lesson she will never forget. We will leave today. An hour should be long enough in which to get ready. Wulf, have a carriage ready and waiting for us in an hour's time, if you please."

"*We?*" Joshua said. "*Us?*"

"You do not think I am going to let you go and face this alone, do you?" she asked haughtily. "I am your *betrothed.* I am going too."

"Oh, yes, Freyja," Eve said. "I *really* believe you ought."

"There is, of course," Bewcastle said, "the small matter of propriety. You are not yet married to Hallmere, Freyja."

She clucked her tongue impatiently, but Alleyne spoke up.

"I'll be your chaperone, Free," he said. "I'll come with the two of you. Actually I would not miss this for worlds."

"And I too," Morgan said firmly. "No, there is no point in grasping your quizzing glass, Wulf. It will not deter *me.* I am eighteen years old, and it is perfectly proper for me to go visiting my future brother-in-law with my sister and brother. Indeed, it is only right that Freyja have female companionship. I do not like the sound of the Marchioness of Hallmere. I want to see her for myself. And I believe *she* should be given the opportunity to discover that the family into which Joshua is about to marry can be a powerful enemy."

"Oh, bravo, Morgan," Eve said. "Though we do not know yet if the marchioness has had anything to do with producing this sudden witness. However, I do like the notion of her finding herself confronted by all the considerable power of the Bedwyns. Of course, Aidan is the most ferocious-looking one of you all. Aidan?" She looked inquiringly at him.

He returned her look with a blank stare for a few

moments before raising his eyebrows and shaking his head slightly.

"We have been planning a sort of belated wedding trip after leaving here," he said, "with the children, of course. Their governess has recently married and we have not yet replaced her. We did think of the Lake District as a possible destination, but I daresay Cornwall would serve just as well—*if* we are invited, that is. Hallmere?"

A house party of Bedwyns determined to be formidable, even ferocious. An iron-willed aunt bent upon a revenge so ruthless that his very life would be snuffed out if she had her way. Accusations of murder rattling around the neighborhood and a mysterious witness and some sort of official investigation pending. Cousin Calvin Moore, the pious heir, riding with furious haste to claim his inheritance from the man who had got it by committing murder most foul. And a fake betrothal that was to be given yet another extension.

What red-blooded, sporting gentleman could possibly resist?

"Certainly you are all invited," Joshua said, "if you care for a little wild excitement rather than more conventional entertainment, that is."

"We *are* Bedwyns," Alleyne said with a grin.

Bewcastle merely raised his eyebrows and resumed his breakfast.

"But we are wasting time while we sit here talking," Freyja said impatiently. "We can be many miles on our way by nightfall if we leave this morning."

The prospect of a long, unexpected journey to Cornwall, beginning on a gloomy day complete with drizzle and a light fog and ending with a potentially nasty murder investigation starring their future brother-in-law as chief and sole suspect appeared to have cheered up the Bedwyns no end. They were all talking at once and pushing away their breakfast dishes as Joshua left the room with Freyja.

"Sweetheart," he said as soon as they were out of earshot, "I presented you with the perfect chance to be rid of me today and the perfect excuse for ridding yourself of me permanently as soon as you are sure circumstances will allow it. Yet you *insist upon coming with me?*"

"*That woman* has gone too far this time," she said, her chin and her nose in the air, a martial gleam in her eyes. "It will give me the greatest pleasure to demonstrate that fact to her."

He chuckled softly. "You may never be rid of me," he said.

"Nonsense," she said briskly. "It will be for just a short while longer. What man in his normal mind would sit alone out on the ocean in his boat during a stormy night just on the chance that someone might row by, not notice him, and then tip his cousin overboard and leave him to drown? And what normal man would not make a great deal of noise and fuss if it *did* happen and at least attempt to rescue the drowning man? What man would keep his mouth shut about the whole thing for five years and then open it at just the moment when the victim's mother happened to be in a royal rage because her hopes of wedding the murderer to her daughter had been foiled? I would like to have a word or two with such a man."

"Lord help him," Joshua said. "You and Alleyne both. And Aidan and Morgan too, I daresay. Not to mention Eve. Do you not realize, my charmer, that we are getting into a deeper and deeper scrape with every passing day?"

"Nonsense," she said again. "And you need not fear that there is going to have to be anything permanent about our connection, Josh. I discovered last night that we have both been spared that fate. *That* was a relief at least."

He stared at her. She was *not* with child? And yet she had just quite deliberately missed her chance to be rid of him permanently within the next few hours? And then he chuckled.

"It is your move next, sweetheart," he said. "*You* are going to have to find a way out of this betrothal. I am quite resigned to being an engaged man until my ninetieth year."

"One hour," she said firmly as they arrived outside the door of her room. "I expect everyone to be ready and downstairs in the hall not one minute later than that."

"Yes, ma'am," Joshua said, grinning at her as she whisked herself inside the room and shut the door firmly in his face.

But his grin faded and his stomach performed an uncomfortable flip-flop as soon as he was alone. He was going to have to go back to Penhallow after all, then, was he?

It was a grim prospect.

THE JOURNEY WAS A LONG AND TEDIOUS ONE. Conversation in the carriage and at the various inns where they stopped for meals and accommodation centered about neutral topics that were probably of no great interest to any of them. Certainly they were not to Freyja.

She could not *believe* this was happening. During the silences that a long journey inevitably brought and even during some of the conversations, she tried to trace back every stage of her relationship with Joshua to understand how she had got herself into this deep scrape, as he called it. How had she got from waking up in the middle of one night to find him invading her room to this moment of riding toward his home in Cornwall with him as his betrothed, half her family with them? Her involvement had all started, she supposed, when she had harbored him in her wardrobe without betraying his presence there to that horrid gray-haired old man, who had not even waited for her to answer his knock on the door.

What would have happened if she *had* betrayed him? Would the whole of her life now be different?

She supposed it would.

So would his.

They arrived at Penhallow late one afternoon, having driven almost all day along the coast road, admiring the views. It was not a brilliantly sunny day. Neither was it entirely cloudy. At one moment the sea below the high cliffs would be steely gray and rather forbidding, and the next it would be a brilliant blue and sparkling in the sunshine. More often its surface was a mixture of the two extremes.

"I would like to paint the sea," Morgan said. "It would be a marvelous challenge, would it not? I suppose most of us usually imagine that it is one color, or at least one color at any particular moment of any particular day. But it is not. One would need a whole palette of colors to paint it well, and even then..."

"And yet if you were to wade into the sea and let a handful of the water trickle through your fingers," Joshua said, "you would see that it is colorless."

"The color is projected onto it from something else," Morgan said.

"The sky?" Alleyne suggested.

"But if you climb a high mountain," Morgan said, "you find that the sky—the air—is also colorless. What gives the sky color? What gives the water color? If we could get inside a blade of grass, as we can get inside water and air, would we find that it too is without color?" Her eyes were shining with the intensity of the puzzle.

"And how many angels can dance on the head of a

pin?" Alleyne said with a chuckle. "Even if I could count them, Morg, I would wonder what was the point."

"Color, interpretation, come from our minds," Freyja said. She held up a staying hand when Morgan drew breath to speak again. "But what gives our minds that capacity, I do not know. Perhaps there is something beyond our minds—something of which we are unaware."

"Awareness itself?" Morgan said.

She was a strange girl, Freyja mused. Beautiful, accomplished, daring, as proud and haughty as any of them, as boldly contemptuous as Freyja herself of some of the starchier rules and conventions of society, she nevertheless had intellectual depths and this almost mystical awareness of the mysteries of existence that most people did not bother to question even if they noticed them.

What would happen to her sister, Freyja wondered, now that she was grown up and about to be launched on society? Would she find a man who would appreciate her, who would allow her enough rein to feel free, who would not clip her wings?

And what would happen to *her*? Once this foolish business of a murder accusation had been cleared up, she was going to have to end her betrothal to Joshua. There must be no more putting it off again for any flimsy reason that presented itself. But *then* what would happen to her?

"You may paint at Penhallow," Joshua said to Morgan, "and probe all the mysteries of the universe with your brush. But, speaking of Penhallow, the house is about to come into view around this bend."

The bend was necessitated by the presence of a river valley cutting across the landscape. The cliff turned sharply inland and then fell gradually away to a steep hillside. The road had been built along the top of it. Below was a river, wide and slow-moving at this point on its course, flowing onward to the sea. The slopes on either side were green and rocky and carpeted in many places with pink thrift and yellow gorse and white clover. On the near side of the valley were the church and houses of a village, close to the sea, climbing the hillside for lack of enough flat land beside the river.

On the far, western side of the valley, perhaps half a mile from the sea, and perched on a wide plateau more than halfway up the hillside, was a large, imposing gray stone mansion. It was half turned to face the sea, smooth-looking lawns all about it and continuing down the hill with beds of brown earth that must be flower gardens in the summer. Surrounded as it was on all four sides as well as above and below by the wild beauties of the Cornish seacoast, the house and park were like a perfect, cultivated gem.

There was something about Freyja's first sight of Penhallow that was pure physical sensation, almost as if a fist had collided with a dull thud into her ribs below the heart. It was almost painful.

The road was descending slowly but rather steeply into the valley and the three-arched stone bridge Freyja could see there. On the other side the road followed the line of the river north for a while before climbing out of the valley on the other side. There was also a steep, curving driveway up to the house and a smaller, though not inconsiderable stone house at the bottom of it—a dower house, perhaps.

Morgan and Alleyne were crowded against the window on their side of the carriage, looking out. Joshua was looking over Freyja's shoulder.

"Impressive indeed," Alleyne said.

"Beautiful!" Morgan said softly.

Joshua was silent. And tense. Freyja could sense his tension even though he did not touch her. This was where his aunt and cousins lived. Where he had spent an unhappy childhood as an orphan in his uncle's home. This was where he had wanted never to return. And where he would fight suspicion and innuendo and hostility and hatred and accusations of murder.

It was his. It was his inheritance, his source of wealth and prestige, his responsibility. It was the millstone about his neck.

She knew almost nothing about his life here, about what had driven him away, about why he had been so reluctant to return. But she was about to discover much, she supposed. She was not sure she wanted to. She had always thought of Joshua as a laughing, carefree, charming man with little depth of character. She had thought of him as pleasant to flirt with, pleasant even to lie with, but not in any way desirable as a lifelong partner. She had always expected to be able to say good-bye to him without any real regrets.

She hoped all that was not about to change, but she had a horrible sinking feeling that perhaps it was.

For no reason she could fathom, and without at all intending to, she sought his hand with her own and held it firmly. He laced his fingers with hers and gripped so tightly that she felt pain. Normally she would have reprimanded him sharply or tried to outgrip him. But she sat quietly and made no protest at all.

The wheels of the carriage rumbled over the bridge and Freyja was aware of a wide and beautiful view along the river to the sea. Both were sparkling like a million diamonds in the sunshine, the clouds having just moved off the face of the sun.

IT WOULD BE DIFFICULT TO APPROACH PENHALLOW unseen unless one climbed to the headland above it and sneaked down the hill on foot. The approach of two grand traveling carriages, another, plainer one for the servants, and two baggage coaches would have been well nigh impossible to miss.

Even so, only Jim Saunders was waiting on the gravel terrace before the front doors when the first carriage, in which Joshua rode with Freyja, Alleyne, and Morgan, drew level with them and then pulled ahead to allow room for Eve and Aidan's carriage too. Grooms were approaching from the stables.

Joshua was first out of the carriage. He shook hands warmly with the steward he had hired in London six months ago and not seen since, and turned to hand Freyja and Morgan down before Alleyne alighted. Aidan was already lifting the children out of their carriage, and the two of them were dashing to the edge of the terrace to gaze downward along the valley to the wide golden beach at the end of it.

"I came as fast as I could," Joshua said after he had presented Saunders to the Bedwyns.

"And a good thing too, my lord," Saunders told him. "The Reverend Calvin Moore arrived last night."

The front doors had opened at last, and glancing up, Joshua saw his aunt standing on the top step, looking frail and wan in her black mourning clothes, a black-bordered handkerchief held to her lips. He wondered if she had expected him. He wondered if she had expected that he would bring Freyja with him. He would wager she had not expected him to bring other guests too. And the Bedwyns were a formidable lot. With the exception of Eve, they were all gazing at the marchioness with their haughtiest expressions. No one could do haughtiness quite like the Bedwyns.

Joshua almost grinned but decided against it.

"Aunt?" he said, striding toward her.

She came down the steps and melted into his arms.

"Joshua, my dearest boy," she said. "What a perfectly delightful surprise—and just when I had given up all hope of your ever coming home. I was just now observing to Cousin Calvin... But you do not know that he has come for a visit, do you? I was just observing to him that it would be more the thing for *you* to receive him since Penhallow is yours and he is your heir, but that you had not found the time to come here since your poor uncle passed on. And then Chastity saw the carriages approaching and I knew that my prayers had been answered."

No, Joshua concluded, she had not expected him. Neither did she realize that he knew what was afoot, or else she chose not to speak of it immediately. She might, of course, have greeted him quite differently if he had come alone.

"I am delighted to be here, Aunt," he said. "I have brought houseguests with me, as you can see. You know my betrothed already. May I present Lord and Lady Aidan Bedwyn, Lady Morgan Bedwyn, and Lord Alleyne Bedwyn? My aunt, the Marchioness of Hallmere."

She welcomed them graciously. For a moment it looked as if she were about to hug Freyja, but something in Freyja's stance caused her to change her mind and she contented herself with a warm, watery smile instead. A stranger would have sworn that she had never been happier in her life than she was at this moment in greeting a number of unexpected guests to the house she considered her own.

"And children!" she exclaimed, clasping her hands to her bosom and gazing fondly at Becky and Davy, who were still admiring the view while their nurse looked on from beside the third carriage. "How delightful it will be to hear the happy voices of children echoing about Penhallow's halls again. It has been many years since you and Albert and the girls were children, Joshua. Those were good days. Will you all come up to the drawing room, where everyone is waiting to meet you? You must be ready for your tea."

Joshua turned to offer his arm to Freyja, but before she could take it, someone came hurtling past his aunt in the doorway. She was ungainly in her haste, her arms clamped to her sides down to the elbows, her hands flapping to the sides in a show of excitement. Her round, childish face beamed with happiness. She was laughing convulsively as children do when deeply involved in a game.

"Josh!" she was saying over and over again. "Josh, Josh, Josh."

He opened his arms and she came into them, coming close to bowling him over. Her arms gripped him tightly about the neck, almost throttling him, and her head came down so that she butted him in the chest with her forehead and fairly robbed him of breath. She was still laughing and repeating his name.

She had grown up in five years—she was eighteen now—but she still looked much the same as she had last time he saw her.

"Prue!" he said, closing his arms about her. "Prue, my sweetest love."

"You have come home," she told his chest. "I knew you would come home. Josh, Josh, Josh."

"Prudence!" his aunt said in awful tones. "How dare you leave the nursery without my permission! Where is Miss Palmer?"

"It is all right, Aunt," Joshua said as his cousin began to make grunting noises of distress. "What better welcome home could I possibly be given? I have brought some people for you to meet, my love. If you will leave off hugging me, I will present them to you."

"Lady Prudence Moore, my cousin," he said, looking

first at Freyja. "This is Lady Freyja Bedwyn, Prue. I daresay she will allow you to call her Freyja just as she will call you Prue. She is going to be my wife."

Now, why the devil had he added that?

Prue smiled her wide, guileless child's smile at each of the Bedwyns in turn and repeated their names quietly to herself so that she would not forget them. When Joshua had finished introducing them, she looked at him and laughed.

"And this is Josh," she said, having noticed that he had not been introduced to anyone.

"And I am Josh," he said, smiling tenderly at her and setting one arm about her shoulders.

"And you have come home."

"And I have come home."

"And you have brought Freyja," Prue said. "I like Freyja. I like everyone. I like Eve best, though. Except Josh. I love Josh most in the world. Except for Chass and Constance and—"

"Prudence!" her mother said a little more faintly.

Joshua chuckled and caught Freyja's eye. She was not looking cold or haughty or shocked or repelled or any of the things he might have expected. She was gazing fully at him, a light of sharp curiosity in her eyes.

His aunt led the way into the house. Eve hurried forward and took Prue's arm, a kind and very genuine smile lighting her pretty face, while Aidan strode across the terrace to fetch the children. Morgan and Alleyne had already stepped inside. Joshua offered Freyja his arm.

"She has always been a child," he said. "She always will be."

"And you love her," Freyja said.

"She is made up of love," he said. "There is nothing else

in her but love. How could one give back to her anything else *but* love?"

"Josh," she said with a sigh, "this is something I really did not need to know about you."

"Sweetheart," he said, laughing softly, "did you think me incapable of loving? How unsporting of you."

CHAPTER XVI

THE PILLARED HALLWAY WAS TWO STORIES HIGH
with marble friezes and marble busts that would be
worth examining more closely some time. The stairway with its wide, gleaming oak stairs and intricately
carved banister was in a separate chamber. The drawing
room to which the Marchioness of Hallmere led them
was a large, square, elegantly classical apartment with an
ornately sculptured marble fireplace, silk-paneled walls
with gilded trim, a high, coved ceiling painted with scenes
from Greek mythology, and a deep bay window with a
breathtaking prospect down over the valley and out toward the sea.

Freyja did not immediately notice the view, but from
the moment she stepped inside the house she realized that
it was far grander than she had expected. Yet it was a place
to which Joshua had never wanted to return.

Lady Constance was waiting in the drawing room. She

smiled with genuine warmth at Joshua and at Freyja. The other lady with her, slender almost to the point of thinness, brown-haired with a long, oval face and large, beautiful, sad eyes, was her younger sister, Lady Chastity Moore. The slightly portly, somewhat balding gentleman with shirt points so stiff and high that he had to move the whole of his upper body when he wished to turn his head, was introduced to the newly arrived guests as the Reverend Calvin Moore, Joshua's second cousin.

The heir, who had been sent for, Freyja supposed.

It was Joshua who made the introductions, not his aunt. Indeed, Freyja noticed with interest, his whole manner had changed as soon as they set foot inside the drawing room. The room became almost visibly his. He became lord of the manor. He invited them all to be seated after the introductions had been made or to look out at the view from the bay window. He asked his aunt if she would be so good as to have tea brought up.

"Prudence," his aunt said, her sweet smile belying the venomous glance she darted at her youngest daughter, "return to Miss Palmer in the nursery immediately."

"Oh, no," Joshua said, the Marquess of Hallmere to his fingertips, "Prue may stay for tea, Aunt."

The girl flapped her hands in excitement, and Lady Chastity took one of them in her own and drew her sister down beside her on a love seat.

"Absolutely," Eve agreed, seating herself close to them and beaming at both. "We came here to see Joshua's home and to meet the members of his family who live here. Prue is one of those."

"A splendid view indeed," Alleyne commented after strolling into the bay window. "I suppose the beach on this side of the valley is a private one, Joshua? Part of the estate? I envy you."

"I still want to paint the sea," Morgan said—she was standing beside Alleyne. "But I want to paint this valley too and the house and the park on the hillside. It is a good thing you are to be my brother-in-law, Joshua. I may have to visit you here several times and at different times of the year before my palette has been satisfied. Oh, Freyja, all this is to be yours too."

"I daresay this is sheep country, is it, Joshua?" Aidan asked. "Your farmland is above the valley? I look forward to viewing it with you and to chatting with your steward."

Freyja was ignoring the view beyond the window for the moment. She was very deliberately viewing the room, standing in the middle of it and turning slowly.

"It is a magnificent apartment," she said in her haughtiest voice. "I daresay I will wish to change some of the furnishings and draperies after we are married, Josh, but those are minor matters. I shall very much enjoy entertaining here. I daresay you enjoyed it in your day too, ma'am." She smiled graciously at the marchioness, who smiled sweetly back but was saved from having to reply by the arrival of the tea trays.

The Bedwyns, Freyja thought, had made their point.

Joshua was talking with his second cousin.

"It is a happy chance that you should be at Penhallow at just the time I have brought my betrothed and some of her family to see the home that will be hers after we wed," he said. "It must be nearly ten years since I saw you last, Calvin. You decided to take a vacation in Cornwall, did you?"

The Reverend Calvin Moore flushed. "I was invited here by Cousin Corinne," he said stiffly.

"Indeed?" Joshua raised his eyebrows and looked at his aunt with a smile. "You guessed that I would bring Freyja here soon, did you, Aunt, and thought to surprise me with a visit from my heir? That was extraordinarily kind of you. Feel free to stay for a week or longer, Calvin—as long as you wish, in fact. It will be pleasant to have my own family about me here as well as Freyja's."

Mr. Moore cleared his throat. "It is good of you to say so, Hallmere," he said.

They all sat down for tea after that and conversed pleasantly enough on a variety of different topics. It was all rather amusing, Freyja thought. The air fairly shouted the unspoken topic. A witness had stepped forward to accuse Joshua of a five-year-old murder. The Reverend Calvin Moore obviously knew about it already. So did the daughters, with the probable exception of Prue. And so, of course, did Joshua and all the Bedwyns. But not a word of the pending scandal was spoken aloud.

The marchioness had been taken by surprise, Freyja guessed—by the sudden arrival of her nephew, by the fact that he had brought her and other houseguests with him, and by his courteously masterful manner. She had hatched the plot, but it obviously had not yet come to full fruition.

And so there was an absurd sense of normality about the whole scene. Two families, about to be connected by marriage, took tea together and made themselves agreeable to one another. The marchioness fairly sparkled with joy.

"Mrs. Richardson will be ready to show you to your rooms," she said when they had finished tea. "You will all wish to rest before dinner, I am sure. How delightful it will be to have so many guests at my table. I have longed for this moment. Have I not, Constance?"

"Rest?" Freyja said, smiling faintly at the woman. "I think not, ma'am. I will change and freshen up and then I will be ready for a tour of the house. You will oblige me, Josh?"

"It would be my pleasure," he said. "Will everyone else

join us? You too, Calvin? And Chass, you must accompany us, if you will. You were always more knowledgeable about the house than anyone else. And yes, Prue, my love, we will certainly not go without you. Shall we all meet in the hall in half an hour?"

The house was far larger than it had appeared to be during their approach to it. It was an elegant, square building. Most of the living apartments were in the front wing, facing toward the southeast and the magnificent views over gardens and valley and sea. The private apartments and bedchambers were in the east wing, the state apartments, the ballroom, and the long gallery in the west wing. The north wing, facing half up the valley and half back toward sloping gardens and hillside, consisted mostly of offices, with servants' quarters on the upper floors.

Joshua did most of the talking as he took them about, though Constance added a few comments of her own. But it was Chastity who made all the explanations once they arrived at the state apartments and the long gallery. She knew the history of every architectural detail, every work of art, every generation of the Moore family who had lived there, both in the old house before it had been pulled down and in the new, which was only four generations old. She spoke softly and clearly and concisely and with obvious warmth for her topic. Freyja found that she rather liked all three daughters. They all seemed surprisingly different from their mother.

Joshua, free of the responsibility of being guide in the state apartments, drew Freyja's hand through his arm and looked down at her with laughter in his eyes.

"The Bedwyns are indeed formidable when they go into action," he said. "You most of all, sweetheart. So you are going to refurnish my drawing room, are you? And enjoy entertaining there?"

"The draperies are the wrong color," she said. "And several of the chairs are in poor taste—they are far too ornate."

He chuckled. *"I shall very much enjoy entertaining here,"* he said softly, quoting her exact words. *"I daresay you enjoyed it in your day too, ma'am.* If one could only have seen into her thoughts at that moment, Free."

"There has been no mention of any suspicion of murder," she said.

"Ah, but there will be." He grinned at her.

He was so very like her, she thought. He was *enjoying* himself. The foolish man—he might hang if convicted, but all he could do was grin at the exciting prospect of danger.

The rest of the day progressed very much as it had since their arrival. Joshua took the head of the table at dinner and seated Freyja at his right, Constance at his left. His aunt sat at the foot of the table. He nodded to her quite firmly when he deemed it time for the ladies to withdraw and leave the gentlemen to their port and their male conversation.

Chastity and Morgan, who appeared to have developed something of a friendly acquaintance, entertained themselves and everyone else at the pianoforte, Eve sat with Prue, whom Joshua had permitted to take dinner with everyone else—Freyja guessed that it had never happened before, and Freyja stood in the bay window looking out onto darkness until the gentlemen joined them.

Eve conversed with the marchioness and Constance. She did not have the chilly hauteur of the Bedwyns, but she did quite well enough in her own quiet, sweet way.

"It must be sad to lose so much more than just one's life's partner when he passes on," she said. "Being mistress of Penhallow must have been a wonderful part of your marriage, ma'am. I am sure Freyja will also find it so. What are your plans for the future? Or is it too soon for you to have decided with any certainty? You are still in mourning, I perceive."

The marchioness dabbed at her eyes. "My dear Hallmere—the *late* Hallmere—is all I can think of at present, Lady Aidan," she said. "I will welcome Lady Freyja here with open arms, of course. There is much I can teach her about the running of so large a household, though I daresay she has learned something at Lindsey Hall."

"The dower house in the valley is a pleasant-looking place," Eve said.

"How prettily your sister plays, Lady Freyja," the marchioness said, raising her voice. "And what beauty she possesses. I daresay she will be married before next summer. All the prettiest girls are snatched up young."

"If they choose to be snatched, ma'am," Freyja said. "I am not sure Morgan is one of their number."

"And you, Lady Constance," Eve continued, "what are your plans now that your mama's year of mourning is drawing to an end? A Season in London, perhaps? Provided Freyja and Joshua are married before the spring, Freyja will be able to sponsor you if your mama still does not feel up to it."

Yes, Freyja thought, smiling to herself, Eve was quite as formidable as any of them.

"It is time you went back to the nursery, Prudence," her mother said in the little-girl whine Freyja remembered so well from Bath.

"Come, Prue." Eve got to her feet and drew the girl to hers. "It is high time I went up and read a few stories to Becky and Davy before tucking them in for the night. Would you like to hear some stories too?"

Later, after the gentlemen had come to the drawing

room and they had all taken tea and prolonged the conversation for a while, the marchioness suggested an early night, which she was sure they would all welcome after such a long journey.

"And I am quite weary myself, I must confess," she said, "from all the excitement of welcoming dear Joshua home, where he belongs, and his dear betrothed and her family too."

No one voiced any objection. It really *had* been a lengthy journey. But Joshua was not ready to retire yet, it seemed.

"Would you care for a breath of fresh air first, Freyja?" he asked.

"Oh, but Joshua, dear," his aunt said faintly, "Lady Freyja would need to take her maid with her."

Alleyne grinned and waggled his eyebrows at Freyja.

"She will be with her betrothed, ma'am," Aidan said, sounding wonderfully arrogant and starchy. "There will be no need of a chaperone."

"And even if there were . . ." Freyja said, arching her eyebrows and leaving the sentence uncompleted. "Yes, I would, Joshua, thank you."

It was a chilly night, as befitted early autumn, but it was lovely nonetheless. The sky, which had been so dark earlier while she stood in the bay window of the drawing room, was now star-studded, and the moon shed its light onto the land and gleamed in a wide, sparkling band across the sea and the lower part of the river.

There was a footpath leading along the hillside on a level with the house, bordered by bushes and flower beds on the inner, hill side, and by a waist-high stone wall half-covered with ivy and other plants on the other. Beyond the wall there was another flower border and then lawn sloping down to bushes and the road below. In the summertime,

Freyja guessed, this must all be a blaze of color. Even now, and even at night, it was beautiful.

"What a foolish woman your aunt is," she said. "You intended never to come back here, did you not? You would have left her to live out her life in peace here and to rule the household as if it were her own. Yet she had to stir up trouble where there was none."

"And now Morgan is to visit us here frequently in order to paint, Alleyne is to come in order to enjoy my private beach, Aidan is interested in my farms, Eve is planning a come-out Season for my cousins, you are planning to remodel my home, and I am here," he said. "Yes, I suppose that if my aunt could go back and ignore Mrs. Lumbard's letter informing her of my presence in Bath, she would perhaps do so. But perhaps not. She always had to feel in complete control."

"Why did you intend never to come back here?" she asked.

She knew very little about him apart from the fact that he was an amusing, attractive companion. It was strange how one could have known a man in the most intimate way physically and yet not really know him at all as a person. She had not wanted to know him. She still did not. Yet it seemed inevitable now. She had made the impulsive, mad decision to accompany him here, and now she had been drawn inextricably into his life.

"I came here at the age of six," he said, "after my parents had died. I was not even told they were dead at first. I was told they had had to go away for a while. The theory was, I suppose, that I would gradually forget them and would never have to be told the searing truth. But my aunt told me the first time I got up to some mischief here. My parents would be very disappointed to know that they had such a bad little boy, she told me. It was a good thing they were dead and would never know."

"Ah, yes," Freyja said. "It is just the sort of thing the marchioness *would* say. I hope you told her to be damned."

"I did," he said, "in words far more colorful than that, I believe. But I knew in that moment what the truth meant to me. I had endured until then with all the patience I could muster. I had lived for the day when my mother and father would come for me and take me back home. There was the truly terrifying emptiness of knowing them gone forever. And there was the knowledge that my present life with my uncle and aunt and cousins was my permanent life."

"I hope," she said tartly, fighting pity for the boy he had been, "you were never abject."

He laughed. "Sweetheart," he said, "you are supposed to be in tears of pitying sentiment by now. No, I never was. I made up my mind that if my aunt was determined to think me bad, I would do all in my power to earn my reputation."

"Your uncle?" she said. "Your cousins? Did they share her low opinion of you?"

"My uncle had no choice," he said. "I *was* bad, Free. I could make your hair stand on end with an account of some of my escapades."

"I doubt it," she said. "I grew up with Bedwyns and Butlers. I was a Bedwyn myself. But in *my* family we were called high-spirited and mischievous before we were punished. Never bad."

"I rubbed along well enough with the girls," he said. "But they were much younger and therefore were never really my companions."

"I suppose," she said, "your aunt hated you because you were the next heir after her son."

"Undoubtedly." He chuckled.

"Oh," she said as they rounded a slight bend in the path and were suddenly buffeted by the wind. They also had a much wider view of the sea—and the village had come into sight on the opposite side of the river. "Magnificent!"

"It is, is it not?" he agreed.

Yet he had never wanted to come back here.

"What was Albert like?" she asked.

"The perfect son," he said. "He learned all there was to learn from my uncle and helped him with estate business whenever he was allowed. He adored his mother and was attentive to his sisters. He excelled at his studies in school and at university. He was an active member of the church and contributed to every charity that arose. He frequently intervened with his mother on my behalf."

"I would have hated him," Freyja said fervently.

He laughed softly. "Yes," he agreed, "I believe you would."

"And yet," she said, "you were always quarreling with him? You told us so at Lindsey Hall."

"Of course," he said. "Badness usually does not appreciate goodness, Free. I was very, very bad. And Albert was very, very good. He frequently lectured me on goodness, and I just as frequently told him what he could do with his lectures."

His voice was full of his usual careless laughter. It was a mask behind which he hid all the darker shadows of his life, Freyja realized. She had wondered before if the mask hid nothing at all or something. She knew the answer now, though she had not yet penetrated those shadows. She did not want to either. She wanted to be able to remember Josh as a light flirt who during one memorable night had become more to her. She did not want to feel any regrets, any pull of darker memories of a person who might have been worth knowing.

They had walked around another bend in the path. The hillside rose above them here in an almost sheer cliff, and they were again sheltered from the wind. They stopped walking, and Joshua leaned over to rest his elbows on the wall and gaze downward. The moonlight lit his profile. He was smiling.

"If you hated life so much here," she asked him, "why did you stay so long? You left here five years ago. You must already have been—what? Two or three and twenty?"

"Three," he said. "I left Penhallow when I was eighteen. I went to live in Lydmere." He nodded his head in the direction of the village. "I apprenticed myself to a carpenter and learned the trade. I was good at it too. I would have made a decent living from it. I was happy enough, and would have continued to be, I believe."

It was a strange thought that Lady Freyja Bedwyn would never have met Joshua Moore, carpenter, from the Cornish village of Lydmere and would have been unaware of his existence even if their paths had somehow crossed. They would have been from different worlds.

"But then Albert died and you became the heir to all this," she said, "and everything changed."

"Yes." He turned his head to look at her, a strangely mocking smile on his lips. "And then I became Hallmere and could aspire to the hand of a duke's daughter even if only in a fake betrothal. Life is strange, would you not agree?"

But he still had not explained why he had left.

Freyja remembered something then, something she had not particularly noticed at the time. He could no longer remember what he and Albert had quarreled about in the boat on the night Albert died, Joshua had told her family back at Lindsey Hall. How could he *not* remember?

Considering how that night had turned out, surely every last detail must be etched on his memory.

But she would not ask. She really did not want to know—though *that* was becoming rather a thin argument even in the privacy of her own thoughts.

"Did you not come to Penhallow at all during the years when you were living in the village?" she asked.

"I came once every week on my half-day off from work," he said. "I came to see Prue."

"Poor girl," Freyja said. "Her mother is not at all fond of her, is she?"

"One need never use the word *poor* to describe Prue," he said. "We tend to view those with physical and mental abilities different from the norm as pitiful creatures with handicaps or disabilities. We talk about cripples and idiots. We view them from our own limited perspective. I once knew a blind person whose sense of wonder at the world put my own limited perceptions to shame. Prue is happy and bubbling over with love—both attributes that many of us allow to lapse with our childhoods. In what sense is she disabled? Or handicapped? Or poor?"

He spoke with an intensity that made him seem unfamiliar to her for a moment. He had been kind and patient with the girl all afternoon as well as during dinner, with no sense of martyrdom or boredom or condescension. Prue had not been the only one brimming over with love. Joshua had reminded her rather strongly of Eve, whom Aidan fondly described as a woman with a bleeding heart and a fondness for lame ducks. Their house was filled with servants whom no one else would employ for one reason or another, including a truly ferocious ex-convict of a housekeeper who would cheerfully die for Eve and whom Freyja admired enormously.

"Perhaps now you *have* returned," she said, "you will

decide to stay—once this nonsense your aunt has been hatching has been cleared up, that is. You would have to have her move elsewhere, of course, but she cannot have been left destitute."

"She has not been," he said. "But she will continue to live here. *I* will not."

And yet if she were in his place, Freyja thought, she would have to have the satisfaction of ousting the marchioness from Penhallow, of stripping from her all that was not rightfully hers. Even if she did not choose to live here herself, she would not allow the other woman to do so instead. She would enjoy the satisfaction of wreaking some revenge.

But it was none of her business what Joshua did or did not do. *He* was none of her business.

"A quiet hillside on a starry night," he said, "with the moonlight dancing on the surface of the sea. And a gorgeous woman at my side. Whatever am I about, holding a polite conversation with her and simply admiring the view? I must be losing my touch—and would quickly lose my reputation too if anyone could see me at it." He straightened up from the wall and turned to grin at her.

"You may imagine, if you will," she said, "that my maid is standing a few feet off."

He chuckled softly. "But Aidan said you did not need a chaperone," he reminded her.

"Because Aidan *trusted* you," she said, "and because he thinks we are betrothed."

"And so we are," he said, "thanks to my aunt and thanks to Bewcastle—and thanks to your decision to accompany me here. Your hair is loose beneath that hood, is it not?"

She had pulled out the pins when she went to her room to fetch her cloak.

"What has that got to do with anything?" she asked

haughtily. Now that he had mentioned it, the surroundings *were* rather conducive to romance—or to dalliance at least. But she had dallied quite enough with Joshua during the past few weeks. They were fortunate indeed that they had not been trapped into having to marry each other. She really ought not to invite any further indiscretions.

But he had closed the distance between them and raised his hands to lift back her hood. Her hair cascaded out about her shoulders and down her back. There was enough wind even in this shaded spot to lift it and waft it about her face.

"It is just, you see," he said, "that a red-blooded male itches to tangle his fingers in such hair, Free. Nothing personal, of course, but I *am* red-blooded." His fingers played with her hair and then twined themselves into it. "But then of course once he does *that*, then he cannot resist doing *this*." He drew her against him and tipped back her head so that she was gazing up into his moonlit face. His eyes, as she fully expected, were dancing with merriment.

"But the trouble is," she said, setting her hands on either side of his waist, "that the woman then feels an almost-irresistible urge to go at that red-blooded male with her fists."

He chuckled. "A good bout of fisticuffs might send us tumbling over the wall and rolling down the hill to get caught in the bushes down there," he said, "all arms and legs and other body parts tangled up together. It might be very interesting indeed. I think I'll take my chances." He lowered his head and rubbed his nose back and forth across hers.

"I cannot think of any reason in the world," she said, "why we should be doing this." *Liar, liar.*

"You see?" he said, licking at her lips and sending raw sensation sizzling into all the wrong parts of her body—

wrong if she wished to walk away from this unscathed, that was. "We are a perfect foil for each other, sweetheart. I cannot think of any reason in the world why we should *not* be doing this."

"This is for courting couples," she said. "For betrothed couples. For married couples. We are none of those things."

"But we *are* a man and a woman," he said, dipping his head and speaking with his lips touching the pulse at the base of her throat. Her toes curled up convulsively inside her shoes and one of her hands clutched at his hair and then lost itself within the soft, silky mass of it. "Alone together on a moonlit night. And panting with desire for each other."

"I am not—"

His mouth stopped her protest. Not his lips, but his mouth, open, hot, moist, tempting, seeking, his tongue pressing against her lips and finding its way through into her mouth. She came against him with a low moan, a dull, aching pulse beating between her thighs and up inside her where he had once been.

She fenced with his tongue and got her hands beneath his cloak and under his coat and waistcoat—why did men wear so many layers of clothing?—while his own fondled her breasts beneath her cloak and then moved behind her to cup her buttocks and pull her hard against him, half lifting her as he did so, rubbing her against him so that the ache inside her almost exploded to add to the starlight.

"You are not—?" he prompted her much later, lifting his mouth perhaps an inch away from hers.

"Panting with desire," she said, ignominiously breathless.

He laughed softly. "Heaven help me if you were, then," he said. "Why do you not want to marry me, Free? You cannot have Ravensberg, but I suppose sooner or later you must have someone. Why not me?"

"Must *you* have someone sooner or later?" she asked sharply, drawing back her head another inch.

"It is different for a man," he said.

"How so?"

"A man likes freedom and no commitment," he said. "He can enjoy dalliance and look for nothing beyond it. Women have nesting instincts. They want homes and fidelity and everlasting romance and babies."

He laughed suddenly and caught her right wrist in his, moving back far enough to look down at her hand.

"What, sweetheart?" he asked. "No fist? I thought that would provoke you if anything could. Ouch!"

Her left fist had caught him a solid blow on the jaw.

"Why do I not want to marry you?" she asked. "Perhaps it is because I feel some pity for your pretty face. If it were within my daily reach for the rest of a lifetime, it would soon be in sorry shape, like the faces of those brutes who are employed to box each other into oblivion for the amusement of gentlemen who choose to wager on blood sports."

He threw back his head and laughed, fingering his jaw and flexing it as he did so.

"We had better get back to the house," he said. "It is perfectly understood, then, is it, that I am footloose and restless and not nearly done with sowing my wild oats, if I ever will be, and that you would rather go through life as a spinster than marry someone who cannot engage your feelings as deeply as they were once engaged? We will never marry, Freyja. But we *are* attracted to each other, and we tend to erupt like a pair of volcanoes when opportunity presents itself. Shall we avoid such opportunities until we can put an end to them altogether? Or shall we *not*, but simply enjoy the moment for what it is worth? The moment being the next few days or weeks or whatever."

"You speak as if the next few days can be taken up with nothing *but* opportunities for dalliance," she said. "There is supposed to be a plot afoot, is there not, to have you accused and convicted of murder. A witness can be a dangerous thing."

"Lord, yes," he agreed. "Half a dozen witnesses could be even more deadly. I wonder if my aunt would be so wise— or so foolish."

"I wonder what really happened that night," she said. But she shook her head even as she was speaking and pulled her hood up over her head again before turning and striding back along the path in the direction of the house. "But I do not want to know."

He fell into step beside her. "Because you fear that I really did kill him?" he asked her.

Was that why she was so reluctant to hear the truth?

"I did *threaten* to kill him," he said.

"But you did not do it," she said firmly. "You told Aidan you did not when he asked at Lindsey Hall, and I believed you. I still believe you. Would you have killed him if he had lived long enough?"

He was a long time answering. They walked around the corner into the wind again, at their backs now.

"I really do not know," he said. "But I very much fear that perhaps I would not have."

There! That was all she wanted to hear on the subject, Freyja thought, lengthening her stride. She had already heard too much. Something horribly serious had happened that night—apart from the nasty fact that someone had died. And she did not want to know what it was.

I wonder if Hallmere has thought to mention to you that he has the most adorable little bastard son living in the village close to Penhallow with his mother.

The remembered words came back to Freyja in the marchioness's whining voice.

She was the girls' governess until the unfortunate incident forced my husband to dismiss her. They appear not to be suffering. I understand that Hallmere still supports them.

The sordid story had nothing to do with her, Freyja decided. He was *not* her betrothed and she felt no inclination whatsoever to stand in judgment on him. But she had a horrible suspicion that the quarrel in the boat that night had been about the governess and her child. Had Albert delivered one of his stuffy, self-righteous lectures on the topic? And had Joshua... Well, how *had* he reacted apart from threatening to kill his cousin? Exactly how and why had Albert died?

She did not want to know.

"I have shocked you, sweetheart," Joshua said. "Does this mean there will be no more dalliance between us? You have slain me."

"Is *nothing* serious to you?" she asked disdainfully.

But she knew the answer to that question now, of course, and really she wished she did not.

Yes, there were many things in his life that were serious to Joshua Moore, Marquess of Hallmere.

She should have said good-bye to him long ago, before she even began to suspect that he was not simply a laughing, carefree rogue too handsome for his own good.

He chuckled softly, found her hand beneath her cloak, and held it as they walked, lacing his fingers with hers.

CHAPTER XVII

WHO IS IT?" JOSHUA ASKED, PROPPING HIMSELF against the edge of his steward's desk and crossing his arms over his chest. It was early in the morning, but Saunders was already at work in his office.

"Hugh Garnett," Saunders said. "His land is on the other side of the valley—his mother was a baron's daughter. He is prospering by all accounts. He bought more land after taking over from his father a couple of years ago. He is not by any means a gentleman without influence."

"Oh, I know Hugh Garnett." Joshua frowned. "He is a nephew, on his father's side, of Mrs. Lumbard, the marchioness's particular friend. I am not overly surprised. But what would be in it for him, do you suppose, apart from the fact that he has reason to dislike me? He is not the sort of man to do something for nothing."

"He has been displaying some interest in Lady Chastity,"

Saunders said, "but without any encouragement from either the lady herself or the marchioness. Yet she did invite him to tea here with his aunt and cousin after the return from Bath. It would be a brilliant match for him, of course, especially if it came with her mother's full blessing."

"And more especially if I were not likely to spoil things by coming here to live now that I am betrothed and likely to marry at any time," Joshua said. "I daresay the Reverend Calvin Moore has been brought here as much to woo Constance as to bring moral support and comfort to the marchioness. She rules her world with as much ruthlessness as she ever did, does she not?"

He got to his feet and crossed to the window. It looked out onto the upward slope of the hill. But it was a pretty view nonetheless. The kitchen gardens and flower gardens were back there, as well as several hothouses. Behind them a footpath snaked its way upward past cultivated bushes to the hardy wildflowers closer to the plateau above.

He remembered then what Constance had told him and swung about to look at Jim Saunders. He was a gentleman of perhaps thirty years, perhaps less, who would inherit a very modest fortune and property on the death of his father, though there were a younger brother and several sisters to provide for. He was a pleasant-looking fellow and a hard worker. It was easy to understand why Constance, living in such isolation from men of her own class, would cast her eyes and her dreams on him. Did he return her regard? He was sitting behind his desk, looking down at a closed ledger, no readable expression on his face.

"You must understand, my lord," Saunders said, his voice carefully formal, "that I am relatively new here and have not yet formed firm opinions on everyone in the house and vicinity. I do not know the marchioness well and do not presume to guess her motives. Neither do I know *you* well. But I am sensible of the fact that I owe my loyalty to you and not to her ladyship."

It was a careful answer. It was not obsequious.

"So you are not sure if there is any truth to these charges you warned me were imminent," he said. "You are wondering if you are employed by a desperate murderer."

"I like to think not," his steward said.

"Thank you." Joshua looked more closely at him. "How did you know? Nothing has been said since my arrival. There has been no constable panting on my doorstep to arrest me. Who told you?"

Saunders straightened the ledger and brought its bottom edge even with the edge of his desk.

"Constance?"

Saunders began to open the book and then let it close again. "She suggested to me that you ought to be informed, my lord," he said.

"Ah," Joshua said softly. "Then I must thank her and thank *you* for complying with her wishes. It would seem that the plot is not quite cooked and that my arrival might have hindered its smooth progress. *Why* is it not cooked, I wonder, if there is a witness, a prosperous gentleman, willing to swear that he saw me murder my cousin?"

Saunders looked back at him but did not venture any suggestion.

"I believe," Joshua said, moving away from the window and grinning, "I am about to make the progress of this plot even less smooth, Saunders. I believe I am going to enjoy my day. Tomorrow you may give me a progress report on the new buildings and the repairs that were to be undertaken as soon as the harvest was in. I will want to see the home farm too and speak with my workers and their wives while I am here."

"Yes, my lord," his steward said, "I am at your command anytime you wish."

Joshua left the office wing of the house to see if any of the family or guests were up yet. But he must have been with Saunders longer than he had realized. Almost everyone was already assembled in the breakfast parlor.

"Good morning," he said, striding inside. "And a crisp, bright one it looks to be. Perhaps we could all drive or ride into Lydmere later? It is a pretty little fishing village with a harbor and beach below it. Ah, Freyja." He took her hand in his, raised it to his lips, and kept it there a little longer than was necessary while he smiled into her eyes.

He might as well amuse himself by annoying both her and his aunt, he thought. Freyja's eyebrows arched upward, Alleyne grinned, Calvin cleared his throat, and his aunt smiled sweetly.

But playing the ardent lover was easier than living the reality of a fake betrothal, he decided, as he helped himself to food from the sideboard and seated himself at the head of the table. Last night's embrace had been more frustrating than satisfying, especially since he now knew what it was like to take an embrace with Freyja to its completion. He was, he had realized last night, in grave danger of falling ever so slightly in love with Freyja Bedwyn. He was going to have to work diligently to keep their relationship to its familiar pattern. The last thing he wanted was to be seriously in love with anyone.

He joined in the general conversation until Eve and Aidan, the last to arrive, since they had been in the nursery with their children, had sat down and begun to eat.

"It has occurred to me," he said, "that my homecoming will be an occasion to be remarked upon in the neighborhood—and I daresay my arrival did not go unnoticed yesterday. When it is known that I have also brought home with me my future bride, the occasion will be seen as one to be celebrated indeed. A grand ball at Penhallow would be in order—perhaps one week hence? I will see to most of the arrangements myself, but I have not been here for five years and doubtless do not know everyone who lives in the neighborhood now. You will help me with the guest list, I trust, Aunt? And Constance and Chastity too?"

Constance, flushed and bright-eyed, nodded her acquiescence. Chastity smiled.

"What a perfectly delightful idea, Joshua," his aunt said, smiling sweetly, "even if I *am* still in mourning for your dear uncle. But you must remember that this is neither London nor Bath. There are very few families of any note living within ten miles of Penhallow. A small dinner and reception will be more in order. I will send out the invitations myself and make arrangements with the cook."

"About the dainties to be served at the ball, yes," he said, smiling at her. "Thank you, Aunt. I would appreciate that. I made many friends during my years in Lydmere. A number of them would enjoy kicking up their heels in the ballroom here, I daresay. And there are all my tenants, as well as the workers on my property. It will be like a village assembly more than a *ton* ball. It is to be hoped that your more genteel friends will not be offended by it, Aunt. I understand that Mrs. Lumbard has returned from Bath with her daughter. We will invite them. Perhaps her nephew will escort them—Hugh Garnett, is it?"

His aunt noticeably paled and stared at him with pinched lips. Chastity's fork clattered to her plate.

"He does escort his aunt about occasionally, I hear," Joshua said. "Indeed, I believe he escorted her here to tea quite recently?"

The Bedwyns were all watching and listening with avid interest, he noticed. Constance was staring at her plate, though she was not eating. Chastity's wide eyes were fixed upon Joshua's face. Calvin cleared his throat again.

"And so he did," his aunt said. "A pleasant young man. Edwina Lumbard dotes on him."

"And yet, Aunt," Joshua said, "I believe he must have upset you badly when he ripped open old wounds that were perhaps beginning to heal."

"Whatever do you mean, Joshua?" She set one hand over her heart while her shoulders sagged and her face looked haggard and pathetic.

"I believe," he said, "Garnett suggested to you, Aunt, that Albert's death five years ago was not accidental, but that he was, in fact, murdered. And I believe that he named me as the murderer."

"Oh, no, Joshua," Eve said, her hand too over her heart.

"Why, the devil!" Alleyne exclaimed.

"If this is correct," Aidan said, "it is a serious charge indeed, Joshua."

"Gracious heavens," Freyja said, raising her coffee cup to her lips with a perfectly steady hand. "Am I betrothed to a murderer? How very diverting!"

Chastity was looking deathly pale. So was Constance.

The Reverend Calvin Moore got to his feet, cleared his throat again, and raised his hands, as if he were about to speak a benediction.

"You are quite right, Hallmere," he said. "Such a suggestion has indeed been made. Mr. Garnett claims to have been a witness to the events of the night on which my cousin died. It was because of this that Cousin Corinne summoned me here. She felt the need of a man, and a relative, to advise her. But this is hardly the time or the place to discuss such a distressing matter."

"I cannot think of a better time or place," Joshua said, smiling at him. "Do sit down again, Calvin. We are all family or potential family here."

The marchioness was clutching her throat, her face suddenly gray. "Joshua, my dear," she said faintly. "I never for a moment believed a word Mr. Garnett said. I do not know why he would say such things. But I did indeed feel the need to consult with someone wiser than I, a man, someone in the family. And Cousin Calvin is a clergyman."

"I hope my unexpected arrival yesterday did not discompose you too severely, Calvin," Joshua said. "But I assure you that you are quite safe here with me. I *was* with Albert the night he drowned, but I did not kill him. When was I to be summoned home to defend myself against these charges, Aunt? Or did your letter to Lindsey Hall pass me while I was on my way here?"

"You must understand, Joshua," she said, "that I was dreadfully upset. I did not know what to do. I urged Cousin Calvin to come to advise me. I did not want to bring you here where you might be in danger."

"That was remarkably thoughtful of you," he said.

"Well." She dabbed at her lips with her napkin. "You *are* my nephew. You have always been like my son."

"Constance," he said, turning his eyes on her, "do you believe that I might have murdered your brother?"

She raised her eyes to his. "No," she said. "No, I do not, Joshua."

"Chass?" He looked at the girl, who was still staring at him with wide eyes in a pale face. "Do you believe it?"

She shook her head slowly. "No," she whispered.

"Calvin?" he asked his cousin, who had just resumed his seat.

Calvin cleared his throat—a habit with him, it seemed. "You were ever a mischievous boy, Hallmere," he said. "But you were never vicious, as far as I recall. I would believe this of you only if the evidence were to prove your guilt beyond any reasonable doubt."

"Fair enough," Joshua said. "Freyja?"

"The morning is slipping by while we talk such nonsense," she said, her nose in the air, her tone haughty. "I am eager for the ride into the village you have promised us."

"Oh, so am I, Joshua," Morgan said.

"And I daresay the children are champing at the bit in their eagerness to be taken outside," Aidan added. "I would be pleased to accompany you on a visit to Mr. Garnett later today, though, Joshua. I suppose you *do* intend to call on him?"

"Indeed," Joshua said. "Calvin, you had better come along too."

His aunt dabbed at her lips again. "Mr. Garnett is from home," she said.

"Indeed, ma'am?" Aidan said.

"I would have invited him here to speak with Cousin Calvin if he had not been," she said. "I am as eager as anyone to hear him admit that he was mistaken. But he has gone away for a few days."

"Indeed." Joshua regarded her with some amusement.

"At such a time?" Alleyne was all amazement. "When he should be going to a magistrate with his evidence? But what I cannot understand, I must confess, Joshua, is why he has waited for five years and why he has decided to come forward now."

"Garnett is from home, I daresay," Joshua said, "in order to think through his evidence with more care. He would be foolish to proceed too hastily, would he not, especially after waiting so long. Any trial would pit his word against mine, and I am, after all, the Marquess of Hallmere. It is to be hoped that he does not prove overzealous, though. He needs to remember that a fishing boat—I assume it *was* a fishing boat from which he witnessed this dastardly crime—would have been perfectly visible to me and, more to the point, to Albert. Why did he row away and offer no assistance? Was he afraid that I would murder him too?"

"You make light of the matter, Joshua," his aunt said in her plaintive whine. "But it may prove serious indeed. I could not bear to lose another son or a nephew who has always been as dear as a son to me. I might almost suggest that you leave now while you may, and disappear. At least you would be safe then."

"Ah, but I would hate myself if I were to take the coward's way out," Joshua said, grinning.

"And I would hate not to be mistress of Penhallow," Freyja said disdainfully as she got to her feet. "But this conversation grows more and more tedious. I am going riding, even if I must do so alone."

The Bedwyns all got to their feet too, and the others followed suit, except for the marchioness, who looked too ill and frail to move.

"Since Garnett is not to be confronted today, then," Joshua said, "we might as well enjoy the good weather. Shall we meet in the hall half an hour from now? The children and Prue too? Come, Aunt, you must not upset yourself further. I shall have a few harsh words for Garnett when I *do* see him for having so preyed upon your delicate sensibilities. Allow me to help you to your room." He offered her his arm and she had little choice but to take it.

"I hope you will talk to him, Joshua," she said, leaning heavily upon him. "I really cannot bear all this."

I T WAS QUICKLY APPARENT TO FREYJA THAT JOSHUA was very well liked both at Penhallow and in the village of Lydmere. The servants, she noticed at the house, had a habit of smiling brightly at him even whenever they served him or were in his line of vision. She could not help but make the comparison between them and the servants at Lindsey Hall, who would no more have dreamed of smiling at Wulfric than they would of breaking into song and dance in his presence.

In Lydmere the reaction was even more marked. He was recognized instantly as he rode along beside Freyja at the head of their party. Everywhere people were curtsying or bowing or tugging at their forelocks. That was not so remarkable in itself since he *was* the Marquess of Hallmere, but, in addition, every face was wreathed in smiles, and some of the bolder villagers even called out greetings. Predictably—oh, utterly so, she thought, half in exasperation, half in a grudging admiration—Joshua was down off his horse at the first opportunity and tossing the reins to Alleyne before shaking hands and clasping shoulders and even kissing a few withered female cheeks.

His face was alight with merriment and affection.

It was the moment at which Freyja realized fully what grave peril she was in. Every minute was revealing more and more of his humanity to her. This morning at breakfast he had been bold and forthright, a hint of ruthlessness behind his courtesy and his smile. She might have been able to resist that man. Now he was full of warmth and laughter and concern for the friendship of people Freyja did not normally consider worthy of notice—it was a strangely shameful realization. *This* man was altogether harder to resist. He was so very different from any other man of her class and acquaintance.

Of course, she might have been forewarned and have avoided all this. He *had* gone rushing to the rescue of a servant girl who had been frightened by a squirrel, had he not?

But he did not neglect the relatives and guests he had brought to the village for an outing. They stabled their horses at the village inn and went inside for tea or ale and muffins. They sat in the public taproom, and he proceeded to point out various details of the view from the window and to describe other attractions they might find of interest. Eve and Aidan did not stay long. They took the children back outside and down onto the beach Joshua had indicated—not as wide as the private beach of Penhallow on the other side of the river, but just as picturesque in its own way with its several jetties and numerous boats bobbing on the sea or stranded on the sand, the water being at half-tide. Chastity took Prue with them. Calvin invited Constance to stroll along the front street with him, and after a while Morgan and Alleyne went to explore the narrow, sloping streets and to look in the few shops the village offered.

Joshua introduced Freyja to Isaac Perrie, the innkeeper—a novel experience for her. He was a bald-headed, gap-toothed, florid-faced giant of a man.

"A fine lady you have found for yourself, lad," he said, pumping Joshua's hand, which looked lost in his huge paw. "And right glad we all will be in Lydmere here when you marry her and come home to Penhallow to stay."

He settled in for a chat, standing wide-legged before them, wiping his hands on his large apron. Freyja could not decide whether to feel amused or outraged but decided upon the former. Life with Joshua was never dull.

"And Hugh Garnett," Joshua was saying when she brought her attention back to the conversation. "He is doing well, I hear."

The innkeeper tutted and tossed his glance ceilingward. "Aye, well enough," he said. "On ill-gotten gains, no doubt. But live and let live is my motto, lad, as you well know."

"He seems not quite prepared to let *me* live, though,"

Joshua said with a chuckle. "In fact, he has been to my aunt recently claiming to have seen me kill my cousin five years ago."

"No!" Mr. Perrie stopped wiping his hands for a moment. "Is he daft?"

"He is from home," Joshua said, "and so I cannot pay him a social call yet. I daresay he has been wise enough to go to round up a few other witnesses. Any wagers on who they will be?"

"I am not daft enough to make any wager," the man said. "There would be no one to bet against me. Leave the matter in my hands, lad. You take your lady out to see the sights. An honor and a privilege to make your acquaintance, ma'am."

The fresh sea breeze caught at Freyja's hat as they stepped out of the inn, and she raised an arm to hold it in place.

"What was that all about?" she asked.

"Hugh Garnett," he explained, "attempted to set up a smuggling business here a number of years ago. There was nothing in that to get excited about—smuggling is big business all along the south coast of England. But his underlings were an imported gang of thugs, and they attempted to rule the trade with an iron fist. They were persuaded of their mistake and took themselves off to other parts."

"I take it," she said, "that you were one of the people who did the persuading. And that Isaac Perrie was another?"

He chuckled and took her elbow.

"There is someone I want you to meet," he said.

He took her to a pretty whitewashed cottage close to the harbor and knocked on the door. It was the home of Richard Allwright, the elderly carpenter who had trained and employed Joshua. He and his wife invited them in and insisted upon their drinking another cup of tea before Mrs. Allwright proudly displayed a small, beautifully carved wooden table that Joshua had made under her husband's tutelage and given her when he finished his apprenticeship.

"It is one of my treasures," she told Freyja.

"You had real talent, Josh," Freyja said, running her hand over the smooth surface of the wood and trying to picture him as he must have been in those days.

"*Have*, ma'am, not *had*," Mr. Allwright assured her. "Carpentry is a talent that does not die even when it is not practiced. And so now, lad, you are going to waste your time being a marquess instead of earning an honest living, are you?" But he laughed heartily and dug Joshua in the ribs with his elbow. "It is good to see you home. I never could understand why you felt you had to leave. You will like it here, ma'am."

"I believe I will," Freyja said, feeling, strangely, that she spoke the truth. Or that it would be the truth if she had any intention of staying. She had not expected to like Cornwall, but there was something about this particular part of it that grabbed at her heart.

"There is someone I want you to meet," Joshua said after they had left the carpenter's house.

"Again?" Freyja said.

He looked at her and grinned.

"This is not quite your idea of an exciting morning, I suppose," he said.

He was like a boy, exuberant with happiness. She tipped her head to one side and regarded him through eyes narrowed against the glare of the sun.

"Josh," she said, "why *did* you leave here?"

Some of the light went out of his eyes as they stood outside the door facing each other.

"Albert was dead and I was the heir," he said. "My aunt and uncle were devastated by grief and inclined to blame me, though murder was never mentioned. I blamed myself. I rowed beside him until he was within his depth, but I did not watch him all the way to shore. He got leg cramps and went under, I suppose. I could not stay here after that."

It did not sound sufficient reason to her. Surely his uncle would have wanted him to stay, to learn his future responsibilities. But it was none of her business.

"Whom did you want me to meet this time?" she asked.

He brightened, offered his arm, and climbed a steep hill with her until they reached another picturesque cottage with rosebushes climbing all over the front wall and a view down over the rooftops to the harbor. He knocked on the door.

The woman who opened it was young and personable. Her eyes lit up as soon as they looked on Joshua.

"Joshua!" she exclaimed, reaching out two slim hands to him. "Is it really you? Oh, it is. What a wonderful surprise."

Freyja guessed in some shock as Joshua presented her to Anne Jewell that this must be the governess who had borne his child. She was introduced as *Miss* Anne Jewell, yet she had a child, a little boy about five years old, who was blond and blue-eyed, with all the potential of being a lady-killer when he grew up. His mother had him make his bow to the Marquess of Hallmere and Lady Freyja Bedwyn before he ducked out of sight behind her skirts.

They did not go inside even though they were invited to do so. They all stood on the threshold for a few minutes, talking. Freyja fought outrage. It was true that she was not really betrothed to Joshua. Nevertheless, it showed poor taste on his part to bring her here.

"Now what have I done, sweetheart?" he asked as they made their way back down the hill in the direction of the harbor. She had not responded to any of his conversational overtures.

"Done?" she said in her frostiest, most quelling tones.

"You were not *jealous*, were you?" he asked, chuckling. "She is not nearly as gorgeous as you, Free."

She was truly angry then and wrenched her arm free of his.

"You might show more loyalty," she said. "She does, after all, mean more to you than I do. As she ought."

He stood still on the pavement and looked quizzically at her.

"Uh-oh," he said. "I perceive my aunt's malice at play here. And you fell for it, Free? Do you not know me better? She always did believe I was Anne Jewell's seducer and father of her son. I let her believe it. I have never cared for her good opinion."

Freyja felt horribly mortified then. For of course she *had* heard it from the marchioness and had not thought of questioning the essential truth of the accusation. How very foolish of her.

"You are *not* the boy's father?" she asked. "But he looks like you."

"And also like his mother," he said. "Did you notice that she has fair hair and blue eyes?"

"Do you *support* her and the child?" she asked. "That is what your aunt told me."

"Not entirely any longer." He smiled at her. "She takes in one or two pupils now, Free, and refuses to take any more from me than she absolutely needs, but the time was when she was not at all well accepted here. These people are kind but not always as tolerant as they might be. They are humans, not saints. She was destitute and had no family to go to."

Freyja drew in a slow breath and turned to walk on, her hands clasped behind her back. But *he* was beginning to look something like a saint, and she did not like it one bit. If she was to have any chance against him, she had to have *something* to despise.

"Let me guess," she said, wondering why the truth had not whacked her over the head long before now. "Albert?"

"Yes, Albert," he said. "And it was *not* with Anne's consent. She has altogether better taste than that."

They had reached the bottom of the hill and turned to stroll along the street that ran parallel to the beach. Becky and Davy were cavorting along the sands with a few other children while Eve and Aidan looked on. They all seemed to be shrieking and making merry. Prue was sitting up on the side of one of the beached fishing boats, swinging her legs and looking excited and happy while Chastity talked with an older woman and a young man hovered close to Prue as if to catch her should she fall. Constance and the Reverend Calvin Moore were at the far end of the street.

"Why did you not simply tell your uncle?" Freyja asked. "Ought he not to have known?"

"What would Bewcastle do," he asked her, "if he discovered that one of your brothers had impregnated your governess or Morgan's?"

"He would thrash the offender within an inch of his life," she said with conviction.

He laughed softly. "Ah, yes," he said, "I believe Bewcastle would. I also believe none of your brothers would put him in such a position. I cannot know how my uncle would have reacted, but I can guess. He would have gone to my aunt, and she would not only have dismissed the governess, but would also have driven her out of the neighborhood. Anne would have found herself destitute and with child and a vagrant to boot. She would have ended up in prison somewhere. Her son would have been fortunate to survive."

"And so you allowed the blame to be put upon you," she said.

"I have broad shoulders," he said, shrugging.

And probably very little money for the past five years—until he inherited the title, she thought. And yet through most of those years he had supported a child who was not his own.

"I find you rather stupid," she said scornfully. "Remarkably stupid, in fact. I am enormously relieved that we will never be married."

And she stuck her nose in the air and went striding off toward Eve and Aidan, trying to convince herself that she had just spoken the truest words she had ever uttered.

She hated him.

She really did.

How *dare* he be so foolishly noble!

How ridiculous all this was.

She wished fervently that she had not so impulsively decided to come here with him. She wished she were back at Lindsey Hall. She wished she had never gone to Bath. She wished she had never met the Marquess of Hallmere.

No, she did not.

"Sweetheart." He was coming along beside her, she realized. "You are doubly gorgeous when your temper is up. No, make that triply gorgeous."

She almost shamed herself by laughing. She lofted her nose into the air instead.

CHAPTER XVIII

CONSTANCE AND CHASTITY SAT DOWN WITH Joshua during the afternoon and helped him draw up a list of guests to invite to the ball. Despite the splendor of the ballroom at Penhallow, he could not remember its ever being used. As his aunt had pointed out at breakfast, there were not enough families close by of sufficiently high social status to merit an invitation.

"We will invite everyone," he explained. "I suppose the inhabitants have not changed a great deal in five years, but you must help me make sure I have forgotten no one."

"A real ball," Chastity said, her eyes shining, "in the splendid Penhallow ballroom. I am so glad you did not allow Mama to talk you out of it, Joshua." She flushed, apparently at her own disloyalty. "And I am *glad* you did not allow her to force you into marrying Constance."

Constance flushed pink too.

"Perhaps," he said, his eyes twinkling, "Constance likes

Cousin Calvin better." He had been right in his guess this morning, of course. His aunt was doing her best to promote a match between them.

"Oh, no, Joshua," Constance said gravely.

"Constance likes *Mr. Saunders* better," Chastity said.

"And you, Chass?" he asked. "Do you like Hugh Garnett?"

He had meant it as a teasing question, one over which they would all laugh. But she stared at him with stricken eyes, her face paling.

"I would not give my consent anyway," he told her hastily. "I am your guardian, remember?"

She smiled, her lips as pale as her face.

"You are Prue's guardian as well," she said. "Will you allow her to be cooped up in the nursery for the rest of her life, Joshua? Or sent to an asylum?"

"An asylum?" he said, frowning. "*That* has not been mentioned again, has it?"

When it had first became obvious that Prue was not as other children were, her mother had wanted her sent to an asylum for the insane. Fortunately it was one of the few matters over which Joshua's uncle had asserted his will, and Prue had stayed. Chastity had devoted most of her girlhood to being a companion to her sister. Joshua had helped, as had Constance to a lesser degree.

"If you come here to live and we have to remove to the dower house, Mama says she will have no choice but to send her away," Chastity said. "Her nerves would not be able to bear having Prue within her sight every day."

Joshua sighed. He had appointed a good and competent steward to look after his estate and had considered his duty to his new position done. But he was Chastity's guardian and Prue's too. Perhaps after all it was neglectful of him to have stayed away—and to be planning to leave again as soon as this business with Garnett had been cleared up. It was an admission he did not want to make.

"Prue will have a home at Penhallow as long as I am alive and marquess here," he said. "And the whole of the house will be hers to use as well as the nursery. Is Miss Palmer good for her?"

"Mama calls her an improper governess," Chastity said, "because she does not even try teaching Prue most of the things governesses usually teach. But she has taught Prue all sorts of things nevertheless, and she takes her outdoors, where Prue loves to be. Prue can tend the sorriest-looking plants and make them grow into a lovely garden. She is not insane, Joshua. She is just... different."

"You are preaching to the converted," he said, smiling at her. "You and she were with Mrs. Turner and Ben Turner down at the harbor this morning?"

"Mrs. Turner adores Prue," Chastity said. She hesitated. "And I believe Ben does too. Mama would have an apoplexy."

Joshua drew a slow breath. Devil take it, it looked as if he was going to have to stay awhile. His aunt was the mother of these girls, of course, and therefore their rightful guardian even if not their legal one. But he could see nothing but unhappiness all around him. Here were two young ladies—both in their twenties—who had not yet been given any chance of a life of their own. And Prue was now grown up—she was eighteen. They could no longer continue to think of her as a child, though he gathered that his aunt preferred not to think of her at all. She seemed incapable of thinking of anyone's happiness but her own.

He wished then that he had not come back after all.

Would the problems vanish, then, if he were not here to see them?

Could he so selfishly ignore his responsibilities?

"I'll speak with Miss Palmer," he said. "And we will talk another time of what is best for Prue. But now, to our list. We have ten names on it so far. I believe we need a few more if we are to outnumber the members of the orchestra."

Constance laughed.

"An orchestra?" Chastity asked, her eyes shining again. "Really, Joshua? How magical this ball is going to be."

Some time later Joshua made his way up the steep path behind the house, the sun warm on his body, though he knew it would feel cooler when he reached the top and was no longer sheltered from the wind. For the first time in seven months he really *felt* like the Marquess of Hallmere. He felt weighted down by responsibility. The really alarming thing, though, was that it did not feel like an oppressive weight. His cousins needed him here even if everything else could be managed by a steward, and he was fond of them. Now he had the power to do something positive to make their lives happier—and the power *not* to do so. He could go away and leave them to his aunt's care, or he could stay and assert his guardianship.

Strangely, he had spared scarcely a thought all afternoon for the murder charge that still hung over his head. It was difficult to take it seriously.

The path brought him up out of the valley, and, as expected, a gust of wind assaulted him. He looked back down toward the house and gardens, to the river and the bridge below them, to the village just visible beyond the headland on the other side of the valley. And he turned to look at the land swelling slightly to his left, rough with stone outcroppings and coarse grass and gorse bushes and wildflowers. The sheep of the home farm were dotted about the land, grazing. To his right the land sloped downward and leveled off into a neat patchwork of fields separated by stone walls and a few hedges. The main road came up out of the valley not far away and snaked its way between the fields and stretched ahead as far as the eye could see, on its way to Land's End.

His land. His farms. And the farms of his tenants.

A totally unexpected love for it all hit him like a low blow to the stomach. Good Lord, had he taken leave of his senses?

He shook his head and turned left to stride in the direction of the cliffs. The Bedwyns were an energetic lot, as he had discovered at Lindsey Hall. The ride into Lydmere during the morning and the romp on the beach had not been enough for them. They had come up here at his direction to see the view. He had promised to join them as soon as he had finished drawing up the guest list for the ball.

Soon he could see them in the distance. The children and Prue were dashing about, a safe distance from the cliff top. It looked as if they were chasing sheep—a favorite childhood pastime of his own. But the sheep—sensible creatures—showed no signs of real panic but merely bobbed off a safe distance just before they could be caught, and then returned to the serious business of grazing. Eve was sitting on a flat rock, her arms clasped about her knees while Aidan sprawled on the ground beside her. Morgan and Alleyne were strolling along the headland some distance away. There was no sign of Freyja.

Prue spotted him first and came lumbering toward him in her characteristic ungainly manner, her elbows clamped to her sides, her hands flapping in the air. She was laughing and excited, and he opened his arms and braced himself as she hurtled into them and took her usual death grip on his neck.

"Josh!" she cried. "Josh, Josh, Josh. I am having such

fun. I like Becky and I like Davy. I love Eve and I love you and—"

He released himself gently from her hold, set an arm about her shoulders, and hugged her to his side.

"You love everyone, Prue," he said. "You should save your breath and just tell me that you love everyone. Are you chasing sheep?"

"Ye-e-es." She laughed. "Eve said we could if we did not hurt them. Davy does not want to hurt them. Becky does not want to hurt them. *I* do not want to hurt them. I love sheep." She beamed up at him.

"Where is Freyja?" he asked.

"Looking at the sea," she said. "She likes it. She likes *me*. She let me hold her hand and pull her up the path."

Freyja had done *that*? he thought in some astonishment.

"I held her hand because she is lonely," Prue said. "I made her feel a bit better. *You* will make her all better, Josh."

Freyja lonely? Now that was a strange notion, but very possibly deadly accurate. Prue sometimes had unexpectedly sharp perceptions, which were quite unhampered by expectations that had been processed through thought and intellect. It was a novel thought, though. Freyja *lonely*?

"Joshua," Eve said as he came up to them, "this is all quite breathtakingly lovely. I am *so* glad we came here instead of going to the Lake District. After you are married to Freyja, we are going to be angling for invitations all the time. Are we not, Aidan?" Her eyes were dancing with laughter.

Aidan reached up with a blade of grass and tickled her behind the ear with it. She laughed out loud as she batted it away.

"I am going to have to teach you some manners, my lady," Aidan said, poker-faced.

Joshua felt a curious lurching sensation low in his abdomen. He tended to think of marriage as an outlet for passion, the sort of sexual passion one might find elsewhere without having to make a lifetime commitment. But here was an aspect of marriage that was altogether more enticing—strangely so, perhaps, when there was no overt sign of the passion that he guessed must flare when the two of them were alone and private together. They were relaxing together, laughing together—Aidan *was* laughing despite the deliberately severe expression—and teasing each other.

"Might I say," Aidan said as Prue skipped off to join the children in their play, "that your handling of that ridiculous situation at breakfast this morning quite won my admiration, Joshua? Bringing the whole thing out into the open as you did was clearly the very best thing to do."

"I learned early," Joshua said, "not to play my aunt's games her way."

"But what if that man—Garnett, is it?—should bring along more witnesses?" Eve asked. "Today is all so lovely and so peaceful that I keep having to remind myself that someone is trying to frame you for murder."

"I have no worries about it." Joshua smiled. "It is just a nuisance of a matter that needs to be cleared up once and for all. Where is Freyja?"

"She found a hollow back there to sit in," Aidan said, indicating the cliffs behind him with his thumb. "I do believe she is awestruck."

Joshua knew just the place she must have found. It was like a scoop of land hollowed out with a giant cup, its floor grassy, its three sides a mixture of rock and firm earth. On the fourth side the cliffs fell away beyond a grassy lip almost sheer to the beach and sea beneath. It was a place that was sheltered from most winds unless they were coming directly from the south.

She was sitting in the middle of the hollow, her legs stretched out before her, her arms braced on the grass behind her taking her weight. She had changed out of the smart riding habit and hat she had worn this morning. Now she was wearing a muslin dress and a warm-looking cloak. Her hair, predictably, was loose down her back.

"This was my childhood fortress," he said, standing on the rim of the hollow above her, "and my ship's mast and my eagle's aerie and my haven for all sorts of dreams."

She lifted her face to the sun as he came down to stand and then sit beside her.

"I have never been fond of the sea," she said. "It has always seemed too vast to me, too mysterious, too . . . powerful. One could never control the sea, could one?"

"And you like to feel in control of everything?" he asked her.

"I am a woman," she said. "Women have very little control over anything in their lives. We are not even persons by right, but the property of some man. We have to fight for every bit of control we can wield over our own destinies. I have four powerful brothers. I have had to fight harder than most. But I could not fight the sea."

"Neither could I, if it is any comfort," he said. "The sea is there to remind us all how little and how powerless we really are. That is not necessarily a bad thing. We do dreadful things with the power we do have. But you sounded when you first spoke as if perhaps you have forgiven the sea."

"It is exalting too," she said. "All that freedom and energy. I feel as if I am gazing into eternity. The beach below is private, is it not? It belongs to Penhallow."

"It does," he said. "I'll take you there one day. It is wide and golden when the tide is out and nonexistent when the tide is in. It can be dangerous. The tide comes in fast at the end and one can be cut off from the valley if one is not careful to be back there in time."

"And if one is not?" she asked. "One drowns?"

"Or one climbs the cliff," he said. "I used to do it sometimes just for the thrill of it, even when the tide was out. It looks sheer, but of course there are numerous foot- and handholds. It's dangerous, though. One slip and I would have been dashed to pieces on my way down and you would never have met me."

"I would have climbed too if I had lived here with you," she said, her teeth bared, the reckless light of a challenge in her eyes. "And I would have raced you to the top."

He chuckled. "We will never know, will we?" he said.

She pointed ahead, out into the sea. "What is that island?" she asked him. "Is it inhabited?"

"It was a smuggling haunt a long time ago," he said. "But no longer, as far as I know. It is wild and deserted."

"Have you ever been there?" she asked.

"I used to row over there once in a while," he told her. "Sometimes with friends, more often alone. I liked the solitude, the chance to think and dream without interruption."

"It must be difficult to get to," she said. "The water looks choppy about it, and there are steep cliffs rising straight from the sea."

"There are a few harbors," he said. "Are you afraid of the sea?"

"I am not afraid of anything," she said, lifting her chin into the air in that characteristically arrogant gesture of hers.

"Liar," he said. "You are afraid."

"Nonsense!" she said while he kept a wary eye on her

hands. But she kept them propped behind her. "Take me there. One day—tomorrow. Just you and me. Just the two of us."

He had not been on water in any small craft since that night. He had not even realized until this moment that he was reluctant to go back out. He gazed down at the sea where he and Albert had sat and argued until Albert had dived overboard and then refused to get back in. He turned his head and gazed at the point beyond the river where Albert had been standing chest-deep in water when he, Joshua, had deemed him safe and gone off around the next headland to clear his head and decide what his next move must be.

He closed his eyes, wishing that the memories would go away. All of them.

"I believe," Freyja said, "that *you* are the one who is afraid, Josh."

He turned his head to grin at her.

"Tomorrow?" he said. "Just the two of us? Are you willing to face such danger? And I am not referring to the boat ride."

She turned and looked at him, her eyebrows arched. She stared at him for long moments before answering, and he felt a distinct tightening in his groin.

"I am willing," she said at last. "But I do wish, Josh, that I could still see you now as I saw you when we were in Bath—as just a charming, shallow rake."

He grinned at her.

"But I am exactly those things, sweetheart," he said. "I just happen to have had an interesting childhood and to have got myself hopelessly entangled in a pile of nonsense before I left here. It has caught up to me now, it seems, and must be dealt with once and for all. But this is a minor hiccup in my frivolous life."

"I wish I could believe you," she said, sitting up and hugging her knees.

And he wished Prue had not suggested to him that Freyja was lonely. He wanted to think of her as strong and independent and contemptuous of all lesser mortals. Yet she had lost the man she had grown up to marry, and she had lost the man she had loved passionately. No, he had not really wanted to get to know Freyja Bedwyn any more than she had wanted to know him.

Their light flirtation in Bath had been so very enjoyable.

He grinned at her, and she continued to look haughtily back at him. But the usual light, flirtatious antagonism was no longer there between them. Something subtle had changed. He thought desperately of a way to lighten the atmosphere. But she foiled him by lifting one hand and setting her fingertips feather-light against his cheek. For a moment he had the absurd feeling that there was not enough air in the hollow to be drawn into his lungs. He lifted his hand to take hers, and turned his head to kiss her palm.

"Are you sure you do not want me to invite anyone else to join us on this island excursion?" he asked her.

"I am sure," she said. "No one else."

Lord! He was fit to explode. Much more of this and he would dive off the cliff to cool himself in the sea—except that the tide was out.

The devil of it was, Joshua thought as she leaned forward and set her lips against his, that he could no longer remember why their betrothal was fake, why they were going to have to end it sooner or later. There *was* a reason, was there not? Something about his not being ready to settle down? Something about her loving someone else?

But his thought processes were made sluggish by the

fact that they were embracing. Somehow he was lying on his back and she was half lying on top of him. They were kissing each other, not with wild passion, or even with lusty hunger, but with soft, almost lazy kisses that seemed far more dangerous to Joshua. He was holding her face cupped in both hands. Her hands were in his hair, her fingertips lightly stroking his head. Both of them had their eyes open.

Lord!

A passionate Freyja was a keg of powder exploding. A tender Freyja was far more deadly.

"Mmm," he said against her lips. "My memories of this hollow will forever be changed."

How long they would have continued to exchange soft kisses he did not know. Someone was clearing his throat above them.

"Lovely view, Morg, would you not agree?" Alleyne asked. "Though I would advise you to look outward rather than downward. You may get vertigo."

"I would advise you to find another lookout point," Joshua said as Freyja sat up and Morgan laughed. "This one is taken."

"Tut, tut," Alleyne said. "Such a gracious host. We are not wanted, Morg. But Davy has caught a sheep, I see, and is attempting to ride it. I had better go to the rescue."

"Of Davy or the sheep?" Morgan asked.

They disappeared.

"That excursion is going to be *very* dangerous, you know," Joshua said, lacing his fingers behind his head while Freyja pushed her hair back from her face and tucked it behind her ears before clasping her knees again.

"I know," she said.

"But you are not afraid?"

"No," she said. "Are you?"

"Mortally." He chuckled, though he was deadly serious. "I may not be able to keep my hands off you, sweetheart."

The sun came out behind her head as she turned it to look down at him, and converted the untamed waves of her hair to a golden halo all about her face. She looked strangely and suddenly beautiful to him.

"Perhaps I will not be able to keep *mine* off *you*," she said, looking steadily down at him.

The hollow felt airless again.

"It should be an interesting day," he said.

"Yes."

God help them, he thought, *now* what were they getting themselves into? Deep waters, no doubt, in more ways than one.

There had to be a reason why they were not going to marry. They had both been so adamant about it.

What the devil *was* the reason? He might be able to save himself if he could remember it.

"When I say my prayers tonight," he said, "I will offer one up for no rain."

He grinned at her.

CHAPTER XIX

FREYJA PRAYED FOR RAIN OR — BETTER YET — SNOW. Then she caught herself playing coward and petitioned the divine weather-maker for cloudless sunshine and midsummer temperatures instead.

Some time very early—it was not even light—she tossed back the bedcovers, crossed her room to the window, and looked out. There was not a cloud in the sky— which did not mean, of course, that it was going to be a lovely day. Often a bright start gave way to clouds and rain later. And a sunny day at this time of year often came with arctic temperatures. But the window was open, she realized, and she was not even shivering.

Whatever had possessed her? She *was* afraid of the sea. She was mortally afraid of being cast adrift on its surface in a small fishing boat. But she had demanded to be taken across to that alarmingly distant island. It was not *that* prospect that had disturbed her sleep, though. After all, she was Freyja Bedwyn, and it was in her nature to confront her fears head-on whenever a challenge presented itself.

Take me there. One day—tomorrow. Just you and me. Just the two of us.

Where had the words come from? Why not an excursion for all of them? It would surely be possible to hire more than one boat. There was safety in numbers.

Just you and me. Just the two of us.

She was in far deeper with Josh than she cared to admit. She had realized that during the night when she had caught herself during one wakeful spell trying to convince herself that she was not over Kit. But she *was*. She was beginning to use her old passion for him as a shield behind which to hide. Kit was happy with Lauren and she with him, and there was no longer any pang of grief or anger in the realization. That part of her life was over and done with.

But if she was over Kit, what was there to stop her from loving Josh?

She *dared* not love him. Even though he was not nearly as shallow a person as she had taken him for when they were in Bath, he nevertheless was not a man it would be wise to fall in love with. He did not intend making his home at Penhallow or anywhere else. He was eager to get back to his life of shiftless wandering. His *frivolous* life, as he had described it yesterday.

And yet yesterday she had not been sure she believed him....

Tomorrow—*today*—she was going to go over to the island with him. Just the two of them. And there could be no pretense of innocence.

Are you willing to face such danger? And I am not referring to the boat ride.

I am willing.

I may not be able to keep my hands off you, sweetheart.

Perhaps I will not be able to keep mine off you.

Freyja shivered after all in the predawn air and went back to bed, but she did little more than doze and wake until she could decently get up and venture from her room.

Early as she was, Joshua had already gone out to the home farm with his steward. Aidan and Alleyne had gone with him. Freyja remembered then that she had promised to spend the morning writing invitations to the ball with Morgan, Constance, and Chastity.

The guest list was a long one, she discovered, when she joined the others in the morning room after breakfast. She wondered if anyone within a five-mile radius of Penhallow had been omitted and realized how typical it was of Joshua to be so egalitarian despite his elevated rank. She tried to imagine Wulfric hosting such a ball and found herself smiling at the absurdity of the thought.

"Can you imagine Wulf with such a guest list, Morgan?" she asked as the four of them settled to their task.

"Or us attending such a ball?" Morgan said. "Wulfric is our brother the duke," she explained to the other two ladies. "He is extremely high in the instep."

"Joshua does not see this ball as an elegant social event for those of elevated rank," Constance said. "He sees it as a neighborhood celebration of his return home and his betrothal. And all these people were his friends—servants, laborers, villagers. He wishes to share his happiness and his good fortune with them. Will such a ball offend you?"

"I do believe," Morgan said, leaning forward across the table, "I am going to enjoy it immensely."

"If it will make Josh happy," Freyja said, "then it will make me happy too."

Gracious heavens, she sounded like a woman meekly in love.

Was she?

Constance looked up from the blank card she had drawn in front of her, her quill pen poised above the ink bottle. "I really believed when we were in Bath, you know, Freyja," she said, "and you helped Joshua foil Mama's plan to talk him into marrying me, that you would soon find some discreet way to put an end to your betrothal. I did not understand that it was *real*, even if the actual announcement was rushed forward. I am so glad it is. You are perfect for Joshua. You are bold and bright enough to challenge him. You will tame him without crushing his spirit, yet you will not allow him to subdue you—he would despise you or soon grow bored with you if you did."

Freyja was startled but had no chance to respond.

"Freyja!" Morgan exclaimed. "Was there more to your sudden betrothal in Bath than you told us? How provoking of you to keep it a secret from *me*. I thought we had no secrets. I shall have it all out of you later—be warned. But I do agree with Constance that Joshua is really quite perfect for you. I hope I will find someone as perfect for myself, though I am sure that will not happen in the foolish atmosphere of a London Season."

"But how wonderful it would be to experience one," Chastity said wistfully. "All those balls and routs and concerts. And *people*. I do envy you, Morgan."

They settled to writing for a while, having divided the list into four equal parts. It was altogether probable, Freyja thought, that many of the recipients of these invitations would not even be able to read them. Doubtless word would spread fast enough, though, and everyone would understand the meaning of the cards even without being able to decipher the writing on them.

She found that she really was looking forward to the ball. It was going to be amusing if nothing else. Life really *was* amusing with Joshua. Certainly it was never predictable.

She broke the silence after fifteen minutes or so, during which there had been nothing to hear but the scratching of four pens.

"Constance," she asked, "do you remember anything about the night your brother died?"

It was strangely easy to forget the reason why they had all come to Penhallow. Only when she saw the marchioness, silent and pale and pathetic—and darting venomous glances at Freyja when no one else was looking—did she remember that they were all waiting for the next development in a bizarre, possibly dangerous game.

"Nothing," Constance said. "It was stormy and got worse as the night went on. I did not even know Albert had not come home until the next morning."

"But you did know he had gone out?" Freyja asked.

"He went to Lydmere," Constance said. "He said he was going to talk to Joshua."

"About what?" Freyja asked.

"I-I do not know," Constance said, dipping her pen into the ink bottle again but not proceeding to write with it. "About Miss Jewell, I believe. She was Chastity's governess and had been turned off because ... Well, it does not matter. Joshua had found a cottage in the village for her and Mama was upset about it. Albert agreed to go and talk to him."

"The governess was with child?" Morgan asked, wide-eyed. "And your mama and your brother thought *Joshua* was responsible? I cannot believe it of him."

"Joshua was *not* the father," Chastity said fiercely. "No one *knows* who the father was. Miss Jewell would never say."

In the rather tense silence that followed, Constance

bent to her task again, and after a moment Morgan followed suit. Chastity was unable to write, Freyja noticed with narrowed gaze. Her hand was shaking. Perhaps she was fearing that her two guests were drawing the conclusion that if the father was not Josh, it must be her brother.

"Do *you* remember anything of that night?" Freyja asked.

Chastity shook her head. "Nothing," she said firmly. "But you must not think ill of Joshua, Freyja. I *know* he did nothing improper with Miss Jewell—he came to the house each week to visit *Prue*, not her. I know—I was always either with Miss Jewell myself whenever he was here or else with him and Prue. And I *know* he did not kill Albert or do anything to cause his death. It was an accident, that is all."

Freyja continued to watch her for a while before resuming her own task—she had four more invitations to write—and giving the girl a chance to recover enough to pick up her own pen.

She wondered if either sister had loved the brother. Certainly neither of them was prepared to suspect foul play in his death, though both had known that he went to the village that night to confront Joshua over the nasty situation concerning the governess. Chastity at least realized that it was her brother who had fathered the child.

Miss Anne Jewell was a sad figure, Freyja thought—somewhat accepted in the village now, though not really one of the villagers. A woman with an illegitimate child, with only a very little of the work with which she had once hoped to make a living, forced to accept at least partial support from a man who was in no way responsible for her. What the woman needed was independence and occupation and a restoration of all her pride. What she needed...

Miss Anne Jewell was none of her concern, she told herself firmly.

The task was finally completed and Constance gathered the folded invitations into a neat pile and took them away to be delivered. Chastity excused herself to go up to the nursery to see Prue.

"Freyja," Morgan said when they were alone together, "there is much here that is still unspoken and unresolved, is there not? As well as a murder charge still looming over Joshua's head. How very challenging and exciting it all is."

A typical Bedwyn reaction, Freyja thought.

"I almost envy you," Morgan said.

"Almost?" Freyja raised her eyebrows.

"Well, I love Joshua dearly," Morgan said, "and he is by far the most handsome man I have ever seen—including Alleyne. But I love him as a brother-in-law. I am going to have to find my own challenge and my own excitement—if there are any still out there somewhere."

It was on the tip of Freyja's tongue to tell her sister that her betrothal was not a real thing at all, but she did not say it. There were a few matters to resolve first, not least of which was the planned boat ride over to the island sometime today.

I may not be able to keep my hands off you, sweetheart.

Perhaps I will not be able to keep mine off you.

Her heart beat faster at the remembered words.

"You will find someone who is perfect for you one of these days," she said. "Everyone does."

Everyone except me.

The only perfect men she seemed to meet, Freyja thought ruefully, were unavailable for a permanent relationship.

FREYJA HAD BEEN ABLE TO SWIM FOR AS FAR BACK AS she could remember. She could jump into lakes from banks, from overhanging tree branches, from the sides of boats. She could swim on the surface or underwater, in a crawl or a backstroke or a simple float. She could hold her own in a fierce water fight. She could sail along in a small, leaky boat, lying, sitting, or standing. It had never occurred to her to be afraid of water.

Until, that was, she had seen the sea for the first time at the age of ten or so.

She had never been sure quite what it was about it that was so terrifying. Its vastness, perhaps. But she had never had to admit her terror, even to herself, until now. She had never before had any opportunity either to swim in or to sail upon the sea.

She was sitting on a narrow wooden seat in a narrow wooden boat, surrounded on all sides by water so close that she could trail her hand in it if she wished—she did not wish. She was very aware that only the thin planking of the boat beneath her feet separated her from unknown depths.

She was so ashamed and so contemptuous of her own terror that she lifted her chin at an arrogant angle as if to say that all this was a crashing bore and clasped her hands loosely in her lap rather than cling for dear life to the sides.

"Nervous?" Joshua asked with a grin.

He was hatless. He was rowing through water that undulated in the breeze and was choppy enough to show the occasional crest of white foam on the waves. He was, of course, looking quite irresistibly gorgeous. The wind was ruffling his blond hair and making it gleam. She tried to concentrate on his good looks, or, better yet, on his wicked, teasing grin. He *knew* she was terrified.

"Ha! Of a little water?" She tried not to notice that the island looked farther away now than when they had started or that the mainland seemed miles away.

"I was not talking about the water." He depressed one eyelid in that slow wink of his.

"Nonsense!" She pressed her lips together and he laughed.

He had explained at the luncheon table that he had promised her he would hire a boat and take her rowing for the afternoon. But before anyone could speak up with the suggestion that they make a party of it, he had added that the boat he had borrowed was very small, only big enough for two, and he was very sorry but he *was* a newly engaged man and needed *some* time alone with his betrothed.

He had smiled engagingly about the table and looked both roguish and charming. No one had uttered a single word of protest, not even Aidan, who might at that moment have chosen to act the part of elder brother since Wulf was not there to give his opinion on such a blatant indiscretion. But of course, she thought, they all believed she was betrothed to Josh. Perhaps they would not have been concerned even if they had known that the island was their destination.

Everyone else had proceeded to make plans of their own. The marchioness was to go visiting and informed Constance that she would accompany her—with the Reverend Calvin Moore. Chastity was to take everyone else down onto the beach. Morgan was going to take canvas and paints with her. Eve had made it clear that no one was even to *think* of going swimming.

Freyja turned her head and was surprised to find that it would still move on her neck. She could see them all there now on the sand, tiny figures looking enviably safe, some of them running, a few walking more sedately. Three of them, on the edge of the water, were waving. Prue and the children? Freyja lifted one hand and waved back.

She was suffocatingly aware that there were two blankets

folded in the bottom of the boat. She had noticed them as soon as Josh and the fisherman whose boat this was had handed her in. She had stepped on them, in fact. If she were to ask what their purpose was, he would tell her that they were there to be wrapped about them if the wind should feel too chilly, but his eyes would laugh at her as he said it.

She did not ask.

"If you wish, sweetheart," Joshua said, "we can turn back right now."

She regarded him haughtily. "I am not afraid," she told him. "Not of anything. Are you?"

But he merely smiled his slow smile at her.

She noticed how the muscles of his arms and thighs flexed as he rowed. If the boat should tip over, she thought, she would simply swim. So would he. He would not let her drown. And she would not let him drown. She felt herself relaxing as she always did when she had once confronted any fear that threatened to daunt her.

At the same time her breath quickened and the blood hummed through her veins. What would happen on the island? Would she let it happen? *Cause* it to happen? Prevent its happening? Or would the question not even arise? Would they simply enjoy an hour of walking about and admiring the views and then return to the safety of the mainland?

For a while she thought they were not going to be able to land at all. The cliffs seemed too high, the shore too rocky, the sea too rough. But Joshua rowed around to a narrow, sandy beach in a small inlet, and he jumped out and pulled the boat up out of the water. He leaned over the side and slung the blankets over one shoulder.

Well, that answered one question at least, she thought, watching him.

"We may want to sit down for a while," he said, grinning at her. "Unless you plan to sit *here* all afternoon."

She ignored his outstretched hand and climbed rather inelegantly over the side to the sand. He hauled the boat even higher before leading the way up over sand and loose pebbles and rough rocks to the land above. She scrambled after him.

The island was larger than she had thought. It stretched ahead in undulating dunes and depressions, a mixture of green, coarse grass, yellow sand, bare rocks, yellow gorse, and pink thrift. Seagulls were screaming overhead and from their perches on rocks and dunes. The air was crisp and salty. The sea was visible all around.

Joshua took her hand in his as they stood on a small promontory drinking in the elemental beauty of it all.

"It is strange," he said. "I had forgotten that there is much I loved about Cornwall."

"In such a place," she said, lifting her face to the breeze, "it is easy to believe in God and eternity without the interference of any religion."

"You had better not let the Reverend Calvin Moore hear you say that," he said. But there was a warmth in his voice, a tenderness that caught at her breathing again and alarmed her.

"Did I give you permission to hold my hand?" she asked.

He chuckled softly and raised their clasped hands to bring the back of hers against his lips.

"Too late for that, sweetheart," he said. "You invited me here, remember? Just the two of us? There is another cove on the eastern side. It will be more sheltered from the wind than the rest of the island. Shall we go and sit there for a while?"

"Of course," she said, her knees feeling decidedly wobbly. What were they *doing*? After this business with Garnett was cleared up and presumably once the ball was over, they were to leave Penhallow and go their separate ways. They would never see each other again. Was she quite sure she wanted this memory? But she realized even as she asked herself the question that really she had no choice now. Whatever happened—or did not happen—this afternoon would be forever seared on her memory.

Would she find Josh as difficult—or as easy—to get over as she had found Kit? She had never lain with Kit.

She stood gazing out at the endless expanse of blue-and-green water as he spread one blanket over the coarse grass above the little cove of a beach to which he had led her. It was indeed more sheltered here. One could almost imagine that it was summer again—a cool summer's day. He set down the other blanket, still folded. Presumably they would cover themselves with it if they were chilly.

Afterward.

She drew a slow breath. It was not too late. He would not force her.

The last time it had been easy. There had been no decision to make. She had been in the throes of an urgent, blind passion occasioned by the pain of the christening party and something he had said to anger her—she could no longer remember what. Today there was too much time for thought.

But one thought pulsed with the beat of her blood. She wanted him. She wanted the memory to take with her into the future. She could no longer think of protecting herself from the sort of pain she had known before with Kit. It was already too late.

She had no wisdom at all, it seemed, in her choice of men to love.

She sat down on the blanket, drew up her knees, and clasped her arms about them, all without looking at him.

He came down beside her, sprawled on his side, his head propped on one hand.

"So, sweetheart," he said softly, "why are we here?"

She shrugged her shoulders and kept them hunched. "To see the island?" she said. "To spend some time together?"

"For what end?" he asked her. "Because we are betrothed?"

"But we are not," she said.

"No." He was silent for a while. "Why are we here, Free?"

He was going to make her spell it out, was he? Well, that was fair enough. She had asked to be brought here. She had asked that they come alone. Was she now to act like a wilting violet and expect the *man* to take charge of the situation? She turned her head to look at him. His eyes were smiling back at her but without either the mockery or the wicked laughter she had expected to see there.

"To make love," she said.

They gazed at each other while the air fairly crackled between them.

"Ah, yes," he said, his voice low. "To make love. We will do it properly, will we, sweetheart, without frenzy, without any haste at all? So that we will both have happy memories of our brief weeks together?"

He sat up and pulled off his Hessian boots and his stockings. He shrugged out of his coat and unbuttoned his waistcoat. Freyja lifted her arms and drew the pins out of her hair. By the time she shook it free, he was pulling his shirt off over his head.

She had hardly had a chance to look at him in the gamekeeper's hut at Alvesley. But his beauty, she discovered now, was not confined to his face. His shoulders, his chest, his arms—all were strongly muscled, beautifully proportioned male perfection. She set one hand on his back and spread her fingers. He was warm and inviting.

"I have wanted this," she admitted, "ever since the last time."

"Can you not do better than that?" he asked her, turning to her, smiling. "I have wanted this since *before* the last time. I believe it all started in a certain inn room when you were barefoot and wild-haired and furious." He moved his head closer until his lips brushed hers. "You must be by far the most desirable woman I have ever known, Freyja Bedwyn." His tongue stroked lightly back and forth across her lips, causing her to sizzle with sensation from her lips down to her toes.

He unclothed her with hands that were clearly very expert indeed at the task. Then he removed the rest of his own garments while his eyes devoured her and hers devoured him. She lay back on the blanket when they were both naked.

She was afraid then that if she touched him, if she initiated anything, she would spoil it all by being in too much of a hurry, as she had been last time. She wanted to discover if there could be any tenderness to lovemaking as well as soaring passion. She wanted to be able to remember him with tenderness. She wanted to remember him as he looked now, gazing down at her with controlled desire. She spread her hands to the sides, palms down.

"Make love to me," she said.

"Oh, I intend to, sweetheart," he said, bending over her.

His hands went to work on her. He was as expert at making love with his hands, she soon realized, as he had been at unclothing her with them. He knew just where to touch her and how, sometimes with such light fingertips that she felt sensation more than his touch. And he knew how to use his mouth too, kissing her pulse points, suckling her breasts, breathing warmly against her navel and flicking it lightly with his tongue, feathering kisses along her inner thighs, sucking one of her big toes before raising his head and grinning at her.

He took her feet in his hands, massaged them in ways that sent desire coursing through her with a faster beat, and then turned them and moved them upward in such a way that her knees fell open before he set her feet back down on the blanket. He came to kneel between her thighs, lifting her legs over his own. And then he slid one hand down between them.

She was wet and hot—his hand felt cool in contrast.

He knew just how to touch her *there* too. His fingers moved lightly, knowingly, and he watched what he did while she watched his face—beautiful, heavy-lidded, absorbed in what he was doing. And then he touched her somewhere with his thumb, rubbing it very lightly. She arched upward, crying out, all her carefully preserved control gone, and exploded into shuddering, utterly pleasurable release.

He laughed softly as he lifted her higher into his lap, opened her with his thumbs, and plunged hard into her. She inhaled slowly. There was no pain at all this time, only incredible pleasure as he pressed against walls still throbbing and sensitive from her recent release. She moved her hands to cup his knees.

"I think it is time I made love to you too," she said, gazing at him through half-closed eyelids. "You feel very good, Josh."

"I do indeed." There was laughter in his eyes, but they were passion-heavy too.

Slowly she clenched inner muscles about him and his nostrils flared.

"Almost," he said, "you tempt me to surrender. *Almost*."

He withdrew to the brink of her and thrust hard inward

again and withdrew and thrust again while she parried with pulsing inner muscles and rocking hips. She bared her teeth, feeling the rise of desire once more, and willed herself to match him stroke for stroke for as long as it lasted. She willed it to last forever.

This time it was he who watched her face while she watched what they did together, her eyes observing what her body felt with such sweet, almost painful intensity. It was all almost unbearably erotic.

"Sweetheart," he said at last, his voice husky and breathless, "a gentleman cannot go riding off into the sunset and leave his lady behind. If I concede defeat, will you let go and allow me to follow you?"

She looked up into his eyes, lost her rhythm, her slender hold on control, and was suddenly defenseless against the firm pounding of his body into her sweet pain. She cried out again and shuddered about him.

He was still deep inside her, she realized a few moments later, and still large and rock-hard. She opened her eyes and he smiled into them. He brought his hands to the blanket on either side of her shoulders and shifted his position without withdrawing from her. He came down flat on top of her, covering her from shoulders to toes, his weight bearing her into the ground. He found her mouth with his and kissed her, not deeply, not passionately as she expected, but with infinite tenderness.

And then he set his head beside hers, his face buried in her hair, and moved in her again with long, deep strokes, covering her so that she felt strangely cherished, strangely loved. Sexually sated as she was, it was an extraordinary sensation, emotional more than physical—and yet she was very much in the body too. When he went still, he was tense for a moment and then relaxed all his weight onto her with a deep sigh. She could feel the hot flow of his release deep inside. She wrapped her arms about him, feeling both giver and gifted.

His breathing was labored against her ear. They were both hot and slick with perspiration. Seagulls were crying overhead. There was the eternal, elemental flow and suck of the sea against the sand. There were the smells of salt and sand and ocean. There were sunlight and sun heat and the welcome coolness of the breeze.

The earth slowed beneath them.

Ah, yes, the memory of this would always remain with her. And she would not allow future pain to sully it. She *would* not.

He reached for the spare blanket as he rolled off her, and she turned onto her side facing away from him as he spread it over them and then slid an arm beneath her neck and curled in behind her.

She gazed at the rocky cliff that formed one side of the cove and at the dark green water beneath it. A white gull was perched on top of a rock, gazing out to sea, opening its beak to cry out. She felt warm, languorous, very aware of every sensation impressing itself upon her memory.

Judging from his breathing, Joshua slept for a while. She was glad. She did not want to talk. Not yet. She did not want to listen to his light teasing or to hear him tell her that they were in a scrape again.

She did not want either to laugh or to fear. She simply wanted to *be* in this endlessly present moment. And when she must move on into the future—well, then. She would *never* forget. She would never allow herself to deny that for one glorious afternoon she had been not just in love. She had also *loved*. Loved with her body and loved with her heart.

Fool, Fool, fool, a faint inner voice tried to tell her. But she drifted off to sleep rather than listen to the voice warn her that she would live to regret this day and this falling over a precipice into love itself.

CHAPTER XX

R EMIND ME, SWEETHEART," JOSHUA SAID, HIS EYES squinting against the glare of sunlight on the water, "why it is we are not going to marry."

She was sitting across from him in the boat, her narrowed gaze on the shoreline, her expression uncommunicative. Since making love for a second time and dressing and returning to the boat, they had exchanged scarcely a word.

She transferred her gaze to his face.

"Don't you dare feel obliged to act the gentleman and offer for me," she said, sounding genuinely angry. "What happened was my fault. It was not done to trap you into marriage."

"Fault?" He grinned at her. "Yours again? I am beginning to feel like a puppet on a string."

"Which is exactly how I felt at the beginning of our acquaintance," she said. "Now we are even."

"Marriage with me would be a trap, would it?" he asked her.

"Of course it would," she said impatiently. "We have been aware of it and wary of it from the start. It would be a horrible mistake for both of us."

He was no longer sure why. She could not mourn her lost love forever, could she? But then he would hate to be married to a woman who felt even leftover traces of such a mourning.

"Why has this afternoon happened, then?" he asked her. "We do not have the excuse of having been swept away by passion, do we? This was planned quite deliberately yesterday—by both of us."

She did not answer him immediately. She stared out over the sea again.

"I am Lady Freyja Bedwyn," she said. "I am the daughter and sister of a duke. Though I have always been known as bold and unconventional and occasionally even rebellious, I am expected to behave in all essential ways with the strictest propriety—both in public and in private. Gentlemen have no such restrictions on their private behavior. All my brothers have had mistresses or casual amours. Wulf has had the same mistress for years without any breath of scandal touching his name. I choose not to marry—not yet, at least, and not unless I meet someone for whom I would willingly sacrifice my freedom. But I am five and twenty and I have all a woman's needs."

"You have used me, then, sweetheart," he asked her, "as a . . . casual amour?"

"Don't be absurd," she said, looking at him again with cold disdain. "You can be remarkably tedious at times, Josh. Change places with me. I want to row."

He grinned at her. "We are not on a lake," he said. "Rowing on the sea takes far more strength and skill.

Besides, you would have to get up from your place and maneuver around me in order to get here. I daresay the boat would rock abominably."

"If you fall overboard," she said, "I will stop the boat and rescue you."

One had to admire the woman. All the way across to the island earlier he had been aware of her terror though she had given no outward sign of it. Yet now she was willing to move around in the boat, somehow shift places with him, and then row them back to the harbor? He could almost smell fear in her arrogant, nonchalant stance.

"That is reassuring, at least," he said, securing the oars and getting to his feet, holding to the sides as he did so. The boat rocked from side to side. "I will do the same for you, Free, though I seem to recall that you can swim like a fish. I only just beat you in our race at Lindsey Hall."

He thought she was going to change her mind when she did not immediately move, but as he approached her she stood up—straight, without clinging to the sides. She held herself upright and balanced as the boat swayed and as he squeezed past her and sat down where she had been sitting. He watched appreciatively as she moved along the boat, keeping perfect balance, before turning and sitting and taking the oars in her hands. Her chin was up, as he had expected, and she was viewing the world along the length of her nose.

She had accused him of wearing a mask, of hiding either his real self or nothing at all behind it. She was no different. Behind the cool, haughty, bold front she displayed to the world was a woman who had been hurt, a woman who was lonely—yes, Prue had been quite right about that—a woman who was perhaps afraid to love again.

He might have guessed that she would row the boat like an expert. She did not expend energy by digging the oars deep and trying to displace the whole ocean with every stroke. They were soon moving along at a steady clip.

So she had not changed her mind about marrying, had she? It was a shame really, as he was beginning to change *his* mind about marrying *her*. Actually, the thought of saying good-bye to her—probably quite soon now—was one his mind shied away from. His life was going to seem very empty indeed without Freyja in it. And now to top everything off he was going to have the memories of this afternoon to live with.

For all her boldness and passion, she was really still a sexual innocent. She probably did not recognize the difference between having sex and making love. They had been making love this afternoon—or at least, he had been even though he had been careful not to utter one word of love.

She had wanted him only for the experience, for the satisfying of her feminine sexual hunger.

It was a humbling thought.

He chuckled.

"I should be wielding a whip in my right hand," he said, laying his arms along the sides of the boat. "This scene would look far more impressive from the harbor if I were."

There were indeed several villagers standing still on the front road or down on the sand among the boats, all watching in curiosity as the Marquess of Hallmere's betrothed rowed him to shore.

Joshua jumped out when they were in shallow water, risking his valet's wrath when he saw his Hessian boots. He dragged the boat up onto dry sand and lifted Freyja out even as Ben Turner came running to haul the boat higher. Someone up on the road whistled shrilly, and there was a burst of good-natured laughter.

"Ah, Ben," Joshua said, "just the man I want to talk to."

Ben looked warily at him and reached into the boat to take out the blankets.

"I understand," Joshua said, "that your mother has been kind to Lady Prudence. She is at your cottage door, I see. Shall we go up?"

He took Freyja by the elbow and indicated one of the cottages on the front road above the harbor. Mrs. Turner was standing in the doorway, her arms crossed over her bosom. She watched them approach before bobbing a curtsy. Ben trailed along behind.

"If he was making you row that boat, my lady," she said, chuckling, "I would give him his marching orders if I was you. Or lay down the law as it is going to be for the rest of your life."

"But she insisted," Joshua protested. "How was a gentleman to say no?"

Freyja, he realized, found this all very strange—this way he had of fraternizing with ordinary folk and their way of being at ease with him. But he had been one of them just five years ago. She stood silently beside him.

"I have heard of all your kindnesses to Lady Prudence," he said to Mrs. Turner.

He had had a lengthy talk with Miss Palmer during the morning while Prue was out walking with Eve and the children. Prue was very much confined to the nursery at the house. Miss Palmer took her out as much as she could. More often than not they walked into the village or took the gig if it was available. Prue had developed a deep attachment to the Turners, who treated her with warm affection. Indeed, Mrs. Turner often suggested that Miss Palmer leave her there for an hour or two and have some time to herself—she often called upon Miss Jewell, she had explained.

Mrs. Turner looked instantly wary.

"She is a sweet child," she said, "and not an imbecile, even though her mother seems to believe she is, begging your pardon, my lord. I know she is *Lady Prudence*, and therefore I ought not to encourage her to set foot over my doorstep, but *someone* has to love her, and Miss Palmer is not always enough."

"I am not here to scold you," Joshua said, clasping his hands behind his back.

"I would think not," she said. "She loves this house. She has her own apron behind the door, and the first thing she does is reach for it and put it on. She sweeps the floors and shakes the mats and washes the dishes and pegs out washing and makes me and Ben tea and is learning how to cook. She even does some mending when she sits down. She brings sunshine into this house."

Joshua looked at Ben, who flushed and dipped his head and worried at a stone buried in the road with the toe of his boot.

"She does that," he said. "And she is not a little girl no longer neither." He looked up into Joshua's face with something like defiance in his own. "She is a woman grown."

Miss Palmer had voiced a concern over the number of times Prue declared that she loved Ben Turner. She said it of everyone, of course, and meant it of everyone. But there was a way she had of saying it with regard to Ben, Miss Palmer had said, that she could not quite explain in words.

"You love her, do you, Ben?" Joshua asked quietly.

Ben's flush deepened, but he did not look away. "It is not my place to love Prue—Lady Prudence," he said. "You need not worry about me, *my lord*. I will not forget my place."

His title was spoken with slight emphasis and some bitterness, Joshua noticed. He sighed.

"No, I did not expect you would, Ben," he said. "I wanted to thank you for befriending her. I *do* love her, you see."

"I have never left her and Ben alone together," Mrs. Turner said. "Nor ever would. I know better than that, though I know Ben wouldn't never forget himself."

Joshua smiled at them both, nodded genially, and offered Freyja his arm. They walked back in the direction of the inn, where they had stabled their horses.

"Strangely," he said, "I had never considered the problem of Prue's growing up. Because she will always be a child in many ways, I suppose I had expected that she would remain a child in every way."

"It is a mistake often made of women in general," she said, "the assumption that they do not have needs to match those of men. Prue is not a child, is she? She is a woman. And Ben Turner has seen that. Probably she has *seen* that he has seen, and the attraction of the cottage is more him than his mother. What will the marchioness do if she discovers the truth?"

"She will try sending Prue to an asylum," he said, "where she will be locked up and chained and beaten and put on public display and treated like an animal."

She looked sharply at him. "Even *she* could not be so cruel," she said.

"She would have done it when Prue was a child," he said, "if my uncle for once in his life had not exerted himself. She is talking of doing it now if she is forced by my return to remove to the dower house with her daughters."

Freyja inhaled audibly. "If I do not take my fists to that woman's face before I leave here," she said, "I will be a candidate for sainthood—and I believe that would be a dreadful fate. What are *you* going to do about it? You are Prue's guardian, are you not?"

"Until I am convicted of murder, yes," he said. "What *ought* I to do, Freyja? Encourage her to marry a fisherman?"

He smiled at the look on her face. Such a prospect must be beyond the wildest imaginings of any member of the proud Bedwyn family. Except that he had learned since going to Lindsey Hall that Aidan had married the daughter of a Welsh coal miner and that Rannulf had married the daughter of an obscure country parson and granddaughter of a London actress. Yet Eve and Judith were as well accepted by the rest of the family as if they had been duchesses.

"Perhaps," she said, "Prue is capable of making her own choices in life. Josh, she held my hand yesterday afternoon when we were climbing up the hill behind the house. It was not because she needed my help but because she believed I needed hers."

"You froze me in my tracks when I once made that mistake," he said. "Though we were about to go down rather than up, I remember."

"I know," she said. "But I was *touched*. I know what you meant when you told me she is full of love and brimming over with it. And so innocent that one fears for her. Perhaps we ought not to fear for such people but for ourselves whose experience has taught us not to trust one another or life itself."

He looked at her in some astonishment. Her voice had lost all its customary hauteur. It was almost shaking with emotion. All because Prue, thinking her lonely, had taken her hand?

"I should talk to her, then?" he asked. "Will you come with me?"

She looked more herself then. "Eve would be a far better choice," she said. "But, yes, I will come. Josh, whatever am I *doing* here at Penhallow? Why am I not still in Bath, promenading in the Pump Room every morning and taking tea in the Assembly Rooms?"

"I believe, sweetheart," he said, "you perceived a rogue and could not resist brightening up your life for a spell by taking on the challenge of trying to keep pace with him. Besides, it is better for you to be here with me than expiring of boredom there, is it not?"

"A rogue," she said as they turned into the cobbled stableyard of the inn and an ostler hastened to lead out their horses. "Is that what you are, Josh? Life was so simple when I had no doubt about the answer."

He turned his head and winked at her.

THE FOLLOWING MORNING WAS CLOUDY, WINDY, AND altogether rather dreary. Joshua had gone out early again with his steward and Aidan. The marchioness had asked Constance to run an errand for her in the village and at the last moment had suggested that the Reverend Calvin Moore accompany her. Alleyne, perhaps seeing the tight look on Constance's face, had asked Chastity if she would like to go too, and the four of them had departed together, the marchioness's dagger glances piercing Alleyne's back.

She was a tedious enemy, Freyja concluded. Very different from Freyja herself or any of the Bedwyns for that matter, she did not simply burst out with open hostility and fight fairly. She had set something in motion, and she was prepared to wait for it to come to fruition. In the meanwhile, she acted the gracious, wilting hostess to everyone. Her gentle smile seemed to have been painted on her face.

Freyja had found refuge in the morning room. She was writing a letter to her solicitor while Morgan, beside her at the table, wrote to Judith.

"This waiting around for something to happen is very

strange, is it not?" Morgan said abruptly after a while. "I expected fireworks as soon as we arrived at Penhallow. I expected excitement and danger and flashing swords and smoking pistols for the first day or two and then the satisfaction of victory."

"Are you disappointed?" Freyja smiled at her.

"Disappointed? No." Morgan frowned. "But a little uneasy, I must confess. The marchioness really does hate Joshua, does she not? And all of us too even though she persists in informing us how delighted she is to have us all here. Why does she hate him so much that she is prepared to put his life in danger?"

"She blames him for her son's death," Freyja said. "She thought him guilty in the sordid business over the governess, and then when her son went to confront him, he died. In a sense, perhaps, one can hardly blame her for wondering if the accident really *was* an accident."

"I suppose," Morgan said, "it was the son who seduced the governess."

"Yes," Freyja said.

"I do not believe I would have liked him," Morgan said. "Indeed, I am quite certain I would have detested him quite as much as I do his mother. How horrid of him to have allowed Joshua to shoulder the blame—and to find a home for that poor lady. But what worries *me*, Freyja, is that witness. How provoking that he is not at home and so cannot be confronted. Alone he is surely no threat at all, but what if he can persuade several other men to corroborate his story? Does Joshua understand the danger he is in? Is he *doing* anything about it?"

"He is indeed," a voice said from the doorway, and they both turned to see Joshua himself standing there. He was still dressed for riding. His face was ruddy from the outdoors, his eyes dancing with laughter.

He liked living on the edge of danger, Freyja thought.

Independent of thought, her body was instantly aware of him, of his virile grace and beauty. She had wanted yesterday to happen so that she would have happy memories to cling to. She had been a fool. How would she live without *that*? How would she live without *him*?

"What, then?" Morgan asked.

"Why spoil the fun by telling?" he said, laughing as he came into the room. "Garnett is still from home, but I have hopes that he will return in time for the ball. Indeed, I am depending upon his having heard of it and upon his having a proper sense of drama. I have sent him an invitation."

"I know," Morgan said. "I *wrote* it. But why?"

But he would only laugh again. "Let me say only," he said, "that if Garnett comes, the ball will be an occasion after the Bedwyns' own heart."

Morgan's eyes shone. "Oh, you *do* have something planned," she said. "Well done."

He reached out a hand and squeezed her shoulder while turning his attention to Freyja.

"I am going down to the river walk with Prue," he said. "Will you come, Freyja?"

"I have to finish this letter to Judith," Morgan said when Freyja looked at her, "and then I must write to Aunt Rochester. I have not done so in ages, but she is to sponsor my come-out in the spring, perish the thought."

Freyja changed into a wool dress and a warm pelisse. She even, after looking out the window to note that the weather had not changed, drew on a bonnet that would cover her ears. Prue too was dressed warmly, in sunshine yellow from head to toe. She was beaming and clearly excited at the prospect of an outing with Josh and Freyja.

They scrambled down over the sloping lawn to the valley without using the more gradual slope of the winding driveway past the dower house. Prue was laughing aloud as she hurtled down the last few feet into Joshua's waiting arms. Freyja glared at him when he would have offered similar assistance to her, and he grinned and turned away.

They walked along the private path that ran beside the river to the beach. They did not go all the way to the beach, though. They stopped frequently to peer into the water, watching the slow currents eddying past stones and small sandbars, seeing the occasional tadpole dart by. Joshua picked up a stone and hurled it in a high arc to hit the opposite bank, some distance away, and Prue laughed and clapped her hands with delight. Freyja, not to be out-done, picked up a flat stone and threw it in such a way that it skimmed the surface of the water, bouncing four times before it sank out of sight. Prue jumped up and down in her excitement.

"I want to do that," she said, and Freyja spent the next ten minutes or so showing her how to select a suitable pebble and how to throw it sideways with just the right flick of the wrist. Prue never did get it right, but she derived a great deal of merriment from trying and collapsed down onto a large rock with uncontrollable mirth when Joshua could not do it either.

Freyja, with a sharp, narrow-eyed look at his abjectly meek face, was convinced that he could make his stones bounce *ten* times if he so chose.

She could not understand the almost painful love she felt for Prue. She was usually embarrassed by what she had always thought of as handicaps. If she had known about Prue in advance, she would have been horrified and would have shied away from her. Even so, she had kept her wary distance for a few days, content to let Eve and Joshua and Chastity converse with the girl.

But there was no guile in her and no stupidity or dullness or negativity. She was a sunny-natured child who simply did not possess whatever it was in most of the rest of mortality that enabled them to move away from the innocent exuberance and loving trust of childhood to a darker place they labeled maturity. Although Prue's sometimes ungainly movements and round, childish face were an outward sign that she was not as other young women were, she nevertheless was a rather pretty young lady.

She was the same age as Morgan.

Joshua looked down at her with a smile of warm affection until she had stopped rocking with laughter.

"Do you like going to the village, Prue?" he asked.

"Ye-es," she said. "I love it."

"What is your favorite part of it?" he asked her. "Your favorite place?"

Prue gazed with bright eyes across the river in the direction of Lydmere.

"The cottage," she said.

"Mrs. Turner's?"

"Yes."

"Why do you like it?" He went down on his haunches before her, selected a few pebbles, and rolled them in one hand.

"I can do things," Prue said. "I can help. It is a dear place."

"But small," Joshua said. "You would not like to live there, would you?"

Prue thought with furrowed brow and then smiled again. "Yes, I would," she said. "I know how to do things."

"You love Mrs. Turner?" Joshua asked.

"Yes." Her smile widened. "And Ben. I *love* Ben."

"Do you?" He turned and flung one of the stones. He obviously forgot that bouncing them was a skill he could not master—it bounced five times. Prue laughed excitedly and pointed. "Why do you love him, Prue? Is he kind to you?"

"Ye-es," Prue said. "He likes me making his tea, and he ate my cake, not Mrs. Turner's. Ben loves me."

"I love you, Prue," Joshua said. "*Freyja* loves you."

"Yes." She looked up at Freyja and beamed. "Josh made you better, Freyja. I saw you in the boat. You went to the island."

Oh, dear. Freyja smiled back and avoided Joshua's eyes.

Prue looked back to Joshua. "Ben kissed me," she said.

His face visibly blanched. "*Kissed* you?"

Prue laughed with delight. "On my birthday," she said. "I was eighteen. Mrs. Turner gave me my apron and she kissed me. And Ben poured my tea—we all laughed—and he kissed me. Here," she added, poking one forefinger at her cheek close to her mouth. "I said, 'I love you, Ben,' and he said, 'I love you, Prue.'" She laughed with delight.

"Prue," Freyja asked, taking the girl by the hand and drawing her to her feet so that they could stroll onward, "do you love Ben in a special way? As Eve loves Aidan?"

"As you love Josh?" Prue laughed. "Ye-es."

Joshua fell into step beside them on Prue's other side.

"Ben has nice hands," Prue said. "They are big. He works with them. He wouldn't hurt me with them, though."

"Of course he would not," Joshua said, drawing her arm through his and patting her hand. "No one will ever hurt you, Prue. Do you know what marriage is? Do you know what married people do together?"

"Ye-es," Prue said. "They look after each other. And they kiss each other. And have babies."

Joshua darted a startled look across her at Freyja.

"Miss Palmer told me," Prue said, "and Chastity. Chastity

took me to see Miss Jewell and *she* told me. Miss Jewell has David. I love David."

"Her son?" Joshua said. "He is a handsome little boy."

"Miss Jewell said there are bad kisses and I must not let anyone give them to me ever again," Prue said. "Ben would not give me bad kisses. Ben loves me. I love Ben."

The women in her life—all except her mother who was most qualified to do it—had been educating Prue in the dangers of her own sexuality, Freyja thought. They clearly had realized that in some ways at least the girl was no longer a child.

"If you lived at the cottage all the time," Joshua said, "you would not have all of Penhallow for your home, Prue. You would sleep there and live there, and the work you do there now would have to be done every day. Lady Prudence Moore should live in a big house, should she not, with servants to look after her and grand clothes to wear all the time?"

"I would like to live in the cottage, Josh," she said. "I would like to live with Mrs. Turner. I would like to live with Ben best of all. I love Ben. He kissed me and it was not a bad kiss. He would not give me bad kisses. He would not hurt me with his hands."

He raised her hand to his lips and held it there for a few moments.

"No, he would not, my sweetest love," he said. "I knew Ben when he was a lad. He would not hurt you or any other woman. And if he ever kisses you again, it will be with good kisses. If he touches you, it will be with gentle hands."

Freyja was startled to notice that his eyes were bright with tears.

"Shall I talk with Ben and Mrs. Turner, then?" he asked Prue. "Would you really choose to live with them if you could?"

She stopped walking, snatched her arm away from Joshua, clasped her hands to her bosom, and regarded first him and then Freyja with wide, excited eyes.

"Miss Palmer said Mama would say no," she said, "and *you* would say no. Mrs. Turner said Mama would say no and you would say no. I asked and she said that. Ben cried and went out."

"But you are a woman, Prue," Joshua said gently. "Sometimes when you are a woman you get to decide things for yourself. But Mrs. Turner and Ben have to decide too. I will talk to them."

Prue smiled sunnily and then laughed and spun around in a circle before offering one of her hands to Joshua and the other to Freyja. They went walking off down the river path—actually it was more skip than walk—swinging their arms like three exuberant children.

Freyja felt raw with love for Joshua. If she had even *suspected* him capable of such gentleness and concern for one of life's lesser mortals—according to the general consensus—she would have fled Sydney Gardens that morning in Bath and left that serving girl to her fate. She would have ignored him in the Pump Room. She would—

No, she would not.

She would perhaps have set about wooing him with every ounce of skill and determination she could muster for the task. She would not have engaged in mere light flirtation with him instead and given him the eternal impression that she wanted no more from him. It was too late now. If she were to try to woo him now, he would feel trapped, obliged to offer for her, obliged to pretend to be happy with her.

And so she could do nothing but skip down the river path with him and Prue, aching with love for him.

Chapter XXI

T HE SERVANTS AT PENHALLOW, BOTH INDOORS and out, had worked extremely hard to prepare for the grand ball. They had grumbled—but only in Joshua's hearing so that he would grin at them and wheedle them and laugh when they occasionally addressed him as "lad." Behind his back they did not waste their time on complaints but threw themselves with great enthusiasm into the preparations for such a novel event.

The state apartments had not been used within the memory of even the oldest servant. They were there for show. The occasional traveler who was bold enough to knock on the door was taken there by the housekeeper and allowed to gaze upon all the treasures while she recited their history. Although they had always been kept clean, there had never seemed to be the necessity of banishing every last speck of dust and making every surface gleam.

It was a huge task to make all ready in time—and all for

the likes of themselves, the cook remarked when she came to peep in on the ballroom when the great chandeliers were down and the hundreds of candles were being replaced. It seemed strangest of all to the servants that they were all invited, as well as all their family members and friends from the village and the surrounding farms. Even those who would need to be on duty in one capacity or another were not too long-faced. The butler, at Joshua's request, had organized the servants into shifts, so that those who worked the start of the evening would be able to feast and dance at the end, and vice versa for those who must work last.

The head gardener had scoured the park for late-blooming flowers and had agreed to sacrifice almost all the contents of his carefully nurtured hothouses for the occasion. The flower arrangements were undertaken by the ladies of the house. Chastity supervised, her cheeks flushed, her eyes bright with the pleasure of such a grand occasion. Prue was allowed to help. Constance and Eve were both competent, but Morgan was the one with the best eye for design. She made a number of suggestions to Chastity, all of which they discussed with much arm gesturing and great good nature. Freyja was content to watch, flower arranging never having been her forte. The marchioness was absent, having declared that flowers made her sneeze and gave her a headache.

The orchestra arrived late in the afternoon and were borne off to their rooms in the back wing of the house after setting up their instruments and tuning them.

Dinner was set for two hours earlier than usual since the guests would be arriving by seven and the ladies preferred to change into their evening finery after eating. This was no London ball, starting late and continuing until dawn. The majority of the guests were ordinary working folk, who would not have the luxury of being able to lie abed until the middle of the next afternoon. And many of them had some distance to travel, either by foot or by gig, though the head groom, at Joshua's direction, had made arrangements to send out every carriage and other vehicle to fetch the more elderly and the more distant folk.

There was to be a receiving line at the entrance of the ballroom, consisting of Joshua and Freyja, the marchioness, Constance, Chastity, and Prue.

Joshua, dressed in dark brown evening coat with dull gold knee breeches, gold-embroidered waistcoat, and white linen and stockings with lace at his neck and cuffs, looked about him with satisfaction from the doorway of the ballroom. He had always thought it a shame that the state rooms were never used. He breathed in the scent of the flowers, noticed how the newly polished floor gleamed under the light of the chandeliers, and looked up at them and beyond them to the ceiling with its richly painted scenes from mythology.

He felt a thrill of exhilaration. This was all his and tonight he would give pleasure to all his people and demonstrate to them that a new age had dawned in their relationship with Penhallow and the Marquess of Hallmere. No longer would there be an impenetrable distance between them and their wealthy, titled, privileged neighbor and overlord. Tonight would begin a new era for those who were dependent upon him, those over whom, like it or not, he had some power—power to give away.

Tonight he would begin *his* new life. It would have horrified him even just a week ago to imagine that he might be bound by Penhallow, which had been an unhappy prison house to him during his growing years, by his title, which he had never wanted, and by his responsibilities, which he had tried to fulfill through the appointment of a competent steward but which he had now discovered extended well beyond what any steward could do. But he *was* bound, and extraordinarily, it was the bonds of love more than duty that would keep him here at Penhallow.

But it was no happily-ever-after that he faced tonight. There was much to be settled before he could even begin to think in terms of happiness, much less happily-ever-after, which was a nonsensical idea anyway. Hugh Garnett had returned home, he had heard. There was no knowing for sure if he would come to the ball, but Joshua would wager on it. Then there was his aunt. And Freyja . . .

He heard sounds behind him and turned to see her approaching with Morgan and Eve—Aidan and Alleyne were coming along behind them, both in black-and-white evening clothes. Freyja was shimmering in a pale green gown embroidered all over with gold thread. It was a low-bosomed gown with loosely flowing skirt and scalloped hem and sleeves. Her hair, elaborately piled and coiled, was threaded with gold. Her long gloves and slippers were also gold-colored.

He caught his breath. When had he started to think of her as beautiful? She was not, was she? But to him she was lovelier than any woman he had ever set eyes upon. He smiled, took her gloved hand in his, bowed over it, and raised it to his lips.

"You look beautiful, my charmer," he said.

Her dark eyebrows arched arrogantly upward.

"So do you, Josh," she said.

He grinned at her and turned to greet the others. His aunt and cousins were approaching too with Calvin. His aunt, in black silk with nodding hair plumes, was smiling about her as if this had been all her idea. Indeed, she had been in a good mood all day even though she had avoided the ballroom while the flowers were being moved about and arranged. Constance, looking prettier than she had in Bath, wore pale blue and looked composed. Chastity, in pink, was sparkling with excitement. Prue, in pale yellow, was almost beside herself.

Almost immediately the guests began to arrive, and soon there was a veritable flood of them, a curious mix of elegantly dressed members of the upper classes and villagers and small farmers and laborers in their Sunday best, looking awkward and pleased with themselves and flustered as they made their bows and curtsies to the marchioness, who greeted them with stiff condescension, and more relaxed as they smiled at Joshua. He shook hands with everyone and had a word for all.

Anne Jewell came, he was pleased to see—Joshua had called upon her personally to urge her to accept her invitation. She entered the ballroom with Miss Palmer and fixed her eyes on the floor as she curtsied to the marchioness. Ben Turner came with his mother. The Allwrights came. Isaac Perrie came with his wife and two daughters. Jim Saunders came. So did Sir Rees Newton, the local magistrate, with Lady Newton and their son.

By the time the new arrivals had slowed to the merest trickle and Joshua announced his intention of getting the dancing started, there was no one he could think of who had *not* come—with the exception of Hugh Garnett. It would be sadly disappointing if he failed to put in any appearance at all. But in the meantime there was a ball to be enjoyed.

He led off the opening set with Freyja. It was a sprightly country dance, as were most of the dances planned for the evening. Everyone would know the steps and would feel no self-consciousness about performing them. There *was* self-consciousness at first, of course, and Joshua had to leave his place in the line, Freyja on his arm, to circle the edge of the dance floor and coax couples to join the revelries. He laughed and teased as he did so, and soon the line stretched the length of the room. Joshua, taking his place again and winking at Freyja, nodded to the leader of the orchestra, and the music began.

After that everyone seemed abandoned to merriment. If those of high rank felt any discomfort in rubbing shoulders with the lower classes, they showed no sign of it. Aidan, Joshua noticed, danced the second set with Anne Jewell, Alleyne with one of the Perrie girls, whose cheeks were such a rosy red that they looked as if they might burst into flame at any moment. Joshua danced with Constance, who had been led into the opening set by Calvin.

"Are you enjoying yourself?" he asked.

"Of course." She smiled.

"I thought," he said, "that Saunders would surely claim this set with you." Jim Saunders had not danced at all.

"Mama would not like it," she said.

"Would she not?" He had meant to have a good talk with Constance but had not found the time for it yet. "But would *you* like it?"

She stared mutely at him.

"And would *Saunders* like it?" he asked.

A frown creased her brow for a moment. "We cannot always do what we want," she said.

"Why not?" He smiled at her.

"Oh, Joshua," she said in a rush, "I wish I could be like you. I wish—"

But the music began and they were obliged to give their attention to the complicated figures of the dance.

It was at the end of the second set that Hugh Garnett strolled into the ballroom, five other men with him, none of whom now lived in the neighborhood. Joshua was talking with Mrs. Turner and Prue at the time and was detained by Prue's excited account of dancing with Ben. But his aunt stepped up to the door and received the new guests with gracious smiles and much nodding of her plumes. She slipped one arm through Garnett's and turned to look about the ballroom with a smile. She beckoned to someone across the room, and Joshua turned his head to see Chastity crossing the floor toward them, a smile still on her face but all the light gone out inside her. Garnett bowed and said something before extending his arm. Chastity set hers along it, and he led her onto the floor, where couples were already gathering for the next set.

The other five men dispersed about the ballroom and were soon lost among the crowds.

Ah, Joshua thought, this was better. He went to claim Morgan, his next partner.

FREYJA DANCED THE SECOND SET WITH SIR REES Newton and the third with Isaac Perrie, the village innkeeper, of all people. She could hardly believe that he would ask and that she would say yes. Gracious heavens, Wulf, if he were here, would have frozen the man with one glance from his silver eyes for even daring to raise his eyes to Lady Freyja Bedwyn. But she discovered that she was enjoying herself enormously. This, she felt, was somehow right. This was how life ought to be. She felt a pang of regret for these people that soon Joshua would be gone—*if* he could ward off the threat that still loomed—and life would return to its dreary norm under the marchioness's rule. She felt a pang of regret for *him*. And for herself.

But she would not think any dreary thoughts tonight. She was going to enjoy herself.

"It is good to see Garnett back from his travels," Mr. Perrie said, nodding his head down the line of dancers.

"Hugh Garnett?" Freyja looked at him, startled. "*He* is here?"

"In person." The innkeeper smiled his gap-toothed smile. "Third from the end."

Hugh Garnett, Freyja saw in one quick glance, was a dark-haired, youngish man and handsome in an oily sort of way. He was dancing with Chastity.

"Don't you worry none, lass," Mr. Perrie said. "Your lad is safe from harm."

Lass? Freyja might well have laughed aloud at the absurdity of it had she not suddenly felt rather alarmed—and strangely exhilarated. At last! Something was going to happen.

That something happened after the set had ended.

When all the dancers moved off the floor, Hugh Garnett did not. And in the lull that succeeded the music and the pounding of the dancers' feet on the floor, he raised his voice and spoke across the room.

"Sir Rees Newton," he said, and waited a moment while everyone's attention swung his way and conversations subsided into a surprised silence, "I wonder if you realize, sir, that this ballroom tonight harbors a murderer and a usurper?"

Freyja, looking sharply across the ballroom to where Joshua stood beside Mr. and Mrs. Allwright, instantly recognized in him the man who had burst into her inn room on the road to Bath and the man who had stood in the Pump Room the morning after the Sydney Gardens incident, waiting for her to finish stalking toward him. He looked alert, ready for danger, very much alive—and enjoying himself.

"I beg your pardon," Sir Rees said, all amazement. "Are you addressing me, Garnett?"

"I am amazed he had the temerity to return to Cornwall,"

Garnett said. "Joshua Moore murdered his cousin five years ago by rowing him out to sea in a small fishing boat and pushing him overboard and holding him under with his oar. He murdered for profit and has reaped all the rewards. You see him tonight as Marquess of Hallmere and in possession of all that has come with it. I am here to denounce him, sir. I was a witness to the killing."

No one, it seemed to Freyja, had moved a muscle except for Chastity, who had sunk onto a chair beside Morgan, and the marchioness, who was half tottering out onto the floor, one hand clutched to her throat.

Sir Rees sounded more irritated than outraged when he spoke.

"This is a serious allegation indeed, Garnett," he said. "But it is hardly the time or the place—"

Another voice interrupted him.

"I was with Hugh Garnett at the time," a squat, rough-looking man said, stepping out of the crowd, "and can corroborate his evidence."

"So was I and so *can* I," said another thin, bald man, stepping forward from the crowd close to the orchestra dais.

"And me, sir."

"And me, sir."

"Me too."

Five of them. And Hugh Garnett himself. Freyja's knees felt weak. She felt suddenly nauseous.

"Mr. Garnett." The marchioness clutched his arm with one hand, her other hand still to her throat. "When you came to me once before with these charges, I told you I would *never* believe them. Not of my dear Joshua, who was like a son to me, even though the victim was my own son. Not unless you could offer me proof that even *I* could not ignore. But I *still* cannot believe it of Joshua. Tell me there is some mistake. Tell me I am dreaming. Tell me this is some joke."

Freyja's hands closed into fists at her sides.

Sir Rees had also stepped forward. He looked deeply troubled, as well he might. *This* was not what he had expected of an evening of celebration. But before he could speak again, Isaac Perrie spoke up.

"Don't trouble yourself, my lady," he said affably. "They are lying rogues, all of them. I was standing in the doorway of my taproom that night, I was, because it was getting stormy and I knew the lads had taken a boat out. I watched it coming back. Young Josh—him that is now marquess—was rowing and your son was swimming beside him. They was close to shore, and I saw your son get to his feet while young Josh rowed off again. I was vexed with him for going back out when the sea was rough, but he was always a sure lad with the oars. I did not worry."

"I saw it too," another voice said. "I came to stand beside you, Isaac, if you recall. Young Josh's cousin was wading in, safe and sound and dripping wet."

"I saw them from the front road," another voice said. "It happened just like Isaac said."

"I was down by our boat with my dad," Ben Turner said. "I saw them too."

"I saw them from the house window," Mrs. Turner said.

Freyja unfurled her fan and fanned her face slowly with it. Her eyes met Morgan's across the room, and they exchanged half-smiles. It was obvious what was happening. At least a dozen other people had witnessed the event from the village exactly as Joshua had told it at the time. And as if that were not sufficient, a few of the servants at Penhallow had been strolling on the private beach the other side of the river and had seen it too, and a couple of the farm laborers had been walking on the cliff top above Penhallow and had seen.

For a stormy night, the area had been literally crawling with people, all with remarkably good vision, assuming there had been no moonlight during the storm.

Freyja met Joshua's eyes, and he depressed one eyelid slowly.

The marchioness and Mr. Hugh Garnett had not, it seemed, taken into account the fact that Penhallow and its environs were filled with Joshua's friends, people who knew him and loved and trusted him and were willing to perjure themselves on his behalf.

"They are lying, Newton, all of them," Hugh Garnett said, still holding his ground, though his face had turned somewhat more purple in hue. The marchioness was swaying on her feet, but no one was rushing toward her. "They are willing to defend a murderer because he has put a fancy ball on for them tonight. He is not the rightful marquess here. He should have hanged long ago. The Reverend Calvin Moore is the rightful marquess."

"You!" Isaac Perrie pointed a large, blunt finger in the direction of the squat, ruffianly individual. "I thought you were told six years ago to take yourself off from here with these fellow rogues of yours. You were told we did not need your bullying, smuggling ways around here. You were warned that if you showed your miserable hides here ever again you would be dragged off to the magistrate and left to your fate—a hanging or transportation most like. Yet you sneaked back one year after that to sail out on the sea with Hugh Garnett here, your former boss, did you, to witness a murder and not lift a finger to help the dying man or to apprehend his dastardly killer? A likely story indeed."

There was a gust of laughter and a smattering of cheers at his words and then rumblings of something uglier.

Sir Rees Newton raised both hands and everyone fell silent.

"I do not know what is at the bottom of all this," he said, "but it all sounds like a piece of malicious nonsense to me. You should be ashamed of yourself, Garnett. And if I discover one trace of your five fellow witnesses within my jurisdiction tomorrow, they are all going to be spending tomorrow night in my jail awaiting my pleasure—or my *displeasure*. As for all you witnesses for the defense, you might want to say an extra prayer for the salvation of your souls in church next Sunday. Lady Hallmere, ma'am, I apologize for the pain this foolishness has caused you. And, my lord." He bowed stiffly in Joshua's direction. "I have always believed your account of what happened that night, and I daresay I always will. You were known as a truthful, reliable boy and I saw no reason to doubt you. I would suggest that you give the word for the ball to resume if you feel the night has not been ruined."

"Not at all," Joshua said, as Hugh Garnett stalked out and his five accomplices slinked after him. "Indeed, I believe it is time for supper in the state dining room, though there will not be seats for everyone in there. Perhaps everyone would fill a plate and find a seat somewhere, and Lady Freyja Bedwyn and I will come around and speak with you all. This ball is partly in celebration of our betrothal, after all."

But just before everyone could rush gratefully into sound and movement, the Reverend Calvin Moore cleared his throat and spoke up unexpectedly, using his pulpit voice, though it shook with indignation.

"This has been a dastardly show of spite," he said, "occasioned, I do not doubt, by some trouble over smuggling in the past in which Joshua took the side of law and peace. I will have it known that I came here to deal as best I could with the understandable distress this looming crisis had caused my cousin, the marchioness. I did *not* come because I coveted the title myself. I did not and I *do* not. I am a man of the cloth and perfectly happy with my lot in life."

There was another smattering of applause, but most people by now were eager for their supper and the chance to astonish one another by repeating every word they had just heard as if they hoped to discover someone who had slept through it all.

Freyja raised her eyebrows as Joshua approached her, his eyes alight with laughter.

"You see, sweetheart?" he said. "Sometimes it is better to keep one's mouth shut and allow one's opponent to ram his foot in his own mouth."

"As I did in the Pump Room?" she said.

He reached out with both hands and circled her wrists with a thumb and forefinger.

"Now, you cannot expect a gentleman to agree with that," he said. "But if the shoe fits..."

"This, I suppose," she said, "is what Mr. Perrie meant that morning when he told you to leave everything to him."

He smiled at her.

"You see," he said, "my aunt and Hugh Garnett are not even worthy foes. It was all somewhat anticlimactic, was it not?"

"It will feed gossip hereabouts for the next fifty years," she said. "It will descend into folklore for generations to come."

He chuckled.

H E HAD ASKED NONE OF THEM TO DO IT, NOT EVEN Perrie. They had done it for him anyway, in an act of blind faith. Because they had known him and had known

Albert, they had not doubted him for one moment. And there was not a one of them who had ever believed that he was the father of Anne Jewell's son, even though he had never denied it and even though it had taken some of them a while to accept her in the village. They had believed in him.

It was hard to believe that he had left such friends behind him and had wanted never to come back.

He spent suppertime circulating among the guests with Freyja, as promised. The only thing that weighed heavily on his heart was the one deception he had perpetrated against everyone. He had even just repeated it—tonight, he had told his friends, was a celebration of his betrothal. But they were not betrothed. Not unless he could persuade her to change her mind about him.

Yet that seemed hardly fair.

Chastity touched his arm just as the people crowded into the dining room were beginning to spill back into the ballroom. She looked ghastly pale. She looked as if she were holding herself upright by sheer willpower.

"Joshua," she said, "will you come to the library? I have asked Mama and Constance and Cousin Calvin and Sir Rees Newton to come too. And Miss Jewell. Freyja, will you come too, please?"

But Joshua grasped her hand and squeezed tightly. "No, Chass!" he said. "No! Don't do this. It is not necessary."

"Yes." She looked dully into his eyes as she withdrew her hand and turned away. "It is."

He closed his eyes briefly and admitted to himself with a deep inward sigh that she was probably right. There was no stopping her now anyway.

"Are we about to find out," Freyja asked quietly, "what *did* happen that night?"

"Let us go and see, shall we?" he asked, offering her his arm.

CHAPTER XXII

N O ONE TOLD THE TRUTH IN THE BALLROOM earlier," Chastity said. She had invited them all to be seated and all of them complied except Joshua, who stood close to the window, his back to it, and Chastity herself, who clung to the end of the desk as if for support. "No one."

"I realized that, Lady Chastity," Sir Rees Newton said. "I beg you not to distress yourself. Hugh Garnett can be a nasty piece of work when he sets his mind to mischief, and the men who spoke up with him are a pack of unsavory rascals. Do not think I was unaware of their smuggling antics years ago even though I said nothing at the time. As for those who spoke up for Lord Hallmere, well, they perjured themselves as surely as I am sitting here, but they know him and trust his word and had clearly decided that there are several kinds of truth. I am quite prepared to pretend I did nothing but dance and feast and enjoy the company of my neighbors here this evening."

"Perhaps that is the trouble," the marchioness said, her voice bitter. For once her mask of gentle sweetness was down. "Everyone has always loved Joshua. Everyone has always believed every word he spoke. No one—not even my husband—would press for a further investigation into what happened that night. Albert went to confront Joshua over his blatant immorality and corruption of our servants, and Albert died. Joshua was the last to see him alive. Is that not suspicious enough to put doubt into anyone's mind?"

"I know everyone was lying," Chastity said, raising her voice and speaking very distinctly even though her eyes were directed at the floor, "because there was no one out that night, either on water or on land, to witness what happened—no one except Joshua and Albert. And me."

Good Lord! Joshua fixed his startled attention on her, as did everyone else. What was this?

"I saw what happened," Chastity said. "*Only* me."

"And me too, Chastity," Anne Jewell said quietly. "I was with you."

What the devil?

Chastity frowned at her but did not contradict her.

"I walked to the village," Chastity said. "I knew Albert was going to talk to Joshua, and I followed. I went to Miss Jewell's house first, and then the two of us went to Joshua's. But we discovered that they had taken a boat out. We went down onto the harbor to wait for them to return. Clouds had already covered the sky and the wind was getting up. There was no one else about. I had a gun with me."

"*What?*"

The marchioness fell back in her chair, but no one paid

her any attention and so she appeared to decide against swooning.

"We were sheltering from the wind beside one of the boats when we saw Joshua coming back," Chastity said. "He was rowing. At first we thought that Albert was not with him, but then we could see him swimming beside the boat. When they were close to shore, Joshua rowed away again and Albert waded toward the harbor."

"*Thank you, Chass,*" Joshua said firmly, taking a step forward. "That is all that needs to be said. It confirms what I have said all along. Shall we——"

Freyja had got up from her chair and come close enough to set a hand on his sleeve.

"We need to know what happened to Albert, then," Calvin said, "if indeed he came safely to shore at that point."

"I confronted him," Chastity said. "With the gun. I pointed it at him and would not let him out of the water. I told him he could stay there and freeze until he had promised to go to Papa and confess and until he had promised to leave Penhallow and never return."

"Oh, Chass," Constance said. She gazed at Anne Jewell, a look of pain on her face. "It was *Albert* who fathered your son, was it not? I suppose I have always known it. I just did not *want* to know it, though I never believed it was Joshua."

"Wicked girl!" the marchioness exclaimed, glaring at Chastity. "I will never believe it. Never! And if this——this *whore* says it is so, she is a liar. And so is Joshua. But even if it were so, would you threaten your own brother, your own flesh and blood, with death or banishment merely because he had taken his pleasure with a woman who was asking for it, always making sheep's eyes at him and tempting him away from the nursery to see something in the schoolroom. Oh, yes, miss. Do not think I did not notice."

"There was no bullet hole in the body," Sir Rees said. "Your brother drowned, Lady Chastity."

"He laughed at me," she said. "He said he did not *need* to come ashore, that he intended to swim some more because it was such a lovely night. He waded back into the water and swam away." She covered her face with both hands. "If anyone killed him, I did."

Constance leaped to her feet and hurried across the room to draw her sister into her arms. Chastity sagged against her for a moment, but then she pushed her gently away.

"It was not just because of Miss Jewell," she said, "though that was bad enough. But Miss Jewell fell prey to Albert only because she deliberately drew him away from the nursery to the schoolroom."

"Ha!" the marchioness said, describing a large arc with one arm.

"Chastity," Anne Jewell warned. "Please, my dear."

"Chass," Joshua said. "Leave it there. Enough has been said now. Leave it."

"I was glad when I found out he was dead," Chastity said. "I was *glad*. God help me, I am still glad. Prue was thirteen years old. *Thirteen!* And his own sister. But he thought that because she had a child's mind and a child's willingness to please and to do whatever she was told, he could get away with doing anything he wished with her. I am . . . I am almost sorry that he did not give me good cause to shoot him."

The marchioness shrieked and fell back in her chair, and this time Constance took notice of her and hurried toward her to take one of her hands in both her own. Chastity sagged against the desk. Calvin cleared his throat.

"I am sorry too, Chastity," Freyja said. "I honor you."

"For what my word is worth," Anne Jewell said, "I corroborate everything Lady Chastity has said."

Sir Rees Newton rose to his feet. "I have heard enough," he said. "I thank you for inviting me here, Lady Chastity, to hear these dreadful family secrets. I did not doubt Lord Hallmere's story, but your account of what happened has banished any shred of doubt that may have lingered. You are not responsible for your brother's death. As a magistrate I absolve you of all blame. As for the pain surrounding the whole tragedy and its revelation tonight to those who did not know before, well, that is none of my concern. I will leave you all and return to my good wife in the ballroom."

He bowed and left the room without further ado.

"That girl, that Prudence," the marchioness said, pushing Constance aside and sitting forward in her chair, "is to be taken from this house and locked up in an asylum where she belongs. This would never have happened if she had not been constantly flaunting herself before Albert—not that I believe he showed her anything more than a filial affection. He was always a loving boy. I never want to set eyes upon Prudence again. She is to be gone by morning. Cousin Calvin, you will see to it, if you please. You are a clergyman. You must know a suitable place where she can be taken."

"If Prue goes, Mama," Chastity said, "I go too."

"Enough now," Joshua said, stepping forward into the middle of the room and speaking with firm authority. "There has been mischief enough here in the past few weeks. I had hoped that the truth might never come out, but perhaps there is something in the old adage that the truth will out no matter what. Perhaps it needed to come out. But it must and *will* be remembered that Prue is the most innocent of innocent victims in all this. She will remain in this house—in *my* house—for as long as she wishes, Aunt, and she will always be welcome here even after she has left."

"Prudence is *my* daughter," his aunt cried.

"And my ward," Joshua reminded her. "But we will not wrangle over her as if she were an inanimate object. Prue is a woman, and she has a mind and a will of her own. She is capable of choosing her own future, her own course in life, and in fact she has already chosen. She is going to wed Ben Turner."

The marchioness stared mutely at him and then got to her feet to confront him, her face pale and distorted with anger.

"You would wed *Lady Prudence Moore* to an uncouth fisherman?" she asked him.

"I will be making the announcement as soon as we have returned to the ballroom, Aunt," he said. "Come with me and smile and look glad. Tomorrow we may discuss all that needs discussing. Tonight we have guests to entertain, and we are neglecting them."

But his aunt had looked beyond his shoulder and her eyes had narrowed to slits and her lips had thinned.

"You!" she said, stepping past Joshua to stand toe to toe with Freyja. "This is all *your* fault! If you had not used your high-and-mighty wiles to seduce Joshua in Bath and snatch him from under Constance's very nose, he would have been betrothed to *her* by now and we would have been the close, happy family we have always been. And now you have come to invade Penhallow itself and to lord it over all of us with your proud, contemptuous family."

Freyja raised her eyebrows and regarded the marchioness with cold, silent disdain.

Joshua watched, appalled, as his aunt raised one hand

and slapped her palm hard across Freyja's cheek. He reached out ineffectually with one hand, but he was too late.

Freyja had drawn back her right arm and punched his aunt in the nose. She went down like a bundle of old rags.

Calvin cleared his throat. The other ladies looked on as if waiting politely for the next scene of the drama. Joshua noticed that one of his aunt's hair plumes had snapped in two.

"I was beginning to be very much afraid," Freyja said, "that she would never give me provocation enough to permit me to do that. I am very glad she did."

B Y MIDNIGHT THE BALL HAD ENDED AND EVERYONE had returned home, all assuring Joshua as they left that they had never enjoyed a grander evening. The drama with Hugh Garnett in the middle of the ball, Freyja guessed, had only enhanced their delight.

So had the announcement of the betrothal of Prue and Ben, and the bubbling happiness of both for the rest of the evening had brought even Freyja to the edge of tears a couple of times. She had blinked them away quite firmly each time. Lady Freyja Bedwyn was certainly not given to shedding sentimental tears.

Incredibly, the marchioness had returned to the ballroom with the rest of her family. Her nose had been rather red for a while—as had one of Freyja's cheeks—and her two remaining hair plumes had had to be rearranged, but she had pulled herself together and smiled her usual sweet martyr's smile.

Constance had danced the final three sets of the evening, Freyja had noticed with interest, with Joshua's steward, James Saunders, who had not danced at all until then. Constance, usually quiet and dignified and self-contained, suddenly made no secret of the glow of love in her eyes and her cheeks. She really had looked very pretty indeed. After the first five minutes or so, Mr. Saunders was returning look for look.

"It was a wonderful evening, Joshua," Eve said when a few of them were alone in the empty ballroom. The marchioness and the Reverend Calvin Moore had withdrawn. Chastity and Miss Palmer had taken Prue off to bed. Constance had disappeared somewhere with Mr. Saunders. "We have attended similar such assemblies at the village inn at home, have we not, Aidan? But tonight has made me realize that we must invite everyone to our own home, perhaps for a summer garden party or a Christmas party or—"

Aidan laughed and set an arm about her waist. "Or both, my love," he said. "Did you know you were to have so many supporters here tonight, Joshua?"

"Let me just say that I was not surprised," Joshua said with a grin.

"It was priceless," Alleyne added. "I just wish it had come to fisticuffs, though. I would have liked nothing better than to lay out that grinning Garnett fellow. But I suppose it would not have been quite the thing with so many ladies present, would it?"

"I at least got to plant the marchioness a facer," Freyja said. "I was never so pleased in my life as I was when she slapped my face."

"You see?" Morgan threw her hands in the air. "I miss all the fun. You do not tell me *anything*, Freyja. Whatever happened?"

"It is a long story," Freyja said, "and not mine to tell."

"You all came here to give me your support when it seemed I was to be charged with murder," Joshua said. "I believe you have earned the right to know the truth. I know I can count upon your discretion."

He gave them a brief, bare account of what had been revealed earlier in the library.

"Oh, Prue," Eve said, closing her eyes when Joshua had finished and setting her arm about Aidan's waist. "My sweet, innocent Prue. But she had Chastity and Miss Jewell and Joshua as her champions, and now she is to have that steady, very nice young man, Ben Turner. She will be happy, I believe. I am ready for bed."

Aidan kissed the top of her head.

Freyja gazed at them rather wistfully. She had never seen any public display of affection between them before now.

"I am not," she said. "I need air and exercise and the wind in my face. Take me down onto the beach, Josh?"

Alleyne grinned at her and waggled his eyebrows, but no one voiced any comment or—more to the point—any protest. They all went off to bed while Freyja changed hastily into a woolen dress and a warm, hooded cloak, and sturdy shoes. It was a chilly night—she knew that much even though it was a light night too. They would have no need of any lantern to light their way down into the valley and along the river path. Joshua had changed out of his evening finery too, she noticed when she met him in the hall.

There was a depressing feeling of anticlimax needing to be blown away in the wind. The danger to Joshua was over—after what really had been a wonderfully satisfying scene in the ballroom. All the uncertainties about that night of Albert's death had been put to rest. It was over. There was nothing left to be done.

Nothing to keep them at Penhallow.

Nothing to keep them together.

"Will you stay for Prue's wedding?" she asked.

"Yes," he told her.

"A whole month while the banns are read?" she said. "You will endure all that time here, Josh, because you love her?"

"Yes," he said.

He was not at all the sort of person she had thought him. The realization had annoyed her just a few days ago. Now she was glad he was not, and she was glad she had been given an opportunity to discover the sort of person he really was.

"And what then?" she asked. "Everything here will go on as it always has, and you will ... what? Wander? Enjoy life again?"

"I have a feeling," he said, "that Constance's marriage will not be long delayed. Her eyes were finally opened to a number of things tonight, I believe. Certainly she was making an almost public acknowledgment of her feelings for Jim Saunders before the evening was over, and he looked as if he was very willing to be persuaded to marry so far above him."

"The match would have your approval, then?" she asked. She wondered what Wulf would have to say if she suddenly embarked upon a romance with one of his stewards.

"It would," he said. "But my approval is supremely unimportant, is it not? Constance is of age and not my ward. And, like Prue, she has a mind of her own and is quite capable of deciding what will give her greatest happiness in life. I cannot think dynastically, Freyja. I was not raised that way."

"You will stay for that wedding too, then?" They were approaching the end of the valley, and the steep hillside no longer protected them from the fresh west wind, which sent their cloaks billowing out to the side.

"Yes," he said. "I would like to settle them in the dower house, but I will need to work out a few details first."

"And so poor Chastity will be left at Penhallow alone with her mother," Freyja said. "But at least she will have her sisters close."

"My aunt can no longer live at Penhallow," he said, turning his head and looking down at her. "Penhallow is going to be *my* home."

"Oh." She looked at him in some surprise. But she could think of nothing else to say. She was feeling a little hurt for some reason she could not yet quite fathom.

"She will have to live at the dower house herself if no other solution presents itself," he said. "But I am going to do all in my power to find her somewhere else to live. And I daresay she will not want to be in such close proximity to me."

"Chastity?" she said.

He sighed. "My ward," he said. "But not my prisoner. *I* cannot decide what she will do, can I? Perhaps she will choose to go wherever my aunt goes. Perhaps she will go to live with Constance—or remain here. I shall give her the chance of a Season in London if she wants it, though I am not sure how I would go about it. I am the Marquess of Hallmere, though, am I not? A man of importance and influence." He grinned at her.

They rounded the headland, and the wide flat sands of the beach stretched before them, the towering cliffs to one side, the sea to the other. It was half out or half in—Freyja did not know which. She could hear the rush of the water and see the moonlight sparkling across its surface. It was chillier here, the air damper and saltier. She lifted her face and drew in great lungfuls of it.

He was going to stay, then. He was going to take on his

responsibilities as head of his family. He was going to settle down. Without her.

"Perhaps I will see you in London next spring, then," she said. "Morgan will be making her come-out."

"I want the first waltz at the first ball," he said. "We have waltzed together only once, Free, and even that was interrupted by the necessity of chasing after the master of ceremonies to announce our betrothal."

They set off across the beach, the wind in their faces.

"The first waltz is reserved, then," she said.

They walked in silence for a while. They were not touching. She had her hands inside her cloak. He had his clasped behind him.

"The tide is on the way in," he said. "But we have plenty of time before we get cut off from the valley."

"Did he commit suicide, do you think?" she asked.

"Albert?" He was silent for a few moments. "He must have realized he was in deep trouble. He also knew that his mother could see no wrong in him and that his father was weak. He did not seem like the sort of man who would take his own life anyway. But who knows? Chass had given him an ultimatum. So had I. I had told him that if he was still within ten miles of Penhallow by nightfall of the next day I would kill him with my bare hands. I don't suppose I would have done it, but I *would* have pounded him within an inch of his life. He knew it too. My guess is that he was overcome by the cold or by cramps. He was a nasty, villainous creature, Freyja—I always suspected that he was in on that attempted smuggling ring too. But enough on that topic. It is over and done with."

He stopped walking and stood looking out to sea. Freyja stood beside him, feeling all the vast wonder of the universe and the exhilaration of the fact that she was part of it.

"Freyja," he said, "what are you doing for the rest of your life?"

Oh, no! She was alerted by his tone and by the fact that he had called her *Freyja* rather than *Free* or *sweetheart*.

"Whatever it is," she said, lifting her chin, "it will be done without you, Josh. I am not one of your loose ends that must be tied up neatly before you can settle peacefully here. It was never a part of our bargain that you feel obligated to offer for me in earnest."

"What if it is not obligation that I feel?" he asked.

But her throat suddenly felt raw and painful and she realized in some horror that if she allowed him to speak one more word she might make an utter idiot of herself by starting to bawl. How dared he! She did not need this. She turned sharply about and eyed the cliffs. The moonlight was full upon them. They did not look quite so sheer from below.

"I am going up," she said.

He sighed. "Very well, then," he said. "It is probably wise to start back anyway. The tide is coming in fast."

"I am going up there." She pointed to the top of the cliffs, and she felt the familiar weakness of the knees and shortness of breath that had assailed her throughout a life of forcing herself to do dangerous things, preferably those that most terrified her. She had climbed trees when she was a girl only because she had been afraid of heights.

Joshua chuckled. "I will come back in the morning, sweetheart," he said, "and sweep up your remains. No, I won't be able to do that, will I? They will have been washed away by the tide. What the devil are you *doing*?"

She was striding straight toward the cliffs.

"I am going up the cliffs," she said.

"Why?" He caught up to her. "We are not even close to being cut off by the tide."

"Why?" she said haughtily. "What a stupid question, Josh. Because they are there, of course."

She pushed her cloak behind her back, found her first foothold and handhold, and raised herself clear of the beach. She looked back over her shoulder.

"I'll race you to the top," she said.

CHAPTER XXIII

W HAT HE OUGHT TO HAVE DONE, JOSHUA
thought, was to have plucked her off the cliff
face and borne her back to the house by the
valley route, by force if necessary. It would have been necessary, of course. He would have had to tuck her under one
arm or toss her over one shoulder and parry her blows as best
he could without retaliating in kind and close his ears to her
curses. But at least she would still have been a live body by
the time he had set her down safely inside Penhallow.

It would have been the responsible thing to do, and he
had drawn responsibility about him like a mantle during
the past week or so. He had become a new person, a ma-
ture adult, a sober marquess with duty as his guiding light.
He had been preparing to fade into stodgy respectability
and premature middle age.

But what was he doing instead of hauling Freyja safely
back home?

He was climbing the cliffs with her, that was what.

In the middle of the night, with a stiff wind blowing.

And with her hampered by a woman's garments.

He was also doing a good deal of laughing. The utter absurdity of it all! And the undeniable rush of exhilaration at the danger of it all!

Not that it was quite as dangerous as it looked—especially from above. Steep as the cliffs were, they provided any number of perfectly steady holds for feet and hands. Of course, there was no going back down once they had started. For one thing, going down a cliff face was infinitely more difficult than going up. For another, the tide was already in at the river mouth, and there would be no way of reaching the valley except by swimming.

He was not engaging in a race. He was keeping as close to her as he could, and slightly below her, almost as if he believed he could catch her if she should happen to slip and hurtle past him. But perhaps he could offer some assistance if she got stuck. Not that he offered out loud. He did not want anger to distract her. When she stopped, sometimes for a whole minute at a time, he stayed quietly where he was.

He knew that as soon as they reached the top they were going to collapse, their legs turned to jelly and quite useless for many minutes. They were also going to lie flat on the blessedly flat land, clinging to it as if expecting to slide off into space at any moment. And they were going to vow, as he had vowed every time he had done this as a boy, that *never again* would they be so foolhardy.

The last few yards were the most difficult, where solid stone became intermingled with earth and grass and loose pebbles and the dangers of finding a false foothold and sliding uncontrollably became very real. He remembered clinging motionless for maybe half an hour a body length from the top the first time he made the climb, unable for all that time to persuade himself to move a muscle while telling himself that he *must* before he disgraced himself by losing control of his bladder.

Freyja did not make the mistake of clinging too long and so becoming paralyzed. He had been trying to decide what to do if she did. He climbed after her over the lip of the very hollow where they had sat a few days ago and lay facedown on the grass, panting, beside her.

She was the first—after perhaps five minutes—to start laughing.

He joined her.

They lay side by side, clinging to the world as if they expected the force of gravity to expend itself at any moment, and shook and snorted with laughter.

"I believe I won," she said—a pronouncement of enormous wit that sent them off into renewed convulsions.

"I suppose," he said, "you are afraid of heights?"

"Always have been," she admitted.

They laughed so hard they wheezed for breath.

He turned onto his side to look at her, and she turned onto hers to look at him.

"You are not finding the night cold, are you?" he asked.

"Cold?" She raised her eyebrows. "*Cold?*"

They met in the middle of the space between them and were soon having tolerable success at trying to occupy the exact same space. Their arms were about each other, their mouths wide on each other's, kissing with the urgency of two madcaps who knew very well that they had just challenged death itself and won.

They came together soon afterward in a tangle of clothes and arms and legs, heat and wetness and enticing urgency at their shared core. They made love with vigor and passion and joy.

"My sweetest heart," he murmured, and other inanities of a like kind, whenever his mouth was free for speech.

"My love. Oh, my dearest love," she murmured back to him.

They exploded into completion together—perhaps all of three minutes after they had begun. As if now, their climb over, they were running a race. Which, appropriately enough, they finished in a dead heat.

They were panting again then, and she was laughing again into his shoulder as he wrapped one arm about her from beneath and both their cloaks about them from above.

"What was this?" he asked, his mouth against her ear. "Has my hearing turned suddenly defective? *My love? My dearest love?* Passion and lust run wild, sweetheart?"

Her laughter subsided, but she said nothing.

"Speechless?" he suggested.

"Don't spoil it, Josh," she said.

"What will spoil things for me," he said, "is to see you leave here in a few days' time, Free, and to smile cheerfully as if I were happy to see you go off to plan our wedding. And then to wait for your letter officially ending our betrothal. And then to waltz with you next spring, having lived all winter for just that one half hour. And then to spend the rest of my life without you."

He heard her drawing a slow, deep breath.

"There is no need—" she began.

"*Dammit!*" He cut her off before she could launch into the expected speech. "Let there be some truth between us at least, Freyja. I have had enough of lies and evasions and secrets to last me a lifetime. If all this has been nothing but a lark to you, then so be it. Say so honestly and I will let you go without another word—*unless*, that is, you have been got with child. But if you are letting me go because you think you ought to honor the temporary clause in our bargain and because you think I am being annoyingly noble in my offer to make our betrothal real, then stuff it, sweetheart. Just stuff it! Give me honesty now. Do you love me?"

Her voice sounded reassuringly normal—it was cold and haughty.

"Well, of course I *love* you," she said.

"Of course." He was back to laughter then. He held her tightly and could not seem to stop laughing for a while. "Are we going to allow a little bargain to ruin the rest of our lives, then?"

"Whenever we would quarrel," she said, "and we *would* quarrel, Josh, each of us would wonder if the other had felt coerced into marrying."

"What poppycock!" he said. "Do you not trust me to say the truth to you, Freyja? I *say* that I love you, that I adore you, that I can imagine no greater happiness than to spend the rest of my life loving you and laughing and quarreling and even fighting with you. I trust you to say what is true to me. You have said that you love me—that *of course* you love me. Does that include the wish to marry me, to live here with me all your life, to have babies with me and fun with me? To share the sorrows of life with me? And all its joys?"

"*Of course* it includes that wish," she said. "But, Josh, I am terrified."

"Why?" he asked. Her face was pressed hard against his shoulder.

"I have never done too well with love and betrothals and marriage prospects," she said. "If I give in to happiness now, it may all evaporate before my very eyes."

"Sweetheart, sweetheart," he said. "What happened the other day when you were afraid of the sea?"

"I was not—"

"What happened?"

There was a short silence.

"I persuaded you to take me over to the island," she said. "And?"

"And I insisted on rowing part of the way back."

"Even though you had to switch places in the boat with me," he said. "What did you do tonight when you were terrified of the height of the cliffs?"

"Climbed them," she said.

"And now," he said, "you are terrified to love me. What are you going to do about it?"

She drew her head back from his shoulder and glared at him.

"Love you anyway," she said. "*Don't* ask the next question, Josh, if you admire the shape of your nose. You remind me of everything I hated about all my governesses, asking their questions, and trying to extract the correct answers out of me by slow degrees and with infinite patience. You are going to ask me what I plan to do about my terror of a real betrothal with you and a real marriage with you."

He gazed back into her eyes and said nothing.

"We are betrothed," she said firmly. "There—*that* is what I am going to do. We are *really* betrothed. But if you should die before our marriage, Josh, I shall pursue you through all of heaven and hell after my own death and throttle you. Do you hear me?"

"Yes, sweetheart," he said meekly, and grinned at her. "I want to hear myself say this, Free. And I want to hear your answer."

He sat up, checked his distance from the edge, and arranged himself in a picturesque kneeling posture. He took one of her hands in his and smiled his most charming smile at her.

"Lady Freyja Bedwyn," he said, "will you do me the great honor of accepting my hand in marriage? On the understanding that it is to be purely a love match on both sides?"

"You look remarkably silly," she said.

"I know, sweetheart," he said, making a kissing gesture with his lips. "But I want you to be able to boast about this to our grandchildren one day—that their grandpapa went down on bended knee and begged you to marry him."

"They will never believe it," she said, "when they look at the old lady I will have grown into and then look at the handsome old gentleman you will have become." She sat up and sighed. "But *I* will remember this moment all my life, and I daresay it will bring tears to my eyes when I know no one is looking. Yes, I will, my love. I will marry you—but only on the understanding that it is to be a mutual love match."

She sat and he knelt, and they grinned at each other like a couple of self-satisfied fools while her hair blew wild about her face and he was very aware of the long, almost sheer drop less than a yard behind his heels.

"I keep expecting to feel the weight of the shackle close about my leg," he said, "but it is simply not happening. I am a betrothed man and have never felt so free. Free with Free! Shall we go back to the house and wake everyone up with the news?"

"It would not be news to them, though, would it?" she said.

"Lord, no," he said, grinning at her. "We have to celebrate *somehow*, though sweetheart. Any suggestions?"

"Oh, Josh," she said, opening her arms, "do stop talking nonsense and come here."

"Brilliant idea," he said.

J OSHUA HAD GONE OUT ON BUSINESS BY THE TIME Freyja asked for him the next morning. She was bubbling with unaccustomed excitement, but though she was surrounded by family and friends, there was no one to confide in. What would she say?

I am *in love*?

I am *betrothed*?

I am going to be *married*?

To Joshua?

Apart from the fact that they would look at her as if she had finally taken leave of her senses, it was all very lowering. She was not a person given to an exuberant outpouring of sentimental drivel.

She went for a walk instead—all the way to the village. This was something she needed to do anyway—and it had to be done alone. No one must know about it. Even the thought that someone might find out gave her the shivers.

"Good morning," she said when Anne Jewell opened the door of her cottage to her knock. "No!" She held up a staying hand when the woman gestured as if to ask her to step inside. "I'll not come in or disturb you longer than I need."

"But—" Anne Jewell began.

"No, thank you." Freyja kept her hand raised. "Correct me if I am wrong, but I do not believe you are entirely happy living here in this village, are you?"

The woman's welcoming smile faded somewhat.

"Everyone has been most kind," she said, "especially Joshua—Lord Hallmere. But you must not fear. I will not continue to accept his support. I am in hope of acquiring some new pupils soon."

Freyja clucked her tongue. "Do you think I care about a little support payment?" she asked. "I have looked at you and seen an intelligent woman who has never complained about her lot even though it was brought on by noble self-sacrifice and injustice—and a woman whose pride has not been broken. Is it your wish to teach?"

Miss Jewell looked wary.

"It was always my wish," she said. "My family was never wealthy, though I was fortunate enough to be educated. I always wanted to teach."

"There is a position for you if you wish for it," Freyja said, "at a girls' school in Bath. It is a quite respectable establishment and pays a salary that will support both you and your son in some comfort. You will be allowed to take him with you, by the way. My solicitor reported to me a week or so ago that there is need of another teacher—of geography, I believe."

Anne Jewell stared at her.

"I have some influence at the school," Freyja explained.

Anne Jewell licked her lips. "I would like it of all things," she said, her voice barely above a whisper. "Do they know that David was born out of wedlock?"

"Yes," Freyja said. "It will not be held against you provided you give good service as a teacher."

"I will." She set one hand flat against her throat and closed her eyes tightly. "Oh, dear God, I will. At a *school*! In *Bath*! How will I ever be able to thank you, Lady Freyja?"

"In just this way," Freyja said firmly. "It is the solicitor, Mr. Hatchard, who has found this position for you and checked your references. You know of no one else, only him. He is the one who answered your letter of inquiry and then wrote to offer you the position. My name is never to be mentioned to anyone, do you understand me? Especially not within the walls of Miss Martin's school. And least of all to Miss Martin herself."

Miss Jewell was regarding her with wide eyes.

"Of course," she said. "Yes, of course."

"Mr. Hatchard will write to you within the next week or two, then, with a formal offer and details and coach tickets for you and your son," Freyja said. "Good day to you, Miss Jewell."

It was at that moment that the half-closed house door opened and the child stepped out—with Joshua right behind him.

"I am ready, Mama," the child cried excitedly. "Look! Clean hands." He displayed them for her inspection, first the palms and then the backs.

Freyja was wishing fervently that she possessed the ability to make herself invisible. Dash it all, *had Josh heard anything*? But he looked at her in cheerful surprise.

"Ah, Freyja," he said, "are you here too? I came to fetch David. I thought to arrange an excursion for the children today."

"I came to bid Miss Jewell farewell," Freyja explained, "since I will be going back to Lindsey Hall soon. To start planning the wedding." Ignominiously she felt herself blush—and then glared at him with flared nostrils when he half depressed one eyelid.

Memories of the night before rushed upon her.

They walked back to the house together, David riding proudly and happily upon the horse as Joshua led it.

"If I had known you were going to see Anne," Joshua said, "I would have waited for you, Free. We could have ridden together."

"Yes, well," she said carelessly, "it was just one of a dozen such errands I must run before I leave."

"Sweetheart," he said softly, "you are a fraud."

She turned her head sharply to look into his laughing eyes.

"But you need not fear," he said. "Your secret is safe with me."

"Secret?" She frowned.

"What connection is Miss Martin to you?" he asked.

"Josh," she said coldly, "I could *kill* you for being at that house this morning. I suppose you had your ear pressed to the keyhole."

"No need, sweetheart," he said. "You are the one who refused to step inside and forced Anne to stand out there with the door half open. If you had come inside, you would have seen me. I was making no attempt to hide."

"She was my governess," she said crossly. "I mistreated her, she was dismissed for being unable to control me, and then she had the effrontery to refuse to allow Wulf to find her other employment. The silly woman opened a school in Bath and was like to starve when I heard about it. What was I to do?" She glared at him.

He grinned at her and winked. The little boy laughed as the horse snorted and tossed its head.

"I suppose," he said, "you have been the patron of the school ever since. The *anonymous* patron."

"Miss Martin hates me," she said. "If she knew, she would refuse all help and starve and I would have to live with my guilt. It would be grossly unfair."

He chuckled again, infuriating her. David was calling out to some villagers and waving importantly to them.

"And I suppose every now and then," he continued, "you see someone who could be helped by that school—a prospective teacher, for example, or a deserving pupil who cannot afford the school fees—and give in to a terrible urge—a shameful urge—to be kind and charitable."

"Josh," she said severely, "if you do not wipe that laughter from your face before I count to three, I shall wipe it off for you. *One*."

"You are nothing but a softie," he said, grinning.

"*Two*."

"I love you, sweetheart," he said, the laughter suddenly gone. "Body, mind, and soul."

She looked at him in exasperation.

"And kind, soft heart," he added.

She chuckled.

"I suppose," she said, "you will hold it against me for the rest of my life."

"To the very last minute," he said, taking her hand in his free one and lacing his fingers with hers.

She laughed out loud.

"I do hate you," she said.

She turned her head to look at him, all blond and handsome and loose-limbed and smiling and gorgeous. *Her* man. Her love.

"Oh, Josh," she said, "I do love you. And you may hold *that* against me for the rest of my life too."

"I intend to, sweetheart," he said, grinning at her.

CHAPTER XXIV

I BELIEVE I MAY WELL CRY," MORGAN ANNOUNCED.
"You had better not do it in public, then," Freyja said.
"It would reflect badly on all of us Bedwyns, and people
might think us soft. They might imagine that we have hearts."

Alice actually was crying, though she sniffed back her
tears as she placed her mistress's white, fur-trimmed bonnet carefully over her elaborate coiffure and tied the wide
white ribbons in a large bow to one side of her chin.

"White fur on white velvet," Judith said. "With a muff!
I am beginning to think that perhaps I should have married in the winter rather than the summer."

But she was smiling and not really serious. And she was,
of course, looking quite gorgeous herself in a dark sage green
gown and pelisse that complemented her bright red hair.
The skirt of her dress flowed loose from its fashionable high
waist to accommodate the slight swelling of her abdomen.

Morgan was wearing a dress of deep rose pink velvet and looked more beautiful than any woman had a right to do.

"Well, *I* am certainly going to shed a few tears," Eve said, "and in public too. People may say what they wish about the Bedwyn wives." She was looking delicately pretty in pale blue.

Alice finally finished her ministrations and stood back with a hiccup of a sob. Freyja stood up and turned to look at herself in the pier glass across one corner of her dressing room.

Oh, gracious goodness, she thought, *is that me?*

Dressed from head to toe in white velvet and fur, she looked almost beautiful. She had scoffed at first when white had been suggested as a color for her wedding dress. Lady Freyja Bedwyn was not a white-wearing person. She would have preferred some bright color.

"You see?" Aunt Rochester said now in her usual strident, no-nonsense voice—their dragon aunt whose veins and arteries ran with pure Bedwyn blood. "Was I not right to insist upon white, Freyja?"

She had not *insisted* exactly. Bedwyns did not insist upon anything with other Bedwyns, who all had iron wills and stubborn ones to boot. But she had pressed her opinion rather forcefully, and she was widely known for her impeccable taste in fashion. Freyja had desperately wanted to look as lovely as it was possible for her to look on her own wedding day.

"I was right to choose it, Aunt," she said.

"Oh, I say, Free," Alleyne said from the doorway. "You look good enough to eat. But it is a good thing it is almost Christmas already and almost the end of the year. Three Bedwyn weddings in one year has been quite a shock to the system, especially for those of us who are left. I vote for its being Morgan's turn next."

"But we will let you have your day first, Freyja," Aidan said from behind his shoulder. "The dress is lovely. The glow in your eyes is lovelier."

Then they both had to step right into the room to make way for Rannulf, who had their grandmother on his arm. Back in the summer, when Judith and Ralf were married, it had seemed that she was close to death, though her dearest wish was to see her first grandchild before she died. Their marriage and Judith's pregnancy and the fact that they lived with her at Grandmaison had given her a new lease on life, at least for the present. She had insisted upon coming all the way to Lindsey Hall from Leicestershire for Freyja's wedding.

"Alleyne," Ralf said, "present me to that very feminine beauty in white, if you will be so good. Ah!" He recoiled theatrically. "Never mind. It is Freyja, is it?"

"You look beautiful and distinguished and happy, Freyja, my dear," their grandmother said. "But I do not believe your dressing room was built to accommodate so many persons. And I do not believe the rector will appreciate our all being late to church. We must leave you with Morgan and your maid."

Morgan was Freyja's bridesmaid.

It was then, when, after a great deal of noise and fuss everyone withdrew, that Freyja began to feel nervous—again. She had been nervous after leaving Penhallow one week after the ball and nervous every day of the weeks that had followed even though Joshua had written to her daily. She had not quite believed in her own happily ever after—or in her own chance for a happy future, anyway. She had opened every letter with trepidation. It had not helped that winter was coming on.

She had *hated* it—the feeling of vulnerability, the

aching love that had not quite been able to trust in a future.

What if he went out boating again and fell in and drowned? What if he climbed those cliffs again—stupid, *stupid* man—and slipped and fell? What if...?

He had stayed for Prue's wedding and for Constance's. He had seen his aunt on her way to her chosen future—managing the large household of her recently widowed brother in Northamptonshire. Chastity had chosen to come to Lindsey Hall for the wedding with Constance and Mr. Saunders before joining her mother. But she was going to be in London during the spring and was to be presented to the queen and have a come-out Season—with Freyja as her sponsor. Anne Jewell and her son had left for Bath a month ago to take up her position as geography teacher at Miss Martin's school.

The weeks while Joshua had remained in Penhallow had seemed endless. But finally he had come.

And today was their wedding day.

She was still nervous—and still hating it.

She lifted her chin. "Wedding days are *such* a bore," she said to Morgan, "with everyone snivelling and being sentimental. I wish we had simply gone to London, purchased a special license, and married without anyone knowing, as Aidan and Eve did."

"No, you do not," Morgan said smiling. "Come, Freyja. Wulf will be waiting for us."

He was. He was standing in the great hall, surrounded by all the pomp and splendor of medieval banners and weaponry, looking positively satanic. He looked them over from head to foot with his cold silver eyes, Morgan first, and then Freyja. Then he surprised Freyja utterly by holding out both his hands to her. She set her own white-gloved ones in them and looked at him with haughtily raised eyebrows as his hands closed tightly about hers.

"You look very lovely, Freyja," he said.

Wulf paying compliments?

"Promise me you will be happy?" he said.

That was when tears sprang to her eyes. She could cheerfully have punched him in the nose. But he did not wait for her answer. He bent his head over her hands and kissed them one at a time.

Well.

Well.

"What are we waiting for?" she asked haughtily. "I would really rather not be late."

They were all in the carriage—the best ducal traveling coach—before she answered his question.

"I promise, Wulf," she said, gazing at him on the opposite seat.

Sometimes she tried to categorize her brothers in order, from her favorite to her least favorite. Aidan was usually on top of her list—perhaps because he had been away at war for so many years that he had had least opportunity to provoke her. But it was all nonsense anyway. She loved them all in different ways, but quite equally. She would have died for any one of them—and for Morgan too. But this morning—just at this precise moment—Wulf was her very favorite brother in all the world. She would do anything in the world, she thought, to see him happy too.

After that everything was a blur of events and sensations. The carriage drew up at the end of the churchyard path, hordes of smiling villagers—or so it seemed—bent to catch their first glimpse of her, she was hurrying up the path beneath the bare old yew tree, the wind blowing the last few crisp, dry leaves across the path in front of her, Morgan was arranging the train of her gown, Wulf was looking austere and emotionless—and as steady as the Rock of Gibraltar—the church organ was playing, and she was walking along the nave of the church on Wulf's arm, people in the pews to either side of her, and . . .

Ah. The blur dissipated and all her scattered, nervous emotions with it.

Joshua was waiting at the end of the nave, looking breathtakingly handsome in black and white. Not that it was his handsome looks that she noticed. It was *him*.

Her love. Her dearest love.

She did not even pause to chide herself for thinking such foolishly sentimental thoughts.

She felt herself smile. She felt happiness bubbling up inside her and threatening to spill over into laughter.

He smiled back, and she saw all the familiar laughter in his eyes. Except that it was not the usual reckless roguery she saw there this morning. It was joy. Simply joy.

She blinked furiously. Foolish sentimentality she would allow herself—this was her wedding day, after all. But tears? No, she must draw the line at tears. He would never let her forget.

"Dearly beloved," the rector began.

I T WAS A COLD, CRISP DECEMBER MORNING. A CHILL wind was blowing. Nevertheless, it was an open carriage that awaited the bride and groom at the end of the church path, and it had been lavishly decorated—by unknown persons, though several of them undoubtedly bore the name of Bedwyn—with ribbons and bows of all colors of the rainbow, and old boots to trail behind.

The church bells were pealing merrily.

Every house in the village must have emptied out its inhabitants, who were gathered in the street in their Sunday best and in festive spirits because they were all to be treated to their own wedding breakfast at the village inn in one hour's time, courtesy of the Duke of Bewcastle.

It was the scene that greeted Freyja and Joshua as they emerged from the church. Someone set up a cheer, and everyone joined in, a little self-consciously at first, but with growing enthusiasm as the congregation began to spill out onto the church steps after the bride and groom and the best man—the Reverend Calvin Moore—and the bridesmaid.

"Shall we wait to be swamped by grinning guests?" Joshua asked. "Or shall we make a dash for it?"

"Let's make a dash for it," she said, and he took her hand in his and ran along the path with her, beneath the great old tree, past applauding, smiling villagers, to the carriage.

It took a while to get her in—her velvet gown came complete with a train. She was laughing and breathless and flushed by the time he climbed in and took his seat beside her.

Everyone was out of the church by then—all her family, the Earl and Countess of Redfield, Viscount and Viscountess Ravensberg—both smiling fondly at Freyja—his grandmother and his aunt and uncle, Lord and Lady Potford, with their children, Constance and Jim Saunders, Chastity, Lord and Lady Holt-Barron with their daughter and her betrothed, a few of his closest friends.

"Drive on," Joshua said to the coachman. It would be time enough to greet everyone back at Lindsey Hall before the wedding breakfast. Right now he had a new bride to gaze upon in some wonder.

Was he really a married man? He had found it hard to believe in the reality of it all after she had left Penhallow with her family. Every day he had half expected that one of her daily letters would be the one breaking off their betrothal.

They were married!

He found her hand inside her large white fur muff and laced his fingers with hers as the carriage rocked on its springs and moved away from the church.

"Have I ever told you how beautiful you are?" he asked.

"What nonsense!" she said. "What utter nonsense, Josh. It is the dress and the hat and all the fur. And the color. Aunt Rochester advised me to wear white, and she was quite correct in her judgment. It is just the clothes."

He laughed. "I'll have to take them off you later tonight, then," he said. "All of them. Every stitch of them. Just to see if you are still beautiful without them. I'll wager you are."

"If you ever tell me lies," she said, looking at him severely, "I will knock your teeth down your throat, Josh. I swear I will."

"You can't," he said, grinning at her. "You are my wife now, my marchioness. You have to do as you are told. It has to be 'Yes, my lord,' and 'No, my lord,' and 'How may I serve you, my lord.' No more fisticuffs, my charmer."

For one moment he thought he was going to have to parry blows right there in full sight of their guests and all the villagers behind them. Her nostrils flared and her eyebrows arched upward and her green eyes glared. But then she threw back her head and laughed.

"You would tire of me in a month," she told him.

"Make that a week," he said.

If she were ever to look at herself in a mirror when she was laughing like this, he thought, she would see for herself how incredibly lovely she was, dark brows and Bedwyn nose notwithstanding. But he would not provoke her again by telling her that. Not now.

"No more complaints about winter?" he asked her.

She shook her head. "It is my favorite season."

"I love you, sweetheart," he told her. "My wife."

Her laughing expression softened into a smile, and she looked even lovelier.

"I am, aren't I?" she said. "And you are my husband. I do love you, Josh. I do."

He winked slowly at her and lowered his head and kissed her.

They both ignored the cheers that rose behind them. They were half drowned by the church bells anyway.

Follow the passionate and spirited
adventures of the Bedwyn family in
Mary Balogh's dazzling novels,
available now from Piatkus

SLIGHTLY MARRIED

Aidan's story

and

SLIGHTLY WICKED

Rannulf's story

Read on for a preview . . .

SLIGHTLY MARRIED

Mary Balogh

THE SCENE WAS ALL TOO FAMILIAR TO THE MAN surveying it. There was not a great deal of difference between one battlefield and another, he had discovered through long experience—not, at least, when the battle was over.

The smoke of the heavy artillery and of the myriad muskets and rifles of two armies was beginning to clear sufficiently to reveal the victorious British and Allied troops establishing their newly won positions along the Calvinet Ridge to the east of the city and turning the big guns on Toulouse itself, into which the French forces under Soult's command had recently retreated. But the acrid smell lingered and mingled with the odors of dust and mud and horse and blood. Despite an ever-present noise—voices bellowing out commands, horses whinnying, swords clanging, wheels rumbling—there was the usual impression of an unnatural, fuzzy-eared silence now that the thunderous pounding of the guns had ceased. The ground was carpeted with the dead and wounded.

It was a sight against which the sensibilities of Col. Lord Aidan Bedwyn never became totally hardened. Tall and solidly built, dark-complexioned, hook-nosed, and granite-faced, the colonel was feared by many. But he always took the time after battle to roam the battlefield, gazing at the dead of his own battalion, offering comfort to the wounded wherever he could.

He gazed downward with dark, inscrutable eyes and grimly set lips at one particular bundle of scarlet, his hands clasped behind him, his great cavalry sword, unsheathed and uncleaned after battle, swinging at his side.

"An officer," he said, indicating the red sash with a curt nod. The man who wore it lay facedown on the ground, spread-eagled and twisted from his fall off his horse. "Who is he?"

His aide-de-camp stooped down and turned the dead officer over onto his back.

The dead man opened his eyes.

"Captain Morris," Colonel Bedwyn said, "you have taken a hit. Call for a stretcher, Rawlings. Without delay."

"No," the captain said faintly. "I am done for, sir."

His commanding officer did not argue the point. He made a slight staying gesture to his aide and continued to gaze down at the dying man, whose red coat was soaked with a deeper red. There could be no more than a few minutes of life remaining to him.

"What may I do for you?" the colonel asked. "Bring you a drink of water?"

"A favor. A promise." Captain Morris closed parchment-pale eyelids over fading eyes, and for a moment the colonel thought he was already gone. He sank down onto one knee beside him, pushing his sword out of the way as he did so. But the eyelids fluttered and half lifted again. "The debt, sir.

I said I would never call it in." His voice was very faint now, his eyes unfocused.

"But I swore I would repay it nonetheless." Colonel Bedwyn leaned over him, the better to hear. "Tell me what I can do."

Captain Morris, then a lieutenant, had saved his life two years before at the Battle of Salamanca, when the colonel's horse had been shot out from under him and he had been about to be cut down from behind while engaging a mounted opponent in a ferocious frontal fight. The lieutenant had killed the second assailant and had then dismounted and insisted that his superior officer take his horse. He had been severely wounded in the ensuing fight. But he had been awarded his captaincy as a result, a promotion he could not afford to purchase. He had insisted at the time that Colonel Bedwyn owed him nothing, that in a battle it was a soldier's duty to watch the backs of his comrades, particularly those of his superior officers. He was right, of course, but his colonel had never forgotten the obligation.

"My sister," the captain said now, his eyes closed again. "Take the news to her."

"I'll do it in person," the colonel assured him. "I'll inform her that your last thoughts were of her."

"Don't let her mourn." The man's breath was being drawn in on slow, audible heaves. "She has had too much of that. Tell her she must not wear black. My dying wish."

"I'll tell her."

"Promise me..." The voice trailed away. But death had still not quite claimed him. Suddenly he opened his eyes wide, somehow found the strength to move one arm until he could touch the colonel's hand with limp, deathly cold fingers, and spoke with an urgency that only imminent death could provoke.

"Promise me you will protect her," he said. His fingers plucked feebly at the colonel's hand. "Promise me! No matter what!"

"I promise." The colonel bent his head closer in the hope that his eyes and his voice would penetrate the fog of death engulfing the agitated man. "I give you my solemn vow."

The last breath sighed out of the captain's lungs even as the words were being spoken. The colonel reached out a hand to close Morris's eyes and remained on one knee for a minute or two longer as if in prayer, though in reality he was considering the promise he had made Captain Morris. He had promised to take the news of her brother's death to Miss Morris in person though he did not even know who she was or where she lived. He had promised to inform her of Morris's dying wish that she not wear mourning for him.

And he had sworn on his most sacred honor to protect her. From what—or from whom—he had no idea.

No matter what!

The echo of those last three words of the dying man rang in his ears. What could they possibly mean? What exactly had he sworn to?

No matter what!

England, 1814

Eve Morris was knee-deep in bluebells. She had decided that it was too glorious a morning to be spent in any of the usual activities about the house and farm or in the village. The bluebells were in bloom for such a short time, and picking them for the house had always been one of her favorite springtime activities. She was not alone. She had persuaded Thelma Rice, the governess, to cancel classes for a few hours and bring her two pupils and her infant son out flower picking. Even Aunt Mari had come despite her arthritic knees and frequent shortness of breath. Indeed, it had been her idea to turn the occasion into an impromptu picnic. She was sitting now on the sturdy chair Charlie had carried down for her, her knitting needles clicking steadily, a large basket of food and drink at her side.

Eve straightened up to stretch her back and savored a conscious feeling of well-being. All of the summer stretched ahead, a summer unmarred by anxiety for the first time in many years. Well, *almost* unmarred. There was, of course, the continuing question of what was keeping John away. He had expected to be home by March, or April at the latest. But he would come as soon as he was able. Of that she was certain. In the meantime, she viewed her surroundings and her companions with placid contentment.

Seven-year-old Davy was picking earnestly, a frown on his thin face, as if he had been set a task of grave importance. Close behind him, as usual, five-year-old Becky, his sister, picked with more obvious enjoyment and less concentration, humming tunelessly as she did so.

Young Benjamin Rice toddled up to his mother, a cluster of azalea and bluebell heads clutched tightly in one outstretched fist. Thelma bent to take them in her cupped hands as if they were some rare and precious treasure—as of course they were.

Eve felt a moment's envy of that mother love, but she shook it off as unworthy of her. She was one of the most fortunate of mortals. She lived in this idyllic place, and she was surrounded by people with whom she shared a reciprocal love, the loneliness of her girlhood a thing of the distant past. Soon—any day now—John would be back, and she could admit to the world at long last that she was in love, love, love. She could have twirled about at the thought, like an exuberant girl, but she contented herself with a smile instead.

And then there was the other prospect to complete her happiness. Percy would be coming home. He had written in his last letter that he would take leave as soon as he was able, and now surely he must be able. A little over a week ago she had heard the glorious news that Napoléon Bonaparte had surrendered to the Allied forces in France and that the long wars were over at last. James Robson, Eve's neighbor, had come in person to Ringwood as soon as he heard himself, knowing what the news would mean to her—the end to years of anxiety for Percy's safety.

Eve stooped to pick more bluebells. She wanted to be able to set a filled vase in every room of the house. They would all celebrate springtime and victory and security and an end to mourning with color and fragrance. If *only* John would come.

"I suppose," Aunt Mari said, "we'd better pack up and take all these flowers back to the house before they wilt. If someone would just hand me my cane as soon as I have my wool and needles in this bag, I could haul these old bones upright."

"Oh, must we?" Eve asked with a sigh as Davy scrambled to offer the cane.

But at that moment someone called her name.

"Miss Morris," the voice called with breathless urgency. "Miss Morris."

"We are still here, Charlie." She swiveled around to watch a large, fresh-faced young man come lumbering over the top of the bank from the direction of the house and crash downward toward them in his usual ungainly manner. "Take your time or you will slip and hurt yourself."

"Miss Morris." He was gasping and ruddy-cheeked by the time he came close enough to deliver his message. "I am sent. By Mrs. Fuller. To fetch you back to the house." He fought for air between each short sentence.

"Did she say why, Charlie?" Eve got unhurriedly to her feet and shook out her skirt. "We are all on our way home anyway."

"Someone's come," Charlie said. He stood very still then, his large feet planted wide, his brow creased in deep furrows of concentration, and tried to bring something else to mind. "I can't remember his name."

Eve felt a lurching of excitement in the pit of her stomach. *John?* But she had been disappointed so many times in the last two months that it was best not to consider the possibility. Indeed, she was even beginning to wonder if he was coming at all, if he had ever intended to come. But she was not yet prepared to draw such a drastic conclusion—she pushed it firmly away.

"Well, never mind," she said cheerfully. "I daresay I will find it out soon enough. Thank you for bringing the message so promptly, Charlie."

"He is a military feller," he said. "I seen him before Mrs. Fuller sent me to fetch you and he was wearing one of them red uniform things."

A military man.

"Oh, Eve, my love," Aunt Mari said, but Eve did not even hear her.

"*Percy!*" she cried in a burst of exuberance. Basket and flowers and companions were forgotten. She gathered up her skirts with both hands and began to run up the bank, leaving her aunt and Thelma and Charlie to gather up the children and the bluebells.

It was not a long way back to the house, but most of the distance was uphill. Eve scarcely noticed.

By the time she burst into the entrance hall, she was flushed and panting and probably looking alarmingly disheveled, even grubby. She did not care one iota. Percy would not care.

The rogue! He had sent no word that he was coming. But that did not matter now. And surprises were wonderful things—at least *happy* surprises were. He was home!

Eve dashed across the checkered floor of the hall, flung open the door of the visitors' parlor, and hurried inside.

"You wretch!" she cried, pulling undone the ribbon of her hat. And then she stopped dead in her tracks, feeling intense mortification. He was not Percy. He was a stranger.

SLIGHTLY WICKED

Mary Balogh

MOMENTS BEFORE THE STAGECOACH OVERTURNED, Judith Law was deeply immersed in a daydream that had effectively obliterated the unpleasant nature of the present reality.

For the first time in her twenty-two years of existence she was traveling by stagecoach. Within the first mile or two she had been disabused of any notion she might ever have entertained that it was a romantic, adventurous mode of travel. She was squashed between a woman whose girth required a seat and a half of space and a thin, restless man who was all sharp angles and elbows and was constantly squirming to find a more comfortable position, digging her in uncomfortable and sometimes embarrassing places as he did so. A portly man opposite snored constantly, adding considerably to all the other noises of travel. The woman next to him talked unceasingly to anyone unfortunate or unwise enough to make eye contact with her, relating the sorry story of her life in a tone of whining complaint. From the quiet man on the other side of her wafted the odors of uncleanness mingled with onions and garlic. The coach rattled and vibrated and jarred over every stone and pothole in its path, or so it seemed to Judith.

Yet for all the discomforts of the road, she was not eager to complete the journey. She had just left behind the lifelong familiarity of Beaconsfield and home and family and did not expect to return to them for a long time, if ever. She was on her way to live at her Aunt Effingham's. Life as she had always known it had just ended. Though nothing had been stated explicitly in the letter her aunt had written to Papa, it had been perfectly clear to Judith that she was not going to be an honored, pampered guest at Harewood Grange, but rather a poor relation, expected to earn her keep in whatever manner her aunt and uncle and cousins and grandmother deemed appropriate. Starkly stated, she could expect only dreariness and drudgery ahead—no beaux, no marriage, no home and family of her own. She was about to become one of those shadowy, fading females with whom society abounded, dependent upon their relatives, unpaid servants to them.

Judith was the one everyone had turned and looked at when Papa came to the sitting room and read Aunt Effingham's letter aloud. Papa had fallen into severe financial straits and must have written to his sister to ask for just the help she was offering. They all knew what it would mean to the one chosen to go to Harewood. Judith had volunteered. They had all cried when she spoke up, and her sisters had all volunteered too—but she had spoken up first.

The sky beyond the coach windows was gray with low, heavy clouds, and the landscape was dreary. The landlord at the inn where they had stopped briefly for a change of horses an hour ago had warned that there had been torrential rain farther north and they were likely to run into it and onto muddy roads, but the stagecoach driver had laughed at the suggestion that he stay at the inn until it was safe to proceed. But sure enough, the road was getting muddier by the minute, even though the rain that had caused it had stopped for a while.

Judith had blocked it all out—the oppressive resentment she felt, the terrible homesickness, the dreary weather, the uncomfortable traveling conditions, and the unpleasant prospect of what lay ahead—and daydreamed instead, inventing a fantasy adventure with a fantasy hero, herself as the unlikely heroine. It offered a welcome diversion for her mind and spirits until moments before the accident.

She was daydreaming about highwaymen. Or, to be more precise, about a highwayman. He was not, of course, like any self-respecting highwayman of the real world—a vicious, dirty, amoral, uncouth robber and cutthroat murderer of hapless travelers. No, indeed. This highwayman was dark and handsome and dashing and laughing—he had white, perfect teeth and eyes that danced merrily behind the slits of his narrow black mask. He galloped across a sun-bright green field and onto the highway, effortlessly controlling his powerful and magnificent black steed with one hand, while he pointed a pistol—unloaded, of course—at the heart of the coachman. He laughed and joked merrily with the passengers as he deprived them of their valuables, and then he tossed back those of the people he saw could ill afford the loss. No . . . No, he returned *all* of the valuables to *all* the passengers since he was not a real highwayman at all, but a gentleman bent on vengeance against one particular villian, whom he was expecting to ride along this very road.

He was a noble hero masquerading as a highwayman, with a nerve of steel, a carefree spirit, a heart of gold, and looks to cause every female passenger heart palpitations that had nothing to do with fear.

And then he turned his eyes upon Judith—and the universe stood still and the stars sang in their spheres. Until, that was, he laughed gaily and announced that he *would* deprive *her* of the necklace that dangled against her bosom even though it must have been obvious to him that it had almost no money value at all. It was merely something that her ... her *mother* had given her on her deathbed, something Judith had sworn never to remove this side of her own grave. She stood up bravely to the highwayman, tossing back her head and glaring unflinchingly into those laughing eyes. She would give him nothing, she told him in a clear, ringing voice that trembled not one iota, even if she must die.

He laughed again as his horse first reared and then pranced about as he brought it easily under control. Then if he could not have the necklace *without* her, he declared, he would have it *with* her. He came slowly toward her, large and menacing and gorgeous, and when he was close enough, he leaned down from the saddle, grasped her by the waist with powerful hands—she ignored the problem of the pistol, which he had been brandishing in one hand a moment ago—and lifted her effortlessly upward.

The bottom fell out of her stomach as she lost contact with solid ground, and ... and she was jerked back to reality. The coach had lost traction on the muddy road and was swerving and weaving and rocking out of control. There was enough time—altogether too much time—to feel blind terror before it went into a long sideways skid, collided with a grassy bank, turned sharply back toward the road, rocked even more alarmingly than before, and finally overturned into a low ditch, coming to a jarring halt half on its side, half on its roof.

When rationality began to return to Judith's mind, everyone seemed to be either screaming or shouting. She was not one of them—she was biting down on both lips instead. The six inside passengers, she discovered, were in a heap together against one side of the coach. Their curses, screams, and groans testified to the fact that most, if not all, of them were alive. Outside she could hear shouts and the whinnying of frightened horses. Two voices, more distinct than any others, were using the most shockingly profane language.

She was alive, Judith thought in some surprise. She was

also—she tested the idea gingerly—unhurt, though she felt considerably shaken up. Somehow she appeared to be on top of the heap of bodies. She tried moving, but even as she did so, the door above her opened and someone—the coachman himself—peered down at her.

"Give me your hand, then, miss," he instructed her. "We will have you all out of there in a trice. Lord love us, stop that screeching, woman," he told the talkative woman with a lamentable lack of sympathy considering the fact that he was the one who had overturned them.

Judith made no complaint. She had chosen to continue her journey even though she had heard the warning and might have waited for a later coach. She had no suggestions to make either. And she had no injuries. She was merely miserable and looked about her for something to take her mind off the fact that they were all stranded in the middle of nowhere and about to be rained upon. She began to tend those in distress, even though most of the hurts were more imaginary than real. Within minutes she had removed her bonnet, which was getting in her way, and tossed it into the still-overturned carriage. Her hair was coming down, but she did not stop to try to restore it to order. Most people, she found, really did behave rather badly in a crisis, though this one was nowhere near as disastrous as it might have been.

Heir attention was diverted by a shout from one of the outside passengers, who was pointing off into the distance from which they had come just a few minutes before. A rider was approaching, a single man on horseback. Several of the passengers began hailing him, though he was still too far off to hear them. What they thought one man could do to improve their plight Judith could not imagine.

Although he was making a lengthy journey, Lord Rannulf Bedwyn was on horseback—he avoided carriage travel whenever possible. His baggage coach, together with his valet, was trundling along somewhere behind him. His valet, being a cautious, timid soul, had probably decided to stop at the inn an hour or so back when warned of rain by an innkeeper intent on drumming up business.

He himself could turn back, he supposed. But it was against his nature to turn tail and flee any challenge, human or otherwise. He must stop at the next inn he came across, though. He might be careless of any danger to himself, but he must be considerate of his horse.

His thoughts were diverted suddenly by the appearance of a black dot ahead of him denser than the prevailing mud and hedgerows. At first he thought it was a building, but as he rode a little closer he realized that it was actually a collection of people and a large, stationary coach. An overturned coach, he soon realized, with a broken axle. The horses were out on the road as well as a few of the people. Many were shouting, waving, and gesticulating in his direction as if they expected him to dismount, set his shoulder to the ruined vehicle, heave it to the road again, magically repairing the axle in the process, and hand them all inside once more before riding off into the proverbial sunset.

It would be churlish, of course, to ride on by without stopping merely because he could not offer any practical assistance. He drew rein when he was close to the group and grinned when almost everyone tried to talk to him at once. He held up a staying hand and asked if anyone had been seriously hurt. No one, it seemed, had been.

"The best I can do for you all, then," he said when the hubbub had subsided again, "is ride on with all the speed I can muster and send help back from the nearest village or town."

"There is a market town no more than three miles ahead, sir," the coachman told him, pointing off along the road.

One of the passengers—a woman—had not joined the others in greeting him. She was bent over a muddy gentleman seated on a wooden crate, pressing some sort of makeshift bandage to his cheek. He took it from her even as Rannulf watched, and the woman straightened up and turned to look at him.

She was young and tall. She was wearing a green cloak, slightly damp, even muddied at the hem. It fell open down the front to reveal a light muslin dress and a bosom that immediately increased Rannulf's body heat by at least a couple of degrees. She was bareheaded. Her hair was disheveled and half down over her shoulders. It was a glorious shade of bright red-gold such as he had never before seen on a human head. The face beneath it was oval and flushed and bright-eyed—the eyes were green, he believed—and quite startlingly lovely. She returned his stare with apparent disdain. What did she expect him to do? Vault down into the mud and play hero?

He grinned lazily and spoke without looking away from her.

"I could, I suppose," he said, "take one person up with me. One lady? Ma'am? How about you?"

The redhead smiled at Rannulf then, an expression that grew slowly even as the color deepened in her cheeks.

"It would be my pleasure, sir," she said in a voice that was warm and husky and crawled up his spine like a velvet-gloved hand.

He rode over to the side of the road, toward her.

Other titles

in

Mary Balogh's

Bedwyn series,

available

from

Piatkus . . .

SLIGHTLY TEMPTED

From the moment he spies Lady Morgan Bedwyn across the glittering ballroom, Gervase Ashford, Earl of Rosthorn, knows he has found the perfect instrument of his revenge. But wedlock is not on the mind of the continent's most notorious rake. Nor is it of interest to the fiercely independent Lady Morgan herself . . . until one night of shocking intimacy erupts in a scandal that could make Gervase's vengeance all the sweeter.

There is only one thing standing in his way: Morgan, who has achieved the impossible – she's melted his coolly guarded heart. For Gervase, only the marriage bed will do, but Morgan simply will not have him. Thus begins a sizzling courtship where two wary hearts are about to be undone by the most scandalous passion of all: all-consuming love.

978-0-7499-3786-7

SLIGHTLY SINFUL

On a Flemish battlefield Lord Alleyne Bedwyn is thrown
from his horse and left for dead, only to awaken in the
bedchamber of a Brussels brothel. The dark, handsome
diplomat has no memory of who he is or how he got there –
yet of one thing he is certain: he owes his life to the
angel of undoubtedly dubious virtue who is
nursing him back to health.

But like him, Rachel York is not who she seems. The havoc
of war has forced Rachel to seek refuge with the 'ladies' of
the house whilst devising a plan to restore her fortunes. The
dashing soldier she rescued from near-death could be her
saviour in disguise. In order to inherit, Rachel needs to be
married and here is a man with no memory – and thus no
ties – willing to do *anything* to help her. However on
returning to England, their marriage charade draws them
both into danger, scandal and a blossoming relationship
that is ever so slightly sinful . . .

978-0-7499-3787-4

SLIGHTLY DANGEROUS

All of London is abuzz over the imminent arrival of
Wulfric Bedwyn – the reclusive, cold-as-ice Duke of
Bewcastle – at the most glittering social event of the season.
Some whisper of a tragic love affair. Others say he is so
aloof and passionless that not even the greatest beauty
could capture his attention. But on this dazzling afternoon,
one woman does catch the duke's eye – and she is the only
female in the room who isn't even trying. Christine Derrick
is intrigued by the handsome duke . . . all the more so when
he invites her to become his mistress.

But Christine has very definite views on men, morals, and
marriage and confounds Wulfric at every turn. Yet even as
the lone wolf of the Bedwyn clan vows to seduce her any
way he can, something strange and wonderful is happening.
Now for a man who thought he'd never lose his heart,
nothing less than love will do.

978-0-7499-3772-0